First published 1979 by
André Deutsch Limited
105 Great Russell Street London WC1

Printed in Great Britain
by W & J Mackay Limited, Chatham

ISBN 0 233 97140 8

V. S. NAIPAUL

A Bend in the River

ANDRE DEUTSCH

A Bend in the River

Contents

I

The Second Rebellion

1

THE WORLD is what it is; men who are nothing, who allow themselves to become nothing, have no place in it.

Nazruddin, who had sold me the shop cheap, didn't think I would have it easy when I took over. The country, like others in Africa, had had its troubles after independence. The town in the interior, at the bend in the great river, had almost ceased to exist; and Nazruddin said I would have to start from the beginning.

I drove up from the coast in my Peugeot. That isn't the kind of drive you can do nowadays in Africa – from the east coast right through to the centre. Too many of the places on the way have closed down or are full of blood. And even at that time, when the roads were more or less open, the drive took me over a week.

It wasn't only the sand-drifts and the mud and the narrow, winding, broken roads up in the mountains. There was all that business at the frontier posts, all that haggling in the forest outside wooden huts that flew strange flags. I had to talk myself and my Peugeot past the men with guns – just to drive through bush and more bush. And then I had to talk even harder, and shed a few more bank-notes and give away more of my tinned food, to get myself – and the Peugeot – out of the places I had talked us into.

Some of these palavers could take half a day. The top man would ask for something quite ridiculous – two or three thousand dollars. I would say no. He would go into his hut, as though there was nothing more to say; I would hang around outside, because there was nothing else for me to do. Then after an hour or two I would go inside the hut, or he would come outside, and we would

9

settle for two or three dollars. It was as Nazruddin had said, when I asked him about visas and he had said that bank-notes were better. 'You can always get into those places. What is hard is to get out. That is a private fight. Everybody has to find his own way.'

As I got deeper into Africa – the scrub, the desert, the rocky climb up to the mountains, the lakes, the rain in the afternoons, the mud, and then, on the other, wetter side of the mountains, the fern forests and the gorilla forests – as I got deeper I thought, 'But this is madness. I am going in the wrong direction. There can't be a new life at the end of this.'

But I drove on. Each day's drive was like an achievement; each day's achievement made it harder for me to turn back. And I couldn't help thinking that that was how it was in the old days with the slaves. They had made the same journey, but of course on foot and in the opposite direction, from the centre of the continent to the east coast. The further away they got from the centre and their tribal area, the less liable they were to cut loose from the caravans and run back home, the more nervous they became of the strange Africans they saw about them, until at the end, on the coast, they were no trouble at all, and were positively anxious to step into the boats and be taken to safe homes across the sea. Like the slave far from home, I became anxious only to arrive. The greater the discouragements of the journey, the keener I was to press on and embrace my new life.

When I arrived I found that Nazruddin hadn't lied. The place had had its troubles: the town at the bend in the river was more than half destroyed. What had been the European suburb near the rapids had been burnt down, and bush had grown over the ruins; it was hard to distinguish what had been gardens from what had been streets. The official and commercial area near the dock and customs house survived, and some residential streets in the centre. But there wasn't much else. Even the African *cités* were inhabited only in corners, and in decay elsewhere, with many of the low, box-like concrete houses in pale blue or pale green abandoned, hung with quick-growing, quick-dying tropical vines, mattings of brown and green.

Nazruddin's shop was in a market square in the commercial

area. It smelt of rats and was full of dung, but it was intact. I had
bought Nazruddin's stock – but there was none of that. I had also
bought the goodwill – but that was meaningless, because so many
of the Africans had gone back to the bush, to the safety of their
villages, which lay up hidden and difficult creeks.

After my anxiety to arrive, there was little for me to do. But
I was not alone. There were other traders, other foreigners; some
of them had been there right through the troubles. I waited with
them. The peace held. People began coming back to the town; the
cité yards filled up. People began needing the goods which we
could supply. And slowly business started up again.

Zabeth was among the earliest of my regular customers. She was a
marchande – not a market-woman, but a retailer in a small way.
She belonged to a fishing community, almost a little tribe, and
every month or so she came from her village to the town to buy
her goods wholesale.

From me she bought pencils and copy-books, razor blades,
syringes, soap and toothpaste and toothbrushes, cloth, plastic
toys, iron pots and aluminium pans, enamel plates and basins.
These were some of the simple things Zabeth's fisherfolk needed
from the outside world, and had been doing without during the
troubles. Not essentials, not luxuries; but things that made ordinary life easier. The people here had many skills; they could get by
on their own. They tanned leather, wove cloth, worked iron; they
hollowed out large tree trunks into boats and smaller ones into
kitchen mortars. But to people looking for a large vessel that
wouldn't taint water and food, and wouldn't leak, imagine what a
blessing an enamel basin was!

Zabeth knew exactly what the people of her village needed and
how much they would be able or willing to pay for it. Traders on
the coast (including my own father) used to say – especially when
they were consoling themselves for some bad purchase – that everything eventually had its buyer. That wasn't so here. People were
interested in new things – like the syringes, which were a surprise
to me – and even modern things; but their tastes had set around
the first examples of these things that they had accepted. They

trusted a particular design, a particular trade-mark. It was useless for me to try to 'sell' anything to Zabeth; I had to stick as far as possible to familiar stock. It made for dull business, but it avoided complications. And it helped to make Zabeth the good and direct businesswoman that, unusually for an African, she was.

She didn't know how to read and write. She carried her complicated shopping list in her head and she remembered what she had paid for things on previous occasions. She never asked for credit – she hated the idea. She paid in cash, taking the money out from the vanity case she brought to town with her. Every trader knew about Zabeth's vanity case. It wasn't that she distrusted banks; she didn't understand them.

I would say to her, in that mixed river language we used, 'One day, Beth, somebody will snatch your case. It isn't safe to travel about with money like that.'

'The day that happens, Mis' Salim, I will know the time has come to stay home.'

It was a strange way of thinking. But she was a strange woman.

'Mis'', as used by Zabeth and others, was short for 'mister'. I was mister because I was a foreigner, someone from the far-off coast, and an English-speaker; and I was mister in order to be distinguished from the other resident foreigners, who were *monsieur*. That was, of course, before the Big Man came along and made us all *citoyens* and *citoyennes*. Which was all right for a while, until the lies he started making us all live made the people confused and frightened and, when a fetish stronger than his was found, made them decide to put an end to it all and go back again to the beginning.

Zabeth's village was only about sixty miles away. But it was some distance off the road, which was little more than a track; and it was some miles in from the main river. By land or by water it was a difficult journey, and took two days. By land during the rainy season it could take three. In the beginning Zabeth came by the land way, trekking with her women assistants to the road and waiting there for a van or truck or bus. When the steamers started up again, Zabeth always used the river; and that wasn't much easier.

The secret channels from the village were shallow, full of snags, humming with mosquitoes. Down these channels Zabeth and her women poled and often pushed their dugouts to the main river. There, close to the bank, they waited for the steamer, the dugouts full of goods – usually food – to be sold to people on the steamer and the barge the steamer towed. The food was mainly fish or monkey, fresh or *boucané* – smoked in the way of the country, with a thick black crust. Sometimes there was a smoked snake or a smoked small crocodile, a black hunk barely recognizable for what it had been – but with white or pale pink flesh below the charred crust.

When the steamer appeared, with its passenger barge in tow, Zabeth and her women poled or paddled out to the middle of the river and stood at the edge of the steamer channel, drifting down with the current. The steamer passed; the dugouts rocked in the swell; and then came the critical moment when the dugouts and the barge came close together. Zabeth and her women threw ropes on to the lower steel deck of the barge, where there were always hands to grab the ropes and tie them to some bulkhead; and the dugouts, from drifting downstream and against the side of the barge, began moving in the other direction, while people on the barge threw down pieces of paper or cloth on the fish or the monkey they wanted to buy.

This attaching of dugouts to the moving steamer or barge was a recognized river practice, but it was dangerous. Almost every trip the steamer made there was a report of a dugout being overturned somewhere along the thousand-mile route and of people being drowned. But the risk was worth taking: afterwards, without labour, as a *marchande* selling goods, Zabeth was towed up the river to the very edge of the town, uncoupling her dugouts by the ruins of the cathedral, a little before the docks, to avoid the officials there, who were always anxious to claim some tax. What a journey! Such trouble and danger to sell simple village things, and to take other goods back to the people of her village.

For a day or two before the steamer came there was a market and a camp in the open space outside the dock gate. Zabeth became part of this camp while she was in the town. If it rained she slept in the verandah of a grocery or a bar; at a later date she put up in an African lodging house, but in the beginning such places didn't exist. When she came to the shop there was nothing in her appearance that spoke of her difficult journey or her nights in the open. She was formally dressed, wrapped in her cotton in the African style that by folds and drapes emphasized the bigness of her bottom. She wore a turban – a piece of down-river style; and she had her vanity case with the creased notes she had got from people in her village and people on the steamer and barge. She shopped, she paid; and some hours before the steamer sailed again her women – thin, short, bald-looking, and in ragged working clothes – came to take the goods away.

This was a quicker journey, down river. But it was just as dangerous, with the same coupling and uncoupling of the dugouts and the barge. In those days the steamer left the town at four in the afternoon; so it was deep night when Zabeth and her women came to where they had to cast off from the steamer. Zabeth took care then not to give away the entrance to her village. She cast off; she waited for the steamer and the barge and the lights to disappear. Then she and her women poled back up or drifted down to their secret channel, and their night-time labour of poling and pushing below the overhanging trees.

Going home at night! It wasn't often that I was on the river at night. I never liked it. I never felt in control. In the darkness of river and forest you could be sure only of what you could see – and even on a moonlight night you couldn't see much. When you made a noise – dipped a paddle in the water – you heard yourself as though you were another person. The river and the forest were like presences, and much more powerful than you. You felt unprotected, an intruder.

In the daylight – though the colours could be very pale and ghostly, with the heat mist at times suggesting a colder climate – you could imagine the town being rebuilt and spreading. You could imagine the forests being uprooted, the roads being laid across creeks and swamps. You could imagine the land being made part of the present: that was how the Big Man put it later, offering us the vision of a two-hundred-mile 'industrial park' along the

14

river. (But he didn't mean it really; it was only his wish to appear a greater magician than any the place had ever known.) In daylight, though, you could believe in that vision of the future. You could imagine the land being made ordinary, fit for men like yourself, as small parts of it had been made ordinary for a short while before independence – the very parts that were now in ruins.

But at night, if you were on the river, it was another thing. You felt the land taking you back to something that was familiar, something you had known at some time but had forgotten or ignored, but which was always there. You felt the land taking you back to what was there a hundred years ago, to what had been there always.

What journeys Zabeth made! It was as though she came out each time from her hidden place to snatch from the present (or the future) some precious cargo to take back to her people – those razor blades, for instance, to be taken out from their packets and sold one by one, miracles of metal – cargo that became more precious the further she got from the town, the nearer she got to her fishing village, the true, safe world, protected from other men by forest and clogged-up waterways. And protected in other ways as well. Every man here knew that he was watched from above by his ancestors, living forever in a higher sphere, their passage on earth not forgotten, but essentially preserved, part of the presence of the forest. In the deepest forest was the greatest security. That was the security that Zabeth left behind, to get her precious cargo; that was the security to which she returned.

No one liked going outside his territory. But Zabeth travelled without fear; she came and went with her vanity case and no one molested her. She was not an ordinary person. In appearance she was not at all like the people of our region. They were small and slight and very black. Zabeth was a big woman with a coppery complexion; there were times when this copper glow, especially on her cheekbones, looked like a kind of make-up. There was something else about Zabeth. She had a special smell. It was strong and unpleasant, and at first I thought – because she came from a fishing village – that it was an old and deep smell of fish. Then I thought

15

it had to do with her restricted village diet. But the people of Zabeth's tribe whom I met didn't smell like Zabeth. Africans noticed her smell. If they came into the shop when Zabeth was there they wrinkled their noses and sometimes they went away.

Metty, the half-African boy who had grown up in my family's house on the coast and had come to join me, Metty said that Zabeth's smell was strong enough to keep mosquitoes away. I thought myself that it was this smell that kept men away from Zabeth, in spite of her fleshiness (which the men here liked) and in spite of her vanity case – because Zabeth wasn't married and, so far as I knew, lived with no man.

But the smell was meant to keep people at a distance. It was Metty – learning local customs fast – who told me that Zabeth was a magician, and was known in our region as a magician. Her smell was the smell of her protecting ointments. Other women used perfumes and scents to attract; Zabeth's ointments repelled and warned. She was protected. She knew it, and other people knew it.

I had treated Zabeth so far as a *marchande* and a good customer. Now that I knew that in our region she was a person of power, a prophetess, I could never forget it. So the charm worked on me as well.

2

Africa was my home, had been the home of my family for centuries. But we came from the east coast, and that made the difference. The coast was not truly African. It was an Arab-Indian-Persian-Portuguese place, and we who lived there were really people of the Indian Ocean. True Africa was at our back. Many miles of scrub or desert separated us from the up-country people; we looked east to the lands with which we traded – Arabia, India, Persia. These were also the lands of our ancestors. But we could no longer say that we were Arabians or Indians or Persians; when we compared ourselves with these people, we felt like people of Africa.

My family was Muslim. But we were a special group. We were distinct from the Arabs and other Muslims of the coast; in our customs and attitudes we were closer to the Hindus of north-western India, from which we had originally come. When we had come no one could tell me. We were not that kind of people. We simply lived; we did what was expected of us, what we had seen the previous generation do. We never asked why; we never recorded. We felt in our bones that we were a very old people; but we seemed to have no means of gauging the passing of time. Neither my father nor grandfather could put dates to their stories. Not because they had forgotten or were confused; the past was simply the past.

I remember hearing from my grandfather that he had once shipped a boatful of slaves as a cargo of rubber. He couldn't tell me when he had done this. It was just there in his memory, float-

17

ing around, without date or other association, as an unusual event
in an uneventful life. He didn't tell it as a piece of wickedness or
trickery or as a joke; he just told it as something unusual that he
had done – not shipping the slaves, but describing them as rubber.
And without my own memory of the old man's story I suppose
that would have been a piece of history lost forever. I believe, from
my later reading, that the idea of rubber would have occurred to
my grandfather at the time, before the first world war, when
rubber became big business – and later a big scandal – in central
Africa. So that facts are known to me which remained hidden or
uninteresting to my grandfather.

Of that whole period of upheaval in Africa – the expulsion of
the Arabs, the expansion of Europe, the parcelling out of the
continent – that is the only family story I have. That was the sort
of people we were. All that I know of our history and the history
of the Indian Ocean I have got from books written by Europeans.
If I say that our Arabs in their time were great adventurers and
writers; that our sailors gave the Mediterranean the lateen sail
that made the discovery of the Americas possible; that an Indian
pilot led Vasco da Gama from East Africa to Calicut; that the
very word *cheque* was first used by our Persian merchants; if I
say these things it is because I have got them from European
books. They formed no part of our knowledge or pride. Without Europeans, I feel, all our past would have been washed
away, like the scuff-marks of fishermen on the beach outside our
town.

There was a stockade on this beach. The walls were of brick.
It was a ruin when I was a boy, and in tropical Africa, land of
impermanent building, it was like a rare piece of history. It was
in this stockade that the slaves were kept after they had been
marched down from the interior in the caravans; there they waited
for the dhows to take them across the sea. But if you didn't
know, then the place was nothing, just four crumbling walls in a
picture-postcard setting of beach and coconut trees.

Once the Arabs had ruled here; then the Europeans had
come; now the Europeans were about to go away. But little had
changed in the manners or minds of men. The fishermen's boats

on that beach were still painted with large eyes on the bows for good luck; and the fishermen could get very angry, even murderous, if some visitor tried to photograph them – tried to rob them of their souls. People lived as they had always done; there was no break between past and present. All that had happened in the past was washed away; there was always only the present. It was as though, as a result of some disturbance in the heavens, the early morning light was always receding into the darkness, and men lived in a perpetual dawn.

The slavery of the east coast was not like the slavery of the west coast. No one was shipped off to plantations. Most of the people who left our coast went to Arabian homes as domestic servants. Some became members of the family they had joined; a few became powerful in their own right. To an African, a child of the forest, who had marched down hundreds of miles from the interior and was far from his village and tribe, the protection of a foreign family was preferable to being alone among strange and unfriendly Africans. This was one reason why the trade went on long after it had been outlawed by the European powers; and why, at the time when the Europeans were dealing in one kind of rubber, my grandfather could still occasionally deal in another. This was also the reason why a secret slavery continued on the coast until the other day. The slaves, or the people who might be considered slaves, wanted to remain as they were.

In my family's compound there were two slave families, and they had been there for at least three generations. The last thing they wanted to hear was that they had to go. Officially these people were only servants. But they wanted it known – to other Africans, and to poor Arabs and Indians – that they were really slaves. It wasn't that they were proud of slavery as a condition; what they were fierce about was their special connection with a family of repute. They could be very rough with people they considered smaller fry than the family.

When I was young I would be taken for walks in the narrow white-walled lanes of the old part of the town, which was where our house was. I would be bathed and dressed; they would put kohl on my eyes and hang a good-luck charm around my neck;

and then Mustafa, one of our old men, would hoist me on his shoulders. That was how I took my walk: Mustafa displaying me on his shoulders, displaying the worth of our family, and at the same time displaying his own trusted position in our family. There were some boys who made a point of taunting us. Mustafa, when we ran into these boys, would set me down, encourage me to speak insults, would add to these insults himself, would encourage me to fight, and then, when things became too hot for me, would lift me out of reach of the boys' feet and fists and place me again on his shoulders. And we would continue our walk.

This talk of Mustafa and Arabia and dhows and slaves might sound like something out of the Arabian Nights. But when I think of Mustafa, and even when I hear the word 'slave', I think of the squalor of our family compound, a mixture of school yard and back yard: all those people, someone always shrieking, quantities of clothes hanging on the lines or spread out on the bleaching stones, the sour smell of those stones running into the smell of the latrine and the barred-off urinal corner, piles of dirty enamel and brass dishes on the washing-up stand in the middle of the yard, children running about everywhere, endless cooking in the blackened kitchen building. I think of a hubbub of women and children, of my sisters and their families, the servant women and their families, both sides apparently in constant competition; I think of quarrels in the family rooms, competitive quarrels in the servants' quarters. There were too many of us in that small compound. We didn't want all those people in the servants' quarters. But they weren't ordinary servants, and there was no question of getting rid of them. We were stuck with them.

That was how it was on the east coast. The slaves could take over, and in more than one way. The people in our servant houses were no longer pure African. It wasn't acknowledged by the family, but somewhere along the line, or at many places along the line, the blood of Asia had been added to those people. Mustafa had the blood of Gujarat in his veins; so had Metty, the boy who later came all the way across the continent to join me. This, though, was a transferring of blood from master to slave. With the Arabs on our coast the process had worked the other way. The

slaves had swamped the masters; the Arabian race of the master
had virtually disappeared.

Once, great explorers and warriors, the Arabs had ruled. They
had pushed far into the interior and had built towns and planted
orchards in the forest. Then their power had been broken by
Europe. Their towns and orchards disappeared, swallowed up in
bush. They ceased to be driven on by their idea of their position
in the world, and their energy was lost; they forgot who they were
and where they had come from. They knew only that they were
Muslims; and in the Muslim way they needed wives and more
wives. But they were cut off from their roots in Arabia and could
only find their wives among the African women who had once
been their slaves. Soon, therefore, the Arabs, or the people who
called themselves Arabs, had become indistinguishable from
Africans. They barely had an idea of their original civilization.
They had the Koran and its laws; they stuck to certain fashions
in dress, wore a certain kind of cap, had a special cut of beard;
and that was all. They had little idea of what their ancestors had
done in Africa. They had only the habit of authority, without the
energy or the education to back up that authority. The authority
of the Arabs – which was real enough when I was a boy – was only
a matter of custom. It could be blown away at any time. The world
is what it is.

I was worried for the Arabs. I was also worried for us. Because,
so far as power went, there was no difference between the Arabs
and ourselves. We were both small groups living under a European
flag at the edge of the continent. In our family house when I was
a child I never heard a discussion about our future or the future
of the coast. The assumption seemed to be that things would
continue, that marriages would continue to be arranged between
approved parties, that trade and business would go on, that Africa
would be for us as it had been.

My sisters married in the traditional way; it was assumed that
I too would marry when the time came and extend the life of our
family house. But it came to me while I was quite young, still at
school, that our way of life was antiquated and almost at an
end.

Small things can start us off in new ways of thinking, and I was started off by the postage stamps of our area. The British administration gave us beautiful stamps. These stamps depicted local scenes and local things; there was one called 'Arab Dhow'. It was as though, in those stamps, a foreigner had said, 'This is what is most striking about this place.' Without that stamp of the dhow I might have taken the dhows for granted. As it was, I learned to look at them. Whenever I saw them tied up at the waterfront I thought of them as something peculiar to our region, quaint, something the foreigner would remark on, something not quite modern, and certainly nothing like the liners and cargo ships that berthed in their own modern docks.

So from an early age I developed the habit of looking, detaching myself from a familiar scene and trying to consider it as from a distance. It was from this habit of looking that the idea came to me that as a community we had fallen behind. And that was the beginning of my insecurity.

I used to think of this feeling of insecurity as a weakness, a failing of my own temperament, and I would have been ashamed if anyone had found out about it. I kept my ideas about the future to myself, and that was easy enough in our house, where, as I have said, there was never anything like a political discussion. My family were not fools. My father and his brothers were traders, businessmen; in their own way they had to keep up with the times. They could assess situations; they took risks and sometimes they could be very bold. But they were buried so deep in their lives that they were not able to stand back and consider the nature of their lives. They did what they had to do. When things went wrong they had the consolations of religion. This wasn't just a readiness to accept Fate; this was a quiet and profound conviction about the vanity of all human endeavour.

I could never rise so high. My own pessimism, my insecurity, was a more terrestrial affair. I was without the religious sense of my family. The insecurity I felt was due to my lack of true religion, and was like the small change of the exalted pessimism of our faith, the pessimism that can drive men on to do wonders. It was the price for my more materialist attitude, my seeking to occupy the middle ground, between absorption in life and soaring above the cares of the earth.

If the insecurity I felt about our position on the coast was due to my temperament, then little occurred to calm me down. Events in this part of Africa began to move fast. To the north there was a bloody rebellion of an up-country tribe which the British seemed unable to put down; and there were explosions of disobedience and rage in other places as well. Even hypochondriacs sometimes have real illnesses, and I don't think it was my nervousness alone that made me feel that the political system we had known was coming to an end, and that what was going to replace it wasn't going to be pleasant. I feared the lies – black men assuming the lies of white men.

If it was Europe that gave us on the coast some idea of our history, it was Europe, I feel, that also introduced us to the lie. Those of us who had been in that part of Africa before the Europeans had never lied about ourselves. Not because we were moral. We didn't lie because we never assessed ourselves and didn't think there was anything for us to lie about; we were people who simply did what we did. But the Europeans could do one thing and say something quite different; and they could act in this way because they had an idea of what they owed to their civilization. It was their great advantage over us. The Europeans wanted gold and slaves, like everybody else; but at the same time they wanted statues put up to themselves as people who had done good things for the slaves. Being an intelligent and energetic people, and at the peak of their powers, they could express both sides of their civilization; and they got both the slaves and the statues.

Because they could assess themselves, the Europeans were better equipped to cope with changes than we were. And I saw, when I compared the Europeans with ourselves, that we had ceased to count in Africa, that really we no longer had anything to offer. The Europeans were preparing to get out, or to fight, or to meet the Africans half-way. We continued to live as we had always done, blindly. Even at this late stage there was never anything like a political discussion in our house or in the houses of families I knew. The subject was avoided. I found myself avoiding it.

I used to go twice a week to play squash in the squash court of my friend Indar. His grandfather had come from the Punjab in India to work on the railway as a contract labourer. The old Punjabi had done well. When he had worked out his contract he had settled on the coast and become a market moneylender, lending twenty or thirty shillings a time to stall-keepers in the market who ran short and depended on these small loans to buy their goods. For ten shillings lent this week twelve or fifteen had to be returned the next. Not the best kind of business; but an active man (and a tough man) could increase his capital many times over in a year. Well, it was a service, and a living. And more than a living. The family had become very grand. They had become merchant-bankers in an unofficial way, staking small prospecting companies, staking trading ventures to India and Arabia and the Persian Gulf (still in the Arab dhows of the postage stamp).

The family lived in a big compound in an asphalted yard. The main house was at the far end; there were smaller houses at the side for members of the family who wished to live by themselves, other houses for the servants (proper servants, hire-and-fire people, not limpets like ours); and there was the squash court. Everything was surrounded by a high ochre-washed wall, and there was a main gate with a watchman. The compound was in a newer part of the town; I didn't think it was possible to be more exclusive or protected.

Rich people never forget they are rich, and I looked upon Indar as a good son of his money-lending or banking family. He was handsome, careful of his appearance, and slightly effeminate, with something buttoned-up in his expression. I put that expression down to his regard for his own wealth and also to his sexual anxieties. I thought he was a great brothel man on the sly and lived in fear of being exposed or catching some disease.

We were having cold orange juice and hot black tea after our game (Indar was already concerned about his weight), when he told me he was leaving. He was going away, going to England to a famous university to do a three-year course. It was like Indar, and his family, to announce important news in this casual way. The news depressed me a little. Indar could do what he was doing not only because he was rich (I associated going abroad to study with great wealth), but also because he had gone right through our local English-language college until he was eighteen. I had left when I was sixteen. Not because I wasn't bright or didn't have the inclination, but because no one in our family had stayed at school after sixteen.

We were sitting on the steps of the squash court, in the shade. Indar said in his quiet way, 'We're washed up here, you know. To be in Africa you have to be strong. We're not strong. We don't even have a flag.'

He had mentioned the unmentionable. And as soon as he spoke I saw the wall of his compound as useless. Two generations had built what I saw; and I mourned for that lost labour. As soon as Indar spoke I felt I could enter his mind and see what he saw – the mocking quality of the grandeur, the gate and the watchman that wouldn't be able to keep out the true danger.

But I gave no sign that I understood what he was talking about. I behaved like the others who had infuriated and saddened me by refusing to acknowledge that change was coming to our part of the world. And when Indar went on to ask, 'What are you going to do?' I said, as though I didn't see any problem, 'I'll stay. I'll go into the business.'

It wasn't true at all. It was the opposite of what I felt. But I found that I was unwilling – as soon as the question had been put to me – to acknowledge my helplessness. I instinctively fell into the attitudes of my family. But with me the fatalism was bogus; I cared very much about the world and wished to renounce nothing. All I could do was to hide from the truth. And that discovery about myself made the walk back through the hot town very disturbing.

The afternoon sun fell on the soft black asphalt road and the tall hibiscus hedges. It was all so ordinary. There was as yet no danger in the crowds, the broken-down streets, the blank-walled lanes. But the place was poisoned for me.

I had an upstairs room in our family house. It was still light when I got back. I looked out over our compound, saw the trees and greenery of the neighbouring yards and open spaces. My aunt was calling to one of her daughters: some old brass vases that had been taken out to the yard to be scoured with limes hadn't been taken back in. I looked at that devout woman, sheltered behind her wall, and saw how petty her concern with the brass vases was. The thin whitewashed wall (thinner than the wall of the slave stockade on the beach) protected her so little. She was so vulnerable – her person, her religion, her customs, her way of life. The squalling yard had contained its own life, had been its own complete world, for so long. How could anyone not take it for granted? How could anyone stop to ask what it was that had really protected us?

I remembered the look of contempt and irritation Indar had given me. And the decision I came to then was this. I had to break away. I couldn't protect anyone; no one could protect me. We couldn't protect ourselves; we could only in various ways hide from the truth. I had to break away from our family compound and our community. To stay with my community, to pretend that I had simply to travel along with them, was to be taken with them to destruction. I could be master of my fate only if I stood alone. One tide of history – forgotten by us, living only in books by Europeans that I was yet to read – had brought us here. We had lived our lives in our way, done what we had to do, worshipped God and obeyed his commandments. Now – to echo Indar's words – another tide of history was coming to wash us away.

I could no longer submit to Fate. My wish was not to be good, in the way of our tradition, but to make good. But how? What did I have to offer? What talent, what skill, apart from the African trading skills of our family? This anxiety began to eat away at me. And that was why, when Nazruddin made his offer, of a shop and business in a far-off country that was still in Africa, I clutched at it.

Nazruddin was an exotic in our community. He was a man of my father's age, but he looked much younger and was altogether more a man of the world. He played tennis, drank wine, spoke French, wore dark glasses and suits (with very wide lapels, the tips of which curled down). He was known among us (and slightly mocked behind his back) for his European manners, which he had picked up not from Europe (he had never been there), but from a town in the centre of Africa where he lived and had his business.

Many years before, following some fancy of his own, Nazruddin had cut down on his business on the coast and begun to move inland. The colonial boundaries of Africa gave an international flavour to his operations. But Nazruddin was doing no more than follow the old Arab trading routes to the interior; and he had fetched up in the centre of the continent, at the bend in the great river.

That was as far as the Arabs had got in the last century. There they had met Europe, advancing from the other direction. For Europe it was one little probe. For the Arabs of central Africa it was their all; the Arabian energy that had pushed them into Africa had died down at its source, and their power was like the light of a star that travels on after the star itself has become dead. Arab power had vanished; at the bend in the river there had grown up a European, and not an Arab, town. And it was from that town that Nazruddin, reappearing among us from time to time, brought back his exotic manners and tastes and his tales of commercial success.

Nazruddin was an exotic, but he remained bound to our community because he needed husbands and wives for his children. I always knew that in me he saw the prospective husband of one of his daughters; but I had lived with this knowledge for so long that it didn't embarrass me. I liked Nazruddin. I welcomed his visits, his talk, his very alienness as he sat downstairs in our drawing room or verandah and spoke of the excitements of his far-off world.

He was a man of enthusiasms. He relished everything he did. He liked the houses he bought (always bargains), the restaurants he chose, the dishes he had ordered. Everything worked out well for him, and his tales of unfailing luck would have made him intolerable if he didn't have the gift of describing things so well. He made me long to do what he had done, to be where he had been. In some ways he became my model.

He was something of a palmist, in addition to everything else, and his readings were valued because he could do them only when the mood took him. When I was ten or twelve he had given me a reading and had seen great things in my hand. So I respected his judgement. He added to that reading from time to time. I remember one occasion especially. He was on the bentwood rocker, rocking unsteadily from the edge of the carpet on to the concrete floor. He broke off what he was saying and asked to see my hand. He felt the tips of my fingers, bent my fingers, looked briefly at my palms, and then let my hand go. He thought for a little about what he had seen – it was his way, thinking about what he had seen rather than looking at the hand all the time – and he said, 'You are the most faithful man I know.' This didn't please me; it seemed to me he was offering me no life at all. I said, 'Can you read your own hand? Do you know what's in store for you?' He said, 'Don't I know, don't I know.' The tone of his voice was different then, and I saw that this man, for whom (according to his talk) everything worked out beautifully, really lived with a vision of things turning out badly. I thought: 'This is how a man should behave,' and I felt close to him after that, closer than I did to members of my own family.

Then came the crash which some people had been quietly prophesying for this successful and talkative man. Nazruddin's adopted country became independent, quite suddenly, and the news from that place for weeks and months was of wars and killings. From the way some people talked you might have believed that if Nazruddin had been another kind of person, if he had boasted less of his success, drunk less wine and been more seemly in his behaviour, events would have taken another turn. We heard that he had fled with his family to Uganda. There was a report that they had driven through the bush for days on the back of a truck and had turned up panic-stricken and destitute at the border town of Kisoro.

At least he was safe. In due course he came to the coast. People looking for a broken man were disappointed. Nazruddin was as sprightly as ever, still with his dark glasses and suit. The disaster appeared not to have touched him at all.

Usually when Nazruddin came to visit efforts were made to receive him well. The drawing room was given a special cleaning, and the brass vases with the hunting scenes were polished up. But this time, because of the belief that he was a man in trouble, and therefore ordinary again, just like us, no one had tried hard. The drawing room was in its usual state of mess, and we sat out on the verandah facing the yard.

My mother brought tea, offering it not in the usual way, as the shamefaced hospitality of simple folk, but behaving as though she was performing some necessary final rite. When she put the tray down she seemed about to burst into tears. My brothers-in-law gathered around with concerned faces. But from Nazruddin – in spite of that tale about the long-distance ride on the back of a truck – there came no stories of disaster, only stories of continuing luck and success. He had seen the trouble coming; he had pulled out months before it came.

Nazruddin said: 'It wasn't the Africans who made me nervous. It was the Europeans and the others. Just before a crash people go crazy. We had a fantastic property boom. Everybody was only talking about money. A piece of bush costing nothing today was selling for half a million francs tomorrow. It was like magic, but with real money. I got caught up in it myself, and nearly got trapped.

'One Sunday morning I went out to the development where I had bought a few lots. The weather was bad. Hot and heavy. The sky was dark but it wasn't going to rain; it was just going to stay like that. The lightning was far away – it was raining somewhere else in the forest. I thought, "What a place to live in!" I could hear the river – the development wasn't too far from the rapids. I listened to the river and looked up at that sky and I thought: "This isn't property. This is just bush. This has always been bush." I could scarcely wait for Monday morning after that. I put everything up for sale. Lower than the going price, but I asked to be paid in Europe. I sent the family to Uganda.

'Do you know Uganda? A lovely country. Cool, three to four thousand feet up, and people say it's like Scotland, with the hills. The British have given the place the finest administration you could ask for. Very simple, very efficient. Wonderful roads. And the Bantu people there are pretty bright.'

That was Nazruddin. We had imagined him done for. Instead, he was trying to excite us with his enthusiasm for his new country, and asking us to contemplate his luck yet again. The patronage, in fact, was all on his side. Though he never said anything openly, he saw us on the coast as threatened, and he had come that day to make me an offer.

He still had interests in his old country – a shop, a few agencies. He had thought it prudent to keep the shop on, while he was transferring his assets out of the country, to prevent people looking at his affairs too closely. And it was this shop and those agencies that he now offered me.

'They aren't worth anything now. But they will be again. I really should be giving it to you for nothing. But that would be bad for you and for me. You must always know when to pull out. A businessman isn't a mathematician. Remember that. Never become hypnotized by the beauty of numbers. A businessman is someone who buys at ten and is happy to get out at twelve. The other kind of man buys at ten, sees it rise to eighteen and does nothing. He is waiting for it to get to twenty. The beauty of numbers. When it drops to ten again he waits for it to get back to eighteen. When it drops to two he waits for it to get back to ten. Well, it gets back there. But he has wasted a quarter of his life. And all he's got out of his money is a little mathematical excitement.'

I said, 'This shop – assuming you bought at ten, what would you say you were selling it to me for?'

'Two. In three or four years it will climb up to six. Business never dies in Africa; it is only interrupted. For me it is a waste of time to see that two get up to six. There is more for me in cotton in Uganda. But for you it will be a trebling of your capital. What you must always know is when to get out.'

Nazruddin had seen faithfulness in my hand. But he had read me wrong. Because when I accepted his offer I was in an important way breaking faith with him. I had accepted his offer because I wanted to break away. To break away from my family and community also meant breaking away from my unspoken commitment to Nazruddin and his daughter.

She was a lovely girl. Once a year, for a few weeks, she came to the coast to stay with her father's sister. She was better educated than I was; there was some talk of her going in for accountancy or law. She would have been a very nice girl to marry, but I admired her as I would have admired a girl of my own family. Nothing would have been easier than to marry Nazruddin's daughter. Nothing, to me, would have been more stifling. And it was from that stifling as well as from everything else that I drove away, when I left the coast in the Peugeot.

I was breaking faith with Nazruddin. Yet he – a relisher of life, a seeker after experience – had been my exemplar; and it was to his town that I drove. All that I knew of the town at the bend of the river I had got from Nazruddin's stories. Ridiculous things can work on us at moments of strain; and towards the end of that hard drive what was often in my head was what Nazruddin had said about the restaurants of the town, about the food of Europe and the wine. 'The wines are Saccone and Speed,' he had said. It was a merchant's observation. He had meant that even there, in the centre of Africa, the wine had come from the shippers on our east coast, and not from the people on the other side. But in my imagination I allowed the words to stand for pure bliss.

I had never been to a real European restaurant or tasted wine – forbidden to us – with any pleasure; and I knew that the life Nazruddin had described had come to an end. But I drove through Africa to Nazruddin's town as to a place where this life might be recreated for me.

When I arrived I found that the town from which Nazruddin had brought back his tales had been destroyed, had returned to the bush he had had a vision of when he had decided to sell. In spite of myself, in spite of all that I had been told about recent events, I felt shocked, let down. My faithlessness hardly seemed to matter.

Wine! It was hard to get the simplest food; and if you wanted vegetables you either got them out of an old – and expensive – tin,

31

or you grew them yourself. The Africans who had abandoned the
town and gone back to their villages were better off; they at least
had gone back to their traditional life and were more or less
self-sufficient. But for the rest of us in the town who needed shops
and services – a few Belgians, some Greeks and Italians, a handful
of Indians – it was a stripped, Robinson Crusoe kind of existence.
We had cars and we lived in proper houses – I had bought a flat
over an empty warehouse for almost nothing. But if we had worn
skins and lived in thatched huts it wouldn't have been too
inappropriate. The shops were empty; water was a problem;
electricity was erratic; and petrol was often short.

Once for some weeks we were without kerosene. Two empty
oil barges had been shanghaied by people down river, towed as
river spoil to a hidden creek, and converted into living quarters.
The people here liked to scrape their yards down to the red earth,
to keep away snakes; and the steel decks of the barges provided
an ideal living surface.

On those kerosene-less mornings I had to boil my water on an
English-made cast-iron charcoal brazier – part of my shop stock,
intended for sale to village Africans. I took the brazier to the
landing of the external staircase at the back of the house, squatted
and fanned. All around me people were doing the same; the
place was blue with smoke.

And there were the ruins. *Miscvique probat populos et foedera
jungi.* These Latin words, whose meaning I didn't know, were all
that remained of a monument outside the dock gates. I knew the
words by heart; I gave them my own pronunciation, and they
ran like a nonsense jingle in my head. The words were carved at
the top of a block of granite, and the rest of the granite was now
bare. The bronze sculpture below the words had been torn away;
the jagged little bits of bronze that remained anchored in the
granite suggested that the sculptor had done banana leaves or
palm branches at the top, to frame his composition. I was told
that the monument had been put up only a few years before,
almost at the end of the colonial time, to mark sixty years of the
steamer service from the capital.

So almost as soon as it had been put up – no doubt with

speeches about a further sixty years of service – the steamer monument had been knocked down. With all the other colonial statues and monuments. Pedestals had been defaced, protective railings flattened, floodlights smashed and left to rust. Ruins had been left as ruins; no attempt had been made to tidy up. The names of all the main streets had been changed. Rough boards carried the new, roughly lettered names. No one used the new names, because no one particularly cared about them. The wish had only been to get rid of the old, to wipe out the memory of the intruder. It was unnerving, the depth of that African rage, the wish to destroy, regardless of the consequences.

But more unnerving than anything else was the ruined suburb near the rapids. Valuable real estate for a while, and now bush again, common ground, according to African practice. The houses had been set alight one by one. They had been stripped – before or afterwards – only of those things that the local people needed – sheets of tin, lengths of pipe, bath tubs and sinks and lavatory bowls (impermeable vessels, useful for soaking cassava in). The big lawns and gardens had returned to bush; the streets had disappeared; vines and creepers had grown over broken, bleached walls of concrete or hollow clay brick. Here and there in the bush could still be seen the concrete shells of what had been restaurants (Saccone and Speed wines) and night clubs. One night club had been called 'Napoli'; the now meaningless name, painted on the concrete wall, was almost bleached away.

Sun and rain and bush had made the site look old, like the site of a dead civilization. The ruins, spreading over so many acres, seemed to speak of a final catastrophe. But the civilization wasn't dead. It was the civilization I existed in and in fact was still working towards. And that could make for an odd feeling: to be among the ruins was to have your time-sense unsettled. You felt like a ghost, not from the past, but from the future. You felt that your life and ambition had already been lived out for you and you were looking at the relics of that life. You were in a place where the future had come and gone.

With its ruins and its deprivations Nazruddin's town was a ghost town. And for me, as a newcomer, there was nothing like

a social life. The expatriates weren't welcoming. They had been
through a lot; they still didn't know how things were going to
turn out; and they were very nervous. The Belgians, especially
the younger ones, were full of resentments and a sense of injustice.
The Greeks, great family men, with the aggressiveness and frustra-
tions of family men, kept to their families and their immediate
friends. There were three houses that I visited, visiting them in
turn on weekdays for lunch, which had become my main meal.
They were all Asian or Indian houses.

There was a couple from India. They lived in a small flat that
smelled of asafoetida and was decorated with paper flowers and
brightly coloured religious prints. He was a United Nations expert
of some sort who hadn't wanted to go back to India and had
stayed on doing odd jobs after his contract had expired. They were
a hospitable couple and they made a point (I feel for religious
reasons) of offering hospitality to frightened or stranded foreigners. They spoilt their hospitality by talking a little too much about
it. Their food was too liquid and peppery for me, and I didn't like
the way the man ate. He bent his head low over his food, keeping
his nose an inch or two away from his plate, and he ate noisily,
slapping his lips together. While he ate like this his wife fanned
him, never taking her eyes off his plate, fanning with her right
hand, resting her chin on the palm of her left hand. Still, I went
there twice a week, more for the sake of having somewhere to go
than for the food.

The other place I went to was a rough, ranch-like house that
belonged to an elderly Indian couple whose family had all gone
away during the troubles. The yard was big and dusty, full of
abandoned cars and trucks, the relics of a transport business in
colonial days. This old couple didn't seem to know where they
were. The bush of Africa was outside their yard; but they spoke
no French, no African language, and from the way they behaved
you would have thought that the river just down the road was
the Ganges, with temples and holy men and bathing steps. But it
was soothing to be with them. They didn't look for conversation,
and were quite happy if you said nothing, if you ate and ran.

Shoba and Mahesh were the people I felt closest to, and I soon thought of them as friends. They had a shop in what ought to have been a prime commercial position, opposite the van der Weyden Hotel. Like me, they were migrants from the east and refugees from their own community. They were an extraordinarily good-looking couple; it was strange, in our town, to find people so careful of their dress and appearance. But they had lived too long apart from their fellows and had forgotten how to be curious about them. Like many isolated people, they were wrapped up in themselves and not too interested in the world outside. And this beautiful couple had their days of tension. Shoba, the lady, was vain and neurotic. Mahesh, the simpler partner, could be in a state of anxiety about her.

That was my life in Nazruddin's town. I had wanted to break away and make a fresh start. But there are degrees in everything, and I felt burdened by the bareness of my days. My life was unconstricted, but narrower than it had ever been; the solitude of my evenings was like an ache. I didn't think I had the resources to last. My comfort was that I had lost little, except time; I could always move on – though where, I didn't yet know. And then I found I couldn't move. I had to stay.

What I had feared would happen on the coast came to pass. There was an uprising; and the Arabs – men almost as African as their servants – had been finally laid low.

I first heard the news from my friends Shoba and Mahesh, who had got it from the radio – that expatriate habit of listening to the BBC news was something I had not yet got into. We treated the news as a secret, as something that had to be kept from the local people; this was one occasion when we were glad there was no local newspaper.

Then newspapers from Europe and the United States came to various people in the town and were passed around; and it was extraordinary to me that some of the newspapers could have found good words for the butchery on the coast. But people are like that about places in which they aren't really interested and where they don't have to live. Some papers spoke of the end of feudalism and the dawn of a new age. But what had happened was not new. People who had grown feeble had been physically destroyed. That, in Africa, was not new; it was the oldest law of the land.

Letters eventually came from the coast – in a batch – from members of my family. They were cautiously written, but their message was plain. There was no place for us on the coast; our life there was over. The family was scattering. Only old people would stay on in our family compound – a quieter life there, at last. The family servants, burdensome to the end, refusing to go away, insisting on their slave status even at this time of revolution, were being split up among the family. And one of the points of the letters was that I had to take my share.

It was not for me to choose who I wanted; apparently I had already been chosen by someone. One of the boys or young men from the servant houses wanted to get as far away from the coast as possible, and he had been firm about being sent 'to stay with Salim'. The boy said he had always had 'a special liking for Salim', and he had made such a fuss that they had decided to send him to me. I could imagine the scene. I could imagine the screaming and the stamping and the sulking. That was how the servants got their way in our house; they could be worse than children. My father, not realizing what other people in the family had written, simply said in his letter that he and my mother had decided to send someone to look after me – he meant, of course, that he was sending me a boy to look after and feed.

I couldn't say no: the boy was on his way. That this boy had 'a special liking' for me was news to me. A better reason for his choice of me was that I was just three or four years older than he was, unmarried, and more likely to put up with his wandering ways. He had always been a wanderer. We had sent him to the Koranic school when he was small, but he was always running off somewhere else, in spite of beatings by his mother. (And how he screamed in the quarters, and how his mother shouted – both of them overdoing the drama, trying to get as much attention as possible from the rest of the compound!) He was nobody's idea of a house servant. With bed and board always provided, he was more a man about town, friendly and unreliable and full of

36

friends, always willing, always offering to help, and never doing a quarter of what he promised.

He turned up at the flat one evening in one of Daulat's trucks, not long after I had got the letters saying that he had been sent. And my heart went out to him: he looked so altered, so tired and frightened. He was still living with the shock of events on the coast; and he hadn't liked the journey across Africa at all.

He had done the first half of the journey by the railway, which travelled at an average speed of ten miles an hour. Then he had transferred to buses and finally to Daulat's trucks – in spite of wars, bad roads and worn-out vehicles, Daulat, a man of our community, maintained a trucking service between our town and the eastern frontier. Daulat's drivers helped the boy past the various officials. But the mixed-race man about town from the coast was still African enough to be unsettled by his passage through the strange tribes of the interior. He couldn't bring himself to eat their food, and he hadn't eaten for days. Without knowing it, he had made in reverse the journey which some of his ancestors had made a century or more before.

He threw himself into my arms, converting the Muslim embrace into a child's clinging. I patted him on the back, and he took this as a signal to scream the place down. Right away, between screams and bawls, he began telling me about the killings he had seen in the market at home.

I didn't take in all that he was saying. I was worried about the neighbours, and trying to get him to tone down the screaming, trying to get him to understand that that kind of showing-off slave behaviour (which it partly was) was all right on the coast, but that people here wouldn't understand. He was beginning to go on a little bit, too, about the savagery of the *kafar*, the Africans, behaving as though my flat was the family compound and he could shout anything he wanted about people outside. And all the time Daulat's friendly African loader was coming up the external staircase with luggage – not much, but in many small, awkward pieces: a few bundles, a wickerwork laundry basket, some cardboard boxes.

I broke away from the bawling boy – to pay attention was to

encourage him – and I dealt with the loader, walking out with him to the street to tip him. The bawling in the flat upstairs died down, as I had expected; solitude and the strangeness of the flat were having their effect; and when I went back up I refused to hear any more from the boy until he had had something to eat.

He became quiet and correct, and while I prepared some baked beans and cheese on toast he brought out, from his bundles and boxes, the things that had been sent me by my family. Ginger and sauces and spices from my mother. Two family photographs from my father, and a wall-print on cheap paper of one of our holy places in Gujarat, showing it as a modern place, though: the artist had put in motor-cars and motor-bikes and bicycles and even trains pell-mell in the surrounding streets. It was my father's way of saying that, modern as I was, I would return to the faith.

'I was in the market, Salim,' the boy said, after he had eaten. 'At first I thought it was just a quarrel around Mian's stall. I couldn't believe what I was seeing. They were behaving as though knives didn't cut, as though people weren't made of flesh. I couldn't believe it. At the end it was as if a pack of dogs had got into a butcher's stall. I saw arms and legs bleeding and lying about. Just like that. They were still there the next day, those arms and legs.'

I tried to stop him. I didn't want to hear more. But it wasn't easy to stop him. He went on about those cut-off arms and legs that belonged to people we had known since we were children. It was terrible, what he had seen. But I was also beginning to feel that he was trying to excite himself to cry a little bit more after he had stopped wanting to cry. I felt that it worried him to find that from time to time he was forgetting, and thinking of other things. He seemed to be wanting to thrill himself again and again; and this disturbed me.

In a few days, though, he thawed out. And the events of the coast were never spoken of again. He settled down more easily than I expected. I had expected him to go sulky and withdrawn; I had thought, especially after his unhappy journey, that he would have hated our backward town. But he liked it; and he liked it because he was himself liked, in a way he hadn't been before.

Physically he was quite different from the local people. He was taller, more muscular, looser and more energetic in his movements. He was admired. The local women, with their usual free ways, made no secret of finding him desirable – calling out to him in the street, and stopping and staring with wicked, half-smiling (and slightly crossed) eyes that appeared to say: 'Consider this a joke, and laugh. Or take it seriously.' My own way of looking at him changed. He ceased to be one of the boys from the servant houses. I saw what the local people saw; in my own eyes he became more handsome and distinctive. To the local people he wasn't quite an African, and he aroused no tribal uneasiness; he was an exotic with African connections whom they wanted to claim. He flourished. He picked up the local language fast, and he even got a new name.

At home we had called him Ali or – when we wanted to suggest the special wild and unreliable nature of this Ali – 'Ali-wa' ('Ali! Ali! But where is this Ali-wa?'). He rejected this name now. He preferred to be called Metty, which was what the local people called him. It was some time before I understood that it wasn't a real name, that it was just the French word *métis*, someone of mixed race. But that wasn't how I used it. To me it was only a name: Metty.

Here, as on the coast, Metty was a wanderer. He had the bedroom just across the passage from the kitchen; it was the first door on the right as you came in from the landing of the external staircase. I often heard him coming in late at night. That was the freedom he had come to me for. But the Metty who enjoyed that freedom was a different person from the boy who had arrived bawling and screaming, with the manners of the servant house. He had quickly shed those manners; he had developed a new idea of his worth. He became useful in the shop; and, in the flat, his wandering habits – which I had dreaded – kept his presence light. But he was always there, and in the town he was like one of my own. He lessened my solitude and made the empty months more bearable – months of waiting for trade to start up again. As, very slowly, it was begininng to do.

We fell into the routine of morning coffee at the flat, shop,

separate lunches, shop, separate evenings. Man and master sometimes met, as equals with equal needs, in the dark little bars that
began to appear in our town, signs of reawakening life: rough little
cells with roofs of corrugated iron, no ceilings, concrete walls
painted dark blue or green, red concrete floors.

In one such place Metty put the seal on our new relationship
one evening. When I entered I saw him dancing fantastically –
slim-waisted, narrow-hipped, wonderfully made. He stopped as
soon as he saw me – his servant's instinct. But then he bowed and
made a show of welcoming me as though he owned the place. He
said, in the French accent he had picked up, 'I must do nothing
indecent in front of the *patron*.' And that was precisely what he
went on to do.

So he learned to assert himself. But there were no strains
between us. And he became, increasingly, an asset. He became
my customs clerk. He was always good with the customers and
won me and the shop much goodwill. As an exotic, a licensed man,
he was the only person in the town who would risk making a joke
with Zabeth, the *marchande* who was also a sorceress.

That was how it was with us, as the town came to life again, as
the steamers started to come up again from the capital, once a
week, then twice a week, as people began coming back from the
villages to the *cités* in the town, as trade grew and my business,
which had stood for so long at zero, climbed (to use Nazruddin's
scale of ten) back up to two, and even gave me glimpses of four.

3

ZABETH, as a magician or sorceress, kept herself from men. But it hadn't always been so; Zabeth hadn't always been a magician. She had a son. She spoke of him sometimes to me, but she spoke of him as part of a life she had put behind her. She made that son seem so far away that I thought the boy might be dead. Then one day she brought him to the shop.

He was about fifteen or sixteen, and already quite big, taller and heavier than the men of our region, whose average height was about five feet. His skin was perfectly black, with nothing of his mother's copper colour; his face was longer and more firmly modelled; and from what Zabeth said I gathered that the boy's father came from one of the tribes of the south.

The boy's father was a trader. As a trader, he had travelled about the country during the miraculous peace of the colonial time, when men could, if they wished, pay little attention to tribal boundaries. That was how, during his travels, he and Zabeth had met; it was from this trader that Zabeth had picked up her trading skills. At independence tribal boundaries had become important again, and travel was not as safe as it had been. The man from the south had gone back to his tribal land, taking the son he had had by Zabeth. A father could always claim his child; there were any number of folk sayings that expressed this almost universal African law. And Ferdinand – that was the name of the boy – had spent the last few years away from his mother. He had gone to school in the south, in one of the mining towns, and had been there through all the troubles that had come after independence, especially the long secessionist war.

Now for some reason – perhaps because the father had died, or had married again and wished to get rid of Ferdinand, or simply because Zabeth had wished it – Ferdinand had been sent back to his mother. He was a stranger in the land. But no one here could be without a tribe; and Ferdinand, again according to tribal custom, had been received into his mother's tribe.

Zabeth had decided to send Ferdinand to the lycée in our town. That had been cleaned up and got going again. It was a solid two-storey, two-courtyard stone building in the colonial-official style, with wide verandahs upstairs and downstairs. Squatters had taken over the downstairs part, cooking on fire stones in the verandah and throwing out their rubbish on to the courtyards and grounds. Strange rubbish, not the tins and paper and boxes and other containers you would expect in a town, but a finer kind of waste – shells and bones and ashes, burnt sacking – that made the middens look like grey-black mounds of sifted earth.

The lawns and gardens had been scuffed away. But the bougainvillaea had grown wild, choking the tall palmiste trees, tumbling over the lycée wall, and climbing up the square pillars of the main gate to twine about the decorative metal arch where, in letters of metal, was still the lycée motto: *Semper Aliquid Novi*. The squatters, timid and half-starved, had moved out as soon as they had been asked. Some doors and windows and shutters had been replaced, the plumbing repaired, the place painted, the rubbish in the grounds carted away, the grounds asphalted over; and in the building which I had thought of as a ruin there had begun to appear the white faces of the teachers.

It was as a lycée boy that Ferdinand came to the shop. He wore the regulation white shirt and short white trousers. It was a simple but distinctive costume; and – though the short trousers were a little absurd on someone so big – the costume was important both to Ferdinand and Zabeth. Zabeth lived a purely African life; for her only Africa was real. But for Ferdinand she wished something else. I saw no contradiction; it seemed to me natural that someone like Zabeth, living such a hard life, should want something better for her son. This better life lay outside the timeless ways of village and river. It lay in education and the acquiring

of new skills; and for Zabeth, as for many Africans of her generation, education was something only foreigners could give.

Ferdinand was to be a boarder at the lycée. Zabeth had brought
him to the shop that morning to introduce him to me. She wanted
me to keep an eye on him in the strange town and take him under
my protection. If Zabeth chose me for this job, it wasn't only because I was a business associate she had grown to trust. It was also
because I was a foreigner, and English-speaking as well, someone
from whom Ferdinand could learn manners and the ways of the
outside world. I was someone with whom Ferdinand could
practise.

The tall boy was quiet and respectful. But I had the feeling
that that would last only while his mother was around. There was
something distant and slightly mocking in his eyes. He seemed
to be humouring the mother he had only just got to know. She
was a village woman; and he, after all, had lived in a mining town
in the south, where he must have seen foreigners a good deal more
stylish than myself. I didn't imagine him having the respect for
my shop that his mother had. It was a concrete barn, with the
shoddy goods spread all over the floor (but I knew where everything was). No one could think of it as a modern place; and it
wasn't as brightly painted as some of the Greek shops.

I said, for Ferdinand's benefit as well as Zabeth's, 'Ferdinand's
a big boy, Beth. He can look after himself without me.'

'No, no, Mis' Salim. Fer'nand will come to you. You beat him
whenever you want.'

There was little likelihood of that. But it was only a way of
speaking. I smiled at Ferdinand and he smiled at me, pulling back
the corners of his mouth. The smile made me notice the neatness
of his mouth and the sharp-cut quality of the rest of his features.
In his face I felt I could see the starting point of certain kinds of
African mask, in which features were simplified and strengthened;
and, with memories of those masks, I thought I saw a special
distinction in his features. The idea came to me that I was looking
at Ferdinand with the eyes of an African, and that was how I
always looked at him. It was the effect on me of his face, which I
saw then and later as one of great power.

I wasn't happy about Zabeth's request. But it had to be assented to. And when I swung my head slowly from side to side, to let them both know that Ferdinand was to look upon me as a friend, Ferdinand began to go down on one knee. But then he stopped. He didn't complete the reverence; he pretended that something had itched him on that leg, and he scratched the back of the knee he had bent. Against the white trousers his skin was black and healthy, with a slight shine.

This going down on one knee was a traditional reverence. It was what children of the bush did to show their respect for an older person. It was like a reflex, and done with no particular ceremony. Outside the town you might see children break off what they were doing and suddenly, as though they had been frightened by a snake, race to the adults they had just seen, kneel, get their little unconsidered pats on the head, and then, as though nothing had happened, run back to what they were doing. It was a custom that had spread from the forest kingdoms to the east. But it was a custom of the bush. It couldn't transfer to the town; and for someone like Ferdinand, especially after his time in the southern mining town, the child's gesture of respect would have seemed old-fashioned and subservient.

I had already been disturbed by his face. Now I thought: 'There's going to be trouble here.'

The lycée wasn't far from the shop, an easy walk if the sun wasn't too hot or if it wasn't raining – rain flooded the streets in no time. Ferdinand came once a week to the shop to see me. He came at about half past three on Friday afternoon, or he came on Saturday morning. He was always dressed as the lycée boy, in white; and sometimes, in spite of the heat, he wore the lycée blazer, which had the *Semper Aliquid Novi* motto in a scroll on the breast pocket.

We exchanged greetings, and in the African way we could make that take time. It was hard to go on after we had finished with the greetings. He offered me nothing in the way of news; he left it to me to ask questions. And when I asked – for the sake of asking – some question like 'What did you do at school today?' or 'Does

44

Father Huismans take any of your classes?' he gave me short and
precise answers that left me wondering what to ask next.

The trouble was that I was unwilling – and very soon unable –
to chat with him as I would have done with another African. I felt
that with him I had to make a special effort, and I didn't know
what I could do. He was a boy from the bush; when the holidays
came he would be going back to his mother's village. But at the
lycée he was learning things I knew nothing about. I couldn't
talk to him about his school work; the advantage there was on his
side. And there was his face. I thought there was a lot going on
behind that face that I couldn't know about. I felt there was a
solidity and self-possession there, and that as a guardian and
educator I was being seen through.

Perhaps, with nothing to keep them going, our meetings would
have come to an end. But in the shop there was Metty. Metty got
on with everybody. He didn't have the problems I had with
Ferdinand; and it was for Metty that Ferdinand soon began to
come, to the shop and then to the flat as well. After his stiff conversation in English or French with me, Ferdinand would, with
Metty, switch to the local patois. He would appear then to undergo
a character change, rattling away in a high-pitched voice, his
laughter sounding like part of his speech. And Metty could match
him; Metty had absorbed many of the intonations of the local
language, and the mannerisms that went with the language.

From Ferdinand's point of view Metty was a better guide to the
town than I was. And for these two unattached young men the
pleasures of the town were what you would expect – beer, bars,
and women.

Beer was part of people's food here; children drank it; people
began drinking from early in the morning. We had no local
brewery, and a lot of the cargo brought up by the steamers was
that weak lager the people here loved. At many points along the
river village dugouts took on cases from the moving steamer; and
the steamer, on the way back to the capital, received the empties.

About women, the attitude was just as matter-of-fact. Shortly
after I arrived my friend Mahesh told me that women slept with
men whenever they were asked; a man could knock on any woman's

door and sleep with her. Mahesh didn't tell me this with any excitement or approval – he was wrapped up in his own beautiful Shoba. To Mahesh the sexual casualness was part of the chaos and corruption of the place.

That was how – after early delight – I had begun to feel myself. But I couldn't speak out against pleasures which were also my own. I couldn't warn Metty or Ferdinand against going to places I went to myself. The restraint, in fact, worked the other way. In spite of the changes that had come to Metty, I still regarded him as a member of my family; and I had to be careful not to do anything to wound him or anything which, when reported back, would wound other members of the family. I had, specifically, not to be seen with African women. And I was proud that, difficult though it was, I never gave cause for offence.

Ferdinand and Metty could drink in the little bars and openly pick up women or drop in at the houses of women they had got to know. It was I – as master of one man and guardian of the other – who had to hide.

What could Ferdinand learn from me? I had heard it said on the coast – and the foreigners I met here said it as well – that Africans didn't know how to 'live'. By that was meant that Africans didn't know how to spend money sensibly or how to keep a house. Well! My circumstances were unusual, but what would Ferdinand see when he considered my establishment?

My shop was a shambles. I had bolts of cloth and oil-cloth on the shelves, but most of the stock was spread out on the concrete floor. I sat on a desk in the middle of my concrete barn, facing the door, with a concrete pillar next to the desk giving me some feeling of being anchored in that sea of junk – big enamel basins, white and blue-rimmed, or blue-rimmed with floral patterns; stacks of white enamel plates with squares of coarse, mud-coloured paper between the plates; enamel cups and iron pots and charcoal braziers and iron bedsteads and buckets in zinc or plastic and bicycle tires and torchlights and oil lamps in green or pink or amber glass.

That was the kind of junk I dealt in. I dealt in it respectfully because it was my livelihood, my means of raising two to four. But it was antiquated junk, specially made for shops like mine; and I doubt whether the workmen who made the stuff – in Europe and the United States and perhaps nowadays Japan – had any idea of what their products were used for. The smaller basins, for instance, were in demand because they were good for keeping grubs alive in, packed in damp fibre and marsh-earth. The larger basins – a big purchase: a villager expected to buy no more than two or three in a lifetime – were used for soaking cassava in, to get rid of the poison.

That was my commercial setting. There was a similar rough-and-ready quality about my flat. The unmarried Belgian lady who had lived there before had been something of an artist. To her 'studio' atmosphere I had added a genuine untidiness – it was like something beyond my control. Metty had taken over the kitchen and it was in a terrible state. I don't believe he ever cleaned the kerosene stove; with his servant-house background he would have considered that woman's work. And it didn't help if I cleaned the stove. Metty wasn't shamed: the stove soon began to smell again and became sticky with all kinds of substances. The whole kitchen smelled, though it was used just for making morning coffee, mainly. I could scarcely bear to go into the kitchen. But Metty didn't mind, though his bedroom was just across the passage from the kitchen.

You entered this passage directly from the landing of the external staircase, which hung at the back of the building. As soon as you opened the landing door you got the warmed-up, shut-in smell of rust and oil and kerosene, dirty clothes and old paint and old timber. And the place smelled like that because you couldn't leave any window open. The town, run down as it was, crawled with thieves, and they seemed able to wriggle through any little opening. To the right was Metty's bedroom: one look showed you that Metty had turned it into a proper little servant's room, with his cot, his bedding-rolls and his various bundles, his cardboard boxes, his clothes hanging on nails and window catches. A little way down the passage, to the left, after the kitchen, was the sitting room.

It was a large room, and the Belgian lady had painted it white all over, ceiling, walls, windows, and even window panes. In this white room with bare floorboards there was a couch upholstered in a coarse-weave, dark-blue material; and, to complete the studio-sitting-room effect, there was an unpainted trestle table as big as a ping-pong table. That had been spread over with my own junk – old magazines, paperbacks, letters, shoes, rackets, spanners, shoe boxes and shirt boxes in which at different times I had tried to sort things. One corner of the table was kept clear, and this was perpetually covered by a scorched white cloth: it was where Metty did his ironing, sometimes with the electric iron (on the table, always), sometimes (when the electricity failed) with the old solid flat iron, a piece of shop stock.

On the white wall at the end of the room was a large oil painting of a European port, done in reds and yellows and blues. It was in slapdash modern style; the lady had painted it herself and signed it. She had given it pride of place in her main room. Yet she hadn't thought it worth the trouble of taking away. On the floor, leaning against the walls, were other paintings I had inherited from the lady. It was as if the lady had lost faith in her own junk and, when the independence crisis came, had been glad to go.

The bedroom was at the end of the passage. It was for me a place of special desolation, with its big fitted cupboards and its very big foam bed. What anticipations that bed had given me, as it had no doubt given the lady! Such anticipations, such an assurance of my own freedom; such let-downs, such a sense of shame. How many African women were hustled away at difficult hours – before Metty came in, or before Metty woke up! Many times on that bed I waited for morning to cleanse me of memory; and often, thinking of Nazruddin's daughter and the faith of that man in my own faithfulness, I promised to be good. In time that was to change; the bed and the room were to have other associations for me. But until then I knew only what I knew.

The Belgian lady had attempted to introduce a touch of Europe and home and art, another kind of life, to this land of rain and heat and big-leaved trees – always visible, if blurred, through the white-painted window panes. She would have had a high idea of herself; but, judged on its own, what she had tried to do wasn't of much value. And I felt that Ferdinand, when he looked at my shop and flat, would come to the same conclusion about me. It would be hard for him to see any great difference between my life and the life he knew. This added to my night-time glooms. I wondered about the nature of my aspirations, the very supports of my existence; and I began to feel that any life I might have anywhere – however rich and successful and better furnished – would only be a version of the life I lived now.

These thoughts could take me into places I didn't want to be. It was partly the effect of my isolation: I knew that. I knew there was more to me than my setting and routine showed. I knew there was something that separated me from Ferdinand and the life of the bush about me. And it was because I had no means in my day-to-day life of asserting this difference, of exhibiting my true self, that I fell into the stupidity of exhibiting my things.

I showed Ferdinand my things. I racked my brains wondering what to show him next. He was very cool, as though he had seen it all before. It was only his manner, the dead tone of voice he used when he spoke to me. But it irritated me.

I wanted to say to him, 'Look at these magazines. Nobody pays me to read them. I read them because I am the kind of person I am, because I take an interest in things, because I want to know about the world. Look at those paintings. The lady took a lot of trouble over them. She wanted to make something beautiful to hang in her house. She didn't hang it there because it was a piece of magic.'

I said it in the end, though not in those words. Ferdinand didn't respond. And the paintings were junk – the lady didn't know how to fill the canvas and hoped to get away with the rough strokes of colour. And the books and magazines were junk – especially the pornographic ones, which could depress me and embarrass me but which I didn't throw away because there were times when I needed them.

Ferdinand misunderstood my irritation.

He said one day, 'You don't have to show me anything, Salim.' He had stopped calling me mister, following Metty's lead.

Metty had taken to calling me *patron* and, in the presence of a third person, could make it sound ironical. Metty was there that day; but Ferdinand, when he told me I didn't have to show him anything, wasn't speaking ironically. He never spoke ironically.

I was reading a magazine when Ferdinand came to the shop one afternoon. I greeted him and went on with the magazine. It was a magazine of popular science, the kind of reading I had become addicted to. I liked receiving these little bits of knowledge; and I often thought, while I read, that the particular science or field I was reading about was the thing to which I should have given my days and nights, adding knowledge to knowledge, making discoveries, making something of myself, using all my faculties. It was as good as the life of knowledge itself.

Metty was at the customs that afternoon, clearing some goods that had arrived by the steamer a fortnight before - that was the pace at which things moved here. Ferdinand hung about the shop for a while. I had felt rebuked by what he had said about not showing him things, and I wasn't going to take the lead in conversation. At last he came to the desk and said, 'What are you reading, Salim?'

I couldn't help myself: the teacher and the guardian in me came out. I said, 'You should look at this. They're working on a new kind of telephone. It works by light impulses rather than an electric current.'

I never really believed in these new wonder things I read about. I never thought I would come across them in my own life. But that was the attraction of reading about them: you could read article after article about these things you hadn't yet begun to use.

Ferdinand said, 'Who are they?'

'What do you mean?'

'Who are the "they" who are working on the new telephone?'

I thought: 'We are here already, after only a few months at the lycée. He's just out of the bush; I know his mother; I treat him like a friend; and already we're getting this political nonsense.' I didn't give the answer I thought he was expecting. I didn't say, 'The white men.' Though with half of myself I felt like saying it, to put him in his place.

I said instead, 'The scientists.'

He said no more. I said no more, and deliberately went back to reading. That was the end of that little passage between us. It was also, as it turned out, the end of my attempts to be a teacher, to show myself and my things to Ferdinand.

Because I thought a lot about my refusal to say 'the white men' when Ferdinand asked me to define the 'they' who were working on the new telephone. And I saw that, in my wish not to give him political satisfaction, I had indeed said what I intended to say. I didn't mean the white men. I didn't mean, I couldn't mean, people like those I knew in our town, the people who had stayed behind after independence. I really did mean the scientists; I meant people far away from us in every sense.

They! When we wanted to speak politically, when we wanted to abuse or praise politically, we said 'the Americans', 'the Europeans', 'the white people', 'the Belgians'. When we wanted to speak of the doers and makers and the inventors, we all – whatever our race – said 'they'. We separated these men from their groups and countries and in this way attached them to ourselves. 'They're making cars that will run on water.' 'They're making television sets as small as a matchbox.' The 'they' we spoke of in this way were very far away, so far away as to be hardly white. They were impartial, up in the clouds, like good gods. We waited for their blessings, and showed off those blessings – as I had shown off my cheap binoculars and my fancy camera to Ferdinand – as though we had been responsible for them.

I had shown Ferdinand my things as though I had been letting him into the deeper secrets of my existence, the true nature of my life below the insipidity of my days and nights. In fact, I – and all the others like me in our town, Asian, Belgian, Greek – were as far away from 'they' as he was.

That was the end of my attempts to be a teacher to Ferdinand. I decided now simply to let him be, as before. I felt that by giving him the run of the shop and the flat I was keeping my promise to his mother.

The rainy-season school holidays came, and Zabeth came to town to do her shopping and to take Ferdinand back with her.

She seemed pleased with his progress. And he didn't seem to mind exchanging the lycée and the bars of the town for Zabeth's village. So he went home for the holidays. I thought of the journey down river by steamer and dugout. I thought of rain on the river; Zabeth's women poling through the unlit waterways to the hidden village; the black nights and the empty days.

The sky seldom cleared now. At most it turned from grey or dark grey to hot silver. It lightened and thundered much of the time, sometimes far away over the forest, sometimes directly overhead. From the shop I would see the rain beating down the flamboyant trees in the market square. Rain like that killed the vendors' trade; it blew all around the wooden stalls and drove people to shelter under the awnings of the shops around the square. Everyone became a watcher of the rain; a lot of beer was drunk. The unsurfaced streets ran red with mud; red was the colour of the earth on which all the bush grew.

But sometimes a day of rain ended with a glorious clouded sunset. I liked to watch that from the viewing spot near the rapids. Once that spot had been a little park, with amenities; but all that remained of the park was a stretch of concrete river-wall and a wide cleared area, muddy in rain. Fishermen's nets hung on great stripped tree trunks buried among the rocks at the edge of the river (rocks like those that, in the river, created the rapids). At one end of the cleared area were thatched huts; the place had become a fishing village again. The sinking sun shot through layers of grey cloud; the water turned from brown to gold to red to violet. And always there was the steady noise of the rapids, innumerable little cascades of water over rock. The darkness came; and sometimes the rain came as well, and to the sound of the rapids was added the sound of rain on water.

Always, sailing up from the south, from beyond the bend in the river, were clumps of water hyacinths, dark floating islands on the dark river, bobbing over the rapids. It was as if rain and river were tearing away bush from the heart of the continent and floating it down to the ocean, incalculable miles away. But the water hyacinth was the fruit of the river alone. The tall lilac flower had appeared only a few years before, and in the local language there was no word for it. The people still called it 'the new thing' or 'the new thing in the river', and to them it was another enemy. Its rubbery vines and leaves formed thick tangles of vegetation that adhered to the river banks and clogged up waterways. It grew fast, faster than men could destroy it with the tools they had. The channels to the villages had to be constantly cleared. Night and day the water hyacinth floated up from the south, seeding itself as it travelled.

I had decided to let Ferdinand be. But in the new term I noticed a change in his attitude to me. He was less distant with me, and when he came to the shop he wasn't so anxious to leave me for Metty. I thought that his mother might have given him a talking-to. I thought also that, though he had been cool when he had gone to his mother's village for the holidays, he had probably been shocked by his time there – how, I wondered, had he spent the days? – and no longer took the town, and the life of the town, for granted.

The truth was simpler. Ferdinand had begun to grow up, and he was finding himself a little bit at sea. He was of mixed tribal heritage, and in this part of the country he was a stranger. He had no group that was really his own, and he had no one to model himself on. He didn't know what was expected of him. He wanted to find out, and he needed me to practise on.

I could see him now trying on various characters, attempting different kinds of manners. His range was limited. For a few days after Zabeth came to town for her goods, he might be the son of his mother, the *marchande*. He would pretend to be my business associate, my equal, might make inquiries about sales and prices. Then he might become the young African on the way up, the lycée student, modern, go-ahead. In this character he liked to wear the blazer with the *Semper Aliquid Novi* motto; no doubt he felt it helped him carry off the mannerisms he had picked up from some of his European teachers. Copying one teacher, he might, in the flat, stand with crossed legs against the white studio wall and, fixed in that position, attempt to conduct a whole conversation. Or, copying another teacher, he might walk around the trestle table, lifting things, looking at them, and then dropping them, while he talked.

He made an effort now to talk to me. Not in the way he talked to Metty; with me he attempted a special kind of serious conversation. Whereas before he had waited for me to ask questions, now it was he who put up little ideas, little debating points, as though he wanted to get a discussion going. It was part of the new lycée character he was working on, and he was practising, treating me almost as a language teacher. But I was interested. I began to get some idea of what was talked about at the lycée – and I wanted to know about that.

He said to me one day, 'Salim, what do you think of the future of Africa?'

I didn't say; I wanted to know what he thought. I wondered whether, in spite of his mixed ancestry and his travels, he really had an idea of Africa; or whether the idea of Africa had come to him, and his friends at school, from the atlas. Wasn't Ferdinand still – like Metty, during his journey from the coast – the kind of man who, among strange tribes, would starve rather than eat their strange food? Did Ferdinand have a much larger idea of Africa than Zabeth, who moved with assurance from her village to the town only because she knew she was especially protected?

Ferdinand could only tell me that the world outside Africa was going down and Africa was rising. When I asked in what way the world outside was going down, he couldn't say. And when I pushed him past the stage where he could repeat bits of what he had heard at the lycée, I found that the ideas of the school discussion had in his mind become jumbled and simplified. Ideas of the past were confused with ideas of the present. In his lycée blazer, Ferdinand saw himself as evolved and important, as in the colonial days. At the same time he saw himself as a new man of Africa, and important for that reason. Out of this staggering idea of his own importance, he had reduced Africa to himself; and the future of Africa was nothing more than the job he might do later on.

The conversations that Ferdinand, in this character, attempted with me had a serial quality, because he wasn't always well briefed. He took a discussion up to a certain point and then dropped it without embarrassment, as though it had been a language exercise in which he would do better next time. Then, returning to old ways, he would look for Metty and leave me.

Though I was learning more of what went on in the lycée (so quickly colonial-snobbish again), and what went on in the mind of Ferdinand, I didn't feel I was getting closer to him. When I had considered him a mystery, distant and mocking behind his mask-like face, I had seen him as a solid person. Now I felt that his affectations were more than affectations, that his personality had become fluid. I began to feel that there was nothing there, and the thought of a lycée full of Ferdinands made me nervous.

Yet there was the idea of his importance. It unsettled me – there wasn't going to be security for anyone in the country. And it unsettled Metty. When you get away from the chiefs and the politicians there is a simple democracy about Africa: everyone is a villager. Metty was a shop assistant and a kind of servant; Ferdinand was a lycée boy with a future; yet the friendship between the two men was like the friendship between equals. That friendship continued. But Metty, as a servant in our family house, had seen playmates grow into masters; and he must have felt himself – with his new idea of his worth – being left behind again.

I was in the flat one day when I heard them come in. Metty was explaining his connection with me and the shop, explaining his journey from the coast.

Metty said: 'My family used to know his family. They used to call me Billy. I was studying book-keeping. I'm not staying here, you know. I am going to Canada. I've got my papers and everything. I'm just waiting for my medical.'

Billy! Well, it was close to Ali. Canada – that was where one of my brothers-in-law had gone; in a letter I received shortly after Metty joined me I had heard about the anxiety of the family about that brother-in-law's 'medical'. That was no doubt where Metty had picked up the talk about Canada.

I made a noise to let them know I was in the flat, and when they came into the sitting room I pretended I had heard nothing.

Not long after this, on an afternoon of settled rain, Ferdinand came to the shop and abruptly, wet and dripping as he was, said, 'Salim, you must send me away to America to study.'

He spoke like a desperate man. The idea had burst inside him; and he clearly had felt that if he didn't act right away, he might never act. He had come through the heavy rain and the flooded streets; his clothes were soaked. I was surprised by the abruptness and the desperation, and by the bigness of his request. To me, going abroad to study was something rare and expensive, something beyond the means of my own family.

I said, 'Why should I send you to America? Why should I spend money on you?'

He had nothing to say. After the desperation and the trip through the rain, the whole thing might just have been another attempt at conversation.

Was it only his simplicity? I felt my temper rising – the rain and the lightning and the unnatural darkness of the afternoon had something to do with that.

I said, 'Why do you think I have obligations to you? What have you done for me?'

And that was true. His attitude, since he had begun to feel towards a character, was that I owed him something, simply because I seemed willing to help.

He went blank. He stood still in the darkness of the shop and looked at me without resentment, as though he had expected me to behave in the way I was behaving, and had to see it through. For a while his eyes held mine. Then his gaze shifted, and I knew he was going to change the subject.

He pulled the wet white shirt – with the lycée monogram embroidered on the pocket – away from his skin, and he said, 'My shirt is wet.' When I didn't reply, he pulled the shirt away in one or two other places and said, 'I walked through the rain.'

Still I didn't reply. He let the shirt go and looked away to the flooded street. It was his way of recovering from a false start: his attempts at conversation could end with these short sentences, irritating observations about what he or I was doing. So now he looked out at the rain and spoke scattered sentences about what he saw. He was pleading to be released.

I said, 'Metty is in the store-room. He will give you a towel. And ask him to make some tea.'

That was not the end of the business, though. With Ferdinand now things seldom ended neatly.

Twice a week I had lunch with my friends Shoba and Mahesh in their flat. Their flat was gaudy and in some ways like themselves. They were a beautiful couple, certainly the most beautiful people in our town. They had no competition, yet they were always slightly overdressed. So, in their flat, to the true beauty of old Persian and Kashmiri carpets and old brassware they had added many flimsy, glittery things – crudely worked modern Moradabad brass, machine-turned wall plaques of Hindu gods, shiny three-pronged wall lights. There was also a heavy carving in glass of a naked woman. This was a touch of art, but it was also a reminder of the beauty of women, the beauty of Shoba – personal beauty being the obsession and theme of that couple, like money for rich people.

At lunch one day Mahesh said, 'What's got into that boy of yours? He's getting *malin* like the others.'

'Metty?'

'He came to see me the other day. He pretended he had known me a long time. He was showing off to the African boy he had with him. He said he was bringing me a customer. He said the African boy was Zabeth's son and a good friend of yours.'

'I don't know about good friend. What did he want?'

'Metty ran away just when I was beginning to get angry, and left the boy with me. The boy said he wanted a camera, but I don't think he wanted anything at all. He just wanted to talk.'

I said, 'I hope he showed you his money.'

'I didn't have any cameras to show him. That was a bad business, Salim. Commission, commission all the way. You hardly get your money back in the end.'

The cameras were one of Mahesh's ideas that had gone wrong. Mahesh was like that, always looking for the good business idea, and full of little ideas he quickly gave up. He had thought that the tourist trade was about to start again, with our town being the base for the game parks in the east. But the tourist trade existed only in the posters printed in Europe for the government in the capital. The game parks had gone back to nature, in a way never meant. The roads and rest houses, always rudimentary, had gone; the tourists (foreigners who might be interested in cut-price photographic equipment) hadn't come. Mahesh had had to send his cameras east, using the staging posts that were still maintained by people like ourselves for the transport (legal or otherwise) of goods in any direction.

Mahesh said, 'The boy said you were sending him to America or Canada to do his studies.'

'What am I sending him to study?'

'Business administration. So he can take over his mother's business. Build it up.'

'Build it up! Buying a gross of razor blades and selling them one by one to fishermen.'

'I knew he was only trying to compromise you with your friends.'

Simple magic: if you say something about a man to his friends, you might get the man to do what you say he is going to do.

I said, 'Ferdinand's an African.'

When I next saw Ferdinand I said, 'My friend Mahesh has been telling me that you are going to America to study business administration. Have you told your mother?'

He didn't understand irony. This version of the story caught him unprepared, and he had nothing to say.

I said, 'Ferdinand, you mustn't go around telling people things that aren't true. What do you mean by business administration?'

He said, 'Book-keeping, typing, shorthand. What you do.'

'I don't do shorthand. And that's not business administration. That's a secretarial course. You don't have to go to America or Canada to do that. You can do that right here. I am sure there are places in the capital. And when the times comes you'll find you want to do more than that.'

He didn't like what I said. His eyes began to go bright with humiliation and anger. But I didn't stay for that. It was with Metty, and not me, that he had to settle accounts, if there were accounts to be settled.

He had found me as I was leaving to play squash at the Hellenic Club. Canvas shoes, shorts, racket, towel around my neck – it was like old times on the coast. I left the sitting room and stood in the passage, to give him the chance to leave, so that I could lock up. But he stayed in the sitting room, doubtless waiting for Metty.

I went out to the staircase landing. It was one of our days without electricity. The smoke from charcoal braziers and other open fires rose blue among the imported ornamental trees – cassia, breadfruit, frangipani, flamboyant – and gave a touch of the forest village to a residential area where, as I had heard, in the old days neither Africans nor Asians were permitted to live. I knew the trees from the coast. I suppose they had been imported there as well; but I associated them with the coast and home, another life. The same trees here looked artificial to me, like the town itself. They were familiar, but they reminded me where I was.

I heard no more about Ferdinand's studies abroad, and soon he even dropped the bright young lycée-man pose. He began trying out something new. There was no more of that standing against the wall with crossed legs, no more walking around the trestle table and lifting and dropping things, no more of that serious conversation.

He came in now with a set face, his expression stern and closed. He held his head up and moved slowly. When he sat down on the couch in the sitting room he slumped so far down that sometimes his back was on the seat of the couch. He was languid, bored. He looked without seeing; he was ready to listen, but couldn't be bothered to talk himself – that was the impression he tried to give. I didn't know what to make of this new character of Ferdinand's, and it was only from certain things that Metty said that I understood what Ferdinand was aiming at.

During the course of the term there had come to the lycée some boys from the warrior tribes to the east. They were an immensely tall people; and, as Metty told me with awe, they were used to being carried around on litters by their slaves, who were of a smaller, squatter race. For these tall men of the forest there had always been European admiration. Ever since I could remember there had been articles about them in the magazines – these Africans who cared nothing about planting or trade and looked down, almost as much as Europeans, on other Africans. This European admiration still existed; articles and photographs continued to appear in magazines, in spite of the changes that had come to Africa. In fact, there were now Africans who felt as the Europeans did, and saw the warrior people as the highest kind of African.

At the lycée, still so colonial in spite of everything, the new boys had created a stir. Ferdinand, both of whose parents were traders, had decided to try out the role of the indolent forest warrior. He couldn't slump around at the lycée and pretend he was used to being waited on by slaves. But he thought he could practise on me.

I knew other things about the forest kingdom, though. I knew that the slave people were in revolt and were being butchered back into submission. But Africa was big. The bush muffled the sound of murder, and the muddy rivers and lakes washed the blood away.

Metty said, 'We must go there, *patron*. I hear it is the last good place in Africa. *Y a encore bien, bien des blancs côté-qui-là.* It have a lot of white people up there still. They tell me that in Bujumbura it is like a little Paris.'

If I believed that Metty understood a quarter of the things he said – if I believed, for instance, that he really longed for the white company at Bujumbura, or knew where or what Canada was – I would have worried about him. But I knew him better; I knew when his chat was just chat. Still, what chat! The white people had been driven out from our town, and their monuments destroyed. But there were a lot of white people up there, in another town, and warriors and slaves. And that was glamour for the warrior boys, glamour for Metty, and glamour for Ferdinand.

I began to understand how simple and uncomplicated the world was for me. For people like myself and Mahesh, and the uneducated Greeks and Italians in our town, the world was really quite a simple place. We could understand it, and if too many

obstacles weren't put in our way we could master it. It didn't
matter that we were far away from our civilization, far away from
the doers and makers. It didn't matter that we couldn't make the
things we liked to use, and as individuals were even without the
technical skills of primitive people. In fact, the less educated we
were, the more at peace we were, the more easily we were carried
along by our civilization or civilizations.

For Ferdinand there was no such possibility. He could never
be simple. The more he tried, the more confused he became. His
mind wasn't empty, as I had begun to think. It was a jumble,
full of all kinds of junk.

With the arrival of the warrior boys, boasting had begun at the
lycée, and I began to feel that Ferdinand – or somebody – had
been boasting about me too. Or what had been got out of me. The
word definitely appeared to have got around that term that I was
interested in the education and welfare of young Africans.

Young men, not all of them from the lycée, took to turning up
at the shop, sometimes with books in their hands, sometimes with
an obviously borrowed *Semper Aliquid Novi* blazer. They wanted
money. They said they were poor and wanted money to continue
their studies. Some of these beggars were bold, coming straight
to me and reciting their requests; the shy ones hung around until
there was no one else in the shop. Only a few had bothered to
prepare stories, and these stories were like Ferdinand's: a father
dead or far away, a mother in a village, an unprotected boy full of
ambition.

I was amazed by the stupidity, then irritated, then unsettled.
None of these people seemed to mind being rebuffed or being
hustled out of the shop by Metty; some of them came again. It
was as if none of them cared about my reactions, as if somewhere
out there in the town I had been given a special 'character', and
what I thought of myself was of no importance. That was what
was unsettling. The guilelessness, the innocence that wasn't
innocence – I thought it could be traced back to Ferdinand, his
interpretation of our relationship and his idea of what I could be
used for.

I had said to Mahesh, lightly, simplifying matters for the benefit of a prejudiced man: 'Ferdinand's an African.' Ferdinand had perhaps done the same for me with his friends, explaining away his relationship with me. And I felt now that out of his lies and exaggerations, and the character he had given me, a web was being spun around me. I had become prey.

Perhaps that was true of all of us who were not of the country. Recent events had shown our helplessness. There was a kind of peace now; but we all – Asians, Greeks and other Europeans – remained prey, to be stalked in different ways. Some men were to be feared, and stalked cautiously; it was necessary to be servile with some; others were to be approached the way I was approached. It was in the history of the land: here men had always been prey. You don't feel malice towards your prey. You set a trap for him. It fails ten times; but it is always the same trap you set.

Shortly after I had arrived Mahesh had said to me of the local Africans, 'You must never forget, Salim, that they are *malins*.' He had used the French word, because the English words he might have used – 'wicked', 'mischievous', 'bad-minded' – were not right. The people here were *malins* the way a dog chasing a lizard was *malin*, or a cat chasing a bird. The people were *malins* because they lived with the knowledge of men as prey.

They were not a sturdy people. They were very small and slightly built. Yet, as though to make up for their puniness in that immensity of river and forest, they liked to wound with their hands. They didn't use their fists. They used the flat of the hand; they liked to push, shove, slap. More than once, at night, outside a bar or little dance-hall I saw what looked like a drunken pushing and shoving, a brawl with slaps, turn to methodical murder, as though the first wound and the first spurt of blood had made the victim something less than a man, and compelled the wounder to take the act of destruction to the end.

I was unprotected. I had no family, no flag, no fetish. Was it something like this that Ferdinand had told his friends? I felt that the time had come for me to straighten things out with Ferdinand, and give him another idea of myself.

I soon had my chance, as I thought. A well dressed young man came into the shop one morning with what looked like a business ledger in his hand. He was one of the shy ones. He hung around, waiting for people to go away, and when he came to me I saw that the ledger was less businesslike than it looked. The spine, in the middle, was black and worn from being held. And I saw too that the man's shirt, though obviously his best, wasn't as clean as I had thought. It was the good shirt he wore on special occasions and then took off and hung up on a nail and wore again on another special occasion. The collar was yellow-black on the inside.

He said, 'Mis' Salim.'

I took the ledger, and he looked away, puckering up his brows. The ledger belonged to the lycée, and it was old. It was something from near the end of the colonial time: a subscription list for a gymnasium the lycée had been planning to build. On the inside of the cover was the lycée label, with the coat of arms and the motto. Opposite that was the principal's appeal, in the stiff and angular European handwriting style which had been passed down to some of the Africans here. The first subscriber was the governor of the province, and he had signed royally, on a whole page. I turned the pages, studying the confident signatures of officials and merchants. It was all so recent, but it seemed to belong to another century.

I saw, with especial interest, the signature of a man of our community about whom Nazruddin had talked a great deal. That man had had old-fashioned ideas about money and security; he had used his wealth to build a palace, which he had had to abandon after independence. The mercenaries who had restored the authority of the central government had been quartered there; now the palace was an army barracks. He had subscribed for an enormous amount. I saw Nazruddin's signature – I was surprised: I had forgotten that he might be here, among these dead colonial names.

The gymnasium hadn't been built. All these demonstrations of loyalty and faith in the future and civic pride had gone for nothing. Yet the book had survived. Now it had been stolen, its money-attracting properties recognized. The date had been altered, very obviously; and Father Huismans's name had been written over the signature of the earlier principal.

I said to the man before me, 'I will keep this book. I will give it back to the people to whom it belongs. Who gave you the book? Ferdinand?'

He looked helpless. Sweat was beginning to run down his puckered forehead, and he was blinking it away. He said, 'Mis' Salim.'

'You've done your job. You've given me the book. Now go.'

And he obeyed.

Ferdinand came that afternoon. I knew he would – he would want to look at my face, and find out about his book. He said, 'Salim?' I didn't acknowledge him. I let him stand. But he didn't have to stand about for long.

Metty was in the store-room, and Metty must have heard him. Metty called out: 'Oo-oo!' Ferdinand called back, and went to the store-room. He and Metty began to chat in the patois. My temper rose as I heard that contented, rippling, high-pitched sound. I took the gymnasium book from the drawer of my desk and went to the store-room.

The room, with one small barred window set high, was half in darkness. Metty was on a ladder, checking stock on the shelves on one wall. Ferdinand was leaning against the shelves on another wall, just below the window. It was hard to see his face.

I stood in the doorway. I made a gesture towards Ferdinand with the book and I said, 'You are going to get into trouble.'

He said, 'What trouble?'

He spoke in his flat, dead way. He didn't mean to be sarcastic; he really was asking what I was talking about. But it was hard for me to see his face. I saw the whites of his eyes, and I thought I saw the corners of his mouth pulling back in a smile. That face, that reminder of frightening masks! And I thought: 'Yes, what trouble?'

To talk of trouble was to pretend there were laws and regulations that everyone could acknowledge. Here there was nothing. There had been order once, but that order had had its own dishonesties and cruelties – that was why the town had been wrecked. We lived in that wreckage. Instead of regulations there were now only officials who could always prove you wrong, until you paid up. All that could be said to Ferdinand was: 'Don't harm me, boy, because I can do you greater harm.'

I began to see his face more clearly.

I said, 'You will take this book back to Father Huismans. If you don't, I will take it back myself. And I will see that he sends you home for good.'

He looked blank, as though he had been attacked. Then I noticed Metty on the ladder. Metty was nervous, tense; his eyes betrayed him. And I knew I had made a mistake, saving up all my anger for Ferdinand.

Ferdinand's eyes went bright, and the whites showed clearly. So that, at this terrible moment, he seemed like a comic in an old-time film. He appeared to lean forward, to be about to lose his balance. He took a deep breath. His eyes never left my face. He was spitting with rage; his sense of injury had driven him mad. His arms hung straight and loose at his side, so that they seemed longer than usual. His hands curled without clenching. His mouth was open. But what I had thought was a smile was no smile at all. If the light had been better I would have seen that at the beginning.

He was frightening, and the thought came to me: 'This is how he will look when he sees his victim's blood, when he watches his enemy being killed.' And, climbing on that thought, was another: 'This is the rage that flattened the town.'

I could have pushed harder, and turned that high rage into tears. But I didn't push. I thought I had given them both a new idea of the kind of man I was, and I left them in the store-room to cool down. After some time I heard them talking, but softly.

At four o'clock, closing time, I shouted to Metty. And he, glad of the chance to come out and be active, said, '*Patron*,' and frowned to show how seriously he took the business of closing up the shop.

Ferdinand came out, quite calm, walking with a light step. He said, 'Salim?' I said, 'I will take the book back.' And I watched him walk up the red street, tall and sad and slow below the leafless flamboyants, past the rough market shacks of his town.

4

FATHER HUISMANS wasn't in when I went to the lycée with the book. There was a young Belgian in the outer office, and he told me that Father Huismans liked to go away for a few days from time to time. Where did he go? 'He goes into the bush. He goes to all those villages,' the young man – secretary or teacher – said, with irritation. And he became more irritated when I gave him the gymnasium book.

He said, 'They come and beg to be admitted to the lycée. As soon as you take them in they start stealing. They would carry away the whole school if you let them. They come and beg you to look after their children. Yet in the streets they jostle you to show you they don't care for you.' He didn't look well. He was pale, but the skin below his eyes was dark, and he sweated as he talked. He said, 'I'm sorry. It would be better for you to talk to Father Huismans. You must understand that it isn't easy for me here. I've been living on honeycake and eggs.'

It sounded as though he had been put on an especially rich diet. Then I understood that he was really telling me he was starving.

He said, 'Father Huismans had the idea this term of giving the boys African food. Well, that seemed all right. There's an African lady in the capital who does wonderful things with prawns and shellfish. But here it was caterpillars and spinach in tomato sauce. Or what looked like tomato sauce. The first day. Of course it was only for the boys, but the sight of it turned my stomach. I couldn't stay in the hall and watch them chew. I can't bring myself to eat anything from the kitchens now. I don't have cooking facilities in my room, and at the van der Weyden there's this sewer smell from the patio. I'm leaving. I've got to go. It's all right for Huismans. He's a priest. I'm not a priest. He goes into the bush. I don't want to go into the bush.'

I couldn't help him. Food was a problem for everybody here. My own arrangements were not of the happiest; I had had lunch that day with the couple from India, in a smell of asafoetida and oil-cloth.

When, a week or so later, I went back to the lycée I heard that just two days after our meeting the young Belgian had taken the steamer and gone away. It was Father Huismans who gave me the news; and Father Huismans, sunburnt and healthy after his own trip, didn't seem put out by the loss of one of his teachers. He said he was glad to have the gymnasium book back. It was part of the history of the town; the boys who had stolen the book would recognize that one day themselves.

Father Huismans was in his forties. He wasn't dressed like a priest, but even in ordinary trousers and shirt there was something about him of the man apart. He had the 'unfinished' face which I have noticed that certain Europeans – but never Arabs or Persians or Indians – have. In these faces there is a babylike quality about the cut of the lips and the jut of the forehead. It might be that these people were born prematurely; they seem to have passed through some very early disturbance, way back. Some of these people are as fragile as they look; some are very tough. Father Huismans was tough. The impression he gave was of incompleteness, fragility, and toughness.

He had been out on the river, visiting some villages he knew, and he had brought back two pieces – a mask and an oldish wood carving. It was about these finds that he wanted to talk, rather than about the teacher who had gone away or the gymnasium book.

The carving was extraordinary. It was about five feet high, a very thin human figure, just limbs and trunk and head, absolutely basic, carved out of a piece of wood no more than six to eight inches in diameter. I knew about carving – it was one of the

A Bend in the River

things we dealt in on the coast; we gave employment to a couple of carving families from a tribe who were gifted that way. But Father Huismans dismissed this information when I gave it to him, and talked instead of what he saw in the figure he had picked up. To me it was an exaggerated and crude piece, a carver's joke (the carvers we employed did things like that sometimes). But Father Huismans knew what the thin figure was about, and to him it was imaginative and full of meaning.

I listened, and at the end he said with a smile, 'Semper aliquid novi.' He had used the lycée motto to make a joke. The words were old, he told me, two thousand years old, and referred to Africa. An ancient Roman writer had written that out of Africa there was 'always something new', semper aliquid novi. And when it came to masks and carvings, the words were still literally true. Every carving, every mask, served a specific religious purpose, and could only be made once. Copies were copies; there was no magical feeling or power in them; and in such copies Father Huismans was not interested. He looked in masks and carvings for a religious quality; without that quality the things were dead and without beauty.

That was strange, that a Christian priest should have had such regard for African beliefs, to which on the coast we had paid no attention. And yet, though Father Huismans knew so much about African religion and went to such trouble to collect his pieces, I never felt that he was concerned about Africans in any other way; he seemed indifferent to the state of the country. I envied him that indifference; and I thought, after I left him that day, that his Africa, of bush and river, was different from mine. His Africa was a wonderful place, full of new things.

He was a priest, half a man. He lived by vows I couldn't make; and I had approached him with the respect that people of my background feel for holy men. But I began to think of him as something more. I began to think of him as a pure man. His presence in our town comforted me. His attitudes, his interests, his knowledge, added something to the place, made it less barren. It didn't worry me that he was self-absorbed, that he had been indifferent to the breakdown of one of his teachers, or that he scarcely seemed to take me in while he was talking to me. To me that was part of his particular religious nature. I sought him out and tried to understand his interests. He was always willing to talk (always looking away slightly) and to show his new finds. He came a few times to the shop and ordered things for the lycée. But the shyness – that wasn't really shyness – never left him. I was never easy with him. He remained a man apart.

He explained the second motto of the town for me – the Latin words carved on the ruined monument near the dock gates: *Miscerique probat populos et foedera jungi.* 'He approves of the mingling of the peoples and their bonds of union': that was what the words meant, and again they were very old words, from the days of ancient Rome. They came from a poem about the founding of Rome. The very first Roman hero, travelling to Italy to found his city, lands on the coast of Africa. The local queen falls in love with him, and it seems that the journey to Italy might be called off. But then the watching gods take a hand; and one of them says that the great Roman god might not approve of a settlement in Africa, of a mingling of peoples there, of treaties of union between Africans and Romans. That was how the words occurred in the old Latin poem. In the motto, though, three words were altered to reverse the meaning. According to the motto, the words carved in granite outside our dock gates, a settlement in Africa raises no doubts: the great Roman god approves of the mingling of peoples and the making of treaties in Africa. *Miscerique probat populos et foedera jungi.*

I was staggered. Twisting two-thousand-year-old words to celebrate sixty years of the steamer service from the capital! Rome was Rome. What was this place? To carve the words on a monument beside this African river was surely to invite the destruction of the town. Wasn't there some little anxiety, as in the original line in the poem? And almost as soon as it had been put up the monument had been destroyed, leaving only bits of bronze and the mocking words, gibberish to the people who now used the open space in front as a market and bivouac, with their goats and crated hens and tethered monkeys (food, like the goats and hens), for the two days or so before the steamer sailed.

But I was glad I didn't speak, because to Father Huismans the words were not vainglorious. They were words that helped him to see himself in Africa. He didn't simply see himself in a place in the bush; he saw himself as part of an immense flow of history. He was of Europe; he took the Latin words to refer to himself. It didn't matter that the Europeans in our town were uneducated, or that there was such a difference between what he stood for in his own life and what the ruined suburb near the rapids had stood for. He had his own idea of Europe, his own idea of his civilization. It was that that lay between us. Nothing like that came between me and the people I met at the Hellenic Club. And yet Father Huismans stressed his Europeanness and his separateness from Africans less than those people did. In every way he was more secure.

He wasn't resentful, as some of his countrymen were, of what had happened to the European town. He wasn't wounded by the insults that had been offered to the monuments and the statues. It wasn't because he was more ready to forgive, or had a better understanding of what had been done to the Africans. For him the destruction of the European town, the town that his countrymen had built, was only a temporary setback. Such things happened when something big and new was being set up, when the course of history was being altered.

There would always have been a settlement at that bend in the river, he said. It was a natural meeting place. The tribes would have changed, power would have shifted, but men would always have returned there to meet and trade. The Arab town would have been only a little more substantial than the African settlements, and technologically not much more advanced. The Arabs, so far in the interior, would have had to build with the products of the forest; life in their town wouldn't have been much more than a kind of forest life. The Arabs had only prepared the way for the mighty civilization of Europe.

For everything connected with the European colonization, the opening up of the river, Father Huismans had a reverence which would have surprised those people in the town who gave him the reputation of being a lover of Africa and therefore, in their way of thinking, a man who rejected the colonial past. That past had been bitter, but Father Huismans appeared to take the bitterness for granted; he saw beyond it. From the ship-repair yard near the customs, long neglected and full of junk and rust, he had taken away pieces of old steamers and bits of disused machinery from the late 1890s and laid them – like relics of an early civilization – in the inner courtyard of the lycée. He was especially pleased with a piece that carried, on a oval steel plate, the name of the makers in the town of Seraing in Belgium.

Out of simple events beside that wide muddy river, out of the mingling of peoples, great things were to come one day. We were just at the beginning. And to Father Huismans colonial relics were as precious as the things of Africa. True Africa he saw as dying or about to die. That was why it was so necessary, while that Africa still lived, to understand and collect and preserve its things.

What he had collected from that dying Africa lay in the gun room of the lycée, where the antiquated rifles of the school cadet corps used to be kept in the old days. The room was as big as a classroom and from the outside looked like one. But there were no windows, only tall panelled doors on two sides; and the only light was from a bare bulb hanging on a long cord.

When Father Huismans first opened the door of that room for me, and I got the warm smell of grass and earth and old fat, and had a confused impression of masks lying in rows on slatted shelves, I thought: 'This is Zabeth's world. This is the world to which she returns when she leaves my shop.' But Zabeth's world was living, and this was dead. That was the effect of those masks lying flat on the shelves, looking up not at forest or sky but at the underside of other shelves. They were masks that had been laid low, in more than one way, and had lost their power.

That was the impression only of a moment, though. Because in that dark, hot room, with the mask smells growing stronger, my own feeling of awe grew, my sense of what lay all around us outside. It was like being on the river at night. The bush was full of spirits; in the bush hovered all the protecting presences of a man's ancestors; and in this room all the spirits of those dead

71

masks, the powers they invoked, all the religious dread of simple men, seemed to have been concentrated.

The masks and carvings looked old. They could have been any age, a hundred years old, a thousand years old. But they were dated; Father Huismans had dated them. They were all quite new. I thought: 'But this one's only 1940. I was born in that year.' Or: 'This is 1963. That was when I came here. While this was being made I was probably having lunch with Shoba and Mahesh.'

So old, so new. And out of his stupendous idea of his civilization, his stupendous idea of the future, Father Huismans saw himself at the end of it all, the last, lucky witness.

5

MOST of us knew only the river and the damaged roads and what lay beside them. Beyond that was the unknown; it could surprise us. We seldom went to places off the established ways. In fact, we seldom travelled. It was as though, having come so far, we didn't want to move about too much. We kept to what we knew – flat, shop, club, bar, the river embankment at sunset. Sometimes we made a weekend excursion to the hippopotamus island in the river, above the rapids. But there were no people there, just the hippopotamuses – seven of them when I first used to go, three now.

We knew the hidden villages mainly by what we saw of the villagers when they came to the town. They looked exhausted and ragged after their years of isolation and want, and seemed glad to be able to move about freely again. From the shop I used to see them idling about the market stalls in the square, gazing at the displays of cloth and ready-made clothes, and wandering back to the food stalls: little oily heaps of fried flying ants (expensive, and sold by the spoonful) laid out on scraps of newspaper; hairy orange-coloured caterpillars with protuberant eyes wriggling in enamel basins; fat white grubs kept moist and soft in little bags of damp earth, five or six grubs to a bag – these grubs, absorbent in body and of neutral taste, being an all-purpose fatty food, sweet with sweet things, savoury with savoury things. These were all forest foods, but the villages had been cleaned out of them (the grubs came from the heart of a palm tree); and no one wanted to go foraging too far in the forest.

More and more of the villagers who came as visitors remained to camp in the town. At night there was cooking in the streets and the squares. On the pavements below shop awnings symbolic walls were put up around sleeping spaces – low fences of cardboard held between stones or bricks, or lengths of string tied (like the ropes of a miniature boxing ring) to sticks kept upright by cairns of stones.

From being abandoned, the town began to feel crowded. It seemed that nothing could stop the movement of people from the villages. Then, from the great unknown outside the town, came the rumour of a war.

And it was the old war, the one we were still recovering from, the semi-tribal war that had broken out at independence and shattered and emptied the town. We had thought it over and done with, the passions burnt out. There was nothing to make us think otherwise. Even local Africans had begun to talk of that time as a time of madness. And madness was the word. From Mahesh and Shoba I had heard dreadful stories of that time, of casual killings over many months by soldiers and rebels and mercenaries, of people trussed up in disgusting ways and being made to sing certain songs while they were beaten to death in the streets. None of the people who came in from the villages seemed ready for that kind of horror. Yet now it was all starting up again.

At independence the people of our region had gone mad with anger and fear – all the accumulated anger of the colonial period, and every kind of reawakened tribal fear. The people of our region had been much abused, not only by Europeans and Arabs, but also by other Africans; and at independence they had refused to be ruled by the new government in the capital. It was an instinctive uprising, without leaders or a manifesto. If the movement had been more reasoned, had been less a movement of simple rejection, the people of our region might have seen that the town at the bend in the river was theirs, the capital of any state they might set up. But they had hated the town for the intruders who had ruled in it and from it; and they had preferred to destroy the town rather than take it over.

Having destroyed their town, they had grieved for it. They

had wished to see it a living place again. And seeing it come to a kind of life again, they had grown afraid once more.

They were like people who didn't know their own mind. They had suffered so much; they had brought so much suffering on themselves. They looked so feeble and crazed when they came out of their villages and wandered about the town. They looked so much like people needing the food and the peace that the town offered. But it was people like them, going back to their villages, who wished to lay the town low again. Such rage! Like a forest fire that goes underground and burns unseen along the roots of trees it has already destroyed and then erupts in scorched land where it has little to feed on, so in the middle of destruction and want the wish to destroy flared up again.

And the war, which we had thought dead, was all at once around us. We heard of ambushes on roads we knew, of villages attacked, of headmen and officials killed.

It was at this time that Mahesh said something which I remembered. It wasn't the kind of thing I was expecting from him – so careful of his looks and clothes, so spoiled, so obsessed with his lovely wife.

Mahesh said to me: 'What do you do? You live here, and you ask that? You do what we all do. You carry on.'

We had the army in our town. They came from a warrior tribe who had served the Arabs as slave-hunters in the region, and had later, with one or two nasty mutinies, served the colonial government as soldiers. So the pattern of policing was old.

But slaves were no longer required, and in post-colonial Africa everybody could get guns; every tribe could be a warrior tribe. So the army was discreet. Sometimes there were trucks with soldiers in the streets – but the soldiers never showed their weapons. Sometimes there was a ceremonial coming and going at the barracks – the palace built by the great man of our community, which now had women's washing hung out in the partitioned verandahs upstairs and downstairs (a Greek had the laundry contract for the soldiers' uniforms). The army was seldom more provocative than that. They couldn't afford to be. They were among their traditional enemies, their former slave-prey; and though they were paid regularly and lived well, they were kept short of equipment. We had a new President, an army man. This was his way of policing the country and controlling his difficult army.

It made for a balance in the town. And a well-paid, domesticated army was good for trade. The soldiers spent. They bought furniture, and they loved carpets – that was a taste they had inherited from the Arabs. But now the balance in our town was threatened. The army had a real war to fight; and no one could say whether those men, given modern weapons again and orders to kill, wouldn't fall into the ways of their slave-hunting ancestors and break up into marauding bands, as they had done at independence, with the collapse of all authority.

No, in this war I was neutral. I was frightened of both sides. I didn't want to see the army on the loose. And though I felt sympathy for the people of our region, I didn't want to see the town destroyed again. I didn't want anybody to win; I wanted the old balance to be maintained.

One night I had a premonition that the war had come close. I woke up and heard the sound of a truck far away. It could have been any truck; it could even have been one of Daulat's, near the end of its hard run from the east. But I thought: 'That is the sound of war.' That sound of a steady, grinding machine made me think of guns; and then I thought of the crazed and half-starved village people against whom the guns were going to be used, people whose rags were already the colour of ashes. This was the anxiety of a moment of wakefulness; I fell asleep again.

When Metty brought me coffee in the morning he said, 'The soldiers are running back. They came to a bridge. And when they got to that bridge their guns began to bend.'

'Metty!'

'I am telling you, *patron*.'

That was bad. If it was true that the army was retreating, it was bad; I didn't want to see that army in retreat. If it wasn't true, it was still bad. Metty had picked up the local rumours; and what he said about the bending guns meant that the rebels, the men in rags, had been made to believe that bullets couldn't kill them, that all the spirits of the forest and the river were on their side. And that meant that at any moment, as soon as someone gave the correct call, there could be an uprising in the town itself.

It was bad, and there was nothing I could do. The stock of the shop – there was no means of protecting that. What other things of value did I have? There were two or three kilos of gold I had picked up in various little deals; there were my documents – my birth certificate and my British passport; there was the camera I had shown Ferdinand, but didn't want to tempt anyone with now. I put these things in a wooden crate. I also put in the wall-print of the holy place my father had sent me by Metty, and I got Metty to put in his passport and money as well. Metty had become the family servant again, anxious, for the sake of prestige, even at this moment, to behave just like me. I had to stop him throwing in all kinds of rubbish. We dug a hole in the yard just at the bottom of the external staircase – it was easy: no stones in the red earth – and buried the crate there.

It was early morning. Our back yard was so drab, so ordinary with sunlight and the smell of the neighbours' chickens, so ordinary with red dust and dead leaves and the morning shadows of trees I knew at home on the coast, that I thought, 'This is too stupid.' A little later I thought: 'I've made a mistake. Metty knows that everything of value that I possess is in that box. I've put myself in his hands.'

We went and opened the shop; I was carrying on. We did a little business in the first hour. But then the market square began to empty and the town began to go silent. The sun was bright and hot, and I studied the contracting shadows of trees and market stalls and buildings around the square.

Sometimes I thought I could hear the noise of the rapids. It was the eternal noise at that bend in the river, but on a normal day it couldn't be heard here. Now it seemed to come and go on the wind. At midday, when we shut the shop for lunch, and I drove through the streets, it was only the river, glittering in the hard light, that seemed alive. No dugouts, though; only the water hyacinths travelling up from the south, and floating away to the west, clump after clump, with the thick-stalked lilac flowers like masts.

I was taking lunch that day with the old Asian couple – they had a transport business until independence, when business just stopped, and the rest of the family went away. Nothing had changed there since I had made the arrangement to have lunch with them twice a week. They were people almost without news, and we still had very little conversation. The view, from the verandah of the rough, ranch-like house, was still of abandoned motor vehicles, relics of the old business, rotting away in the yard. I would have minded that view, if it had been my business. But the old people didn't seem to mind or know that they had lost a lot. They seemed content just to live out their lives. They had done all that their religion and family customs had required them to do; and they felt – like the older people of my own family – that they had lived good and complete lives.

On the coast I used to grieve for people of our community who were like that, indifferent to what lay around them. I wanted to shake them up and alert them to danger. But it was soothing now to be with these calm old people; and it would have been nice, on a day like this, not to have to leave that house, to be a child again, protected by the wisdom of the old, and to believe that what they saw was true.

Who wanted philosophy or faith for the good times? We could all cope with the good times. It was for the bad that we had to be equipped. And here in Africa none of us were as well equipped as the Africans. The Africans had called up this war; they would suffer dreadfully, more than anybody else; but they could cope. Even the raggedest of them had their villages and tribes, things that were absolutely theirs. They could run away again to their secret worlds and become lost in those worlds, as they had done before. And even if terrible things happened to them they would die with the comfort of knowing that their ancestors were gazing down approvingly at them.

But this was not true of Ferdinand. With his mixed parentage he was almost as much a stranger in the town as I was. He came to the flat in the afternoon, and he was wild, close to hysteria, possessed by all the African terror of strange Africans.

Classes had been suspended at the lycée; thoughts there were of the safety of the boys and the teachers. Ferdinand had decided that the lycée wasn't safe; he thought it would be one of the first places to be attacked if there was an uprising in the town. He had dropped all his characters, all his poses. The blazer, which he had worn with pride as a young man of new Africa, he had discarded as dangerous, something that made him more a man apart; and he was wearing long khaki trousers, not the white shorts of the school uniform. He talked in a frantic way of returning to the south, to his father's people. But that was impossible – he knew it was impossible; and there was no question either of sending him down river to his mother's village.

The big boy, almost a man, sobbed, 'I didn't want to come here. I don't know anyone here. My mother wanted me to come. I didn't want to be in the town or go to the lycée. Why did she send me to the lycée?'

It was a comfort to us, Metty and myself, to have someone to comfort. We decided that Ferdinand was to sleep in Metty's room, and we dug out some bedding for him. The attention calmed Ferdinand down. We ate early, while it was still light. Ferdinand was silent then. But later, when we were in our different rooms, he and Metty talked.

I heard Metty say: 'They came to a bridge. And all the trucks stalled and the guns began to bend.'

Metty's voice was high-pitched and excited. That wasn't the voice he had used when he had given me the news in the morning. He was talking now like the local Africans, from whom he had got the story.

In the morning the market square outside the shop didn't come to life at all. The town remained empty. The squatters and campers in the street seemed to have gone into hiding.

When I went to Shoba and Mahesh's flat for lunch I noticed that their better carpets had disappeared, and some of the finer glassware and silver, and the crystal figure of the nude woman. Shoba looked strained, especially around her eyes, and Mahesh

seemed more nervous of her than of anything else. Shoba's mood
always dictated the mood of our lunch, and she seemed that day
to want to punish us for the good lunch she had prepared. We ate
for some time in silence, Shoba looking down at the table with her
tired eyes, Mahesh constantly looking at her.

Shoba said, 'I should have been at home this week. My father
is sick. Did I tell you, Salim? I should have been with him. And
it is his birthday.'

Mahesh's eyes hopped about the table. Spoiling the effect of
the words which I had found so wise, he said, 'We'll carry on.
It will be all right. The new President's not a fool. He isn't just
going to stay in his house like the last man, and do nothing.'

She said, 'Carry on, carry on. That's all I've been doing. That's
how I've spent my life. That's how I've lived in this place, among
Africans. Is that a life, Salim?'

She looked at her plate, not at me. And I said nothing.

Shoba said, 'I've wasted my life, Salim. You don't know how
I've wasted my life. You don't know how I live in fear in this
place. You don't know how frightened I was when I heard about
you, when I heard that a stranger had come to the town. I've got
to be frightened of everybody, you know.' Her eyes twitched.
She stopped eating, and pressed her cheekbones with the tips of
her fingers, as though pressing away a nervous pain. 'I come from
a well-to-do family, a rich family. You know that. My family
had plans for me. But then I met Mahesh. He used to own a
motor-cycle shop. Something terrible happened. I slept with him
almost as soon as I met him. You know us and our ways well
enough to know that that was a terrible thing for me to do. But
it was terrible for me in another way as well. I didn't want to
get to know anybody else after that. That has been my curse.
Why aren't you eating, Salim? Eat, eat. We must carry on.'

Mahesh's lips came together nervously, and he looked a little
foolish. At the same time his eyes brightened at the praises contained in the complaining words; yet he and Shoba had been
together for nearly ten years.

'My family beat up Mahesh terribly. But that just made me
more determined. My brothers threatened to throw acid on me.

They were serious. They also threatened to kill Mahesh. That was why we came here. I watched for my brothers every day. I still do. I wait for them. You know that with families like ours certain things are no joke. And then, Salim, while we were here, something worse happened. Mahesh said one day that I was stupid to be watching out for my brothers. He said, "Your brothers wouldn't come all the way here. They'll send somebody else." '

Mahesh said, 'That was a joke.'

'No, that wasn't a joke. That was true. Anybody could come here – they could send anybody. It doesn't have to be an Asian. It could be a Belgian or a Greek or any European. It could be an African. How am I to know?'

She did all the talking at lunch, and Mahesh let her; he seemed to have handled this kind of situation before. Afterwards I drove him back to the centre of the town – he said he didn't want to take his car in. His nervousness disappeared as soon as we left Shoba. He didn't seem embarrassed by what Shoba had said about their life together, and made no comment about it.

He said, as we drove through the dusty red streets, 'Shoba exaggerates. Things are not as bad as she believes. The new man's no fool. The steamer came in this morning with the white men. You didn't know? Go across to the van der Weyden and you'll see a few of them. The new man might be a maid's son. But he's going to hold it together. He's going to use this to put a lot of people in their place. Go to the van der Weyden. It will give you an idea of what things were like after independence.'

Mahesh was right. The steamer had arrived; I had a glimpse of it when we drove by the docks. It hadn't hooted and I hadn't looked for it earlier. Low-decked, flat-bottomed, it was almost hidden by the customs sheds, all but the top of the superstructure at the rear. And when I stopped outside Mahesh's shop, which was opposite the van der Weyden, I saw a number of army vehicles, and some civilian trucks and taxis that had been commandeered.

Mahesh said, 'It's a good thing Africans have short memories. Go and have a look at the people who've come to save them from suicide.'

The van der Weyden was a modern building, four storeys high, concrete and straight lines, part of the pre-independence boom; and in spite of all that it had gone through it still pretended to be a modern hotel. It had many glass doors at pavement level; the lobby had a mosaic floor; there were lifts (not reliable now); there was a reception desk with a pre-independence airline advertisement and a permanent *Hotel Complet* ('No Vacancies') sign – which hadn't been true for some years.

I had expected a crowd in the lobby, noise, rowdiness. I found the place looking emptier than usual, and it was almost hushed. But the hotel had guests: on the mosaic floor there were about twenty or thirty suitcases with identical blue tie-on labels printed *Hazel's Travels*. The lifts weren't working, and a single hotel boy – a small old man wearing the servant costume of the colonial time: short khaki trousers, short-sleeved shirt, and a large, coarse white apron over that – had the job of taking the suitcases up the terrazzo steps at the side of the lift. He was working under the direct supervision of the big-bellied African (from down river somewhere) who normally stood behind the reception desk cleaning his teeth with a toothpick and being rude to everybody, but was now standing by the suitcases and trying to look busy and serious.

Some of the hotel's new guests were in the patio bar, where there were a few green palms and creepers in concrete pots. The terrazzo floor here sloped from all sides to a central grille, and from this grille there always came, but especially after rain, a smell of the sewer. In this smell – not particularly bad now: it was dry and hot, a triangle of sunlight dazzled on one wall – the white men sat, eating the van der Weyden's sandwiches and drinking lager.

They wore civilian clothes, but they would have been a noticeable crowd anywhere. An ordinary bar crowd would have had some flabby types and would have been more mixed in age. These men were all in fine physical condition, and even the few grey-haired ones among them didn't look over forty; they could have passed as some kind of sports team. They sat in two distinct groups. One group was rougher-looking, noisier, with a few flashy dressers; two or three very young men in this group were pretending to be drunk, and clowning. The men in the other group were graver, cleaner shaved, more educated in face, more conscious of their appearance. And you might have thought the two groups had accidentally come together in the bar, until you saw that they were all wearing the same kind of heavy brown boots.

Normally at the van der Weyden the hotel boys drooped around. The old ones, with their squashed and sour little faces, sat on their stools and expected only to be tipped, wearing their shorts and very big aprons like a pensioner's uniform (and sometimes, in their great stillness, hiding their arms below their aprons and looking like men at the barber's); the younger, post-independence boys wore their own clothes and chatted behind the counter as though they were customers. Now they were all alert and jumping about.

I asked for a cup of coffee, and no cup of coffee ever came to me more quickly at the van der Weyden. It was a tiny old man who served me. And I thought, not for the first time, that in colonial days the hotel boys had been chosen for their small size, and the ease with which they could be manhandled. That was no doubt why the region had provided so many slaves in the old days: slave peoples are physically wretched, half men in everything except in their capacity to breed the next generation.

The coffee came fast, but the stainless steel jug the old man brought me had only a stale-looking trickle of powdered milk. I lifted the jug. The old man saw before I could show him, and he looked so terrified that I put the jug down and sipped the awful coffee by itself.

The men in the bar had come to do a job. They – or their fellows – had probably already begun. They knew they were dramatic figures. They knew I had come to see what they looked like; they knew the boys were terrified of them. Until this morning those hotel servants had been telling one another stories about the invincibility of their people in the forest; and those hotel servants were men who, given an uprising in the town, would have done terrible things with their small hands. Now, so quickly, they had become abject. In one way it was good; in another way it was pitiful. This was how the place worked on you: you never knew what to think or feel. Fear or shame – there seemed to be nothing in between.

I went back to the shop. It was a way of carrying on, and a way of passing the time. The flamboyant trees were in new leaf, feathery, a delicate green. The light changed; shadows began to angle across the red streets. On another day at this time I would have been starting to think of tea at the flat, squash at the Hellenic Club, with cold drinks afterwards in the rough little bar, sitting at the metal tables and watching the light go.

When Metty came in, just before four, closing time, he said, 'The white men came this morning. Some of them went to the barracks and some of them went to the hydro.' This was the hydro-electric station, some miles up river from the town. 'The first thing they did at the barracks was to shoot Colonel Yenyi. It was what the President asked them to do. He doesn't play, this new President. Colonel Yenyi was running out to meet them. They didn't let him talk. They shot him in front of the women and everybody. And Iyanda, the sergeant – he bought that bolt of curtain material with the apple pattern – they shot him too, and a few other soldiers as well.'

I remembered Iyanda with his overstarched uniform, his broad face, and his smiling, small, malicious eyes. I remembered the way he had rubbed the palm of his hand over the cloth with the big red apples, the proud way he had pulled out the rolled-up notes to pay – such a small sum, really. Curtain material! The news of his execution would have pleased the local people. Not that he was a wicked man; but he belonged to that detested slave-hunting tribe, like the rest of the army, like his colonel.

The President had sent terror to our town and region. But at the same time, by terrorizing the army as well, he was making a gesture to the local people. The news of the executions would have spread fast, and people would already have become confused and nervous. They would have felt – as I began to feel – that for the first time since independence there was some guiding intelligence in the capital, and that the free-for-all of independence had come to an end.

I could see the change in Metty. He had brought quite bloody

news. Yet he seemed calmer than in the morning; and he made
Ferdinand calmer. Late in the afternoon we began to hear guns.
In the morning that sound would have panicked us all. Now we
were almost relieved – the guns were far away, and the noise was
a good deal less loud than thunder, to which we were accustomed.
The dogs were disturbed by the strange noise, though, and set
up a barking that rolled back and forth, at times drowning the
sound of the guns. Late sunlight, trees, cooking smoke: that was
all we could see when we went out to the landing of the external
staircase to look.

No lights came on at sunset. There was no electricity. The
machinery had failed again, or the power had been deliberately
turned off, or the power station had been captured by the rebels.
But it wasn't bad to be without lights now; it meant that at least
there would be no uprising during the night. People here didn't
like the dark, and some could sleep only with lights in their rooms
or huts. And none of us – neither Metty nor Ferdinand nor myself – believed that the station had been captured by the rebels.
We had faith in the President's white men. The situation, so
confused for us in the morning, had become as simple as that
now.

I stayed in the sitting room and read old magazines by an oil
lamp. In their room Metty and Ferdinand talked. They didn't use
their day-time voices or the voices they might have used in
electric light. They both sounded slow, contemplative, old; they
talked like old men. When I went out to the passage I saw, through
the open door, Metty sitting on his cot in vest and pants, and
Ferdinand, also in vest and pants, lying on his bedding on the
floor, one raised foot pressed against the wall. In lamplight it was
like the interior of a hut; their leisurely, soft talk, full of pauses
and silences, matched their postures. For the first time for days
they were relaxed, and they felt so far from danger now that they
began to talk of danger, war, and armies.

Metty said he had seen the white men in the morning.

Ferdinand said, 'There were a lot of white soldiers in the
south. That was a real war.'

'You should have seen them this morning. They just raced to

85

the barracks and they were pointing their guns at everybody. I never saw soldiers like that before.'

Ferdinand said, 'I saw soldiers for the first time when I was very young. It was just after the Europeans went away. It was in my mother's village, before I went to stay with my father. These soldiers came to the village. They had no officers and they began to behave badly.'

'Did they have guns?'

'Of course they had guns. They were looking for white people to kill. They said we were hiding white people. But I think they only wanted to make trouble. Then my mother spoke to them and they went away. They just took a few women.'

'What did she say to them?'

'I don't know. But they became frightened. My mother has powers.'

Metty said, 'That was like the man we had on the coast. He came from somewhere near here. He was the man who made the people kill the Arabs. It began in the market. I was there. You should have seen it, Ferdinand. The arms and legs lying about in the streets.'

'Why did he kill the Arabs?'

'He said he was obeying the god of Africans.'

Metty had never told me about that. Perhaps he hadn't thought it important; perhaps it had frightened him. But he had remembered.

They went silent for a while – I had the feeling that Ferdinand was examining what he had heard. When they spoke again it was of other things.

The gunfire went on. But it came no nearer. It was the sound of the weapons of the President's white men, the promise of order and continuity; and it was oddly comforting, like the sound of rain in the night. All that was threatening, in that great unknown outside, was being held in check. And it was a relief, after all the anxiety, to sit in the lamplit flat and watch the shadows that electric lights never made; and to hear Ferdinand and Metty talk in their leisurely old men's voices in that room which they had turned into a warm little cavern. It was a little like being transported to the hidden forest villages, to the protection and secrecy of the huts at night – everything outside shut out, kept beyond some magical protecting line; and I thought, as I had thought when I had had lunch with the old couple, how nice it would be if it were true. If in the morning we could wake up and find that the world had shrunken only to what we knew and what was safe.

In the morning there came the fighter plane. Almost as soon as you heard it, before you had time to go out and look for it, it was overhead, flying low, and screaming at such a pitch that you barely felt yourself in possession of your body; you were close to a cutting-out of the senses. A jet fighter flying low, so low that you clearly see its triangular silver underside, is a killing thing. Then it was gone, and was soon hardly visible in the sky, white with the heat of the day that had just begun. It made a few more passes over the town, that one plane, like a vicious bird that wouldn't go away. Then it flew over the bush. At last it lifted, and just a little while later, at some distance, the missiles it had released exploded in the bush. And that was like the thunder we were used to.

It came back more than once during the week, that single plane, to fly low over the town and the bush and to drop its explosives at random in the bush. But the war was over that first day. Though it was a month before the army began to come back from the bush, and a full two months before the van der Weyden began to lose its new guests.

In the beginning, before the arrival of the white men, I had considered myself neutral. I had wanted neither side to win, neither the army nor the rebels. As it turned out, both sides lost.

Many of the soldiers – from the famous warrior tribe – were killed. And afterwards many more lost their guns and over-starched uniforms and the quarters they had spent so much of their money furnishing. The army was reorganized by the President, far away in the capital; in our town the army became more mixed, with men from many tribes and different regions. The men of the warrior tribe were turned out unprotected into the town. There were dreadful scenes at the barracks; the women wailed in the forest way, lifting their bellies and letting them drop heavily again. A famous tribe, now helpless among their traditional prey: it was as though some old law of the forest, something that came from Nature itself, had been overturned.

As for the starveling rebels of our region, they soon began to reappear in the town, more starved and abject, their blackened rags hanging on them, men who only a few weeks before had thought they had found a fetish powerful enough to cause the guns of their enemies to bend and to turn bullets to water. There was bitterness in their wasted faces, and for a little while they were withdrawn, like people slightly crazed. But they needed the town they had wanted to destroy; as Mahesh said, they had been saved from suicide. They recognized the new intelligence that ran the country from afar, and they returned to their old habit of obedience.

For the first time since I had arrived there was something like life at the van der Weyden. The steamers brought up not only supplies for the President's white men, but also very plump and fantastically dressed women from the down-river peoples, beside whom the women of our region, polers of dugouts and carriers of loads, looked like bony boys.

Eventually we were allowed to drive out to the dam and the hydro-electric station, near where there had been fighting. The installations were untouched; but we had lost one of our new night clubs. It had been started by a refugee from the Portuguese territory to the south (a man avoiding conscription), and it was beautifully sited, on a cliff overlooking the river. It was a place to which we had just begun to get accustomed. The trees were hung with small coloured bulbs and we sat out at metal tables and drank light Portuguese white wine and looked at the gorge and the floodlit dam; it was like luxury to us, and made us feel stylish. That place had been captured by the rebels and pillaged. The main building was basic and very ordinary – walls of concrete blocks around an unroofed dance floor with a covered bar at one side. The walls still stood (though they had tried to set the concrete alight: there were fire-marks in many places); but all the fittings had been destroyed. The rage of the rebels was like a rage against metal, machinery, wires, everything that was not of the forest and Africa.

There were signs of that rage in other places as well. After the earlier war a United Nations agency had repaired the power station and the causeway at the top of the dam. A metal plaque set on a small stone pyramid, some distance from the dam itself, recorded this fact. That plaque had been defaced, battered with some heavy metal piece, individual letters filed away. At the beginning of the causeway old cast-iron lamp standards from Europe had been placed as a decorative feature – old lamps at a site of new power. A pretty idea; but the lamp standards had also received a battering, and again attempts had been made to file away the lettering – the name of the nineteenth-century makers in Paris.

It was the rage that made an impression – the rage of simple men tearing at metal with their hands. And already, after only a few weeks of peace, with so many people from the villages hungry and scrounging in the town, it seemed far away, hard to imagine.

It was during these early days of the peace that Father Huismans went out on one of his trips and was killed. His death need never have been discovered; he could easily have been buried somewhere in the bush. But the people who killed him wanted the fact to be known. His body was put in a dugout, and the dugout drifted down the main river until it caught against the bank in a tangle of water hyacinths. His body had been mutilated, his head cut off and spiked. He was buried quickly, with the minimum of ceremony.

It was terrible. His death made his life seem such a waste. So much of his knowledge was buried with him, and what to me was more than knowledge – his attitudes, his relish for Africa, his feeling for the beliefs of the forest. A little bit of the world was lost with him.

I had admired him for his purity, but now I had to ask whether in the end it had been of value. A death like that makes us question everything. But we are men; regardless of the deaths around us we continue to be flesh and blood and mind, and we cannot stay with that questioning mood for long. When the mood went away I felt – what deep down, as a life-loving man, I had never doubted – that he had passed his time better than most of us. The idea Father Huismans had of his civilization had made him live his particular kind of dedicated life. It had sent him looking, inquiring; it had made him find human richness where the rest of us saw bush or had stopped seeing anything at all. But his idea of his civilization was also like his vanity. It had made him read too much in that mingling of peoples by our river; and he had paid for it.

Little was said about the way he had died. But the body had floated down the main river in a dugout and must have been seen by many people. Word got around the lycée. In our town Father Huismans had the reputation – though most people were rather vague about him – of being a lover of Africa; and some of the boys at the lycée were embarrassed and ashamed. Some were aggressive. Ferdinand – recovered from the days of fright, his wish to be back in his father's or mother's village – was one of the aggressive ones. I wasn't surprised.

Ferdinand said, 'It is a thing of Europeans, a museum. Here it is going against the god of Africans. We have masks in our houses and we know what they are there for. We don't have to go to Huismans's museum.'

'The god of Africans' – the words were Metty's, and Metty had got them from the leader of the uprising against the Arabs on the coast. I had heard the words for the first time that night when we heard the gunfire from the hydro-electric station and knew that we were safe. The words, occurring when they did, seemed to have released certain things in Ferdinand. Those days in the flat had been days of special crisis for Ferdinand, and he had ever since been settling into a new character. This one fitted, or made more sense. He was no longer concerned about being a particular kind of African; he was simply an African, himself, ready to acknowledge all sides of his character.

It didn't make him easier. He abandoned politeness; he became aggressive and perverse, over a secret nervousness. He began to stay away from the shop and flat. I expected that; it was his way of demonstrating, after the great fright of the rebellion, that he could do without me. But then one day Metty brought me a letter from Ferdinand, and the letter moved me. It was a one-sentence letter writen in very big letters on a lined sheet roughly torn out from an exercise book, and sent without an envelope, the sheet just folded small and tight. 'Salim! You took me in that time and treated me as a member of your own family. F.'

It was his letter of thanks. I had given him shelter under my own roof, and to him, as an African, that hospitality was extraordinary and had to be acknowledged. But he didn't want to appear fawning or weak, and everything in the letter was deliberately crude – no envelope, the lined paper torn down one side, the very big and careless handwriting, the absence of the direct word of thanks, the 'Salim!' and not 'Dear Salim', the 'F.' and not 'Ferdinand'.

I found it funny and moving. Yet there was something ironical about the whole thing. The action which had drawn that softness from Ferdinand was the simple gesture of a man from the coast whose family had lived close, too close, to their servants, once their slaves, descendants of people snatched from this part of Africa. Ferdinand would have been outraged if he knew. Still, the letter, and his unapologetic new character, showed how far, as a man, he had rounded out. And that was what his mother Zabeth had had in mind when she brought him to the shop and asked me to look after him.

What Ferdinand had said about Father Huismans's collection, other people began to say. While he lived, Father Huismans, collecting the things of Africa, had been thought a friend of Africa. But now that changed. It was felt that the collection was an affront to African religion, and no one at the lycée took it over. Perhaps there was no one there with the knowledge and the eye that were required.

Visitors were sometimes shown the collection. The wooden carvings remained as they were; but in the unventilated gun room the masks began to deteriorate and the smell became more unpleasant. The masks themselves, crumbling on the slatted shelves, seemed to lose the religious power Father Huismans had taught me to see in them; without him, they simply became extravagant objects.

In the long peace that now settled on the town, we began to receive visitors from a dozen countries, teachers, students, helpers in this and that, people who behaved like discoverers of Africa, were happy with everything they found, and looked down quite a bit on foreigners like ourselves who had been living there. The collection began to be pillaged. Who more African than the young American who appeared among us, who more ready to put on African clothes and dance African dances? He left suddenly by the steamer one day; and it was discovered afterwards that the bulk of the collection in the gun room had been crated and shipped back with his belongings to the United States, no doubt to be the nucleus of the gallery of primitive art he often spoke of starting. The richest products of the forest.

II

The New Domain

6

IF you look at a column of ants on the march you will see that there are some who are stragglers or have lost their way. The column has no time for them; it goes on. Sometimes the stragglers die. But even this has no effect on the column. There is a little disturbance around the corpse, which is eventually carried off – and then it appears so light. And all the time the great busyness continues, and that apparent sociability, that rite of meeting and greeting which ants travelling in opposite directions, to and from their nest, perform without fail.

So it was after the death of Father Huismans. In the old days his death would have caused anger, and people would have wanted to go out to look for his killers. But now we who remained – outsiders, but neither settlers nor visitors, just people with nowhere better to go – put our heads down and got on with our business.

The only message of his death was that we had to be careful ourselves and remember where we were. And oddly enough, by acting as we did, by putting our heads down and getting on with our work, we helped to bring about what he had prophesied for our town. He had said that our town would suffer setbacks but that they would be temporary. After each setback, the civilization of Europe would become a little more secure at the bend in the river; the town would always start up again, and would grow a little more each time. In the peace that we now had the town wasn't only re-established; it grew. And the rebellion and Father Huismans's death receded fast.

We didn't have Father Huismans's big views. Some of us had our own clear ideas about Africans and their future. But it occurred to me that we did really share his faith in the future. Unless we believed that change was coming to our part of Africa, we couldn't have done our business. There would have been no point. And – in spite of appearances – we also had the attitude to ourselves that he had to himself. He saw himself as part of a great historical process; he would have seen his own death as unimportant, hardly a disturbance. We felt like that too, but from a different angle.

We were simple men with civilizations but without other homes. Whenever we were allowed to, we did the complicated things we had to do, like the ants. We had the occasional comfort of reward, but in good times or bad we lived with the knowledge that we were expendable, that our labour might at any moment go to waste, that we ourselves might be smashed up; and that others would replace us. To us that was the painful part, that others would come at the better time. But we were like the ants; we kept on.

People in our position move rapidly from depression to optimism and back down again. Now we were in a period of boom. We felt the new ruling intelligence – and energy – from the capital; there was a lot of copper money around; and these two things – order and money – were enough to give us confidence. A little of that went a long way with us. It released our energy; and energy, rather than quickness or great capital, was what we possessed.

All kinds of projects were started. Various government departments came to life again; and the town at last became a place that could be made to work. We already had the steamer service; now the airfield was re-commissioned and extended, to take the jets from the capital (and to fly in soldiers). The *cités* filled up, and new ones were built, though nothing that was done could cope with the movement of people from the villages; we never lost the squatters and campers in our central streets and squares. But there were buses now, and many more taxis. We even began to get a new telephone system. It was far too elabarate for our needs, but it was what the Big Man in the capital wanted for us.

The growth of the population could be gauged by the growth of the rubbish heaps in the *cités*. They didn't burn their rubbish in oil drums, as we did; they just threw it out on the broken streets – that sifted, ashy African rubbish. Those mounds of rubbish, though constantly flattened by rain, grew month by month into increasingly solid little hills, and the hills literally became as high as the box-like concrete houses of the *cités*.

Nobody wanted to move that rubbish. But the taxis stank of disinfectant; the officials of our health department were fierce about taxis. And for this reason. In the colonial days public vehicles had by law to be disinfected once a year by the health department. The disinfecters were entitled to a personal fee. That custom had been remembered. Any number of people wanted to be disinfecters; and now taxis and trucks weren't disinfected just once a year; they were disinfected whenever they were caught. The fee had to be paid each time; and disinfecters in their official jeeps played hide and seek with taxis and trucks among the hills of rubbish. The red dirt roads of our town, neglected for years, had quickly become corrugated with the new traffic we had; and these disinfectant chases were in a curious kind of slow motion, with the vehicles of hunters and hunted pitching up and down the corrugations like launches in a heavy sea.

All the people – like the health officials – who performed services for ready money were energetic, or could be made so – the customs people, the police, and even the army. The administration, however hollow, was fuller; there were people you could appeal to. You could get things done, if you knew how to go about it.

And the town at the bend in the river became again what Father Huismans had said it had always been, long before the peoples of the Indian Ocean or Europe came to it. It became the trading centre for the region, which was vast. *Marchands* came in now from very far away, making journeys much more difficult than Zabeth's; some of those journeys took a week. The steamer didn't go beyond our town; above the rapids there were only dugouts (some with outboard motors) and a few launches. Our town became a goods depot, and I acquired a number of agencies (re-assuming some that Nazruddin had had) for things that until then I had more or less been selling retail.

There was money in agencies. The simpler the product, the simpler and better the business. It was a different kind of business from the retail trade. Electric batteries, for instance – I bought and sold quantities long before they arrived; I didn't have to handle them physically or even see them. It was like dealing in words alone, ideas on paper; it was like a form of play – until one day you were notified that the batteries had arrived, and you went to the customs warehouse and saw that they existed, that workmen somewhere had actually made the things. Such useful things, such necessary things – they would have been acceptable in a plain brown-paper casing; but the people who had made them had gone to the extra trouble of giving them pretty labels, with tempting slogans. Trade, goods! What a mystery! We couldn't make the things we dealt in; we hardly understood their principles. Money alone had brought these magical things to us deep in the bush, and we dealt in them so casually!

Salesmen from the capital, Europeans most of them, preferring to fly up now rather than spend seven days on the steamer coming up and five going down, began to stay at the van der Weyden, and they gave a little variety to our social life. In the Hellenic Club, in the bars, they brought at last that touch of Europe and the big city – the atmosphere in which, from his stories, I had imagined Nazruddin living here.

Mahesh, with his shop just across the road from the van der Weyden, saw the comings and goings, and his excitement led him into a series of little business ventures. It was strange about Mahesh. He was always on the look-out for the big break, but he could spend weeks on things that were quite petty.

He acquired at one time a machine for cutting out or engraving letters and numbers, and he acquired a stack of the very tough plastic plates on which the numbers or letters were to be engraved. His idea was to supply name-plates to the town. He practised at home; Shoba said the noise was terrible. Mahesh, in his flat and in his shop, showed off the practice name-plates as though it was he, rather than the machine, that had made the beautiful letters. The modernity and precision – and, above all, the 'manufactured' look of the plates – really excited him, and he was sure it would excite everybody else as well.

He had bought the equipment from a salesman who had stayed at the van der Weyden. And it was typical of Mahesh's casual approach to business that, when it came to getting engraving orders, he could only think of crossing the road back to the van der Weyden – reversing the trip of the salesman who had sold him the equipment. He had pinned all his hopes on the van der Weyden. He was going to re-do the room numbers, all the *Hommes* and *Dames* signs, and he was going to affix descriptive plates on almost every door downstairs. The van der Weyden alone was going to keep him busy for weeks and pay back for the machine. But the van der Weyden owners (a middle-aged Italian couple who kept themselves in the background and hid behind their African front-men) didn't want to play. And not many of us felt the need to have our names on triangular sections of wood on our desks. So that idea was dropped; that tool was forgotten.

Mahesh, broaching a new idea, liked to be mysterious. The time, for instance, he wanted to import a machine from Japan for cutting little flat wood sticks and spoons for ice cream, he didn't say so right out. He began by offering me a sample spoon in a paper wrapper which the salesman had given him. I looked at the little shoe-shaped spoon. What was there to say? He asked me to smell the spoon and then to taste it; and while I did so he looked at me in a way that made me feel that I was going to be surprised. There was no surprise: he was just demonstrating to me – something I must say I had never stopped to think about – that ice cream spoons and sticks shouldn't taste or smell.

He wanted to know whether there was a local wood which was like that nice Japanese wood. To import the wood from Japan with the machine would be too complicated, and might make the sticks and spoons cost more than the ice cream. So for some weeks we thought and talked about wood. The idea interested me; I got taken up with it, and began to look at trees in a different way. We had tasting sessions, smelling and tasting different kinds of wood, including some varieties that Daulat, the man with the trucks, picked up for us on his runs east. But then it occurred to me that it was important to find out – before the spoon-making machine came down – whether the local people, with their own tastes in food, were ready for ice cream. Perhaps there was a good reason why the ice cream idea hadn't occurred to anybody else; and we had Italians in the town, after all. And how was the ice cream going to be made? Where were the milk and the eggs?

Mahesh said, 'Do you need eggs to make ice cream?'

I said, 'I don't know. I was asking you.'

It wasn't the ice cream that attracted Mahesh. It was the idea of that simple machine, or rather the idea of being the only man in the town to own such a machine. When Shoba had met him he had been a motor-cycle repair man; and he had been so flattered by her devotion that he had not risen above that kind of person. He remained the man who loved little machines and electrical tools and saw them as magical means of making a living.

I knew a number of men like that on the coast, men of our community; and I believe people like that exist wherever machines are not made. These men are good with their hands and gifted in their own way. They are dazzled by the machines they import. That is part of their intelligence; but they soon start behaving as though they don't just own the machines, but the patents as well; they would like to be the only men in the world with such magical instruments. Mahesh was looking for the wonderful imported thing which he would own exclusively, the simple thing which would provide a short-cut to power and money. So that in this respect Mahesh was only a notch or two above the *marchands* who came to the town to buy modern goods to take back to their villages.

I used to wonder how someone like Mahesh had survived all that he had survived in our town. There was a kind of quiet wisdom or canniness there, no doubt of that. But I also began to feel that he had survived because he was casual, without doubts or deep anxieties, and – in spite of his talk of getting out to a better country (standard talk among us) – without deeper ambitions. He suited the place; he would have found it hard to survive anywhere else.

Shoba was his life. She told him – or by her devotion showed him – how fine he was; and I believe he saw himself as she saw him. Outside that, he took things as they came. And now in the most casual way, with almost no attempt at secrecy or guile, he became involved in 'business' deals that frightened me when he told me about them. He seemed unable to resist anything that might be described as a business offer. And most of those business offers came to him now from the army.

I wasn't too happy with our new army. I preferred the men from the warrior tribe, for all their roughness. I understood their tribal pride and – always making allowance for that – I had found them straight. The officers of the new army were a different breed. No warrior code there; no code. They were all in varying ways like Ferdinand, and they were often as young as Ferdinand. They were as aggressive, but without Ferdinand's underlying graciousness.

They wore their uniforms the way Ferdinand had at one time worn his lycée blazer: they saw themselves both as the new men of Africa and the men of the new Africa. They made such play with the national flag and the portrait of the President – the two now always going together – that in the beginning I thought these new officers stood for a new, constructive pride. But they were simpler. The flag and the President's portrait were only like their fetishes, the sources of their authority. They didn't see, these young men, that there was anything to build in their country. As far as they were concerned, it was all there already. They had only to take. They believed that, by being what they were, they had earned the right to take; and the higher the officer, the greater the crookedness – if that word had any meaning.

With their guns and jeeps, these men were poachers of ivory and thieves of gold. Ivory, gold – add slaves, and it would have been like being back in oldest Africa. And these men would have dealt in slaves, if there was still a market. It was to the traders in the town that the army turned when they wished to clear their gold or, more especially, the ivory they had poached. Officials and governments right across the continent were engaged in this ivory trade which they themselves had declared illegal. It made smuggling easy; but I was nervous of getting involved, because a government that breaks its own laws can also easily break you. Your business associate today can be your jailer or worse tomorrow.

But Mahesh didn't mind. Like a child, as it seemed to me, he accepted all the poisoned sweets that were offered him. But he wasn't a child; he knew the sweets were poisoned.

He said, 'Oh, they will let you down. But if they let you down, you pay up. That is all. In your costing you make allowances for that. You just pay. I don't think you understand, Salim. And it isn't an easy thing to understand. It isn't that there's no right and wrong here. There's no right.'

Twice, miraculously interpreting a nonsense telephone call from him as an appeal for help, I had to take away things from his flat.

The first time, one afternoon, after some inconsequential talk from him about tennis and the shoes I had asked for, I drove to his flat and blew my horn. He didn't come down. He opened a window of his sitting room and shouted down to me in the street, 'I'm sending the boy down with the tennis shoes for you. Right, Salim!' And, still standing before the window, he turned and shouted in patois to someone inside: *"Phonse! Aoutchikong pour Mis' Salim!"* *Aoutchikong*, from *caoutchouc*, the French word for rubber, being patois for canvas shoes. With many people looking on, the boy Ildephonse brought down something roughly wrapped in newspaper. I threw it on the back seat and drove off without hanging around. It turned out, when I examined it later, to be a bundle of foreign bank-notes; and it went, as soon as it was dark, into the hole in the ground at the foot of my external staircase. To help Mahesh like this, though, was only to encourage him. The next time I had to bury some ivory. Burying ivory! What age were we living in? What did people want ivory for, apart from carving it – and not too well these days – into cigarette holders and figurines and junk like that?

Still, these deals made Mahesh money, and he acknowledged

my help and put me in the way of adding to my little store of gold. He had said that there was no right. It was hard for me to adapt to that; but he managed it beautifully. He was always cool and casual, never ruffled. I had to admire him for it. Though the casualness could lead him into situations that were quite ridiculous.

He said to me one day, with the mysterious, over-innocent manner he put on when he was about to tell about some deal: 'You read the foreign papers, Salim. Are you keeping an eye on the copper market? What's it like?' Well, copper was high. We all knew that; copper was at the bottom of our little boom. He said, 'It's that war the Americans are fighting. I hear they've used up more copper in the last two years than the world has used in the last two centuries.' This was boom talk, salesmen's chat from the van der Weyden. Mahesh, just across the road, picked up a fair amount of that chat; without it, he might have had less idea than he had of what was happening in the world.

From copper he turned to the other metals, and we talked for a while, quite ignorantly, about the prospects for tin and lead. Then he said, 'Uranium – what about that? What are they quoting that at now?'

I said, 'I don't think they quote that.'

He gave me his innocent look. 'But it must be pretty high? A chap here wants to sell a piece.'

'Do they sell uranium in pieces? What does it look like?'

'I haven't seen it. But the chap wants to sell it for a million dollars.'

That was what we were like. One day grubbing for food, opening rusty tins, cooking on charcoal braziers and over holes in the ground; and now talking of a million dollars as though we had talked of millions all our lives.

Mahesh said, 'I told the general it could be sold only to a foreign power, and he told me to go ahead. You know old Mancini. He is consul for quite a few countries here – that's a nice line of business, I always think. I went to see him. I told him straight out, but he wasn't interested. In fact, Mancini went crazy. He ran to the door and closed it and stood with his back against it and told me to get out. His face was red, red. Everybody's frightened of the Big Man in the capital. What do you think I should tell the general, Salim? He's frightened too. He told me he stole it from some top security place. I wouldn't like to make an enemy of the general. I wouldn't like him to think I hadn't tried. What do you think I should tell him? Seriously, seriously.'

'You say he's frightened?'

'Very frightened.'

'Then tell him he's being watched and he mustn't come to see you again.'

I looked in my science magazines and children's encyclopaedia parts (I had grown to love those) and read up about uranium. Uranium is one of those things we all hear about but not many of us know about. Like oil. I used to think, from hearing and reading about oil reservoirs, that oil ran in trapped underground streams. It was my encyclopaedia parts which told me that oil reservoirs were of stone and could even be of marble, with the oil in tiny pockets. It was in just such a way, I suppose, that the general, hearing of the immense value of uranium, had thought of it as a kind of super-precious metal, a kind of gold nugget. Mancini, the consul, must have thought so too. My reading told me of tons and tons of ore that had to be processed and reduced – but reduced to hefty blocks.

The general, offering a 'piece', might have been duped himself. But for some reason – Mahesh might have told him he was being watched – he never troubled Mahesh again. And not long afterwards he was posted away from our town. It was the method of the new President: he gave his men power and authority, but he never allowed them to settle in anywhere and become local kings. He saved us a lot of trouble.

Mahesh went on as coolly as before. The only man who had had a fright was Mancini, the consul.

That was what we were like in those days. We felt that there was treasure around us, waiting to be picked up. It was the bush that gave us this feeling. During the empty, idle time we had been indifferent to the bush; during the days of the rebellion it had depressed us. Now it excited us – the unused earth, with the promise of the unused. We forgot that others had been here before us, and had felt like us.

I shared in the boom. I was energetic in my own modest way. But I was also restless. You so quickly get used to peace. It is like being well – you take it for granted, and forget that when you were ill to be well again had seemed everything. And with peace and the boom I began to see the town as ordinary, for the first time.

The flat, the shop, the market outside the shop, the Hellenic Club, the bars, the life of the river, the dugouts, the water hyacinths – I knew it so well. And especially on hot sunny afternoons – that hard light, those black shadows, that feeling of stillness – it seemed without further human promise.

I didn't see myself spending the rest of my days at that bend in the river, like Mahesh and the others. In my own mind I separated myself from them. I still thought of myself as a man just passing through. But where was the good place? I couldn't say. I never thought constructively about it. I was waiting for some illumination to come to me, to guide me to the good place and the 'life' I was still waiting for.

From time to time now letters from my father on the coast reminded me of his wish to see me settled – married to Nazruddin's daughter: that was almost like a family commitment. But I was less prepared than ever for that. Though it was a comfort on occasion to play with the idea that outside this place a whole life waited for me, all the relationships that bind a man to the earth and give him a feeling of having a place. But I knew that it wasn't like that, really. I knew that for us the world was no longer as safe as that.

And again events caught up with my anxieties. There was trouble in Uganda, where Nazruddin had a cotton-ginning business. Uganda up till then had been the secure and well-run country Nazruddin had tried to excite us about, the country which received refugees from neighbouring countries. Now in Uganda itself a king was overthrown and forced to flee; Daulat brought back stories of yet another army on the loose. Nazruddin, as I remembered, lived with the knowledge that, after all his luck, things were going to end badly for him; and I thought that his luck had run out now. But I was wrong; Nazruddin's luck was still with him. The trouble in Uganda didn't last; only the king suffered. Life there went back to normal. But I began to fear for Nazruddin and his family, and the idea of marriage to his daughter ceased to be the idea of a correct family duty. It became a more oppressive kind of responsibility, and I pushed it to the back of my mind as something I would face when I absolutely had to.

So in the midst of the boom I had my anxieties and became almost as dissatisfied and restless as I had been at the beginning. It wasn't only outside pressures, or my solitude and my temperament. It also had to do with the place itself, the way it had altered with the peace. It was nobody's fault. It was something that had just happened. During the days of the rebellion I had had the sharpest sense of the beauty of the river and the forest, and had promised myself that when the peace came I would expose myself to it, learn it, possess that beauty. I had done nothing of the sort; when the peace came I had simply stopped looking about me. And now I felt that the mystery and the magic of the place had gone.

In those days of fear I felt we had been in touch, through the Africans, with the spirits of the river and forest; and that everything had been full of tension. But all the spirits seemed now to have left the place, as, after Father Huismans's death, the spirits appeared to have left his masks. We had been so nervous of the Africans during those days; we hadn't taken any man for granted. We had been the intruders, the ordinary men, they the inspired ones. Now the spirits had left them; they were ordinary, squalid, poor. Without effort we had become, in a real way, the masters, with the gifts and skills they needed. And we were so simple. On the land now ordinary again we had arranged such ordinary lives for ourselves – in the bars and brothels, the night clubs. Oh, it was unsatisfactory. Yet what else could we do? We did only what we could do. We followed Mahesh's motto: we carried on.

Mahesh did more than that. He pulled off a coup. He continued to consult catalogues, fill in coupons, write off for further information; and at last he found the package he had been looking for, the thing he could import whole and use as a short-cut to business and money. He got the Bigburger franchise for our town.

It wasn't what I was expecting. He had been running an odd little shop that dealt in ironmongery of various sorts, electrical goods, cameras, binoculars, lots of little gadgets. Hamburgers – Bigburgers – didn't seem to be his thing. I wasn't even sure that the town would go for Bigburgers. But he had no doubts.

He said, 'They've done their market research and they've decided to make a big push in Africa. They have an area office now in one of the French places on the west coast. The chap came the other day and measured up and everything. They don't just send you the sauce, you know, Salim. They send you the whole shop.'

And that was what they did. The crates that came up on the steamer in a couple of months did contain the whole shop: the stoves, the milk-shake machines, the coffee machine, the cups and plates, the tables and chairs, the made-to-measure counter, the stools, the made-to-measure wall panelling with the Bigburger design. And after all this serious stuff there were the toys: the Bigburger cruets, the Bigburger ketchup containers, the Bigburger menus and menu-holders, and the lovely advertisements – 'Bigburger – The Big One – The Bigwonderful One', with pictures of different kinds of Bigburgers.

I thought the Bigburger pictures looked like smooth white lips of bread over mangled black tongues of meat. But Mahesh didn't like it when I told him, and I decided not to say anything disrespectful about Bigburgers again. Mahesh had been full of jokes about the project; but as soon as the stuff arrived he became deadly serious – he had become Bigburger.

Mahesh's shop was structurally quite simple, the standard concrete box of our town; and in no time the local Italian builder had cleared it of Mahesh's shelves, re-wired, put in new plumbing, and fitted up a dazzling snack bar that seemed to have been imported from the United States. The whole prefabricated business did work; and it was great fun to be in Bigburger, to leave the sewer smells of the street, and the dust and the rubbish, and to step into this modern interior, with the advertisements and everything. So Mahesh did, after all, pull it off.

The prettiness had an effect on Shoba too. It made her energetic and brought out something of her family business talents. She organized the place and soon had it running smoothly. She arranged for the deliveries of meat from our new supermarket (the meat came from South Africa, like our eggs now) and she arranged with an Italian for the loaves. She trained the boys and worked out their schedules.

Ildephonse, the house-boy, was taken from the flat and given a Bigburger chef's cap and a yellow Bigburger jacket and put behind the counter. It was Mahesh's idea to give Ildephonse a label for his jacket with his name and the designation – in English, for the extra style – 'Manager'. Mahesh did little things like that sometimes which showed you that, casual as he was, he knew instinctively how to operate in our town. He said he called Ildephonse the manager to ward off African resentment of the new, rich-looking place, and also to attract African customers. And he made a point of leaving Ildephonse in charge for some hours every day.

It was strange about Ildephonse, though. He loved his Bigburger costume and he loved his new job. No one was quicker and more friendly and more anxious to please than he was, when Shoba or Mahesh was around. They trusted Ildephonse; they boasted of their trust in him, in his presence. Yet as soon as he was left alone he became a different person. He went vacant. Not rude, just vacant. I noticed this alteration in the African staff in other places as well. It made you feel that while they did their jobs in their various glossy settings they were only acting for the people who employed them; that the job itself was meaningless to them; and that they had the gift – when they were left alone, and had no one to act for – of separating themselves in spirit from their setting, their job, their uniform.

Bigburger was a success. The van der Weyden, across the road, was content to make money from its beds and rooms. The service and the kitchens there drove people out to look for food, and Bigburger was perfectly placed to capture that refugee trade.

Bigburger attracted a lot of African officials and army people as well – they liked the décor and the modernity. So that Mahesh, from running a nondescript little hardware shop, found himself at the centre of things in our town.

All this happened quickly, in less than a year. Everything happened quickly now. It was as though everyone felt he had to make up for the lost years, or as though everyone felt that time was short, that the place might close down at any moment again.

Mahesh said to me one day, 'Noimon offered me two million. But you know Noimon. When he offers two, you know it's worth four.'

Noimon was one of our local big Greeks. The new furniture shop – doing fantastic business – was just one of his ventures. The two million he offered were local francs, which were thirty-six to the dollar.

Mahesh said, 'I suppose your place is worth a lot now. Nazruddin offered it to me, you know. A hundred and fifty thousand. What do you think you'll get for it now?'

You heard that kind of property talk everywhere now. Everyone was totting up how much he had gained with the boom, how much he was worth. People learned to speak huge figures calmly.

There had been a boom before, just at the end of the colonial period, and the ruined suburb near the rapids was what it had left behind. Nazruddin had told a story about that. He had gone out there one Sunday morning, had thought that the place was bush rather than real estate, and had decided to sell. Lucky for him then; but now that dead suburb was being rehabilitated. That development or redevelopment had become the most important feature of our boom. And it had caused the big recent rise in property values in the town.

The bush near the rapids was being cleared. The ruins which had seemed permanent were being levelled by bulldozers; new avenues were being laid out. It was the Big Man's doing. The government had taken over all that area and decreed it the domain of the State, and the Big Man was building what looked like a little town there. It was happening very fast. The copper money was pouring in, pushing up prices in our town. The deep, earth-shaking burr of bulldozers competed with the sound of the rapids. Every steamer brought up European builders and artisans, every aeroplane. The van der Weyden seldom had vacant rooms.

Every thing the President did had a reason. As a ruler in what was potentially hostile territory, he was creating an area where he and his flag were supreme. As an African, he was building a new town on the site of what had been a rich European suburb – but what he was building was meant to be grander. In the town the only 'designed' modern building was the van der Weyden; and to us the larger buildings of the Domain were startling – concrete louvres, pierced concrete blocks of great size, tinted glass. The smaller buildings – houses and bungalows – were more like what we were used to. But even they were on the large side and, with air-conditioners sticking out in many places like building blocks that had slipped, looked extravagant.

No one was sure, even after some of the houses were furnished, what the Domain was to be used for. There were stories of a great new model farm and agricultural college; a conference hall to serve the continent; holiday houses for loyal citizens. From the President himself there came no statement. We watched and wondered while the buildings were run up. And then we began to understand that what the President was attempting was so stupendous in his own eyes that even he would not have wanted to proclaim it. He was creating modern Africa. He was creating a miracle that would astound the rest of the world. He was by-passing real Africa, the difficult Africa of bush and villages, and creating something that would match anything that existed in other countries.

Photographs of this State Domain – and others like it in other parts of the country – began to appear in those magazines about Africa that were published in Europe but subsidized by governments like ours. In these photographs the message of the Domain was simple. Under the rule of our new President the miracle had occurred: Africans had become modern men who built in concrete and glass and sat in cushioned chairs covered in imitation velvet. It was like a curious fulfilment of Father Huismans's prophecy about the retreat of African Africa, and the success of the European graft.

Visitors were encouraged, from the *cités* and shanty towns, from the surrounding villages. On Sundays there were buses and army trucks to take people there, and soldiers acted as guides, taking people along one-way paths marked with directional arrows, showing the people who had recently wished to destroy the town what their President had done for Africa. Such shoddy buildings, after you got used to the shapes; such flashy furniture – Noimon was making a fortune with his furniture shop. All around, the life of dugout and creek and village continued; in the bars in the town the foreign builders and artisans drank and made easy jokes about the country. It was painful and it was sad.

The President had wished to show us a new Africa. And I saw Africa in a way I had never seen it before, saw the defeats and humiliations which until then I had regarded as just a fact of life. And I felt like that – full of tenderness for the Big Man, for the ragged villagers walking around the Domain, and the soldiers showing them the shabby sights – until some soldier played the fool with me or some official at the customs was difficult, and then I fell into the old way of feeling, the easier attitudes of the foreigners in the bars. Old Africa, which seemed to absorb everything, was simple; this place kept you tense. What a strain it was, picking your way through stupidity and aggressiveness and pride and hurt!

But what was the Domain to be used for? The buildings gave pride, or were meant to; they satisfied some personal need of the President's. Was that all they were for? But they had consumed millions. The farm didn't materialize. The Chinese or the Taiwanese didn't turn up to till the land of the new model African farm; the six tractors that some foreign government had given remained in a neat line in the open and rusted, and the grass grew high about them. The big swimming pool near the building that was said to be a conference hall developed leaks and remained empty, with a wide-meshed rope net at the top. The Domain had been built fast, and in the sun and the rain decay also came fast. After the first rainy season many of the

111

young trees that had been planted beside the wide main avenue died, their roots waterlogged and rotted.

But for the President in the capital the Domain remained a living thing. Statues were added, and lamp standards. The Sunday visits went on; the photographs continued to appear in the subsidized magazines that specialized in Africa. And then at last a use was found for the buildings.

The Domain became a university city and a research centre. The conference-hall building was turned into a polytechnic for people of the region, and other buildings were turned into dormitories and staff quarters. Lecturers and professors began to come from the capital, and soon from other countries; a parallel life developed there, of which we in the town knew little. And it was to the polytechnic there – on the site of the dead European suburb that to me, when I first came, had suggested the ruins of a civilization that had come and gone – that Ferdinand was sent on a government scholarship, when he had finished at the lycée.

The Domain was some miles away from the town. There was a bus service, but it was irregular. I hadn't been seeing much of Ferdinand, and now I saw even less of him. Metty lost a friend. That move of Ferdinand's finally made the difference between the two men clear, and I thought that Metty suffered.

My own feelings were more complicated. I saw a disordered future for the country. No one was going to be secure here; no man of the country was to be envied. Yet I couldn't help thinking how lucky Ferdinand was, how easy it had been made for him. You took a boy out of the bush and you taught him to read and write; you levelled the bush and built a polytechnic and you sent him there. It seemed as easy as that, if you came late to the world and found ready-made those things that other countries and peoples had taken so long to arrive at – writing, printing, universities, books, knowledge. The rest of us had to take things in stages. I thought of my own family, Nazruddin, myself – we were so clogged by what the centuries had deposited in our minds and hearts. Ferdinand, starting from nothing, had with one step made himself free, and was ready to race ahead of us.

The Domain, with its shoddy grandeur, was a hoax. Neither
the President who had called it into being nor the foreigners who
had made a fortune building it had faith in what they were creating. But had there been greater faith before? *Miscerique probat
populos et foedera jungi*: Father Huismans had explained the
arrogance of that motto. He had believed in its truth. But how
many of the builders of the earlier city would have agreed with
him? Yet that earlier hoax had helped to make men of the country
in a certain way; and men would also be made by this new hoax.
Ferdinand took the polytechnic seriously; it was going to lead
him to an administrative cadetship and eventually to a position of
authority. To him the Domain was fine, as it should be. He was as
glamorous to himself at the polytechnic as he had been at the lycée.

It was absurd to be jealous of Ferdinand, who still after all
went home to the bush. But I wasn't jealous of him only because
I felt that he was about to race ahead of me in knowledge and
enter realms I would never enter. I was jealous more of that idea
he had always had of his own importance, his own glamour. We
lived on the same patch of earth; we looked at the same views.
Yet to him the world was new and getting newer. For me that
same world was drab, without possibilities.

I grew to detest the physical feel of the place. My flat remained
as it had always been. I had changed nothing there, because I
lived with the idea that at a moment's notice I had to consider it
all as lost – the bedroom with the white-painted window panes and
the big bed with the foam mattress, the roughly made cupboards
with my smelly clothes and shoes, the kitchen with its smell of
kerosene and frying oil and rust and dirt and cockroaches, the
empty white studio-sitting-room. Always there, never really mine,
reminding me now only of the passing of time.

I detested the imported ornamental trees, the trees of my childhood, so unnatural here, with the red dust of the streets that
turned to mud in rain, the overcast sky that meant only more heat,
the clear sky that meant a sun that hurt, the rain that seldom
cooled and made for a general clamminess, the brown river with
the lilac-coloured flowers on rubbery green vines that floated on
and on, night and day.

Ferdinand had moved only a few miles away. And I, so recently his senior, felt jealous and deserted.

Metty, too, was like a man with preoccupations. Freedom had its price. Once he had had the slave's security. Here he had gained an idea of himself as a man to be measured against other men. That had so far brought him only pleasure. But now it seemed to have brought him a little bitterness as well. He seemed to be staying away from his friends.

He was full of friends, and all kinds of people came to the shop and the flat to ask about him. Or sometimes they sent others to ask about him. One such messenger I grew to recognize. She was like a very thin boy, the kind of girl you would see poling the dugouts, someone regarded by her people just as labour, a pair of hands. Hard work and bad food appeared to have neutered her, worn away her feminine characteristics, and left her almost bald.

She used to come for Metty at the shop, hanging around outside. Sometimes he spoke to her; sometimes he was rough with her. Sometimes he made as if to chase her away, bending down to pick up an imaginary stone, the way people did here when they wanted to frighten away a pariah dog. No one like the slave for spotting the slave, or knowing how to deal with the slave. This girl was among the lowest of the low; her status, in whatever African household she was, would have been close to that of a slave.

Metty succeeded in driving her away from the shop. But one afternoon, when I went to the flat after closing the shop, I saw her on the pavement outside, standing among the dusty hummocks of wild grass near the side entrance to our back yard. An ashy, unwashed cotton smock, wide-sleeved and wide-necked, hung loosely from her bony shoulders and showed she was wearing nothing else below. Her hair was so sparse her head looked shaved. Her thin little face was set in a frown which wasn't a frown but was only meant to say she wasn't looking at me.

She was still there when, after making myself some tea, and changing, I went down again. I was going to the Hellenic Club for my afternoon squash. It was my rule: whatever the circumstances, however unwilling the spirit, never give up the day's exercise. Afterwards I drove out to the dam, to the Portuguese night club on the cliff, now got going again, and had some fried fish there – I am sure they did it better in Portugal. It was too early for the band and the town crowd, but the dam was floodlit, and they turned on the coloured lights on the trees for me.

The girl was still on the pavement when I went back to the flat. This time she spoke to me. She said, '*Metty-ki là?*'

She had only a few words of the local patois, but she could understand it when it was spoken, and when I asked her what she wanted she said, '*Popo malade. Dis-li Metty.*'

Popo was 'baby'. Metty had a baby somewhere in the town, and the baby was sick. Metty had a whole life out there, separate from his life with me in the flat, separate from his bringing me coffee in the mornings, separate from the shop.

I was shocked. I felt betrayed. If we had been living in our compound on the coast, he would have lived his own life, but there would have been no secrets. I would have known who his woman was; I would have known when his baby was born. I had lost Metty to this part of Africa. He had come to the place that was partly his home, and I had lost him. I felt desolate. I had been hating the place, hating the flat; yet now I saw the life I had made for myself in that flat as something good, which I had lost.

Like the girl outside, like so many other people, I waited for Metty. And when, very late, he came in, I began to speak at once.

'Oh Metty, why didn't you tell me? Why did you do this to me?' Then I called him by the name we called him at home. 'Ali, Ali-wa! We lived together. I took you under my roof and treated you as a member of my own family. And now you do this.'

Dutifully, like the servant of the old days, he tried to match his mood to mine, tried to look as though he suffered with me.

'I will leave her, *patron*. She's an animal.'

'How can you leave her? You've done it. You can't go back on that. You've got that child out there. Oh Ali, what have you done? Don't you think it's disgusting to have a little African child running about in somebody's yard, with its *toto* swinging from side to side? Aren't you ashamed, a boy like you?'

'It is disgusting, Salim.' He came and put his hand on my shoulder. 'And I am very ashamed. She's only an African woman. I will leave her.'

'How can you leave her? That is now your life. Didn't you know it was going to be like that? We sent you to school, we had the mullahs teach you. And now you do this.'

I was acting. But there are times when we act out what we really feel, times when we cannot cope with certain emotions, and it is easier to act. And Metty was acting too, being loyal, reminding me of the past, of other places, reminding me of things I could scarcely bear that night. When I said, acting, 'Why didn't you tell me, Metty?' he acted back for my sake. He said, 'How could I tell you, Salim? I knew you were going to get on like this.'

How did he know?

I said, 'You know, Metty, the first day you went to school I went with you. You cried all the time. You began to cry as soon as we left the house.'

He liked being reminded of this, being remembered from so far back. He said, almost smiling, 'I cried a lot? I made a lot of noise?'

'Ali, you screamed the place down. You had your white cap on, and you went down the little alley at the side of Gokool's house, and you were bawling. I couldn't see where you had gone. I just heard you bawling. I couldn't stand it. I thought they were doing terrible things to you, and I begged for you not to go to school. Then the trouble was to get you to come back home. You've forgotten, and why should you remember? I've been noticing you since you've been here. You've been very much getting on as though you're your own man.'

'Oh, Salim! You mustn't say that. I always show you respect.'

That was true. But he had returned home; he had found his new life. However much he wished it, he couldn't go back. He had shed the past. His hand on my shoulder – what good was that now?

I thought: 'Nothing stands still. Everything changes. I will inherit no house, and no house that I build will now pass to my children. That way of life has gone. I have lost my twenties, and what I have been looking for since I left home hasn't come to me. I have only been waiting. I will wait for the rest of my life. When I came here, this flat was still the Belgian lady's flat. It wasn't my home; it was like a camp. Then that camp became mine. Now it has changed again.'

Later, I woke to the solitude of my bedroom, in the unfriendly world. I felt all the child's heartache at being in a strange place. Through the white-painted window I saw the trees outside – not their shadows, but the suggestion of their forms. I was homesick, had been homesick for months. But home was hardly a place I could return to. Home was something in my head. It was something I had lost. And in that I was like the ragged Africans who were so abject in the town we serviced.

7

DISCOVERING the ways of pain, the ageing that it brings, I wasn't surprised that Metty and myself should have been so close just at that moment when we understood that we had to go our separate ways. What had given the illusion of closeness that evening was only our regret for the past, our sadness that the world doesn't stand still.

Our life together didn't change. He continued to live in his room in the flat, and he continued to bring me coffee in the mornings. But now it was understood that he had a whole life outside. He altered. He lost the brightness and gaiety of the servant who knows that he will be looked after, that others will decide for him; and he lost what went with that brightness – the indifference to what had just happened, the ability to forget, the readiness for every new day. He seemed to go a little sour inside. Responsibility was new to him; and with that he must also have discovered solitude, in spite of his friends and his new family life.

I too, breaking out of old ways, had discovered solitude and the melancholy which is at the basis of religion. Religion turns that melancholy into uplifting fear and hope. But I had rejected the ways and comforts of religion; I couldn't turn to them again, just like that. That melancholy about the world remained something I had to put up with on my own. At some times it was sharp; at some times it wasn't there.

And just when I had digested that sadness about Metty and the past, someone from the past turned up. He walked into the shop one morning, Metty leading him in, Metty calling out in high excitement, 'Salim! Salim!'

It was Indar, the man who had first brought out my panic on the coast, confronted me – after that game of squash in the squash court of his big house – with my own fears about our future, and had sent me away from his house with a vision of disaster. He had given me the idea of flight. He had gone to England, to his university; I had fled here.

And I felt now, as Metty led him in, that he had caught me out again, sitting at my desk in the shop, with my goods spread out on the floor, as they had always been, and with my shelves full of cheap cloth and oil-cloth and batteries and exercise books.

He said, 'I heard some years ago in London that you were here. I wondered what you were doing.' His expression was cool, balanced between irritation and a sneer, and it seemed to say that he didn't have to ask now, and that he wasn't surprised by what he had found.

It had happened so quickly. When Metty came running in saying, 'Salim! Salim! Guess who's here,' I had at once had an idea that it would be someone we had both known in the old days. I thought it would be Nazruddin, or some member of my family, some brother-in-law or nephew. And I had thought: 'But I can't cope. The life here is no longer the old life. I cannot accept this responsibility. I don't want to run a hospital.'

Expecting, then, someone who was about to make a claim on me in the name of family and community and religion, and preparing a face and an attitude for that person, I was dismayed to find Metty leading Indar into the shop, Metty beside himself with joy, not pretending now, but for that moment delighted to re-create something of the old days, being the man in touch with great families. And from being myself the man full of complaint, the man who was going to pour out his melancholy in harsh advice to a new arrival who was perhaps already half crushed – 'There is no place for you here. There is no place here for the homeless. Find somewhere else' – from being that kind of man, I had to be the opposite. I had to be the man who was doing well and more than well, the man whose drab shop concealed some bigger operation that made millions. I had to be the man who had planned it all, who had come to the destroyed town at the bend in the river because he had foreseen the rich future.

I couldn't be any other way with Indar. He had always made me feel so backward. His family, though new on the coast, had outstripped us all; and even their low beginnings – the grandfather who was a railway labourer, then a market moneylender – had become (from the way people spoke) a little sacred, part of their wonderful story. They invested adventurously and spent money well; their way of living was much finer than ours; and there was their unusual passion for games and physical exercise. I had always thought of them as 'modern' people, with a style quite different from ours. You get used to differences like that; they can even begin to appear natural.

When we had played squash that afternoon, and Indar had told me he was going to England to a university, I hadn't felt resentful or jealous of him for what he was doing. Going abroad, the university – that was part of his style, what might have been expected. My unhappiness was the unhappiness of a man who felt left behind, unprepared for what was coming. And my resentment of him had to do with the insecurity he had made me feel. He had said, 'We're washed up here, you know.' The words were true; I knew they were true. But I disliked him for speaking them – he had spoken as someone who had foreseen it all and had made his dispositions.

Eight years had passed since that day. What he had said would happen had happened. His family had lost a lot; they had lost their house; they (who had added the name of the town on the coast to their family name) had scattered, like my own family. Yet now, as he came into the shop, it seemed that the distance between us had remained the same.

There was London in his clothes, the trousers, the striped cotton shirt, the way his hair was cut, his shoes (ox-blood in colour, thin-soled but sturdy, a little too narrow at the toes). And I – well, I was in my shop, with the red dirt road and the market square outside. I had waited so long, endured so much, changed; yet to him I hadn't changed at all.

So far I had remained sitting. As I stood up I had a little twinge of fear. It came to me that he had reappeared only to bring me bad news. And all I could find to say was: 'What brings you to the back of beyond?'

He said, 'I wouldn't say that. You are where it's at.'

' "Where it's at"?'

'Where big things are happening. Otherwise I wouldn't be here.'

That was a relief. At least he wasn't giving me my marching orders again, without telling me where to go.

Metty all this while was smiling at Indar and swinging his head from side to side, saying, 'Indar! Indar!' And it was Metty who remembered our duty as hosts. He said, 'You would like some coffee, Indar?' As though we were on the coast, in the family shop, and he just had to step down the lane to Noor's stall and bring back the little brass cups of sweet and muddy coffee on a heavy brass tray. No coffee like that here; only Nescafé, made in the Ivory Coast, and served in big china cups. Not the same kind of drink – you couldn't chat over it, sighing at each hot sweet sip.

Indar said, 'That would be very nice, Ali.'

I said, 'His name here is Metty. It means "half-caste".'

'You let them call you that, Ali?'

'African people, Indar. *Kafar*. You know what they give.'

I said, 'Don't believe him. He loves it. It makes him a great hit with the girls. Ali's a big family man now. He's lost.'

Metty, going to the store-room to boil the water for the Nescafé, said, 'Salim, Salim. Don't let me down too much.'

Indar said, 'He was lost a long time ago. Have you heard from Nazruddin? I saw him in Uganda a few weeks ago.'

'What's it like out there now?'

'Settling down. For how long is another matter. Not one bloody paper has spoken up for the king. Did you know that? When it comes to Africa, people don't want to know or they have their principles. Nobody cares a damn about the people who live in the place.'

'But you do a lot of travelling.'

'It's my business. How are things with you here?'

121

'It's been very good since the rebellion. The place is booming. Property is fantastic. Land is two hundred francs a square foot in some parts now.'

Indar didn't look impressed – but the shop wasn't an impressive place. I felt, too, I had run on a little bit and was doing the opposite of what I intended to do with Indar. Wishing to let him know that his assumptions about me were wrong, I was in fact acting out the character he saw me as. I was talking the way I had heard traders in the town talk, and even saying the things they said.

I said, attempting another kind of language, 'It's a specialized business. A sophisticated market would be easier in some ways. But here you can't follow your personal likes and dislikes. You have to know exactly what is needed. And of course there are the agencies. That's where the real money is.'

Indar said, 'Yes, yes. The agencies. It's like old times for you, Salim.'

I let that pass. But I decided to tone the whole thing down. I said, 'I don't know how long it's going to last, though.'

'It will last as long as your President wants it to last. And no one can tell how long that will be. He's a strange man. He seems to be doing nothing at all, and then he can act like a surgeon. Cutting away some part he doesn't like.'

'That's how he settled the old army. It was terrible, Indar. He sent a message to Colonel Yenyi telling him to stay at the barracks and to welcome the commander of the mercenaries. So he stayed on the steps in full uniform, and when they arrived he began to walk to the gate. They shot him as he walked. And everybody with him.'

'It saved your bacon, though. I have something for you, by the way. I went to see your father and mother before I came here.'

'You went home?' But I dreaded hearing about it from him.

He said, 'Oh, I've been there a few times since the great events. It isn't so bad. You remember our house? They've painted it in the party colours. It's some kind of party building now. Your mother gave me a bottle of coconut chutney. It isn't for you alone. It is for Ali and you. She made that clear.' And to Metty, coming back then with the jug of hot water and the cups and the tin of Nescafé and the condensed milk, he said, 'Ma sent you some coconut chutney, Ali.'

Metty said, 'Chutney, coconut chutney. The food here is *horrible*, Indar.'

We sat all three around the desk, stirring coffee and water and condensed milk together.

Indar said, 'I didn't want to go back. Not the first time. I didn't think my heart could stand it. But the aeroplane is a wonderful thing. You are still in one place when you arrive at the other. The aeroplane is faster than the heart. You arrive quickly and you leave quickly. You don't grieve too much. And there is something else about the aeroplane. You can go back many times to the same place. And something strange happens if you go back often enough. You stop grieving for the past. You see that the past is something in your mind alone, that it doesn't exist in real life. You trample on the past, you crush it. In the beginning it is like trampling on a garden. In the end you are just walking on ground. That is the way we have to learn to live now. The past is here.' He touched his heart. 'It isn't there.' And he pointed at the dusty road.

I felt he had spoken the words before, or had gone over them in his mind. I thought: 'He fights to keep his style. He's probably suffered more than the rest of us.'

We sat, the three of us, drinking Nescafé. And I thought the moment beautiful.

Still, the conversation had so far been one-sided. He knew everything about me; I knew nothing about his recent life. When I had first arrived in the town I had noticed that for most people conversation meant answering questions about themselves; they seldom asked you about yourself; they had been cut off for too long. I didn't want Indar to feel that way about me. And I really wanted to know about him. So, a little awkwardly, I began to ask.

He said he had been in the town for a couple of days and was going to stay for a few months. Had he come up by the steamer? He said, 'You're crazy. Cooped up with river Africans for seven days? I flew up.'

Metty said, 'I wouldn't go anywhere by the steamer. They tell me it's horrible. And it's even worse on the barge, with the latrines and the people cooking and eating everywhere. It's horrible-horrible, they tell me.'

I asked Indar where he was staying – it had occurred to me that I should make the gesture of offering him hospitality. Was he staying at the van der Weyden?

This was the question he was waiting to be asked. He said in a soft and unassuming voice, 'I'm staying at the State Domain. I have a house there. I'm a guest of the government.'

And Metty behaved more graciously than I. Metty slapped the desk and said, 'Indar!'

I said, 'The Big Man invited you?'

He began to scale it down. 'Not exactly. I have my own outfit. I am attached to the polytechnic for a term. Do you know it?'

'I know someone there. A student.'

Indar behaved as though I had interrupted him; as though – although I lived in the place, and he had just arrived – I was trespassing, and had no right to know a student at the polytechnic.

I said, 'His mother's a *marchande*, one of my customers.'

That was better. He said, 'You must come and meet some of the other people there. You may not like what's going on. But you mustn't pretend it isn't happening. You mustn't make that mistake again.'

I wanted to say: 'I live here. I have lived through quite a lot in the last six years.' But I didn't say that. I played up to his vanity. He had his own idea of the kind of man I was – and indeed he had caught me in my shop, at my ancestral business. He had his own idea of who he was and what he had done, the distance he had put between himself and the rest of us.

His vanity didn't irritate me. I found I was relishing it, in the way that years before, on the coast, as a child, I had relished Nazruddin's stories of his luck and of the delights of life here, in the colonial town. I hadn't slapped the desk like Metty, but I was impressed by what I saw of Indar. And it was a relief to put aside the dissatisfactions he made me feel, to forget about being caught out, and to give him a straight admiration for what he had made of himself – for his London clothes and the privilege they spoke of, his travelling, his house in the Domain, his position at the polytechnic.

To give him admiration, to appear not to be competing or resisting, was to put him at his ease. As we chatted over our Nescafé, as Metty exclaimed from time to time, expressing in his servant's manner the admiration which his master also felt, Indar's edginess wore off. He became gentle, full of manners, concerned. At the end of the morning I felt I had at last made a friend of my kind. And I badly needed such a friend.

And far from being his host and guide, I became the man who was led about. It wasn't all that absurd. I had so little to show him. All the key points of the town I knew could be shown in a couple of hours, as I discovered when I drove him around later that morning.

There was the river, with a stretch of broken promenade near the docks. There were the docks themselves; the repair yards with open corrugated-iron sheds full of rusting pieces of machinery; and some way down river the ruined cathedral, beautifully overgrown and looking antique, like something in Europe – but you could only look from the road, because the bush was too thick and the site was famous for its snakes. There were the scuffed squares with their defaced and statue-less pedestals; the official buildings from the colonial time in avenues lined with palmiste trees; the lycée, with the decaying masks in the gun room (but that bored Indar); the van der Weyden and Mahesh's Bigburger place, which were hardly things to show to a man who had been to Europe.

There were the *cités* and the squatters' settlements (some of them I was driving into for the first time) with their hills of rubbish, their corrugated dusty lanes, and a lot of old tyres lying in the dust. To me the rubbish hills and the tyres were features of the *cités* and shanty towns. The spidery little children that we had here did wonderful somersaults off those tyres, running, jumping on the tyres, and then springing high in the air. But it was nearly noon. There were no children doing somersaults when we drove by; and I realized that (after a monument with nothing on it, and pedestals without statues) I was literally just showing Indar a lot of rubbish. I cut short the tour at that point. The rapids and the fishermen's village – that had been incorporated into the State Domain; that he had already seen.

As we drove to the Domain – the intervening area, once empty, now filling up with the shacks of new arrivals from the villages: shacks which, in Indar's company, I seemed to be seeing for the first time: the red ground between the shacks stained with rivulets of black or grey-green filth, maize and cassava planted in every free space – as we drove, Indar said, 'How long did you say you've been living here?'

'Six years.'

'And you've shown me everything?'

What hadn't I shown him? A few interiors of shops and houses and flats, the Hellenic Club – and the bars. But I wouldn't have shown him the bars. And really, looking at the place with his eyes, I was amazed at the little I had been living with. And I had stopped seeing so much. In spite of everything, I had thought of the town as a real town; I saw it now as an agglomeration of shack settlements. I thought I had been resisting the place. But I had only been living blind – like the people I knew, from whom in my heart of hearts I had thought myself different.

I hadn't liked it when Indar had suggested that I was living like our community in the old days, not paying attention to what was going on. But he wasn't so far wrong. He was talking about the Domain; and for us in the town the Domain had remained only a source of contracts. We knew little of the life there, and we hadn't wanted to find out. We saw the Domain as part of the waste and foolishness of the country. But, more importantly, we saw it as part of the President's politics; and we didn't want to become entangled with that.

We were aware of the new foreigners on the periphery of our town. They were not like the engineers and salesmen and artisans we knew, and we were a little nervous of them. The Domain people were like tourists, but they were not spenders – every-

thing was found for them on the Domain. They were not interested in us; and we, thinking of them as protected people, looked
upon them as people separate from the true life of the place, and
for this reason not quite real, not as real as ourselves.

Without knowing it, and thinking all the time that we were
keeping our heads down and being wise and protecting our
interests, we had become like the Africans the President ruled.
We were people who felt only the weight of the President's power.
The Domain had been created by the President; for reasons of his
own he had called certain foreigners to live there. For us that was
enough; it wasn't for us to question or look too closely.

Sometimes, after Ferdinand had come to the town to see his
mother during one of her shopping trips, I had driven him back
to his hostel in the Domain. What I saw then was all that I knew,
until Indar became my guide.

It was as Indar had said. He had a house in the Domain and he
was a guest of the government. His house was carpeted and
furnished show-room style – twelve hand-carved dining chairs,
upholstered chairs in fringed synthetic velvet in two colours in
the sitting room, lamps, tables, air-conditioners everywhere. The
air-conditioners were necessary. The Domain houses, naked in
levelled land, were like grander concrete boxes, with roofs that
didn't project at all, so that at any hour of a bright day one wall,
or two, got the full force of the sun. With the house there was
also a boy, in the Domain servant costume – white shorts, white
shirt, and a white *jacket de boy* (instead of the apron of colonial
days). It was the Domain style for people in Indar's position. The
style was the President's. It was he who had decided on the
costumes for the boys.

And in the strange world of the Domain Indar appeared to be
well regarded. Part of this regard was due to the 'outfit' to which
he belonged. He couldn't quite explain to me what the outfit was
that sent him on African tours – or I might have been too naïve
to understand. But a number of people on the Domain seemed to
belong to outfits that were as mysterious; and they looked upon
Indar not as a man of our community or a refugee from the coast,

but as one of themselves. It was all a little extraordinary to me.

These were the new-style foreigners whom we, in the town, had seen arriving for some time past. We had seen them putting on African clothes; we had noticed their gaiety, so unlike our own caution; their happiness with everything they found. And we had considered them parasites and half dangerous, serving some hidden cause of the President's, people we had to be careful with.

But now, being with them in the Domain, which in every way was their resort, and being admitted so easily to their life, their world of bungalows and air-conditioners and holiday ease, catching in their educated talk the names of famous cities, I swung the other way and began to see how shut-in and shabby and stagnant we in the town would have seemed to them. I began to get some sense of the social excitements of life on the Domain, of people associating in a new way, being more open, less concerned with enemies and danger, more ready to be interested and entertained, looking for the human worth of the other man. On the Domain they had their own way of talking about people and events; they were in touch with the world. To be with them was to have a sense of adventure.

I thought of my own life and Metty's; of Shoba and Mahesh and their overheated privacy; of the Italians and Greeks – especially the Greeks – bottled up and tense with their family concerns and their nervousness of Africa and Africans. There was hardly anything new there. So, to travel those few miles between the town and the Domain was always to make some adjustment, to assume a new attitude, and each time almost to see another country. I was ashamed of myself for the new judgements I found myself making on my friends Shoba and Mahesh, who had done so much for me for so many years, and with whom I had felt so safe. But I couldn't help those thoughts. I was tilting the other way, to the life of the Domain, as I saw it in the company of Indar.

I was aware, in the Domain, that I belonged to the other world. When I met people with Indar I found I had little to say. There were times when I thought that I might be letting him down. But there seemed to be no such thought in his head. He introduced

me round as a friend of his family's from the coast, a member of
his community. He didn't only want me to witness his success
with the people of the Domain; he seemed to want me to share
it as well. It was his way of rewarding me for my admiration, and
I saw a delicacy in him that I had never seen on the coast. His
manners were like a form of consideration; and however small the
occasion, his manners never failed. They were the manners of an
impresario, a little bit. But it was also his old family style; it was
as though he had needed security and admiration to bring it out
again. In the artificiality of the Domain he had found his perfect
setting.

We in the town could offer Indar nothing like the regard and
the social excitements he enjoyed at the Domain; we could
scarcely appreciate what he enjoyed there. With our cynicism,
created by years of insecurity, how did we look on men? We
judged the salesmen in the van der Weyden by the companies
they represented, their ability to offer us concessions. Knowing
such men, having access to the services they offered, and being
flattered by them that we were not ordinary customers paying
the full price or having to take our place in the queue, we thought
we had mastered the world; and we saw those salesmen and
representatives as men of power who had to be courted. We
judged traders by their coups, the contracts they landed, the
agencies they picked up.

It was the same with Africans. We judged them by their
ability, as army men or officials in the customs or policemen, to
do us services; and that was how they also judged themselves.
You could spot the powerful in Mahesh's Bigburger place. They,
sharing in our boom, and no longer as shoddy as they once were,
wore gold, as much as possible – gold-rimmed glasses, gold rings,
gold pen and pencil sets, gold watches with solid gold wristlets.
Among ourselves we scoffed at the vulgarity and pathos of that
African lust for gold. Gold – how could it alter the man, who was
only an African? But we wanted gold ourselves; and we regularly
paid tribute to the Africans who wore gold.

Our ideas of men were simple; Africa was a place where we
had to survive. But in the Domain it was different. There they

could scoff at trade and gold, because in the magical atmosphere of the Domain, among the avenues and new houses, another Africa had been created. In the Domain Africans – the young men at the polytechnic – were romantic. They were not always present at the parties or gatherings; but the whole life of the Domain was built around them. In the town 'African' could be a word of abuse or disregard; in the Domain it was a bigger word. An 'African' there was a new man whom everybody was busy making, a man about to inherit – the important man that years before, at the lycée, Ferdinand had seen himself as.

In the town, when they were at the lycée, Ferdinand and his friends – certainly his friends – were still close to village ways. When they were off duty, not at the lycée or with people like myself, they had merged into the African life of the town. Ferdinand and Metty – or Ferdinand and any African boy – could become friends because they had so much in common. But in the Domain there was no question of confusing Ferdinand and his friends with the white-uniformed servants.

Ferdinand and his friends had a clear idea of who they were and what was expected of them. They were young men on government scholarships; they would soon become administrative cadets in the capital, serving the President. The Domain was the President's creation; and in the Domain they were in the presence of foreigners who had a high idea of the new Africa. Even I, in the Domain, began to feel a little of the romance of that idea.

So foreigners and Africans acted and reacted on one another, and everyone became locked in an idea of glory and newness. Everywhere the President's photograph looked down at us. In the town, in our shops and in government buildings, it was just the photograph of the President, the ruler, something that had to be there. In the Domain the glory of the President brushed off on to all his new Africans.

And they were bright, those young men. I had remembered them as little tricksters, pertinacious but foolish, with only a kind of village cunning; and I had assumed that for them studying meant only cramming. Like other people in the town, I believed that degree courses had been scaled down or altered for Africans.

It was possible; they did go in for certain subjects – international relations, political science, anthropology. But those young men had sharp minds and spoke wonderfully – and in French, not the patois. They had developed fast. Just a few years before Ferdinand had been incapable of grasping the idea of Africa. That wasn't so now. The magazines about African affairs – even the semi-bogus, subsidized ones from Europe – and the newspapers – though censored – had spread new ideas, knowledge, new attitudes.

Indar took me one evening to one of his seminars, in a lecture room in the big polytechnic building. The seminar was not part of any course. It was an extra, and was described on the door as an exercise in English speaking. But more must have been expected from Indar. Most of the desks were taken. Ferdinand was there, in a little group of his own.

The biscuit-coloured walls of the lecture room were bare except for a photograph of the President – not in army uniform, but in a chief's leopard-skin cap, a short-sleeved jacket and a polka-dotted cravat. Indar, sitting below this photograph, began to speak, easily, about the other parts of Africa he had visited, and the young men were fascinated. Their innocence and eagerness were astonishing. In spite of the wars and coups they were hearing about, Africa was still to them the new continent, and they behaved as though Indar felt like them, was almost one of them. The language exercise turned into a discussion about Africa, and I could feel polytechnic topics, lecture topics, coming to the surface. Some of the questions were dynamite; but Indar was very good, always calm, never surprised. He was like a philosopher; he tried to get the young men to examine the words they were using.

They talked for a while about the coup in Uganda, and about the tribal and religious differences there. Then they began to talk more generally about religion in Africa.

There was some movement in the group around Ferdinand. And Ferdinand – not unaware of me – stood up and asked, 'Would the honourable visitor state whether he feels that Africans have been depersonalized by Christianity?'

Indar did what he had done before. He restated the question. He said, 'I suppose you are really asking whether Africa can be served by a religion which is not African. Is Islam an African religion? Do you feel that Africans have been depersonalized by that?'

Ferdinand didn't reply. It was as in the old days – he hadn't thought beyond a certain point.

Indar said, 'Well, I suppose you can say that Islam has become an African religion. It has been on the continent for a very long time. And you can say the same for the Coptic Christians. I don't know – perhaps you might feel that those people have been so depersonalized by those religions that they are out of touch with Africa. Would you say that? Or would you say they are Africans of a special sort?'

Ferdinand said, 'The honourable visitor knows very well the kind of Christianity I mean. He is trying to confuse the issue. He knows about the low status of African religion, and he knows very well that this is a direct question to him about the relevance or otherwise of African religion. The visitor is a gentleman sympathetic to Africa who has travelled. He can advise us. That is why we ask.'

A number of desk lids were banged in approval.

Indar said, 'To answer that question you must allow me to ask you one. You are students. You are not villagers. You cannot pretend you are. You will soon be serving your President and his government in different capacities. You are men of the modern world. Do you need African religion? Or are you being sentimental about it? Are you nervous of losing it? Or do you feel you have to hold on to it just because it's yours?'

Ferdinand's eyes went hard. He banged the lid of his desk and stood up. 'You are asking a complicated question.'

And 'complicated', among these students, was clearly a word of disapproval.

Indar said, 'You are forgetting. I didn't raise the question. You raised it, and I merely asked for information.'

That restored order, put an end to the banging of the desk lids. It made Ferdinand friendly again, and he remained friendly for the rest of the seminar. He went to Indar at the end, when the boys in the *jackets de boy* pushed in chromium-plated trolleys and began serving coffee and sweet biscuits (part of the style the President had decreed for the Domain).

I said to Ferdinand, 'You've been heckling my friend.'

He said, 'I wouldn't have done it if I had known he was your friend.'

Indar said, 'What are your own feelings about African religion?'

Ferdinand said, 'I don't know. That's why I asked. It is not an easy question for me.'

Later, when Indar and I left the polytechnic building to walk back to his house, Indar said, 'He's pretty impressive. He's your *marchande*'s son? That explains it. He's got that little extra background.'

In the asphalted space outside the polytechnic building the flag was floodlit. Slender lamp standards lifted fluorescent arms down both sides of the main avenue; and the avenue was also lit with lights at grass level, like an airport runway. Some of the bulbs had been broken and grass had grown tall around the fittings.

I said, 'His mother's also a magician.'

Indar said, 'You can't be too careful. They were tough tonight, but they didn't ask the really difficult question. Do you know what that is? Whether Africans are peasants. It's a nonsense question, but big battles are fought about that one. Whatever you say you get into trouble. You see why my outfit is needed. Unless we can get them thinking, and give them real ideas instead of just politics and principles, these young men will keep our world in turmoil for the next half century.'

I thought how far we had both come, to talk about Africa like this. We had even learned to take African magic seriously. It hadn't been like that on the coast. But as we talked that evening about the seminar, I began to wonder whether Indar and I weren't fooling ourselves and whether we weren't allowing the Africa we talked about to become too different from the Africa we knew. Ferdinand didn't want to lose touch with the spirits; he was nervous of being on his own. That had been at the back of his question. We all understood his anxiety; but it was as though, at the

seminar, everyone had been ashamed, or fearful, of referring to it
directly. The discussion had been full of words of another kind,
about religion and history. It was like that on the Domain; Africa
there was a special place.

I wondered, too, about Indar. How had he arrived at his new
attitudes? I had thought of him, since the coast, as a hater of
Africa. He had lost a lot; I didn't think he had forgiven. Yet he
flourished on the Domain; it was his setting.

I was less 'complicated'; I belonged to the town. And to leave
the Domain and drive back to the town, to see the shacks, acres
and acres of them, the rubbish mounds, to feel the presence of the
river and the forest all around (more than landscaping now), to
see the ragged groups outside the drinking booths, the squatters'
cooking fires on the pavements in the centre of the town, to do
that drive back was to return to the Africa I knew. It was to climb
down from the exaltation of the Domain, to grasp reality again.
Did Indar believe in the Africa of words? Did anyone on the
Domain believe? Wasn't the truth what we in the town lived
with – the salesmen's chat in the van der Weyden and the bars,
the photographs of the President in government offices and in our
shops, the army barracks in the converted palace of the man of
our community?

Indar said, 'Does one believe in anything? Does it matter?'

There was a ritual I went through whenever I had to clear a
difficult consignment through the customs. I filled in the declaration form, folded it over five hundred francs, and handed it to the
official in charge. He would – as soon as he had got his subordin-
ates out of the room (and they of course knew why they had been
asked to leave the room) – check the notes with his eyes alone.
The notes would then be taken; the entries on the form would be
studied with exaggerated care; and soon he would say, '*C'est bien,
Mis' Salim. Vous êtes en ordre.*' Neither he nor I would refer to
the bank-notes. We would talk only about the details on the
declaration form, which, correctly filled, correctly approved,
would remain as proof of both our correctness. Yet what had lain
at the heart of the transaction would be passed over in silence,
and would leave no trace in the records.

So, in my talks with Indar about Africa – the purpose of his outfit, the Domain, his anxieties about imported doctrines, the danger to Africa of its very newness, first ideas being caught most securely by new minds as sticky as adhesive tape – I felt that between us lay some dishonesty, or just an omission, some blank, around which we both had to walk carefully. That omission was our own past, the smashed life of our community. Indar had referred to that at our first meeting that morning in the shop. He said that he had learned to trample on the past. In the beginning it had been like trampling on a garden; later it had become like walking on ground.

I became confused myself. The Domain was a hoax. But at the same time it was real, because it was full of serious men (and a few women). Was there a truth outside men? Didn't men make the truth for themselves? Everything men did or made became real. So I moved between the Domain and the town. It was always reassuring to return to the town I knew, to get away from that Africa of words and ideas as it existed on the Domain (and from which, often, Africans were physically absent). But the Domain, and the glory and the social excitements of the life there, always called me back.

8

INDAR said, 'We are going to a party after dinner. It's being given by Yvette. Do you know her? Her husband Raymond keeps a low profile, but he runs the whole show here. The President, or the Big Man, as you call him, sent him down here to keep an eye on things. He's the Big Man's white man. In all these places there's someone like that. Raymond's a historian. They say the President reads everything he writes. That's the story anyway. Raymond knows more about the country than anyone on earth.'

I had never heard of Raymond. The President I had seen only in photographs – first in army uniform, then in the stylish short-sleeved jacket and cravat, and then with his leopard-skin chief's cap and his carved stick, emblem of his chieftaincy – and it had never occurred to me that he might be a reader. What Indar told me brought the President closer. At the same time it showed me how far away I, and people like me, were from the seat of power. Considering myself from that distance, I saw how small and vulnerable we were; and it didn't seem quite real that, dressed as I was, I should be strolling across the Domain after dinner to meet people in direct touch with the great. It was strange, but I no longer felt oppressed by the country, the forest and the waters and the remote peoples – I felt myself above it all, considering it from this new angle of the powerful.

From what Indar had said I had expected that Raymond and Yvette would be middle-aged. But the lady – in black slacks in some shiny material – who came to meet us after the white-jacketed boy had let us in was young, in her late twenties, near

136

my own age. That was the first surprise. The second was that she
was barefooted, feet white and beautiful and finely made. I looked
at her feet before I considered her face and her blouse, black silk,
embroidered round the low-cut collar – expensive stuff, not the
sort of goods you could get in our town.

Indar said, 'This lovely lady is our hostess. Her name is
Yvette.'

He bent over her and appeared to hold her in an embrace. It
was a piece of pantomime. She playfully arched her back to receive
his embrace, but his cheek barely brushed hers, he never touched
her breast, and only the tips of his fingers rested on her back, on
the silk blouse.

It was a house of the Domain, like Indar's. But all the upholstered furniture had been cleared out of the sitting room and had
been replaced by cushions and bolsters and African mats. Two or
three reading lamps had been put on the floor, so that parts of
the room were in darkness.

Yvette said, referring to the furniture, 'The President has an
exaggerated idea of the needs of Europeans. I've dumped all that
velvety stuff in one of the bedrooms.'

Remembering what Indar had told me, I ignored the irony in
her voice, and felt that she was speaking with privilege, the
privilege of someone close to the President.

A number of people were already there. Indar followed Yvette
deeper into the room, and I followed Indar.

Indar said, 'How's Raymond?'

Yvette said, 'He's working. He'll look in later.'

We sat down all three next to a bookcase. Indar lounged
against a bolster, a man at ease. I concentrated on the music. As
so often when I was with Indar on the Domain, I was prepared
only to watch and listen. And this was all new to me. I hadn't been
to a Domain party like this. And the atmosphere itself in that room
was something I had never experienced before.

Two or three couples were dancing; I had visions of women's
legs. I had a vision especially of a girl in a green dress who sat on
a straight-backed dining chair (one of the house set of twelve).
I studied her knees, her legs, her ankles, her shoes. They were not

particularly well made legs, but they had an effect on me. All my
adult life I had looked for release in the bars of the town. I knew
only women who had to be paid for. The other side of the life of
passion, of embraces freely given and received, I knew nothing of,
and had begun to consider alien, something not for me. And so
my satisfactions had only been brothel satisfactions, which hadn't
been satisfactions at all. I felt they had taken me further and
further away from the true life of the senses and I feared they had
made me incapable of that life.

I had never been in a room where men and women danced for
mutual pleasure, and out of pleasure in one another's company.
Trembling expectation was in that girl's heavy legs, the girl in
the green dress. It was a new dress, loosely hemmed, not ironed
into a crease, still suggesting the material as it had been measured
out and bought. Later I saw her dancing, watched the movements
of her legs, her shoes; and such a sweetness was released in me
that I felt I had recovered a part of myself I had lost. I never
looked at the girl's face, and it was easy in the semi-gloom to let
that remain unknown. I wanted to sink into the sweetness; I
didn't want anything to spoil the mood.

And the mood became sweeter. The music that was being
played came to an end, and in the wonderfully lit room, blurred
circles of light thrown on to the ceiling from the lamps on the
floor, people stopped dancing. What next came on went straight
to my heart – sad guitars, words, a song, an American girl singing
'Barbara Allen'.

That voice! It needed no music; it hardly needed words. By
itself it created the line of the melody; by itself it created a whole
world of feeling. It is what people of our background look for in
music and singing – feeling. It is what makes us shout '*Wa-wa!*
Bravo!' and throw bank-notes and gold at the feet of a singer.
Listening to that voice, I felt the deepest part of myself awakening,
the part that knew loss, homesickness, grief, and longed for love.
And in that voice was the promise of a flowering for everyone who
listened.

I said to Indar, 'Who is the singer?'

He said, 'Joan Baez. She's very famous in the States.'

'And a millionaire,' Yvette said.

I was beginning to recognize her irony. It made her appear to be saying something when she had said very little – and she was, after all, playing the record in her house. She was smiling at me, perhaps smiling at what she had said, or perhaps smiling at me as Indar's friend, or smiling because she believed it became her.

Her left leg was drawn up; her right leg, bent at the knee, lay flat on the cushion on which she sat, so that her right heel lay almost against her left ankle. Beautiful feet, and their whiteness was wonderful against the black of her slacks. Her provocative posture, her smile – they became part of the mood of the song, too much to contemplate.

Indar said, 'Salim comes from one of our old coast families. Their history is interesting.'

Yvette's hand lay white on her right thigh.

Indar said, 'Let me show you something.'

He leaned across my legs and reached up to the bookcase. He took out a book, opened it and showed me where I was to read. I held the book down to the floor, to catch the light from the reading lamp, and saw, among a list of names, the names of Yvette and Raymond, acknowledged by the writer of the book as 'most generous of hosts' at some recent time in the capital.

Yvette continued to smile. No embarrassment or playing it down, though; no irony now. Her name in the book mattered to her.

I gave the book back to Indar, looked away from Yvette and him, and returned to the voice. Not all the songs were like 'Barbara Allen'. Some were modern, about war and injustice and oppression and nuclear destruction. But always in between there were the older, sweeter melodies. These were the ones I waited for, but in the end the voice linked the two kinds of song, linked the maidens and lovers and sad deaths of bygone times with the people of today who were oppressed and about to die.

It was make-believe – I never doubted that. You couldn't listen to sweet songs about injustice unless you expected justice and received it much of the time. You couldn't sing songs about the end of the world unless – like the other people in that room, so beautiful with such simple things: African mats on the floor and African hangings on the wall and spears and masks – you felt that the world was going on and you were safe in it. How easy it was, in that room, to make those assumptions!

It was different outside, and Mahesh would have scoffed. He had said, 'It isn't that there's no right and wrong here. There's no right.' But Mahesh felt far away. The aridity of that life, which had also been mine! It was better to pretend, as I could pretend now. It was better to share the companionship of that pretence, to feel that in that room we all lived beautifully and bravely with injustice and imminent death and consoled ourselves with love. Even before the songs ended I felt I had found the kind of life I wanted; I never wanted to be ordinary again. I felt that by some piece of luck I had stumbled on the equivalent of what years before Nazruddin had found right here.

It was late when Raymond came in. I had, at Indar's insistence, even danced with Yvette and felt her skin below the silk of her blouse; and when I saw Raymond my thoughts – leaping at this stage of the evening from possibility to possibility – were at first only about the difference in their ages. There must have been thirty years between Yvette and her husband; Raymond was a man in his late fifties.

But I felt possibilities fade, felt them as dreams, when I saw the immediate look of concern on Yvette's face – or rather in her eyes, for her smile was still on, a trick of her face; when I saw the security of Raymond's manner, remembered his job and position, and took in the distinction of his appearance. It was the distinction of intelligence and intellectual labours. He looked as though he had just taken off his glasses, and his gentle eyes were attractively tired. He was wearing a long-sleeved safari jacket; and it came to me that the style – long sleeves rather than short – had been suggested to him by Yvette.

After that look of concern at her husband, Yvette relaxed again, with her fixed smile. Indar got up and began fetching a dining chair from against the opposite wall. Raymond motioned to us to stay where we were; he rejected the chance of sitting next to Yvette and, when Indar returned with the dining chair, sat on that.

Yvette said, without moving, 'Would you like a drink, Raymond?'

He said, 'It will spoil it for me, Evie. I'll be going back to my room in a minute.'

Raymond's presence in the room had been noted. A young man and a girl had begun to hover around our group. One or two other people came up. There were greetings.

Indar said, 'I hope we haven't disturbed you.'

Raymond said, 'It made a pleasant background. If I look a little troubled, it is because just now, in that room, I became very dejected. I began to wonder, as I've often wondered, whether the truth ever gets known. The idea isn't new, but there are times when it becomes especially painful. I feel that everything one does is just going to waste.'

Indar said, 'You are talking nonsense, Raymond. Of course it takes time for someone like yourself to be recognized, but it happens in the end. You are not working in a popular field.'

Yvette said, 'You tell him that for me, please.'

One of the men standing around said, 'New discoveries are constantly making us revise our ideas about the past. The truth is always there. It can be got at. The work has to be done, that's all.'

Raymond said, 'Time, the discoverer of truth. I know. It's the classical idea, the religious idea. But there are times when you begin to wonder. Do we really know the history of the Roman Empire? Do we really know what went on during the conquest of Gaul? I was sitting in my room and thinking with sadness about all the things that have gone unrecorded. Do you think we will ever get to know the truth about what has happened in Africa in the last hundred or even fifty years? All the wars, all the rebellions, all the leaders, all the defeats?'

There was a silence. We looked at Raymond, who had introduced this element of discussion into our evening. Yet the mood was only like an extension of the mood of the Joan Baez songs. And for a little while, but without the help of music, we contemplated the sadness of the continent.

Indar said, 'Have you read Muller's article?'

Raymond said, 'About the Bapende rebellion? He sent me a proof. It's had a great success, I hear.'

The young man with the girl said, 'I hear they're inviting him to Texas to teach for a term.'

Indar said, 'I thought it was a lot of rubbish. Every kind of cliché parading as new wisdom. The Azande, that's a tribal uprising. The Bapende, that's just economic oppression, rubber business. They're to be lumped with the Budja and the Babwa. And you do that by playing down the religious side. Which is what makes the Bapende dust-up so wonderful. It's just the kind of thing that happens when people turn to Africa to make the fast academic buck.'

Raymond said, 'He came to see me. I answered all his questions and showed him all my papers.'

The young man said, 'Muller's a bit of whiz-kid, I think.'

Raymond said, 'I liked him.'

Yvette said, 'He came to lunch. As soon as Raymond left the table, he forgot all about the Bapende and said to me, "Do you want to come out with me?" Just like that. The minute Raymond's back was turned.'

Raymond smiled.

Indar said, 'I was telling Salim, Raymond, that you are the only man the President reads.'

Raymond said, 'I don't think he has much time for reading these days.'

The young man, his girl now close to him, said, 'How did you meet him?'

'It is a story at once simple and extraordinary,' Raymond said. 'But I don't think we have time for that now.' He looked at Yvette.

She said, 'I don't think anybody is rushing off anywhere right at this minute.'

'It was long ago,' Raymond said. 'In colonial times. I was teaching at a college in the capital. I was doing my historical work. But of course in those days there was no question of publishing. There was the censorship that people pretended didn't exist, in

spite of the celebrated decree of 1922. And of course in those days
Africa wasn't a subject. But I never made any secret of what I felt
or where I stood, and I suppose the word must have got around.
One day at the college I was told that an old African woman had
come to see me. It was one of the African servants who brought
me the message, and he wasn't too impressed by my visitor.

'I asked him to bring her to me. She was middle-aged rather
than old. She worked as a maid in the big hotel in the capital, and
she had come to see me about her son. She belonged to one of the
smaller tribes, people with no say in anything, and I suppose she
had no one of her own kind to turn to. The boy had left school.
He had joined some political club and had done various odd jobs.
But he had given up all that. He was doing nothing at all. He was
just staying in the house. He didn't go out to see anybody. He
suffered from headaches, but he wasn't ill. I thought she was going
to ask me to get the boy a job. But no. All she wanted me to do
was to see the boy and talk to him.

'She impressed me a great deal. Yes, the dignity of that hotel
maid was quite remarkable. Another woman would have thought
that her son was bewitched, and taken appropriate measures. She,
in her simple way, saw that her son's disease had been brought
on by his education. That was why she had come to me, the
teacher at the college.

'I asked her to send the boy to me. He didn't like the idea of
his mother talking to me about him, but he came. He was as
nervous as a kitten. What made him unusual – I would even say
extraordinary – was the quality of his despair. It wasn't just a
matter of poverty and the lack of opportunity. It went much
deeper. And, indeed, to try to look at the world from his point of
view was to begin to get a headache yourself. He couldn't face the
world in which his mother, a poor woman of Africa, had endured
such humiliation. Nothing could undo that. Nothing could give
him a better world.

'I said to him, "I've listened to you, and I know that one day
the mood of despair will go and you will want to act. What you
mustn't do then is to become involved in politics as they exist.
Those clubs and associations are talking shops, debating societies,

where Africans posture for Europeans and hope to pass as evolved. They will eat up your passion and destroy your gifts. What I am going to tell you now will sound strange, coming from me. You must join the Defence Force. You won't rise high, but you will learn a real skill. You will learn about weapons and transport, and you will also learn about men. Once you understand what holds the Defence Force together, you will understand what holds the country together. You might say to me, 'But isn't it better for me to be a lawyer and be called *maître?*' I will say, 'No. It is better for you to be a private and call the sergeant sir.' This isn't advice I will want to give to anybody else. But I give it to you." '

Raymond had held us all. When he stopped speaking we allowed the silence to last, while we continued to look at him as he sat on the dining chair in his safari jacket, distinguished, his hair combed back, his eyes tired, a bit of a dandy in his way.

In a more conversational voice, as though he was commenting on his own story, Raymond said at last, breaking the silence, 'He's a truly remarkable man. I don't think we give him enough credit for what he's done. We take it for granted. He's disciplined the army and brought peace to this land of many peoples. It is possible once again to traverse the country from one end to the other – something the colonial power thought it alone had brought about. And what is most remarkable is that it's been done without coercion, and entirely with the consent of the people. You don't see policemen in the streets. You don't see guns. You don't see the army.'

Indar, sitting next to Yvette, who was still smiling, seemed about to change the position of his legs prior to saying something. But Raymond raised his hand, and Indar didn't move.

'And there's the freedom,' Raymond said. 'There's the remarkable welcome given to every kind of idea from every kind of system. I don't think,' he said, addressing Indar directly, as though making up to him for keeping him quiet, 'that anyone has even hinted to you that there are certain things you have to say and certain things you mustn't say.'

Indar said, 'We've had an easy ride here.'

'I don't think it would have occurred to him to try to censor

144

you. He feels that all ideas can be made to serve the cause. You might say that with him there's an absolute hunger for ideas. He uses them all in his own way.'

Yvette said, 'I wish he would change the boys' uniforms. The good old colonial style of short trousers and a long white apron. Or long trousers and a jacket. But not that carnival costume of short trousers and jacket.'

We all laughed, even Raymond, as though we were glad to stop being solemn. And Yvette's boldness was also like proof of the freedom Raymond had been talking about.

Raymond said, 'Yvette goes on about the boys' uniforms. But that's the army background, and the mother's hotel background. The mother wore a colonial maid's uniform all her working life. The boys in the Domain have to wear theirs. And it isn't a colonial uniform – that's the point. In fact, everybody nowadays who wears a uniform has to understand that. Everyone in uniform has to feel that he has a personal contract with the President. And try to get the boys out of that uniform. You won't succeed. Yvette has tried. They want to wear that uniform, however absurd it is to our eyes. That's the amazing thing about this man of Africa – this flair, this knowledge of what the people need, and when.

'We have all these photographs of him in African costume nowadays. I must confess I was disturbed when they began to appear in such number. I raised the issue with him one day in the capital. I was shattered by the penetration of his answer. He said, "Five years ago, Raymond, I would have agreed with you. Five years ago our African people, with that cruel humour which is theirs, would have laughed, and that ridicule would have destroyed our country, with its still frail bonds. But times have changed. The people now have peace. They want something else. So they no longer see a photograph of a soldier. They see a photograph of an African. And that isn't a picture of me, Raymond. It is a picture of all Africans." '

This was so like what I felt, that I said, 'Yes! None of us in the town liked putting up the old photograph. But it is different seeing the new photographs, especially in the Domain.'

Raymond permitted this interruption. His right hand was being raised though, to allow him to go on. And he went on.

'I thought I would check this. Just last week, as a matter of fact. I ran into one of our students outside the main building. And just to be provocative, I dropped some remark about the number of the President's photographs. The young man pulled me up quite sharply. So I asked him what he felt when he saw the President's photograph. You will be surprised by what he said to me, that young man, holding himself as erect as any military cadet. "It is a photograph of the President. But here on the Domain, as a student at the polytechnic, I also consider it a photograph of myself." The very words! But that's a quality of great leaders – they intuit the needs of their people long before those needs are formulated. It takes an African to rule Africa – the colonial powers never truly understood that. However much the rest of us study Africa, however deep our sympathy, we will remain outsiders.'

The young man, sitting now on a mat with his girl, asked, 'Do you know the symbolism of the serpent on the President's stick? Is it true that there's a fetish in the belly of the human figure on the stick?'

Raymond said, 'I don't know about that. It is a stick. It is a chief's stick. It is like a mace or a mitre. I don't think we have to fall into the error of looking for African mysteries everywhere.'

The critical note jarred a little. But Raymond seemed not to notice.

'I have recently had occasion to look through all the President's speeches. Now, what an interesting publication that would make! Not the speeches in their entirety, which inevitably deal with many passing issues. But selections. The essential thoughts.'

Indar said, 'Are you working on that? Has he asked you?'

Raymond lifted a palm and hunched a shoulder, to say that it was possible, but that he couldn't talk about a matter that was still confidential.

'What is interesting about those speeches when read in sequence is their development. There you can see very clearly what I have described as the hunger for ideas. In the beginning

the ideas are simple. Unity, the colonial past, the need for peace.
Then they become extraordinarily complex and wonderful about
Africa, government, the modern world. Such a work, if adequately
prepared, might well become the handbook for a true revolution
throughout the continent. Always you can catch that quality of
the young man's despair which made such an impression on me
so long ago. Always you have that feeling that the damage can
never perhaps be undone. Always there is that note, for those
with the ears to hear it, of the young man grieving for the humiliations of his mother, the hotel maid. He's always remained true to
that. I don't think many people know that earlier this year he
and his entire government made a pilgrimage to the village of that
woman of Africa. Has that been done before? Has any ruler
attempted to give sanctity to the bush of Africa? This act of piety
is something that brings tears to the eyes. Can you imagine the
humiliations of an African hotel maid in colonial times? No
amount of piety can make up for that. But piety is all we have to
offer.'

'Or we can forget,' Indar said. 'We can trample on the past.'

Raymond said, 'That is what most of the leaders of Africa do.
They want to build skyscrapers in the bush. This man wants to
build a shrine.'

Music without words had been coming out of the speakers.
Now 'Barbara Allen' began again, and the words were distracting.
Raymond stood up. The man who had been sitting on the mat
went to lower the volume. Raymond indicated that he wasn't to
bother, but the song went faint.

Raymond said, 'I would like to be with you. But unfortunately
I have to get back to my work. Otherwise I might lose something.
I find that the most difficult thing in prose narrative is linking one
thing with the other. The link might just be a sentence, or even a
word. It sums up what has gone before and prepares one for what
is to come. As I was sitting with you I had an idea of a possible
solution to a problem that was beginning to appear quite intract-
able. I must go and make a note. Otherwise I might forget.'

He began to move away from us. But then he stopped and said,
'I don't think it is sufficiently understood how hard it is to write

about what has never been written about before. The occasional academic paper on a particular subject, the Bapende rebellion or whatever – that has its own form. The larger narrative is another matter. And that's why I have begun to consider Theodor Mommsen the giant of modern historical writing. Everything that we now discuss about the Roman Republic is only a continuation of Mommsen. The problems, the issues, the very narrative, especially of those extraordinarily troubled years of the later Republic – you might say the German genius discovered it all. Of course Theodor Mommsen had the comfort of knowing that his subject was a great one. Those of us who work in our particular field have no such assurance. We have no idea of the value posterity will place on the events we attempt to chronicle. We have no idea where the continent is going. We can only carry on.'

He ended abruptly, turned, and went out of the room, leaving us in silence, looking after where he had disappeared, and only slowly directing our attention to Yvette, now his representative in that room, smiling, acknowledging our regard.

After a little Indar said to me, 'Do you know Raymond's work?'

Of course he knew the answer to that one. But, to give him his opening, I said, 'No, I don't know his work.'

Indar said, 'That's the tragedy of the place. The great men of Africa are not known.'

It was like a formal speech of thanks. And Indar had chosen his words well. He had made us all men and women of Africa; and since we were not Africans the claim gave us a special feeling for ourselves which, so far as I was concerned, was soon heightened by the voice of Joan Baez, turned up again, reminding us sweetly, after the tensions Raymond had thrown among us, of our common bravery and sorrows.

Indar was embraced by Yvette when we left. And I was embraced, as the friend. It was delicious to me, as the climax to that evening, to press that body close, soft at this late hour, and to feel the silk of the blouse and the flesh below the silk.

There was a moon now – there had been none earlier. It was small and high. The sky was full of heavy clouds, and the moon-

light came and went. It was very quiet. We could hear the rapids;
they were about a mile away. The rapids in moonlight! I said to
Indar, 'Let's go to the river.' And he was willing.

In the wide levelled land of the Domain the new buildings
seemed small, and the earth felt immense. The Domain seemed the
merest clearing in the forest, the merest clearing in an immensity
of bush and river – the world might have been nothing else.
Moonlight distorted distances; and the darkness, when it came,
seemed to drop down to our heads.

I said to Indar, 'What do you think of what Raymond said?'

'Raymond tells a story well. But a lot of what he says is true.
What he says about the President and ideas is certainly true. The
President uses them all and somehow makes them work together.
He is the great African chief, and he is also the man of the people.
He is the modernizer and he is also the African who has redis-
covered his African soul. He's conservative, revolutionary, everything. He's going back to the old ways, and he's also the man who's
going ahead, the man who's going to make the country a world
power by the year 2000. I don't know whether he's done it
accidentally or because someone's been telling him what to do.
But the mish-mash works because he keeps on changing, unlike the
other guys. He is the soldier who decided to become an old-
fashioned chief, and he's the chief whose mother was a hotel
maid. That makes him everything, and he plays up everything.
There isn't anyone in the country who hasn't heard of that hotel-
maid mother.'

I said, 'They caught me with that pilgrimage to the mother's
village. When I read in the paper that it was an unpublicized
pilgrimage, I thought of it as just that.'

'He makes these shrines in the bush, honouring the mother.
And at the same time he builds modern Africa. Raymond says he
doesn't build skyscrapers. Well, he doesn't do that. He builds
these very expensive Domains.'

'Nazruddin used to own some land here in the old days.'

'And he sold it for nothing. Are you going to tell me that?
That's an African story.'

'No, Nazruddin sold well. He sold at the height of the boom

before independence. He came out one Sunday morning and said, "But this is only bush." And he sold.'

'It could go that way again.'

The sound of the rapids had grown louder. We had left the new buildings of the Domain behind and were approaching the fishermen's huts, dead in the moonlight. The thin village dogs, pale in the moonlight, their shadows black below them, walked lazily away from us. The fishermen's poles and nets were dark against the broken glitter of the river. And then we were on the old viewing point, repaired now, newly walled; and around us, drowning everything else, was the sound of water over rocks. Clumps of water hyacinths bucked past. The hyacinths were white in the moonlight, the vines dark tangles outlined in black shadow. When the moonlight went there was nothing to be seen; the world was then only that old sound of tumbling water.

I said, 'I've never told you why I came here. It wasn't just to get away from the coast or to run that shop. Nazruddin used to tell us wonderful stories of the times he used to have here. That was why I came. I thought I would be able to live my own life, and I thought that in time I would find what Nazruddin found. Then I got stuck. I don't know what I would have done if you hadn't come. If you hadn't come I would never have known about what was going on here, just under my nose.'

'It's different from what we used to know. To people like us it's very seductive. Europe in Africa, post-colonial Africa. But it isn't Europe or Africa. And it looks different from the inside, I can tell you.'

'You mean people don't believe in it? They don't believe in what they say and do?'

'No one is as crude as that. We believe and don't believe. We believe because that way everything becomes simpler and makes more sense. We don't believe – well, because of this.' And Indar waved at the fishermen's village, the bush, the moonlit river.

He said after a time, 'Raymond's in a bit of a mess. He has to keep on pretending that he is the guide and adviser, to keep himself from knowing that the time is almost here when he will just be receiving orders. In fact, so as not to get orders, he is beginning to anticipate orders. He will go crazy if he has to acknowledge that that's his situation. Oh, he's got a big job now. But he's on the slippery slope. He's been sent away from the capital. The Big Man is going his own way, and he no longer needs Raymond. Everybody knows that, but Raymond thinks they don't. It's a dreadful thing for a man of his age to have to live with.'

But what Indar was saying didn't make me think of Raymond. I thought of Yvette, all at once brought nearer by this tale of her husband's distress. I went over the pictures I had of her that evening, ran the film over again, so to speak, reconstructing and reinterpreting what I had seen, re-creating that woman, fixing her in the posture that had bewitched me, her white feet together, one leg drawn up, one leg flat and bent, re-making her face, her smile, touching the whole picture with the mood of the Joan Baez songs and all that they had released in me, and adding to it this extra mood of moonlight, the rapids, and the white hyacinths of this great river of Africa.

9

IT was on that evening, by the river, after he had spoken about Raymond, that Indar began to tell me about himself. The evening that had excited me had enervated and depressed him; he had become irritable as soon as we had left Yvette's house.

Earlier in the evening, as we had walked across to the house for the party, he had spoken of Raymond as a star, someone close to power, the Big Man's white man; but then, by the rapids, he had spoken of Raymond in quite another way. As my guide Indar had been anxious for me truly to understand the nature of life on the Domain, and his own position there. Now that I had seized the glamour of his world he was like a guide who had lost faith in what he showed. Or like a man who, because he had got someone else to believe, had felt he could let go of some of his own faith.

The moonlight that made me light-headed deepened his depression, and it was out of this depression that he began to speak. The mood of the evening didn't stay with him, though; the next day he had bounced back, and was like the man he had always been. But he was more ready to acknowledge his depression when it came; and what he outlined that evening he returned to and filled in at other times, when the occasion suited, or when he drifted back to that earlier mood.

'We have to learn to trample on the past, Salim. I told you that when we met. It shouldn't be a cause for tears, because it isn't just true for you and me. There may be some parts of the world – dead countries, or secure and by-passed ones – where men can cherish the past and think of passing on furniture and china to

152

their heirs. Men can do that perhaps in Sweden or Canada. Some peasant department of France full of half-wits in châteaux; some crumbling Indian palace-city, or some dead colonial town in a hopeless South American country. Everywhere else men are in movement, the world is in movement, and the past can only cause pain.

'It isn't easy to turn your back on the past. It isn't something you can decide to do just like that. It is something you have to arm yourself for, or grief will ambush and destroy you. That is why I hold on to the image of the garden trampled until it becomes ground – it is a small thing, but it helps. That perception about the past came to me at the end of my third year in England. And oddly enough, it came to me beside another river. You've told me that I've led you here to the kind of life you've always felt you needed. It was something like that, too, that I began to feel beside that river in London. I made a decision about myself then. And it was as an indirect result of that decision that I came back to Africa. Though when I left, it was my intention never to return.

'I was very unhappy when I left. You remember that. I tried to depress you – in fact, I tried to wound you – but that was only because I was myself so depressed. The thought of the work of two generations going to waste – it was very painful. The thought of losing that house built by my grandfather, the thought of the risks he and my father had taken to build up a business from nothing, the bravery, the sleepless nights – it was all very painful. In another country such effort and such talent would have made us millionaires, aristocrats, or at any rate secure for some generations. There it was all going up in smoke. My rage wasn't only with the Africans. It was also with our community and our civilization, which gave us energy but in every other way left us at the mercy of others. How do you rage against a thing like that?

'I thought when I went to England I would put all that behind me. I had no plans beyond that. The word "university" dazzled me, and I was innocent enough to believe that after my time in the university some wonderful life would be waiting for me. At that age three years seems a long time – you feel that anything can happen. But I hadn't understood to what extent our civilization had also been our prison. I hadn't understood either to what extent we had been made by the place where we had grown up, made by Africa and the simple life of the coast, and how incapable we had become of understanding the outside world. We have no means of understanding a fraction of the thought and science and philosophy and law that have gone to make that outside world. We simply accept it. We have grown up paying tribute to it, and that is all that most of us can do. We feel of the great world that it is simply there, something for the lucky ones among us to explore, and then only at the edges. It never occurs to us that we might make some contribution to it ourselves. And that is why we miss everything.

'When we land at a place like London Airport we are concerned only not to appear foolish. It is more beautiful and more complex than anything we could have dreamed of, but we are concerned only to let people see that we can manage and are not overawed. We might even pretend that we had expected better. That is the nature of our stupidity and incompetence. And that was how I spent my time at the university in England, not being overawed, always being slightly disappointed, understanding nothing, accepting everything, getting nothing. I saw and understood so little that even at the end of my time at the university I could distinguish buildings only by their size, and I was hardly aware of the passing of the seasons. And yet I was an intelligent man, and could cram for examinations.

'In the old days, after three years like that, and with some scraped-through degree, I would have returned home and hung up my board and devoted myself to the making of money, using the little half-skill I had picked up, the half-knowledge of other men's books. But of course I couldn't do that. I had to stay where I was and I had to get a job. I hadn't acquired a profession, you understand; nothing at home had pushed me in that direction.

'For some time the boys of my year at the university had been talking of jobs and interviews. The more precocious ones had even been talking about the interview expenses various companies paid. In the porter's lodge the pigeon-holes of these boys were full of long brown envelopes from the University Appointments Committee. The dimmest boys were naturally the ones with the most varied prospects; they could be anything; and in their pigeon-holes the brown envelopes fell as thick as autumn leaves. That was my attitude to those adventurous boys – slightly mocking. I had to get a job, but I never thought of myself as someone who would have to go through the brown-envelope adventure. I don't know why; I just didn't; and then, almost at the end of my time, with bewilderment and shame I realized that I had. I made an appointment with the Appointments Committee and on the morning put on a dark suit and went.

'As soon as I got there I knew my errand was fruitless. The Committee was meant to put English boys in English jobs; it wasn't meant for me. I realized that as soon as I saw the look on the face of the girl in the outer office. But she was nice, and the dark-suited man inside was also nice. He was intrigued by my African background, and after a little talk about Africa he said, "And what can this great organization do for you?" I wanted to say, "Couldn't you send me some brown envelopes too?" But what I said was: "I was hoping you would tell me." He seemed to find this funny. He took down my details, for the form of the thing; and then he tried to get a conversation going, senior dark suit to junior dark suit, man to man.

'He had little to tell me, though. And I had less to tell him. I had hardly looked at the world. I didn't know how it worked or what I might do in it. After my three unamazed student years, I was overwhelmed by my ignorance; and in that quiet little office full of peaceful files I began to think of the world outside as a place of horror. My dark-suited interviewer became impatient. He said, "Good heavens, man! You must give me some guidance. You must have some idea of the kind of job you see yourself doing."

'He was right, of course. But that "Good heavens, man!" seemed to me affected, something he might have picked up in the past from someone his senior and was now throwing at me as someone lesser. I became angry. The idea came to me that I should fix him with a look of the utmost hostility and say, "The job I want is your job. And I want your job because you enjoy it so much." But I didn't speak the words; I didn't speak any words at all; I just gave him the hostile look. So our interview ended inconclusively.

'I became calmer outside. I went to the café where I used to go for coffee in the mornings. As a consolation, I bought myself a piece of chocolate cake as well. But then, to my surprise, I found I wasn't consoling myself; I was celebrating. I found I was positively happy to be in the café in the middle of the morning, drinking coffee and eating cake, while my tormentor fussed about with his brown envelopes in his office. It was only escape, and it couldn't last long. But I remember that half hour as one of pure happiness.

'After this I didn't expect anything from the Appointments Committee. But the man was, after all, a fair man; a bureaucracy is a bureaucracy; and a couple of brown envelopes did arrive for me, unseasonably, not as part of the autumn rush, choking the pigeon-holes in the porter's lodge, but like the last dead leaves of the year, torn away by the gales of January. An oil company, and two or three other large companies with connections in Asia or Africa. With each job description I read I felt a tightening of what I must call my soul. I found myself growing false to myself, acting to myself, convincing myself of my rightness for whatever was being described. And this is where I suppose life ends for most people, who stiffen in the attitudes they adopt to make themselves suitable for the jobs and lives that other people have laid out for them.

'None of those jobs came my way. There again I found myself amusing my interviewers unintentionally. Once I said, "I don't know anything about your business, but I can put my mind to it." For some reason this brought the house down – in this case it was a three-man board. They laughed, the oldest man leading the laughter and in the end even wiping away tears; and they dismissed me. With each rejection came a feeling of relief; but with each rejection I became more anxious about the future.

'Once a month or so I had lunch with a woman lecturer. She was about thirty, not bad-looking, and very kind to me. She was unusual because she was so much at peace with herself. That was why I liked her. It was she who made me do the absurd thing I am going to describe.

'This lady had the idea that people like myself were at sea because we were men of two worlds. She was right, of course. But at the time it didn't seem so to me – I thought I saw everything very clearly – and I thought she had got the idea from some young man from Bombay or thereabouts who was trying to make himself interesting. But this lady also thought that my education and background made me extraordinary, and I couldn't fight the idea of my extraordinariness.

'An extraordinary man, a man of two worlds, needed an extraordinary job. And she suggested I should become a diplomat. That was what I decided to do, and the country I decided to serve – since a diplomat has to have a country – was India. It was absurd; I knew it was absurd, even while I was doing it; but I wrote a letter to the Indian High Commission. I got a reply, and was given an appointment.

'I went up to London by train. I didn't know London very well, and didn't like what I knew; and I liked it less that morning. There was Praed Street with its pornographic bookshops that didn't deal in real pornography; there was the Edgware Road where the shops and restaurants seemed continually to be changing hands; there were the shops and crowds of Oxford Street and Regent Street. The openness of Trafalgar Square gave me a lift, but it reminded me that I was almost at the end of my journey. And I had begun to be very embarrassed by my mission.

'The bus took me down the Strand and dropped me at the curve of the Aldwych, and I crossed the road to the building that had been pointed out to me as India House. How could I have missed it, with all the Indian motifs on the outside wall? At this stage my embarrassment was acute. I was in my dark suit and my university tie, and I was entering a London building, an English building, which pretended to be of India – an India quite different from the country my grandfather had spoken about.

'For the first time in my life I was filled with a colonial rage. And this wasn't only a rage with London or England, it was also a rage with the people who had allowed themselves to be coralled into a foreign fantasy. My rage didn't die down when I went inside. There again were the oriental motifs. The uniformed messengers were English and middle-aged; they clearly had been taken on by the old management, if you can call it that, and were working out their time under the new. I had never felt so involved with the land of my ancestors, and yours, and so far from it. I felt in that building I had lost an important part of my idea of who I was. I felt I had been granted the most cruel knowledge of where I stood in the world. And I hated it.

'It was a minor official who had written me. The receptionist spoke to one of the elderly English messengers, and he led me, with no great ceremony and a lot of asthmatic breathing, to a room that contained many desks. At one of these my man was sitting. His desk was bare, and the man himself seemed quite vacant and easy in his mind. He had small smiling eyes, a superior manner, and he didn't know what I had come about.

'In spite of his jacket and tie he wasn't what I was expecting. He wasn't the kind of man I would have worn a dark suit for. I thought he belonged to another kind of office, another kind of building, another kind of city. His name was the name of his merchant caste, and it was easy for me to imagine him in a dhoti reclining against a bolster in a cloth shop in a bazaar lane, with his feet bare, and his fingers massaging his toes, rubbing off the dead skin. He was the kind of man who would say, "Shirtings? You want shirtings?" and, barely moving his back from the bolster, would throw a bolt of cloth across the sheet spread on the floor of his stall.

'It wasn't shirtings that he flung across the desk at me, but my letter, the letter he had written himself, which he had asked to see. He understood that I was looking for a job and his small eyes twinkled with amusement. I felt very shabby in my suit. He said, "You had better go and see Mr Verma." The English messenger, breathing heavily, and seeming to choke with every breath, led me to another office. And there he abandoned me.

'Mr Verma wore horn-rimmed glasses. He sat in a less crowded office and he had many papers and folders on his desk. On the walls there were photographs, from the British days, of Indian buildings and Indian landscapes. Mr Verma looked more worried than the first man. He was higher in the service; and he had probably taken the name Verma to conceal his caste origins. He was puzzled by my letter; but he was also made uneasy by my dark suit and university tie and he attempted in a half-hearted way to interview me. The telephone rang a lot and our interview never got going. At one stage, after talking on the telephone, Mr Verma left me and went out of the room. He was away for a while and when he came back, with some papers, he seemed surprised to see me. He told me then that I should go to an office on another floor; and, giving me real attention for the first time, told me how to get there.

'The room I knocked at turned out to be a dark little antechamber, with a small man sitting before an old-fashioned standard typewriter with a wide carriage. He looked at me with something like terror – it was the effect of my dark suit and the tie, my man-of-two-worlds garb – and he calmed down only when he had read my letter. He asked me to wait. There was no chair. I remained standing.

'A buzzer rang, and the typist-secretary jumped. He seemed, after this jump, to land on the tips of his toes; he very quickly drew his shoulders up and then down into a kind of cringe, making himself smaller than he already was; and with a curious long tiptoeing stride, a lope, he reached the great wooden doors that separated us from the room on the other side. He knocked, opened; and with his hunched gait, his prepared cringe, disappeared.

'My wish for the diplomatic life had by now vanished. I studied the large framed photographs of Gandhi and Nehru and wondered how, out of squalor like this, those men had managed to get themselves considered as men. It was strange, in that building in the heart of London, seeing those great men in this new way, from the inside, as it were. Up till then, from the outside, without knowing more of them than I had read in newspapers and magazines, I had admired them. They belonged to me; they ennobled me and gave me some place in the world. Now I felt the opposite. In that room the photographs of those great men made me feel that I was at the bottom of a well. I felt that in that building complete manhood was permitted only to those men and denied to everybody else. Everyone had surrendered his manhood, or a part of it, to those leaders. Everyone willingly made himself smaller the better to exalt those leaders. These thoughts surprised and pained me. They were more than heretical. They destroyed what remained of my faith in the way the world was ordered. I began to feel cast out and alone.

'When the secretary came back to the room, I noticed that he still walked on tiptoe, still cringed, still leaned forward. I saw then that what had looked like a cringe, that humping of the shoulders as he had jumped off his chair and loped across to the door, wasn't something he had put on, but was natural. He was a hunchback. This was a shock. I began confusedly to think back to my earlier impressions of the man, and I was in a state of confusion when he motioned me through the door into the inner office, where a fat black man in a black suit, one of our black Indians, was sitting at a big black table, opening envelopes with a paper knife.

'His shiny cheeks were swollen with fat and his lips appeared to pout. I sat down on a chair placed some distance away from his desk. He didn't look up at me and he didn't speak. And I didn't speak; I let him open his letters. Not an hour's exercise had he taken in his life, this devout man of the South. He reeked of caste and temple, and I was sure that below that black suit he wore all kinds of amulets.

'At last, but still not looking up, he said, "So?"

'I said, "I wrote in about joining the diplomatic service. I had a letter from Aggarwal and I came to see him."

'Opening his letters, he said, "*Mister* Aggarwal."

'I was glad he had found something we might fight about.

' "Aggarwal didn't seem to know too much. He sent me to Verma."

'He almost looked at me. But he didn't. He said, "Mister Verma."

' "Verma didn't know too much either. He spent a long time with someone called Divedi."

' "Mister Divedi."

'I gave up. He could outplay me. I said, wearily, "And he sent me to you."

' "But you say in your letter you are from Africa. How can you join our diplomatic service? How can we have a man of divided loyalties?"

'I thought: "How dare you lecture me about history and loyalty, you slave? We have paid bitterly for people like you. Who have you ever been loyal to, apart from yourself and your family and your caste?"

'He said, "You people have been living the good life in Africa. Now that things have got a little rough you want to run back. But you must throw in your lot with the local people."

'That was what he said. But I don't have to tell you that what he was really talking about was his own virtue and good fortune. For himself the purity of caste, arranged marriage, the correct diet, the services of the untouchables. For everybody else, pollution. Everybody else was steeped in pollution, and had to pay the price. It was like the message of the photographs of Gandhi and Nehru in the room outside.

'He said, "If you become a citizen of India, there are the examinations. We have arranged for them to be taken at some of the universities here. Mr Verma should have told you. He shouldn't have sent you to me."

'He pressed a buzzer on his desk. The door opened, and the hunchback secretary sent in a tall thin man with bright anxious eyes and a genuine cringe. The new man carried an artist's zip-up portfolio, and he had a long green woollen scarf wound about his neck, although the weather was warm. Without reference to me, with eyes only for the black man, he unzipped his portfolio and began taking out drawings. He held them one by one against his chest, giving the black man an anxious open-mouthed smile every time, and then looking down at what he was showing, so that, with this head bowed over his drawings, and with the cringe that was already there, he looked like a man doing penance, displaying one sin after another. The black man didn't look at the artist, only at the drawings. They were of temples and of smiling women picking tea – perhaps for some window display about the new India.

'I had been dismissed. The hunchback secretary, tense over his old big typewriter, but not typing, his bony hands like crabs on the keys, gave me one last look of terror. This time, though, in his look I thought there was also a question: "Do you understand now about me?"

'Walking down the steps, surrounded by the motifs of imperial India, I saw Mr Verma, away from his desk again, and with more papers; but he had forgotten me. The idle merchant-caste man in the office downstairs remembered me, of course. I received his mocking smile, and then I went out through the revolving door into the London air.

'My crash course in diplomacy had lasted a little over an hour. It was past twelve, too late for the comfort of coffee and cake, as a sign in a snack bar reminded me. I set to walking. I was full of rage. I followed the curve of Aldwych to the end, crossed the Strand, and went down to the river.

'As I walked, the thought came to me: "It is time to go home." It wasn't our town that I thought of, or our stretch of the African coast. I saw a country road lined with tall shady trees. I saw fields, cattle, a village below trees. I don't know what book or picture I had got that from, or why a place like that should have seemed to me safe. But that was the picture that came to me, and I played with it. The mornings, the dew, the fresh flowers, the shade of the trees in the middle of the day, the fires in the evening. I felt I had known that life, and that it was waiting for me again somewhere. It was fantasy, of course.

'I awakened to where I was. I was walking on the Embankment, beside the river, walking without seeing. On the Embankment wall there are green metal lamp standards. I had been examining the dolphins on the standards, dolphin by dolphin, standard by standard. I was far from where I had started, and I had momentarily left the dolphins to examine the metal supports of the pavement benches. These supports, as I saw with amazement, were in the shape of camels. Camels and their sacks! Strange city – the romance of India in that building, and the romance of the desert here. I stopped, stepped back mentally, as it were, and all at once saw the beauty in which I had been walking – the beauty of the river and the sky, the soft colours of the clouds, the beauty of light on water, the beauty of the buildings, the care with which it had all been arranged.

'In Africa, on the coast, I had paid attention only to one colour in Nature – the colour of the sea. Everything else was just bush, green and living, or brown and dead. In England so far I had walked with my eyes at shop level; I had seen nothing. A town, even London, was just a series of streets or street names, and a street was a row of shops. Now I saw differently. And I understood that London wasn't simply a place that was there, as people say of mountains, but that it had been made by men, that men had given attention to details as minute as those camels.

'I began to understand at the same time that my anguish about being a man adrift was false, that for me that dream of home and security was nothing more than a dream of isolation, anachronistic and stupid and very feeble. I belonged to myself alone. I was going to surrender my manhood to nobody. For someone like me there was only one civilization and one place – London, or a place like it. Every other kind of life was make-believe. Home – what for? To hide? To bow to our great men? For people in our situation, people led into slavery, that is the biggest trap of all. We have nothing. We solace ourselves with that idea of the great men of our tribe, the Gandhi and the Nehru, and we castrate ourselves. "Here, take my manhood and invest it for me. Take my manhood and be a greater man yourself, for my sake!" No! I want to be a man myself.

'At certain times in some civilizations great leaders can bring out the manhood in the people they lead. It is different with slaves. Don't blame the leaders. It is just part of the dreadfulness of the situation. It is better to withdraw from the whole business, if you can. And I could. You may say – and I know, Salim, that you have thought it – that I have turned my back on my community and sold out. I say, "Sold out to what and from what? What do you have to offer me? What is your own contribution? And can you give me back my manhood?" Anyway, that was what I decided that morning, beside the river of London, between the dolphins and the camels, the work of some dead artists who had been adding to the beauty of their city.

'That was five years ago. I often wonder what would have happened to me if I hadn't made that decision. I suppose I would have sunk. I suppose I would have found some kind of hole and tried to hide or pass. After all, we make ourselves according to the ideas we have of our possibilities. I would have hidden in my hole and been crippled by my sentimentality, doing what I was doing, and doing it well, but always looking for the wailing wall. And I would never have seen the world as the rich place that it is. You wouldn't have seen me here in Africa, doing what I do. I wouldn't have wanted to do it, and no one would have wanted me to do it. I would have said: "It's all over for me, so why should I let myself be used by anybody? The Americans want to win the world. It's their fight, not mine." And that would have been stupid. It is stupid to talk of *the* Americans. They are not a tribe, as you might think from the outside. They're all individuals fighting to make their way, trying as hard as you or me not to sink.

'It wasn't easy after I left the university. I still had to get a job, and the only thing I knew now was what I didn't want to do. I didn't want to exchange one prison for another. People like me have to make their own jobs. It isn't something that's going to come to you in a brown envelope. The job is there, waiting. But it doesn't exist for you or anyone else until you discover it, and you discover it because it's for you and you alone.

'I had done a little acting at the university – that had begun with a walk-on part in a little film somebody had made about a boy and girl walking in a park. I fell in with the remnants of that group in London and began to do a certain amount of acting. Not in any important way. London is full of little theatrical groups. They write their own plays, and they get grants from firms and local councils here and there. A lot of them live on the dole. Sometimes I played English parts, but usually they wrote parts for me, so that as an actor I found myself being the kind of person I didn't want to be in real life. I played an Indian doctor visiting a dying working-class mother; I did another Indian doctor who had been charged with rape; I was a bus conductor no one wanted to work with. And so on. Once I did Romeo. Another time there was an idea of rewriting *The Merchant of Venice* as *The Malindi Banker*, so that I could play Shylock. But it became too complicated.

'It was a Bohemian life, and it was attractive at first. Then it became depressing. People dropped out and took jobs and you understood that they had had pretty solid connections all along. That was always a let-down, and there were times during those two years when I felt lost and had to fight hard to hold on to that mood that had come to me beside the river. Among all those nice people I was the only real drop-out. And I didn't want to be a drop-out at all. I'm not running these people down. They did what they could to make room for me, and that is more than any outsider can say for us. It's a difference in civilization.

'I was taken one Sunday to lunch at the house of a friend of a friend. There was nothing Bohemian about the house or the lunch, and I discovered that I had been invited for the sake of one of the other guests. He was an American and he was interested in Africa. He spoke about Africa in an unusual way. He spoke of Africa as though Africa was a sick child and he was the parent. I later became very close to this man, but at that lunch he irritated me and I was rough with him. This was because I had never met that kind of person before. He had all this money to spend on Africa, and he desperately wanted to do the right thing. I suppose the idea of all that money going to waste made me unhappy. But he also had the simplest big-power ideas about the regeneration of Africa.

'I told him that Africa wasn't going to be saved or won by promoting the poems of Yevtushenko or by telling the people about the wickedness of the Berlin Wall. He didn't look too surprised. He wanted to hear more, and I realized I had been invited to the lunch to say the things I had been saying. And it was there that I began to understand that everything which I had thought had made me powerless in the world had also made me of value, and that to the American I was of interest precisely because I was what I was, a man without a side.

'That was how it began. That was how I became aware of all

the organizations that were using the surplus wealth of the western world to protect that world. The ideas I put forward, aggressively at that lunch, and more calmly and practically later, were quite simple ones. But they could only have come from someone like myself, someone of Africa, but with no use at all for the kind of freedom that had come to Africa.

'My idea was this. Everything had conspired to push black Africa into every kind of tyranny. As a result Africa was full of refugees, first-generation intellectuals. Western governments didn't want to know, and the old Africa hands were in no position to understand – they were still fighting ancient wars. If Africa had a future, it lay with those refugees. My idea was to remove them from the countries where they couldn't operate and send them, if only for a little while, to those parts of the continent where they could. A continental interchange, to give the men themselves hope, to give Africa the better news about itself, and to make a start on the true African revolution.

'The idea has worked beautifully. Every week we get requests from one university or the other where they would like to keep some kind of intellectual life going without getting involved in local politics. Of course we've attracted the usual free-loaders, black and white, and we've run into trouble with the professional anti-Americans. But the idea is good. I don't feel I have to defend it. Whether it's doing any good as of now is another matter. And perhaps we don't have the time. You've seen the boys at the Domain here. You've seen how bright they are. But they only want jobs. They'll do anything for that, and that's where it may all end. There are times when I feel that Africa will simply have its own way – hungry men are hungry men. And that is when I can get very low.

'To work for an outfit like this is to live in a construct – you don't have to tell me that. But all men live in constructs. Civilization is a construct. And this construct is my own. Within it, I am of value, just as I am. I have to put nothing on. I exploit myself. I allow no one to exploit me. And if it folds, if tomorrow the people at the top decide we're getting nowhere, I've now learned that there are other ways in which I might exploit myself.

'I'm a lucky man. I carry the world within me. You see, Salim, in this world beggars are the only people who can be choosers. Everyone else has his side chosen for him. I can choose. The world is a rich place. It all depends on what you choose in it. You can be sentimental and embrace the idea of your own defeat. You can be an Indian diplomat and always be on the losing side. It's like banking. It is stupid setting up as a banker in Kenya or the Sudan. That was more or less what my family did on the coast. What do the banks say in their annual reports about those places? That many of the people are "outside the monetary sector"? You're not going to be a Rothschild there. The Rothschilds are what they are because they chose Europe at the right time. The other Jews, just as talented, who went to bank for the Ottoman Empire, in Turkey or Egypt or wherever, didn't do so well. Nobody knows their names. And that's what we've been doing for centuries. We've been clinging to the idea of defeat and forgetting that we are men like everybody else. We've been choosing the wrong side. I'm tired of being on the losing side. I don't want to pass. I know exactly who I am and where I stand in the world. But now I want to win and win and win.'

10

INDAR had begun his story at the end of that evening at Raymond and Yvette's. He had added to it at different times later. He had begun his story on the first evening I had seen Yvette, and whenever I saw Yvette afterwards she was in his company. I had trouble with both their personalities: I could pin down neither.

In my mind I had my own picture of Yvette, and this never varied. But the person I saw, at different times of day, in different kinds of light and weather, in circumstances so different from those in which I had first seen her, was always new, always a surprise. I was nervous of looking at her face – I was becoming obsessed with her.

And Indar too began to change for me. His personality too had a dissolving quality. As he filled in his story he became in my eyes quite unlike the man who had presented himself in my shop many weeks before. In his clothes then I had seen London and privilege. I had seen that he was fighting to keep up his style, but I hadn't thought of his style as something he had created for himself. I had seen him more as a man touched by the glamour of the great world; and I had thought that, given the chance to be in his world, I too would have been touched by the same glamour. In those early days I had often wanted to say to him: 'Help me to get away from this place. Show me how to make myself like you.'

But that wasn't so now. I could no longer envy his style or his stylishness. I saw it as his only asset. I felt protective towards him. I felt that since that evening at Yvette's – the evening which had lifted me up but cast him down – we had exchanged roles. I no longer looked on him as my guide; he was the man who needed to be led by the hand.

That perhaps was the secret of his social success which I had envied. My wish – which must have been like the wish of the people in London he had told me about, who had made room for him – was to clear away the aggressiveness and the depression that choked the tenderness I knew was there. I was protective towards him and towards his stylishness, his exaggerations, his delusions. I wished to keep all those from hurt. It saddened me that in a little while he would have to leave, to carry on with his lecturer's duties elsewhere. That was what, from his story, I judged him to be – a lecturer, as uncertain of his future in this role as he had been in his previous roles.

The only friends in the town I had introduced him to were Shoba and Mahesh. They were the only people I thought he would have had something in common with. But that hadn't worked. There was suspicion on both sides. These three people were in many ways alike – renegades, concerned with their personal beauty, finding in that beauty the easiest form of dignity. Each saw the other as another version of himself; and they were like people – Shoba and Mahesh on one side, Indar on the other – sniffing out the falseness in one another.

At lunch in their flat one day – a good lunch: they had gone to a lot of trouble: silver and brass polished, the curtains drawn to keep out the glare, the three-stemmed standard lamp lighting up the Persian carpet on the wall – Shoba asked Indar, 'Is there any money in what you do?' Indar said, 'I get by.' But outside, in the sunlight and red dust, he had raged. As we drove back to the Domain, his home, he said, 'Your friends don't know who I am or what I've done. They don't even know where I've been.' He wasn't referring to his travels; he meant they hadn't appreciated the kind of battles he had fought. 'Tell them that my value is the value I place on myself. There is no reason why it couldn't be fifty thousand dollars a year, a hundred thousand dollars a year.'

That was his mood as his time at the Domain came to an end. He was more easily irritated and depressed. But for me, even during those racing days, the Domain remained a place of possibility. I was looking for a repeat of the evening I had had – the mood of the Joan Baez songs, reading lamps and African mats on the floor, a disturbing woman in black slacks, a walk to the rapids below a moon and drifting cloud. It began to feel like fantasy; I kept it secret from Indar. And Yvette, whenever I saw her, in harsher electric light or ordinary daylight, confounded me again and again, so different from what I remembered.

The days passed; the polytechnic term was over. Indar said goodbye abruptly one afternoon, like a man who didn't want to make too much fuss about a goodbye; he didn't want me to see him off. And I felt that the Domain, and the life there, had been closed to me forever.

Ferdinand too was going away. He was going to the capital to take up his administrative cadetship. And it was Ferdinand that I went to see off on the steamer at the end of the term. The hyacinths of the river, floating on: during the days of the rebellion they had spoken of blood; on heavy afternoons of heat and glitter they had spoken of experience without savour; white in moonlight, they had matched the mood of a particular evening. Now, lilac on bright green, they spoke of something over, other people moving on.

The steamer had arrived the previous afternoon with its passenger barge in tow. It hadn't brought Zabeth and her dugout. Ferdinand hadn't wanted her to be there. I had told Zabeth this was only because Ferdinand was at the age when he wanted to appear quite independent. And this was true up to a point. The journey to the capital was important to Ferdinand; and, because it was important, he wished to play it down.

He had always seen himself as important. But this was part of the new unsurprised attitude to himself that he had developed. From dugout to a first-class cabin on the steamer, from a forest village to the polytechnic to an administrative cadetship – he had leapt centuries. His passage hadn't always been easy; during the rebellion he had wanted to run away and hide. But he had since learned to accept all sides of himself and all sides of the country;

he rejected nothing. He knew only his country and what it offered; and all that his country offered him he wished now to take as his due. It was like arrogance; but it was also a form of ease and acceptance. He was at home in every setting; he accepted every situation; and he was himself everywhere.

That was what he demonstrated that morning when I picked him up from the Domain to drive him to the dock. The change from the Domain to the shanty settlements outside – with their scattered plantings of maize, their runnels of filth and mounds of sifted rubbish – jarred more on me than on him. I would have preferred, being with him, and thinking of his pride, to ignore them; he spoke about them, not critically, but seeing them as part of his town. At the Domain, saying goodbye to people he knew, he had behaved like the administrative cadet; with me in the car he had been like an old friend; and then outside the dock gates he had become a reasonably happy, and patient, member of an African crowd, taken with the market bustle.

Miscerique probat populos et foedera jungi. I had long since ceased to reflect on the vainglory of the words. The monument had only become part of the market scene on steamer days. Through that crowd we now began to make our way, accompanied by an old man, feebler than either of us, who had taken possession of Ferdinand's suitcases.

Basins of grubs and caterpillars; baskets of trussed-up hens, squawking when they were lifted by one wing by the vendor or a prospective buyer; dull-eyed goats on the bare, scuffed ground, chewing at rubbish and even paper; damp-haired young monkeys, full of misery, tethered tightly around their narrow waists and nibbling at peanuts and banana skin and mango skin, but nibbling without relish, as though they knew that they themsleves were soon to be eaten.

Nervous passengers from the bush, barge passengers, travelling from one far-off village to another, and being seen off by families or friends; the established vendors in their established places (two or three at the foot of the monument), with their box seats, cooking stones, pots and pans, bundles, babies; idlers, cripples, and scroungers. And officials.

There were many more officials nowadays, and most of them appeared to be active in this area on steamer days. Not all of them were in police or army uniform, and not all of them were men. In the name of his dead mother, the hotel maid, 'the woman of Africa', as he called her in his speeches, the President had decided to honour as many women as possible; and he had done so by making them government servants, not always with clear duties.

Ferdinand and myself and the porter made a noticeable group (Ferdinand much taller than the men of the region), and we were stopped about half a dozen times by people who wanted to see our papers. Once we were stopped by a woman in a long African-style cotton dress. She was as small as her sisters who poled the dugouts in village creeks, and fetched and carried; her head was as hairless and looked as shaved; but her face had plumped out. She spoke to us roughly. She held Ferdinand's steamer tickets (one for the fare, one for the food) upside down when she examined them; and she frowned.

Ferdinand's face registered nothing. When she gave him back the tickets he said, 'Thank you, *citoyenne*.' He spoke without irony; the woman's frown was replaced by a smile. And that seemed to have been the main point of the exercise – the woman wanted to be shown respect and to be called *citoyenne*. *Monsieur* and *madame* and *boy* had been officially outlawed; the President had decreed us all to be *citoyens* and *citoyennes*. He used the two words together in his speeches, again and again, like musical phrases.

We moved through the waiting crowd – people made room for us simply because we were moving – to the dock gates. And there our porter, as though knowing what was to follow, dropped his load, asked for a lot of francs, quickly settled for less, and bolted. The gates, for no reason, were closed against us. The soldiers looked at us and then looked away, refusing to enter into the palaver Ferdinand and I tried to get going. For half an hour or more we stood there in the crowd, pressed against the gate, in the stinging sun, in the smell of sweat and smoked food; and then, for no apparent reason, one of the soldiers opened the gate and let us in, but just us, not anyone behind, as though, in spite of Ferdinand's tickets and my own dock pass, he was doing us a great favour.

The steamer was still pointing towards the rapids. The white superstructure, with the first-class cabins, just visible above the customs-shed roof, was at the stern end of the steamer. On the steel-plated deck below, just a few feet above the water, a range of iron-clad barrack-like structures ran all the way to the rounded bow. The iron barracks were for the lesser passengers. And for passengers who were least of all there was the barge – tiers of cages on a shallow iron hull, the cages wire-netted and barred, the wire netting and bars dented and twisted, the internal organization of the cages hidden, lost in gloom, in spite of the sunlight and the glitter of the river.

The first-class cabins still suggested luxury. The iron walls were white; the timbered decks were scrubbed and tarred. The doors were open; there were curtains. There were stewards and even a purser.

I said to Ferdinand, 'I thought those people down there were going to ask you for your certificate of civic merit. In the old days you had to have one before they let you up here.'

He didn't laugh, as an older man might have done. He didn't know about the colonial past. His memories of the larger world began with the mysterious day when mutinous soldiers, strangers, had come to his mother's village looking for white people to kill, and Zabeth had frightened them off, and they had only taken away a few of the village women.

To Ferdinand the colonial past had vanished. The steamer had always been African, and first class on the steamer was what he could see now. Respectably dressed Africans, the older men in suits, the evolved men of an earlier generation; some women with families, everyone dressed up for the journey; one or two of the old ladies of such families, closer to the ways of the forest, already sitting on the floor of their cabins and preparing lunch, breaking the black hulls of smoked fish and smoked monkeys into enamel plates with coloured patterns, and releasing strong, salty smells. Rustic manners, forest manners, in a setting not of the forest.

173

But that was how, in our ancestral lands, we all began – the prayer mat on the sand, then the marble floor of a mosque; the rituals and taboos of nomads, which, transferred to the palace of a sultan or a maharaja, become the traditions of an aristocracy.

Still, I would have found the journey hard, especially if, like Ferdinand, I had to share a cabin with someone else, someone in the crowd outside who had not yet been let in. But the steamer was not meant for me or – in spite of the colonial emblems embroidered in red on the frayed, much laundered sheets and pillowcase on Ferdinand's bunk – for the people who had in the old days required certificates of civic merit, with good reason. The steamer was now meant for the people who used it, and to them it was very grand. The people on Ferdinand's deck knew they were not passengers on the barge.

From the rear end of the deck, looking past the lifeboats, we could see people going aboard the barge with their crates and bundles. Above the roof of the customs sheds the town showed mainly as trees or bush – the town which, when you were in it, was full of streets and open spaces and sun and buildings. Few buildings showed through the trees and none rose above them. And from the height of the first-class deck you could see – from the quality of the vegetation, the change from imported ornamental trees to undifferentiated bush – how quickly the town ended, what a narrow strip of the river bank it occupied. If you looked the other way, across the muddy river to the low line of bush and the emptiness of the other bank, you could pretend that the town didn't exist. And then the barge on this bank was like a miracle, and the cabins of the first-class deck an impossible luxury.

At either end of that deck was something even more impressive – a *cabine de luxe*. That was what the old, paint-spattered metal plates above the doors said. What did these two cabins contain? Ferdinand said, 'Shall we have a look?' We went into the one at the back. It was dark and very hot; the windows were sealed and heavily curtained. A baking bathroom; two armchairs, rather beaten up, and one with an arm missing, but still armchairs; a table with two shaky chairs; sconces with bulbs missing; torn curtains screening off the bunks from the rest of the cabin;

174

and an air-conditioner. Who, in that crowd outside, had such a
ridiculous idea of his needs? Who required such privacy, such
cramping comforts?

From the forward end of the deck came the sound of a disturbance. A man was complaining loudly, and he was complaining
in English.

Ferdinand said, 'I think I hear your friend.'

It was Indar. He was carrying an unusual load, and he was
sweating and full of anger. With his forearms held out at the
horizontal – like the fork of a fork-lift truck – he was supporting
a shallow but very wide cardboard box, open at the top, on which
he could visibly get no grip. The box was heavy. It was full of
groceries and big bottles, ten or twelve bottles; and after the long
walk from the dock gates and up all the steamer steps Indar seemed
to be at the end of all physical resource and on the verge of
tears.

With a backward lean he staggered into the *cabine de luxe*, and
I saw him drop – almost throw – the cardboard box on the bunk.
And then he began to do a little dance of physical agony, stamping
about the cabin and flexing his arms violently from the elbows
down, as though to shake out the ache from all kinds of yelping
muscles.

He was overdoing the display, but he had an audience. Not
me, whom he had seen but was yet in no mood to acknowledge.
Yvette was behind him. She was carrying his briefcase. He
shouted at her, with the security that the English language gave
him here, 'The suitcase – is the bugger bringing the suitcase?'
She looked sweated and strained herself, but she said soothingly,
'Yes, yes.' And a man in a flowered shirt whom I had taken to be
a passenger appeared with the suitcase.

I had seen Indar and Yvette together many times, but never in
such a domestic relationship. For a dislocating moment the
thought came to me that they were going away together. But then
Yvette, straightening up, and remembering to smile, said to me,
'Are you seeing someone off too?' And I understood that my
anxiety was foolish.

Indar was now squeezing his biceps. Whatever he had planned

175

for this moment with Yvette had been destroyed by the pain of
the cardboard box.

He said, 'They had no carrier bags. They had no bloody
carrier bags.'

I said, 'I thought you had taken the plane.'

'We waited for hours at the airport yesterday. It was always
coming and coming. Then at midnight they gave us a beer and
told us that the plane had been taken out of service. Just like that.
Not delayed. Taken away. The Big Man wanted it. And no one
knows when he is going to send it back. And then, buying this
steamer ticket – have you ever done that? There are all kinds of
rules about when they can sell and when they can't sell. The man
is hardly ever there. The damned door is always locked. And every
five yards somebody wants to see your papers. Ferdinand, explain
this to me. When the man was totting up the fare, all the de luxe
supplements, he worked the sum out twenty times on the adding
machine. The same sum, twenty times. Why? Did he think the
machine was going to change its mind? That took half an hour.
And then, thank God, Yvette reminded me about the food. And
the water. So we had to go shopping. Six bottles of Vichy water
for the five days. It was all they had – I've come to Africa to drink
Vichy water. One dollar and fifty cents a bottle, U.S. Six bottles
of red wine, the acid Portuguese stuff you get here. If I had known
I would have to carry it all in that box, I would have done without
it.'

He had also bought five tins of sardines, one for each day of
the journey, I suppose; two tins of evaporated milk; a tin of
Nescafé, a Dutch cheese, some biscuits and a quantity of Belgian
honeycake.

He said, 'The honeycake was Yvette's idea. She says it's full of
nourishment.'

She said, 'It keeps in the heat.'

I said, 'There was a man at the lycée who used to live on
honeycake.'

Ferdinand said, 'That's why we smoke nearly everything. Once
you don't break the crust it lasts a long time.'

'But the food situation in this place is appalling,' Indar said.

'Everything in the shops is imported and expensive. And in the market, apart from the grubs and things that people pick up, all you have are two sticks of this and two ears of that. And people are coming in all the time. How do they make out? You have all this bush, all this rain. And yet there could be a famine in this town.'

The cabin was more crowded than it had been. A squat barefooted man had come in to introduce himself as the steward of the *cabine de luxe*, and after him the purser had come in, with a towel over one shoulder and a folded tablecloth in his hand. The purser shooed away the steward, spread the tablecloth on the table – lovely old material, but mercilessly laundered. Then he addressed Yvette.

'I see that the gentleman has brought his own food and water. But there is no need, madame. We follow the old rules still. Our water is purified. I myself have worked on ocean liners and been to countries all over the world. Now I am old and work on this African steamer. But I am accustomed to white people and know their ways well. The gentleman has nothing to fear, madame. He will be looked after well. I will see that the gentleman's food is prepared separately, and I will serve him with my own hands in his cabin.'

He was a thin, elderly man of mixed race; his mother or father might have been mulatto. He had conscientiously used the forbidden words – *monsieur, madame*; he had spread a tablecloth. And he stood waiting to be rewarded. Indar gave him two hundred francs.

Ferdinand said, 'You've given him too much. He called you *monsieur* and *madame*, and you tipped him. As far as he's concerned his account has been settled. Now he will do nothing for you.'

And Ferdinand seemed to be right. When we went down one deck to the bar, the purser was there, leaning against the counter, drinking beer. He ignored all four of us; and he did nothing for us when we asked for beer and the barman said, '*Terminé.*' If the purser hadn't been drinking, and if another man with three well-dressed women hadn't been drinking at one of the tables, it would have looked convincing. The bar – with a framed photograph of the President in chief's clothes, holding up the carved stick with the fetish – was stripped; the brown shelves were bare.

I said to the barman, '*Citoyen.*' Ferdinand said, '*Citoyen.*' We got a palaver going, and beer was brought from the back room.

Indar said, 'You will have to be my guide, Ferdinand. You will palaver for me.'

It was past noon, and very hot. The bar was full of reflected river light, with dancing veins of gold. The beer, weak as it was, lulled us. Indar forgot his aches and pains; a discussion he started with Ferdinand about the farm at the Domain that the Chinese or Taiwanese had abandoned trailed away. My own nervousness was soothed; my mood was buoyant – I would leave the steamer with Yvette.

The light was the light of the very early afternoon – everything stoked up, the blaze got truly going, but with a hint of the blaze about to consume itself. The river glittered, muddy water turned to white and gold. It was busy with dugouts with outboard motors, as always on steamer days. The dugouts carried the extravagant names of their 'establishments' painted in large letters down their sides. Sometimes, when a dugout crossed a patch of glitter, the occupants were all silhouetted against the glitter; they appeared then to be sitting very low, to be shoulders and round heads alone, so that for a while they were like comic figures in a cartoon strip, engaged on some quite ridiculous journey.

A man teetered into the bar on platform shoes with soles about two inches thick. He must have been from the capital; that style in shoes hadn't reached us as yet. He was also an official, come to check our tickets and passes. Not long after he had teetered out, panic appeared to seize the purser and the barman and some of the men drinking at tables. It was this panic that finally distinguished crew and officials, none of them in uniform, from the other people who had come in and palavered for their beer; and it meant only that the steamer was about to leave.

Indar put his hand on Yvette's thigh. When she turned to him he said gently, 'I'll see what I can find out about Raymond's book. But you know those people in the capital. If they don't reply to your letters, it's because they don't want to reply. They're not going to say yes or no. They're going to say nothing. But I'll see.'

Their embrace, just before we got off, was no more than formal. Ferdinand was cool. No handshake, no words of farewell. He simply said, 'Salim.' And to Yvette he gave a nod rather than a bow.

We stood on the dock and watched. After some manoeuvring the steamer was clear of the dock wall. Then the barge was attached; and steamer and barge did a slow, wide turn in the river, the barge revealing at its stern tiers, slices, of a caged backyard life, a mixture of kitchens and animal pens.

A departure can feel like a desertion, a judgement on the place and people left behind. That was what I had been accustoming myself to since the previous day, when I thought I had said good-bye to Indar. For all my concern for him, I had thought of him – as I had thought of Ferdinand – as the lucky man, the man moving on to richer experience, leaving me to my little life in a place once again of no account.

But I didn't think so now, standing with Yvette on the exposed dock, after the accident and luck of that second goodbye, watching the steamer and barge straighten in the brown river, against the emptiness of the far bank, which was pale in the heat and like part of the white sky. The place where it was all going on after all was where we were, in the town on the river bank. Indar was the man who had been sent away. The hard journey was his.

11

It was past two, a time when, on sunny days, it hurt to be in the open. We had neither of us had anything to eat – we had only had that bloating beer – and Yvette didn't reject the idea of a snack in a cool place.

The asphalt surfacing of the dock area was soft underfoot. Hard black shadows had pulled back to the very edges of buildings, buildings which here on the dock were of the colonial time and substantial – ochre-washed stone walls, green shutters, tall, iron-barred windows, green-painted corrugated-iron roofs. A scratched blackboard outside the closed steamer office still gave the time of the steamer sailing. But the officials had gone; the crowd outside the dock gates had gone. The market around the granite wall of the ruined monument was being dismantled. The feathery leaves of the flamboyant trees made no shade; the sun struck right through. The ground, hummocked around tufts of grass, scuffed to dust elsewhere, was littered with rubbish and animal droppings and patches of wet which, coated and bound on the underside with fine dust, seemed to be curling back on themselves, peeling off the ground.

We didn't go to Mahesh's Bigburger bar. I wanted to avoid the complications – Shoba hadn't approved of Yvette's connection with Indar. We went instead to the Tivoli. It wasn't far away, and I hoped that Mahesh's boy Ildephonse wouldn't report. But that was unlikely; it was the time of day when Ildephonse was normally vacant.

The Tivoli was a new or newish place, part of our continuing boom, and was owned by a family who had run a restaurant in the capital before independence. Now, after some years in Europe, they had come back to try again here. It was a big investment for them – they had skimped on nothing – and I thought they were taking a chance. But I didn't know about Europeans and their restaurant habits. And the Tivoli was meant for our Europeans. It was a family restaurant, and it served the short-contract men who were working on various government projects in our region – the Domain, the airport, the water supply system, the hydro-electric station. The atmosphere was European; Africans kept away. There were no officials with gold watches and gold pen and pencil sets, as at Mahesh's. While you were at the Tivoli you could live without that tension.

But you couldn't forget where you were. The photograph of the President was about three feet high. The official portraits of the President in African garb were getting bigger and bigger, the quality of the prints finer (they were said to be done in Europe). And once you knew about the meaning of the leopard skin and the symbolism of what was carved on the stick, you were affected; you couldn't help it. We had all become his people; even here at the Tivoli we were reminded that we all in various ways depended on him.

Normally the boys – or citizen waiters – were friendly and welcoming and brisk. But the lunch period was more or less over; the tall, fat son of the family who stood behind the counter by the coffee machine, superintending things, was probably having his siesta; no other member of the family was present; and the waiters stood about idly, like aliens in their blue waiter's jackets. They weren't rude; they were simply abstracted, like people who had lost a role.

The air-conditioning was welcome, though, and the absence of glare, and the dryness after the humidity outside. Yvette looked less harassed; energy returned to her. We got the attention of a waiter. He brought us a jug of red Portuguese wine, chilled down and then allowed to lose its chill; and two wooden platters with Scottish smoked salmon on toast. Everything was imported; everything was expensive; smoked salmon on toast was in fact the Tivoli's plainest offering.

I said to Yvette, 'Indar's a bit of an actor. Were things really as bad as he said?'

'They were much worse. He left out cashing the traveller's cheques.'

She was sitting with her back to the wall. She made a small arresting gesture – like Raymond's – with the palm of her hand against the edge of the table, and gave a slight tilt of her head to her right.

Two tables away a family of five were finishing lunch and talking loudly. Ordinary people, the kind of family group I had been used to seeing at the Tivoli. But Yvette seemed to disapprove, and more than disapprove; a little rage visited her.

She said, 'You can't tell about them. I can.'

And yet that face, of rage, still seemed close to a smile; and those slanting eyes, half closed above the small cup of coffee which she was holding at the level of her mouth, were quite demure. What had irritated her about the family group? The district she had judged them to come from? The job the man did, the language, the loud talk, the manners? What would she have said about the people in our night clubs?

I said, 'Did you know Indar before?'

'I met him here.' She put the cup down. Her slanting eyes considered it and then, as though she had decided on something, she looked at me. 'You live your life. A stranger appears. He is an encumbrance. You don't need him. But the encumbrance can become a habit.'

My experience of women outside my family was special, limited. I had had no experience of dealing with a woman like this, no experience of language like this, no experience of a woman with such irritations and convictions. And in what she had just said I saw an honesty, a daringness which, to a man of my background, was slightly frightening and, for that reason, bewitching.

I was unwilling for us to have Indar in common, as Indar and she seemed to have had Raymond in common. I said, 'I can't tell you how much I liked being in your house that evening. I've never forgotten the blouse you wore. I've always been hoping to see you in it again. Black silk, beautifully cut and embroidered.'

I couldn't have touched a better subject. She said, 'There hasn't been the occasion. But I assure you it's still there.'

'I don't think it was Indian. The cut and the work were European.'

'It's from Copenhagen. Margit Brandt. Raymond went there for a conference.'

And at the door of the Tivoli, before we went out again into the heat and the light, during that moment of pause which in the tropics is like the pause we make before we finally go out into the rain, she said to me, as though it were an afterthought, 'Would you like to come to lunch at the house tomorrow? We have to have one of the lecturers, and Raymond finds that kind of occasion very trying these days.'

The steamer would have been about fifteen miles down river. It would have been travelling through bush; it would have passed the first bush settlement. There, though the town was so close, they would have been waiting for the steamer since morning, and there would have been the atmosphere of a fair until the steamer passed. Boys would have dived off dugouts and swum towards the moving steamer and barge, trying to get the attention of passengers. Trading dugouts, poling out from their stations on the bank with their little cargoes of pineapples and roughly made chairs and stools (disposable furniture for the river journey, a speciality of the area), would have been attached in clusters to the sides of the steamer; and these dugouts would be taken – were being taken – miles down river, to paddle back for hours, after that brief excitement, through the fading afternoon, dusk, and night, in silence.

Yvette had cancelled the lunch. But she hadn't let me know. The white-jacketed servant led me to a room which obviously awaited no visitors and was not at all like the room I remembered. The African mats were on the floor, but some of the upholstered chairs that had been taken away for that evening (and, as I remembered Yvette saying, stored in a bedroom), had been brought out again – fringed imitation velvet, in the 'old bronze' colour that was everywhere in the Domain.

The buildings of the Domain had been run up fast, and the

flaws that lamplight had hidden were noticeable in the midday brightness. The plaster on the walls had cracked in many places, and in one place the cracks followed the stepped pattern of the hollow clay bricks below. The windows and doorways, without architraves or wooden facings, were like holes unevenly cut out of the masonry. The ceiling panels, compressed cardboard of some sort, bellied here and there. One of the two air-conditioners in the room had leaked down the wall; they were not on. The windows were open; with no projecting roof, no trees outside, just the levelled land, the room was full of light and glare and there was no feeling of shelter. What fantasies I had built around this room, around the music that had come out of the record player – there, against the wall next to the bookcase, with its smoked perspex cover showing dust in the bright light!

To see the room like this, as Yvette lived in it every day, to add my knowledge of Raymond's position in the country, was to catch her unawares and get some idea of her housewifely ordinariness, some idea of the tensions and dissatisfactions of her life at the Domain, which had until then seemed so glamorous to me. It was to fear to be entangled with her and this life of hers; and it was to be surprised and relieved at the disappearance of my fantasies. But relief and fear lasted only until she came in. The surprise then, as always for me, was herself.

She was more amused than apologetic. She had forgotten, but she knew there was something she had had to remember about that lunch. There had been so many changes of plan about that lunch – which was in fact taking place in the staff-room of the polytechnic. She went away to make us some scrambled South African eggs. The servant came in to clear some receipts from the oval table, which was dark and highly polished, and to lay the table. 'You live your life. A stranger appears. He is an encumbrance.'

On the upper shelf of the bookcase I saw the book Indar had shown me that evening in which there was a mention of Raymond and Yvette as generous hosts at one time in the capital – a mention which had mattered to Yvette. The bright light and the altered room seemed to make it a different book. Colour had faded from the backs of books. One book I took out carried Raymond's sig-

nature and the date, 1937 – a note of ownership, but also perhaps
at that date a statement of intent, Raymond's expression of faith
in his own future. That book felt very tarnished now, with the
paper brown at the edges, the red letters on the paper spine almost
bleached away – something dead, a relic. Another, newer book
carried Yvette's signature with her unmarried name – very stylish
that Continental handwriting, with a fancy *Y*, and speaking in
much the same way as Raymond's signature of twenty-three years
before.

I said to Yvette while we were eating the scrambled eggs, 'I
would like to read something by Raymond. Indar says he knows
more about the country than any man living. Has he published
any books?'

'He's working on this book, and has been for some years now.
The government were going to publish it, but now apparently
there are difficulties.'

'So there are no books.'

'There's his thesis. That's been published as a book. But I
can't recommend it. I couldn't bear to read it. When I told
Raymond that, he said he could scarcely bear to write it. There are
a few articles in various journals. He hasn't had time for many of
those. He's spent all his time on that big book about the history
of the country.'

'Is it true that the President has read parts of that book?'

'That used to be said.'

But she couldn't tell me what the difficulties now were. All I
learned was that Raymond had temporarily put aside his history to
work on a selection of the President's speeches. Our lunch began
to feel sad. Understanding Yvette's position in the Domain now,
knowing that the stories I had heard about Raymond would have
been heard by others, I began to feel that the house must have
been like a prison to her. And that evening when she gave a party
and wore her Margit Brandt blouse began to appear like an
aberration.

I said, as I was getting ready to leave, 'You must come with me
to the Hellenic Club one afternoon. You must come tomorrow.
The people there are people who have been here a long time.

They've seen it all. The last thing they want to talk about is the situation of the country.'

She agreed. But then she said, 'You mustn't forget them.'

I had no idea what she was talking about. She left the room, going through the door that Raymond had gone through after he had made his exit speech that evening; and she came back with a number of magazines, *Cahiers* of this and that, some of them printed by the government printery in the capital. They were magazines with articles by Raymond. Already, then, we had Raymond in common; it was like a beginning.

The rough-bladed grass of the lawns or open areas of this part of the Domain was high; it almost buried the low-level lights housed in mushroom-like aluminium structures that lined the asphalted avenues. A number of those lights had been smashed, some a long time ago; but there seemed to be no one to mend them. On the other side of the Domain the land for the model farm had become overgrown; all that remained of the project was the Chinese gateway that the now absent Taiwanese or Chinese had built, and the six tractors standing in a line and rotting. But the area where the public walked on Sundays, following a fixed one-way route – watched now by the Youth Guard and not the army – was maintained. New statues were still added from time to time to this public walk. The most recent, at the end of the main avenue, was a bulky sculpture in stone, unfinished-looking, of a mother and child.

Nazruddin's old words came to me. 'This is nothing. This is just bush.' But my alarm wasn't like Nazruddin's. It had nothing to do with my business prospects. I saw the empty spaces of the Domain, and the squatters from the villages camping just outside; and my thoughts were of Yvette and her life on the Domain. Not Europe in Africa, as it had seemed to me, when Indar was there. Only a life in the bush. And my fear was at once the fear of failing with her, being left with nothing, and the fear of the consequences of success.

But that alarm vanished the next afternoon when she came to the flat. She had been there before with Indar; in that setting, my own, she had for me a good deal of her old glamour. She had seen the ping-pong table with my household junk and with one corner left clear for Metty's ironing. She had seen the paintings of European ports that the Belgian lady had bequeathed me with the white studio-sitting-room.

It was against this white wall that, after some talk about the paintings and the Hellenic Club, both of us standing, she showed me her profile, turning away when I drew close, not rejecting me or encouraging me, just seeming weary, accepting a new encumbrance. That moment – as I read it – was the key to all that followed. The challenge that I saw then was what I always saw; it was the challenge to which I never failed to respond.

Until then my fantasies were brothel fantasies of conquest and degradation, with the woman as the willing victim, the accomplice in her own degradation. It was all that I knew. It was all that I had learned from the brothels and night clubs of our town. It had been no hardship to me to give these places up while Indar was around. I had grown to find those occasions of vice enervating. For some time, in fact, though it still excited me to see these women in groups in a bar or a brothel front room, I had shrunk from true sex with bought women, and restricted myself to subsidiary sexual satisfactions. Familiarity of this kind with so many women had bred something like contempt for what they offered; and at the same time, like many men who use brothels alone, I had grown to think of myself as feeble, critically disadvantaged. My obsession with Yvette had taken me by surprise; and the adventure with her (unbought but willing) that began in the white sitting room was for me quite new.

What I have called my brothel fantasies hurried me through the initial awkwardness. But in the bedroom with the very large bed with the foam mattress – at last serving the purpose for which I was certain the Belgian lady painter had intended it – in the bedroom those fantasies altered. The self-regard of those fantasies dropped away.

Women make up half the world; and I thought I had reached the stage where there was nothing in a woman's nakedness to surprise me. But I felt now as if I was experiencing anew, and seeing a woman for the first time. I was amazed that, obsessed with

Yvette as I had been, I had taken so much for granted. The body on the bed was to me like the revelation of woman's form. I wondered that clothes, even the apparently revealing tropical clothes I had seen on Yvette, should have concealed so much, should have broken the body up, as it were, into separate parts and not really hinted at the splendour of the whole.

To write about the occasion in the manner of my pornographic magazines would be more than false. It would be like trying to take photographs of myself, to be the voyeur of my own actions, to reconvert the occasion into the brothel fantasy that, in the bedroom, it ceased to be.

I was overwhelmed, but alert. I did not wish to lose myself in the self-regard and self-absorption of that fantasy, the blindness of that fantasy. The wish that came to me – consuming the anxiety about letting myself down – was the wish to win the possessor of that body, the body which, because I wished to win its possessor, I saw as perfect, and wanted continuously, during the act itself, to see, holding myself in ways that enabled me to do so, avoiding crushing the body with my own, avoiding that obliteration of sight and touch. All my energy and mind were devoted to that new end of winning the person. All my satisfactions lay in that direction; and the sexual act became for me an extraordinary novelty, a new kind of fulfilment, continuously new.

How often before, at such moments, moments allegedly of triumph, boredom had fallen on me! But as a means of winning, rather than the triumph in itself, the present act required constant alertness, a constant looking outward from myself. It wasn't tender, though it expressed a great need for tenderness. It became a brute physical act, an act almost of labour; and as it developed it became full of deliberate brutality. This surprised me. But I was altogether surprised by my new self, which was as far from the brothel man I had taken myself to be, with all his impulses to feebleness, as this act was from the brothel act of surrender, which was all I had so far known.

Yvette said, 'This hasn't happened to me for years.' That statement, if it were true, would have been a sufficient reward; my own climax was not important to me. If what she said were true! But

I had no means of gauging her response. She was the experienced one, I was the beginner.

And there was a further surprise. No fatigue, no drowsiness overcame me at the end. On the contrary. In that room with the window panes painted white, a white that now glowed with the late afternoon light, in that heated room, at the end of one of our heavy, hot days, sweating as I was, with a body slippery with sweat, I was full of energy. I could have gone and played squash at the Hellenic Club. I felt refreshed, revitalized; my skin felt new. I was full of the wonder of what had befallen me. And awakening from minute to minute to the depth of my satisfactions, I began to be aware of my immense previous deprivation. It was like discovering a great, unappeasable hunger in myself.

Yvette, naked, wet, unembarrassed, her hair lank, but already herself again, her flush gone, her eyes calm, sat with crossed legs on the edge of the bed and telephoned. She spoke in patois. It was to her house servant: she was coming home right away: he was to tell Raymond. She dressed and made up the bed. This housewifely attention reminded me – painfully, already – of attentions like this that she gave elsewhere.

Just before she left the bedroom she stooped and kissed me briefly on the front of my trousers. And then it was over – the corridor, Metty's dreadful kitchen, the landing, the yellowing afternoon light, the trees of back yards, the dust in the air, the cooking smoke, the active world, and the sound of Yvette's feet pattering down the external staircase. That gesture, of kissing my trousers, which elsewhere I would have dismissed as a brothel courtesy, the gesture of an overtipped whore, now moved me to sadness and doubt. Was it meant? Was it true?

I thought of going to the Hellenic Club, to use up the energy that had come to me, and to sweat a little more. But I didn't go. I wandered about the flat, letting the time pass. The light began to fade; and a stillness fell over me. I felt blessed and remade; I wanted to be alone for a while with that sensation.

Later, thinking of dinner, I drove out to the night club near the dam. It was doing better than ever now, with the boom and the expatriates. But the structure hadn't been added to and still had a temporary look, the look of a place that could be surrendered without too much loss – just four brick walls, more or less, around a cleared space in the bush.

I sat outside at one of the tables under the trees on the cliff and looked at the floodlit dam; and until someone noticed me and turned on the coloured bulbs strung about the trees, I sat in the darkness, feeling the newness of my skin. Cars came and parked. There were the French accents of Europe and Africa. African women, in twos and threes, came up in taxis from the town. Turbanned, lazy, erect, talking loudly, they dragged their slippers over the bare ground. It was the other side of the expatriate family scene that had offended Yvette at the Tivoli. To me it all felt far away – the night club, the town, the squatters, the expatriates, 'the situation of the country'; everything had just become background.

The town, when I drove back, had settled down to its own night life. At night now, in the increasingly crowded main streets, there was the atmosphere of the village, with unsteady groups around the little drinking stalls in the shanty areas, the cooking fires on the pavements, the barring off of sleeping places, the lunatic or drunken old men in rags, ready to snarl like dogs, taking their food to dark corners, to eat out of the sight of others. The windows of some shops – especially clothing shops, with their expensive imported goods – were brightly lit, as a precaution against theft.

In the square not far from the flat a young woman was bawling – a real African bawl. She was being hustled along the pavement by two men, each one twisting an arm. But no one in the square did anything. The men were of our Youth Guard. The officers got a small stipend from the Big Man, and they had been given a couple of government jeeps. But, like the officials at the docks, they really had to look for things to do. This was their new 'Morals Patrol'. It was the opposite of what it said. The girl would have been picked up from some bar; she had probably answered back or refused to pay.

In the flat I saw that Metty's light was on. I said, 'Metty?' He said through the door, '*Patron*.' He had stopped calling me

Salim; we had seen little of one another outside the shop for some time. I thought there was sadness in his voice; and going on to my own room, considering my own luck, I thought: 'Poor Metty. How will it end for him? So friendly, and yet in the end always without friends. He should have stayed on the coast. He had his place there. He had people like himself. Here he is lost.'

Yvette telephoned me at the shop late the next morning. It was our first telephone call, but she didn't speak my name or give her own. She said, 'Will you be at the flat for lunch?' I seldom had lunch at the flat during the week, but I said, 'Yes.' She said, 'I'll see you there.' And that was all.

She had allowed no pause, no silence, had given me no time for surprise. And indeed, waiting for her in the white sitting room just after twelve, standing at the ping-pong table, turning over a magazine, I felt no surprise. I felt the occasion – for all its unusualness, the oddity of the hour, the killing brightness of the light – to be only a continuation of something I had long been living with.

I heard her hurry up the steps she had pattered down the previous afternoon. Out of every kind of nervousness I didn't move. The landing door was open, the sitting-room door was open – her steps were brisk and didn't falter. I was utterly delighted to see her; that was an immense relief. There was still briskness in her manner; but though her face seemed set for it, she wore no smile. Her eyes were serious, with a disturbing, challenging hint of greed.

She said, 'I've been thinking of you all morning. I haven't been able to get you out of my head.' And as though she had entered the sitting room only to leave it, as though her arrival at the flat was a continuation of the directness of her telephone call, and she wanted to give neither of us time for words, she went into the bedroom and began to undress.

It was as before with me. Confronted with her, I shed old fantasies. My body obeyed its new impulses, discovered in itself resources that answered my new need. New – it was the word. It was always new, familiar though the body and its responses

191

became, and as physical as the act was, requiring such roughness, control and subtlety. At the end (which I willed, as I had willed all that had gone before), energized, revivified, I felt I had been taken far beyond the wonder of the previous afternoon.

I had closed the shop at twelve. I got back just after three. I hadn't had any lunch. That would have delayed me further, and Friday was a big day for trade. I found the shop closed. Metty hadn't opened up at one, as I had expected him to. Barely an hour of trade remained, and many of the retailers from the outlying villages would have done their shopping and started back on the long journey home by dugout or truck. The last pickup vans in the square, which left when they had a load, were more or less loaded.

I had my first alarm about myself, the beginning of the decay of the man I had known myself to be. I had visions of beggary and decrepitude: the man not of Africa lost in Africa, no longer with strength or purpose to hold his own, and with less claim to anything than the ragged, half-starved old drunks from the villages who wandered about the square, eyeing the food stalls, cadging mouthfuls of beer, and the young trouble-makers from the shanty towns, a new breed, who wore shirts stamped with the Big Man's picture and talked about foreigners and profit and, wanting only money (like Ferdinand and his friends at the lycée in the old days), came into shops and bargained aggressively for goods they didn't want, insisting on the cost price.

From this alarm about myself – exaggerated, because it was the first – I moved to a feeling of rage against Metty, for whom the previous night I had felt such compassion. Then I remembered. It wasn't Metty's fault. He was at the customs, clearing the goods that had arrived by the steamer that had taken Indar and Ferdinand away, the steamer that was still one day's sailing from the capital.

For two days, since my scrambled-eggs lunch with Yvette at her house in the Domain, the magazines with Raymond's articles had lain in the drawer of my desk. I hadn't looked at them. I did so now, reminded of them by thoughts of the steamer.

When I had asked Yvette to see something Raymond had
written, it was only as a means of approaching her. Now there was
no longer that need; and it was just as well. The articles by
Raymond in the local magazines looked particularly difficult. One
was a review of an American book about African inheritance laws.
The other, quite long, with footnotes and tables, seemed to be a
ward-by-ward analysis of tribal voting patterns in the local council
elections in the big mining town in the south just before independence; some of the names of the smaller tribes I hadn't even
heard of.

The earlier articles, in the foreign magazines, seemed easier.
'Riot at a Football Match', in an American magazine, was about a
race riot in the capital in the 1930s that had led to the formation
of the first African political club. 'Lost Liberties', in a Belgian
magazine, was about the failure of a missionary scheme, in the late
nineteenth century, to buy picked slaves from the Arab slave
caravans and resettle them in 'liberty villages'.

These articles were a little more in my line – I was especially
interested in the missionaries and the slaves. But the bright opening paragraphs were deceptive; the articles weren't exactly shop-
time, afternoon reading. I put them aside for later. And that
evening, as I read in the large bed which Yvette a few hours earlier
had made up, and where her smell still lingered, I was appalled.

The article about the race riot – after that bright opening para-
graph which I had read in the shop – turned out to be a compila-
tion of government decrees and quotations from newspapers.
There was a lot from the newspapers; Raymond seemed to have
taken them very seriously. I couldn't get over that, because from
my experience on the coast I knew that newspapers in small
colonial places told a special kind of truth. They didn't lie, but
they were formal. They handled big people – businessmen, high
officials, members of our legislative and executive councils – with
respect. They left out a lot of important things – often essential
things – that local people would know and gossip about.

I didn't think that the papers here in the 1930s would have
been much different from ours on the coast; and I was always
hoping that Raymond was going to go behind the newspaper

stories and editorials and try to get at the real events. A race riot in the capital in the 1930s – that ought to have been a strong story: gun-talk in the European cafés and clubs, hysteria and terror in the African *cités*. But Raymond wasn't interested in that side. He didn't give the impression that he had talked to any of the people involved, though many would have been alive when he wrote. He stuck with the newspapers; he seemed to want to show that he had read them all and had worked out the precise political shade of each. His subject was an event in Africa, but he might have been writing about Europe or a place he had never been.

The article about the missionaries and the ransomed slaves was also full of quotations, not from newspapers, but from the mission's archives in Europe. The subject wasn't new to me. At school on the coast we were taught about European expansion in our area as though it had been no more than a defeat of the Arabs and their slave-trading ways. We thought of that as English-school stuff; we didn't mind. History was something dead and gone, part of the world of our grandfathers, and we didn't pay too much attention to it; even though, among trading families like ours, there were still vague stories – so vague that they didn't feel real – of European priests buying slaves cheap from the caravans before they got to the depots on the coast. The Africans (and this was the point of the stories) had been scared out of their skins – they thought the missionaries were buying them in order to eat them.

I had no idea, until I read Raymond's article, that the venture had been so big and serious. Raymond gave the names of all the liberty villages that had been established. Then, quoting and quoting from letters and reports in the archives, he tried to fix the date of the disappearance of each. He gave no reasons and looked for none; he just quoted from the missionary reports. He didn't seem to have gone to any of the places he wrote about; he hadn't tried to talk to anybody. Yet five minutes' talk with someone like Metty – who, in spite of his coast experience, had travelled in terror across the strangeness of the continent – would have told Raymond that the whole pious scheme was cruel and very ignorant, that to set a few unprotected people down in strange territory was to expose them to attack and kidnap and worse. But Raymond didn't seem to know.

Yet he knew so much, had researched so much. He must have spent weeks on each article. Yet he had less true knowledge of Africa, less feel for it, than Indar or Nazruddin or even Mahesh; he had nothing like Father Huismans's instinct for the strangeness and wonder of the place. Yet he had made Africa his subject. He had devoted years to those boxes of documents in his study that I had heard about from Indar. Perhaps he had made Africa his subject because he had come to Africa and because he was a scholar, used to working with papers, and had found this place full of new papers.

He had been a teacher in the capital. Chance – in early middle age – had brought him into touch with the mother of the future President. Chance – and something of the teacher's sympathy for the despairing African boy, a sympathy probably mixed with a little bitterness about the more successful of his own kind: the man perhaps seeing himself in the boy: that advice he had given the boy about joining the Defence Force appeared to have in it something of a personal bitterness – chance had given him that extraordinary relationship with the man who became President and had raised him, after independence, to a glory he had never dreamed of.

To Yvette, inexperienced, from Europe, and with her own ambitions, he must have glittered. She would have been misled by her ambitions, much as I had been by her setting, in which I had seen such glamour. Really, then, we did have Raymond in common, from the start.

The Big Man

12

I OFTEN thought about the chance that had shown me Yvette for the first time that evening in her house, in that atmosphere of Europe in Africa, when she had worn her black Margit Brandt blouse and had been lighted by the reading lamps placed on the floor, and every kind of yearning had been stirred in me by the voice of Joan Baez.

Perhaps in another setting and at another time she would not have made such an impression on me. And perhaps if I had read Raymond's articles on the day Yvette had given them to me, nothing would have happened the following afternoon when she came to the flat. I wouldn't have given her cause to show me her profile against the white wall of the studio-sitting-room; we might instead have simply gone to the Hellenic Club. Seeing her house in the light of midday had already given me a little alarm. To have understood more about Raymond immediately after might have made me see her more clearly – her ambition, her bad judgement, her failure.

And failure like that wasn't what I would have chosen to be entangled with. My wish for an adventure with Yvette was a wish to be taken up to the skies, to be removed from the life I had – the dullness, the pointless tension, 'the situation of the country'. It wasn't a wish to be involved with people as trapped as myself.

But that was what I had now. And it wasn't open to me to withdraw. After that first afternoon, my first discovery of her, I was possessed by Yvette, possessed by that person I never stopped wanting to win. Satisfaction solved nothing; it only opened up a new void, a fresh need.

The town changed for me. It had new associations. Different memories and moods attached to places, to times of day, weather. In the drawer of my desk in the shop, where Raymond's magazines had once lain forgotten for two days, there were now photographs of Yvette. Some of them were quite old and must have been precious to her. These photographs were her gifts to me, made at various times, as favours, rewards, gestures of tenderness; since, just as we never embraced when we met, never wasted the sense of touch (and in fact seldom kissed), so, as if by unspoken agreement, we continued as we had begun and never exchanged words of tenderness. In spite of the corrupt physical ways our passion had begun to take, the photographs of Yvette that I preferred were the chastest. I was especially interested in those of her as a girl in Belgium, to whom the future was still a mystery.

With these photographs in my drawer, the view from my shop had a different feel: the square with the bedraggled trees, the market stalls, the wandering villagers, the unpaved roads dusty in the sun or running red in the rain. The broken-down town, in which I had felt neutered, became the place where it had all come to me.

With that I developed a new kind of political concern, almost a political anxiety. I could have done without that, but it couldn't be helped. Through Yvette I was bound to Raymond, and through Raymond I was bound more closely than ever to the fact or the knowledge of the President's power. Seeing the President's photograph everywhere had already made me feel that, whether African or not, we had all become his people. To that was now added, because of Raymond, the feeling that we were all dependent on the President and that – whatever job we did and however much we thought we were working for ourselves – we all were serving him.

For that brief moment when I had believed Raymond to be as Indar had described him – the Big Man's white man – I had been thrilled to feel so close to the highest power in the land. I felt I had been taken far above the country I knew and its everyday worries –

the mountainous rubbish dumps, bad roads, tricky officials, shanty towns, the people coming in every day from the bush and finding nothing to do and little to eat, the drunkenness, the quick murders, my own shop. Power, and the life around the President in the capital, had seemed to be what was real and essential about the country.

When I understood what Raymond's position was, the President had once again appeared to zoom away and to be high above us. But now there remained a link with him: the sense of his power as a personal thing, to which we were all attached as with strings, which he might pull or let dangle. That was something I had never felt before. Like other expatriates in the town, I had done what was expected of me. We hung up the official photographs in our shops and offices; we subscribed to the various Presidential funds. But we tried to keep all that as background, separate from our private lives. At the Hellenic Club, for instance, though there was no rule about it, we never talked of local politics.

But now, taken deep into the politics through Raymond and Yvette, and understanding the intent behind each new official photograph, each new statue of the African madonna with child, I could no longer consider statues and photographs as background. I might be told that thousands were owed in Europe to the printers of those photographs; but to understand the President's purpose was to be affected by it. The visitor might snigger about the African madonna; I couldn't.

The news about Raymond's book, the history, was bad – there was no news. Indar, in spite of his promise to find out about the book (and that farewell hand on Yvette's thigh on the steamer) hadn't written. It didn't console Yvette to hear that he hadn't written me either, that he was a man with big problems of his own. It wasn't Indar she was worried about; she wanted news, and long after Indar had left the country she continued to wait for some word from the capital.

Raymond in the meantime had finished his work on the President's speeches and had gone back to his history. He was good at hiding his disappointments and strains. But they were reflected in Yvette. Sometimes when she came to the flat she looked years older than she was, with her young skin looking bleached, the flesh below her chin sagging into the beginning of a double chin, the little wrinkles about her eyes more noticeable.

Poor girl! It wasn't at all what she had expected from a life with Raymond. She was a student in Europe when they had met. He had gone there with an official delegation. His role as the adviser of the man who had recently made himself President was supposed to be secret, but his eminence was generally known and he had been invited to lecture at the university where Yvette was. She had asked a question – she was writing a thesis about the theme of slavery in French African writing. They had met afterwards; she had been overwhelmed by his attentions. Raymond had been married before; but there had been a divorce some years before independence, while he was still a teacher, and his wife and daughter had gone back to Europe.

'They say that men should look at the mother of the girl they intend to marry,' Yvette said. 'Girls who do what I did should consider the wife a man has discarded or worn out, and know they are not going to do much better. But can you imagine? This handsome and distinguished man – when Raymond took me out to dinner for the first time he took me to one of the most expensive places. He did it all in a very absent-minded way. But he knew the kind of family I came from and he knew exactly what he was doing. He spent more on that dinner than my father earned in a week. I knew it was delegation money, but it didn't matter. Women are stupid. But if women weren't stupid the world wouldn't go round.

'It was wonderful when we came out, I must say that. The President invited us to dinner regularly and for the first two or three times I sat on his right. He said he could do no less for the wife of his old *professeur* – but that wasn't true: Raymond never taught him: that was just for the European press. He was extraordinarily charming, the President, and there was never any hint of nonsense, I should add. The first time we talked about the table, literally. It was made of local wood and carved with African motifs at the edge. Rather horribly, if you want to know. He said the Africans had prodigious skills as wood-carvers and that the country could supply the whole world with high-quality furniture. It was like the recent talk about an industrial park along the river – it was just an idea to talk about. But I was new then and I wanted to believe everything I was told.

'Always there were the cameras. Always the cameras, even in those early days. He was always posing for them – you knew that, and it made conversation difficult. He never relaxed. He always led the conversation. He never let you start a new topic; he simply turned away. The etiquette of royalty – he had learned it from somebody, and I learned it from him, the hard way. He had this very abrupt way of turning away from you; it was like a piece of personal style. And he seemed to enjoy the stylishness of turning and walking straight out of a room at the appointed time.

'We used to go out on tours with him. We appeared in the background in a few of the old official pictures – white people in the background. I noticed that his clothes were changing, but I thought it was only his way of wearing more comfortable clothes, African-style country clothes. Everywhere we went there used to be these welcoming *séances d'animation*, tribal dancing. He was very keen on that. He said he wanted to give dignity to those dances that Hollywood and the West had maligned. He intended to build modern theatres for them. And it was during one of those animations that I got into trouble. He had put his stick on the ground. I didn't know that had a meaning. I didn't know I had to shut up, that in the old days of the chiefs to talk when that stick was down was something you could be beaten to death for. I was close to him and I said something perfectly banal about the skill of the dancers. He just curled his lips in anger and looked away, lifting up his head. There wasn't any stylishness in that. All the Africans were horrified at what I had done. And I felt that the make-believe had turned horrible and that I had come to a horrible place.

'After that I couldn't appear with him in public. But of course that wasn't why he broke with Raymond. In fact, he was friendlier than ever with Raymond afterwards. He broke with Raymond when he decided that he didn't need him, that in the new direction he was taking the white man was an embarrassment to him in the capital. As for me, he never spoke to me. But he always made a point of sending me his regards, of having some official come to ask how I was getting on. He needs a model in everything, and I believe he heard that de Gaulle used to send personal regards to the wives of his political enemies.

'That was why I thought that if Indar made some inquiries about Raymond's book in the capital, it would get back to him. Everything gets back to the President here. The place is a one-man show, as you know. And I was expecting to get some indirect word. But in all these months he hasn't even sent me his regards.'

She suffered more than Raymond appeared to. She was in a country that was still strange to her and she was dangling, doubly dependent. Raymond was in a place that had become his home. He was in a situation that he had perhaps lived through before, when he was a neglected teacher in the colonial capital. Perhaps he had returned to his older personality, the self-containedness he had arrived at as a teacher, the man with the quiet but defiant knowledge of his own worth. But I felt there was something else. I felt that Raymond was consciously following a code he had prescribed for himself, and the fact that he was following this code gave him his serenity.

This code forbade him expressing disappointment or envy. In this he was different from the young men who continued to come to the Domain and called on him and listened to him – Raymond still had his big job. He still had those boxes of papers that many people wanted to look through; and after all his years as the Big Man's white man, all those years as the man who knew more about the country than any man living, Raymond still had a reputation.

When one of these visitors spoke critically about somebody's book or a conference that somebody had organized somewhere (Raymond wasn't invited to conferences these days), Raymond would say nothing, unless he had something good to say about the book or the conference. He would look steadily at the eyes of the visitor, as though only waiting for him to finish. I saw him do this many times; he gave the impression then of hearing out an interruption. Yvette's face would register the surprise or the hurt.

As it did on the evening when I understood, from something one of our visitors said, that Raymond had applied for a job in the United States and had been rejected. The visitor, a bearded man with mean and unreliable eyes, was speaking like a man on Raymond's side. He was even trying to be a little bitter on Raymond's behalf, and this made me feel that he might be one of those visiting scholars Yvette told me about, who, while they were going through Raymond's papers, also took the opportunity of making a pass at her.

Times had changed since the early 1960s, the bearded man said. Africanists were not so rare now, and people who had given their life to the continent were being passed over. The great powers had agreed for the time being not to wrangle over Africa, and as a result attitudes to Africa had changed. The very people who had said that the decade was the decade of Africa, and had scrambled after its great men, were now giving up on Africa.

Yvette lifted her wrist and looked carefully at her watch. It was like a deliberate interruption. She said, 'The decade of Africa finished ten seconds ago.'

She had done that once before, when someone had spoken of the decade of Africa. And the trick worked again. She smiled; Raymond and I laughed. The bearded man took the hint, and the subject of Raymond's rejected application was left alone.

But I was dismayed by what I had heard, and when Yvette next came to the flat I said, 'But you didn't tell me you were thinking of leaving.'

'Aren't you thinking of leaving?'

'Eventually, yes.'

'Eventually we all have to leave. Your life is settled. You're practically engaged to that man's daughter, you've told me. Everything is just waiting for you. My life is still fluid. I must do something. I just can't stay here.'

'But why didn't you tell me?'

'Why talk of something you know isn't going to come off? And it wouldn't do us any good if it got around. You know that. Raymond doesn't stand a chance abroad now anyway.'

'Why did he apply then?'

'I made him. I thought there was a possibility. Raymond wouldn't do a thing like that by himself. He's loyal.'

The closeness to the President that had given Raymond his reputation, that had made people call him out to conferences in different parts of the world, now disqualified him from serious consideration abroad. Unless something extraordinary happened he would have to stay where he was, dependent on the power of the President.

His position in the Domain required him to display authority. But at any moment he might be stripped of this authority, reduced to nothing, with nothing to fall back on. In his place I don't think I would have been able to pretend to have any authority – that would have been the hardest thing for me. I would have just given up, understanding the truth of what Mahesh had told me years before: 'Remember, Salim, the people here are *malins*.'

But Raymond showed no uncertainty. And he was loyal – to the President, to himself, his ideas and his work, his past. My admiration for him grew. I studied the President's speeches – the daily newspapers were flown up from the capital – for signs that Raymond might be called back to favour. And if I became Raymond's encourager, after Yvette, if I became his champion and promoted him even at the Hellenic Club as the man who hadn't published much but really *knew*, the man every intelligent visitor ought to see, it wasn't only because I didn't want to see him go away, and Yvette with him. I didn't want to see him humiliated. I admired his code and wished that when my own time came I might be able to stick to something like it.

Life in our town was arbitrary enough. Yvette, seeing my life as settled, with everything waiting for me somewhere, had seen her own life as fluid. She felt she wasn't as prepared as the rest of us; she had to look out for herself. That was how we all felt, though: we saw our own lives as fluid, we saw the other man or person as solider. But in the town, where all was arbitrary and the law was what it was, all our lives were fluid. We none of us had certainties of any kind. Without always knowing what we were doing we were constantly adjusting to the arbitrariness by which we were surrounded. In the end we couldn't say where we stood.

We stood for ourselves. We all had to survive. But because we felt our lives to be fluid we all felt isolated, and we no longer felt accountable to anyone or anything. That was what had happened to Mahesh. 'It isn't that there's no right and wrong here. There's no right.' That was what had happened to me.

It was the opposite of the life of our family and community on the coast. That life was full of rules. Too many rules; it was a pre-packed kind of life. Here I had stripped myself of all the rules. During the rebellion – such a long time ago – I had also discovered that I had stripped myself of the support the rules gave. To think of it like that was to feel myself floating and lost. And I preferred not to think about it – it was too much like the panic you could at any time make yourself feel if you thought hard enough about the physical position of the town in the continent, and your own place in that town.

To see Raymond answering arbitrariness with a code like the one he had worked out for himself seemed to me extraordinary.

When I said so to Yvette she said, 'Do you think I would have married someone who was not extraordinary?'

Strange, after all the criticism, or what I had seen as criticism! But everything that was strange in my relationship with Yvette quickly stopped being strange. Everything about the relationship was new to me; I took everything as it came.

With Yvette – and with Yvette and Raymond together – I had acquired a kind of domestic life: the passion in the flat, the quiet family evening in the house in the Domain. The idea that it was my domestic life came to me when the life itself was disturbed. While it went on I simply lived it. At the time nothing seemed settled. And it was only when the life was disturbed that amazement came to me at the coolness with which I had accepted a way of living which, if it had been reported to me about someone else when I was younger, would have seemed awful. Adultery was horrible to me. I continued to think of it in the setting of family and community on the coast, and saw it as sly and dishonourable and weak-willed.

It was Yvette who had suggested, after an afternoon in the flat, that I should have dinner with them that evening in the house. She had done so out of affection, and a concern for my lonely evening; and she seemed not to see any problems. I was nervous; I didn't think I would be able to face Raymond in his house so soon afterwards. But Raymond was in his study when I arrived, and remained there until it was time to eat; and my nervousness disappeared in the novel excitement I felt at seeing Yvette, so recently naked, corrupt with pleasure, in the role of wife.

I sat in the sitting room. She came and went. Those moments were utterly delicious to me. I was stirred by every housewifely gesture; I loved the ordinariness of her clothes. Her movements in her house were brisker, more assertive, her French speech (with Raymond now at the table) more precise. Even while (all anxiety gone) I was listening to Raymond, it was a thrill to me to distance myself from Yvette, to try to see her as a stranger, and then to look through that stranger to the other woman I knew.

On the second or third occasion like this I made her drive back with me to the flat. No subterfuge was necessary: immediately after eating Raymond had gone back to his study.

Yvette had thought I had only wanted to go for a drive. When she understood what I had in mind she made an exclamation, and her face – so mask-like and housewifely at the dinner table – was transformed with pleasure. All the way to the flat she was close to laughter. I was surprised by her reaction; I had never seen her so easy, so delighted, so relaxed.

She knew she was attractive to men – those visiting scholars drove home that message. But to be desired and needed again after all that had happened during our long afternoon seemed to touch her in a way she hadn't been touched before. She was pleased with me, absurdly pleased with herself, and so companionable that I might have been an old school friend rather than a lover. I tried to put myself in her place, and just for a while I had the illusion of entering her woman's body and mind and understanding her delight. And I thought then, knowing what I did of her life, that I had been given an idea of her own needs and deprivations.

Metty was in. In the old days, following old manners, I had taken care to keep this side of my life secret from him, or at any rate to appear to be trying to do so. But now secrecy wasn't possible and didn't seem to matter. And we never worried about Metty in the flat again.

What was extraordinary that evening became part of the pattern of many of the days we were together. The dinner with Raymond in the house, or the after-dinner gathering with Raymond, occurred in a kind of parenthesis, between the afternoon in the flat and the late evening in the flat. So that in the house, when Raymond appeared, I was able to listen with a clear mind and real concern to whatever he had to say.

His routine didn't change. He tended to be working in his study when I – and visitors, if there were visitors – arrived. He took his time to appear, and in spite of his absent-minded air his hair was always freshly damped, nicely combed backwards, and he was neatly dressed. His exits, when they were preceded by a little speech, could be dramatic; but his entrances were usually modest.

He liked, especially at after-dinner gatherings, to begin by pretending to be a shy guest in his own house. But it didn't take much to draw him out. Many people wanted to hear about his position in the country and his relations with the President; but Raymond no longer talked about that. He talked instead about his work, and from that he moved on to general intellectual topics. The genius of Theodor Mommsen, the man Raymond said had rewritten the history of Rome, was a favourite theme. I grew to recognize the way Raymond built up to it.

He never avoided making a political comment, but he never raised the subject of politics himself and never became involved in political argument. However critical our guests were of the country, Raymond allowed them to have their say, in that way he had of hearing out an interruption.

Our visitors were becoming increasingly critical. They had a lot to say about the cult of the African madonna. Shrines had been set up – and were being set up – in various places connected with the President's mother, and pilgrimages to these places had been decreed for certain days. We knew about the cult, but in our region we hadn't seen too much of it. The President's mother came from one of the small down-river tribes, far away, and in our town we had only had a few statues in semi-African style, and photographs of shrines and processions. But visitors who had been to the capital had a lot to report, and it was easy enough for them as outsiders to be satirical.

More and more they included us – Raymond and Yvette and people like myself – in their satire. It began to appear that in their eyes we were people not of Africa who had allowed ourselves to be turned into Africans, accepting whatever was decreed for us. Satire like this from people who were just passing through, people we weren't going to see again but did our best for, people who were safe in their own countries, satire like this was sometimes wounding. But Raymond never allowed himself to be provoked.

To one crass man he said, 'What you are failing to understand is that this parody of Christianity you talk so warmly about can only make sense to people who are Christians. In fact that is why, from the President's point of view, it may not be such a good idea. The point of the message may be lost in the parody. Because, at the heart of this extraordinary cult, is an immense idea about the redemption of the woman of Africa. But this cult, presented as it has been, may antagonize people for different reasons. Its message may be misinterpreted, and the great idea it enshrines may be set back for two or three generations.'

That was Raymond – still loyal, trying hard to make sense of events which must have bewildered him. It did him no good; all the labour that went into those thoughts was wasted. No word came from the capital. He and Yvette continued to dangle.

But then, for a month or so, their spirits appeared to lift. Yvette told me that Raymond had reason to believe that his selections from the President's speeches had found favour. I was delighted. It was quite ridiculous – I found myself looking in a different way at the President's pictures. And though no direct word came,

Raymond, after being on the defensive for so long, and after all the talking he had had to do about the madonna cult, began to be more argumentative with visitors and to hint, with something of his old verve, that the President had something up his sleeve that would give a new direction to the country. Once or twice he even spoke about the possible publication of a book of the President's speeches, and its effect on the people.

The book was published. But it wasn't the book Raymond had worked on, not the book of longish extracts with a linking commentary. It was a very small, thin book of thoughts, *Maximes*, two or three thoughts to a page, each thought about four or five lines long.

Stacks of the book came to our town. They appeared in every bar and shop and office. My shop got a hundred; Mahesh got a hundred and fifty at Bigburger; the Tivoli got a hundred and fifty. Every pavement huckster got a little stock – five or ten: it depended on the Commissioner. The books weren't free; we had to buy them at twenty francs a copy in multiples of five. The Commissioner had to send the money for his entire consignment back to the capital, and for a fortnight or so, big man as he was, he ran around everywhere with his Land-Rover full of *Maximes*, trying to place them.

The Youth Guard used up a lot of its stock on one of its Saturday-afternoon children's marches. These marches were hurried, ragged affairs – blue shirts, hundreds of busy little legs, white canvas shoes, some of the smaller children frantic, close to tears, regularly breaking into a run to keep up with their district group, everybody anxious to get to the end and then to get back home, which could be many miles away.

The march with the President's booklet was raggeder than usual. The afternoon was overcast and heavy, after early morning rain; and the mud in the streets, drying out, had reached the nasty stage where bicycles and even footsteps caused it to fly about in sticky lumps and pellets. Mud stained the children's canvas shoes red and looked like wounds on their black legs.

The children were meant to hold up the President's book as they marched and to shout the long African name the President had given himself. But the children hadn't been properly drilled; the shouts were irregular; and since the clouds had rolled over black, and it looked as though it was going to rain again soon, the marchers were in a greater hurry than usual. They just held the little book and scampered in the gloom, spattering one another with mud, shouting only when the Youth Guard shouted at them.

The marches were already something of a joke to our people, and this didn't help. Most people, even people from the deep bush, understood what the madonna cult was about. But I don't think anyone in the squares or the market had any idea what the *Maximes* march was about. I don't think, to tell the truth, that even Mahesh knew what it referred to or was modelled on, until he was told.

So *Maximes* failed with us. And it must have been so in other parts of the country as well, because shortly after reporting the great demand for the book the newspapers dropped the subject.

Raymond, speaking of the President, said, 'He knows when to pull back. That has always been one of his great virtues. No one understands better than he the cruel humour of his people. And he may finally decide that he is being badly advised.'

Raymond was still waiting, then. In what I had seen as his code I began to recognize a stubbornness and something like vanity. But Yvette now didn't even bother to conceal her impatience. She was bored with the subject of the President. Raymond might have nowhere else to go. But Yvette was restless. And that was a bad sign for me.

13

MAHESH was my friend. But I thought of him as a man who had been stunted by his relationship with Shoba. That had been achievement enough for him. Shoba admired him and needed him, and he was therefore content with himself, content with the person she admired. His only wish seemed to be to take care of this person. He dressed for her, preserved his looks for her. I used to think that when Mahesh considered himself physically he didn't compare himself with other men, or judge himself according to some masculine ideal, but saw only the body that pleased Shoba. He saw himself as his woman saw him; and that was why, though he was my friend, I thought that his devotion to Shoba had made him half a man, and ignoble.

I had longed myself for an adventure, for passion and physical fulfilment, but I never thought that it would take me in that way, that all my idea of my own worth would be bound up with the way a woman responded to me. But that was how it was. All my self-esteem came from being Yvette's lover, from serving her and pleasing her in the physical way I did.

That was my pride. It was also my shame, to have reduced my manhood just to that. There were times, especially during slack periods in the shop, when I sat at my desk (Yvette's photographs in the drawer) and found myself mourning. Mourning, in the midst of a physical fulfilment which could not be more complete! There was a time when I wouldn't have thought it possible.

And so much had come to me through Yvette. I had got to know so much more. I had lost the expatriate businessman's way of not appearing to take too much notice of things, which could end up in genuine backwardness. I had been given so many ideas about history, political power, other continents. But, with all my new knowledge, my world was narrower than it had ever been. In events around me – like the publication of the President's book, and the book march – I looked only to see whether the life I had with Yvette was threatened or was going to go on. And the narrower my world became the more obsessively I lived in it.

Even so, it was a shock when I heard that Noimon had sold up and left, to go to Australia. Noimon was our biggest businessman, the Greek with a finger in every pie. He had come out to the country as a very young man at the end of the war to work on one of the Greek coffee plantations in the deep bush. Though speaking only Greek when he came, he had done very well very quickly, acquiring plantations of his own and then a furniture business in the town. Independence had appeared to wipe him out; but he had stayed put. At the Hellenic Club – which he treated like his private charity, and ruled, having kept it going through very bad times – he used to say that the country was his home.

All during the boom Noimon had been re-investing and expanding; at one time he had offered Mahesh a lot of money for the Bigburger property. He had a way with officials and was good at getting government contracts (he had furnished the houses in the Domain). And now he had sold up secretly to some of the new-fangled state trading agencies in the capital. We could only guess at the foreign-exchange ins and outs, and the hidden beneficiaries, of that deal – the newspaper in the capital announced it as a kind of nationalization, with fair compensation.

His departure left us all feeling a little betrayed. We also felt foolish, caught out. Anybody can be decisive during a panic; it takes a strong man to act during a boom. And Nazruddin had warned me. I remembered his little lecture about the difference between the businessman and the man who was really only a mathematician. The businessman bought at ten and was happy to get out at twelve; the mathematician saw his ten rise to eighteen, but didn't sell because he wanted to double his ten to twenty.

I had done better than that. What (using Nazruddin's scale) I had bought at two I had taken over the years to twenty. But now, with Noimon's departure, it had dropped to fifteen.

Noimon's departure marked the end of our boom, the end of confidence. We all knew that. But at the Hellenic Club – where only a fortnight before, throwing dust in our eyes, Noimon had been talking in his usual practical way about improving the swimming pool – we put a brave face on things.

I heard it said that Noimon had sold up only for the sake of his children's education; it was also said that he had been pressured by his wife (Noimon was rumoured to have a second, half-African family). And then it began to be said that Noimon would regret his decision. Copper was copper, the boom was going to go on, and while the Big Man was in charge everything would keep on running smoothly. Besides, though Australia and Europe and North America were nice places to visit, life there wasn't as rosy as some people thought – and Noimon, after a lifetime in Africa, was going to find that out pretty soon. We lived better where we were, with servants and swimming pools, luxuries that only millionaires had in those other places.

It was a lot of nonsense. But they had to say what they said, though that point about the swimming pools was especially stupid, because in spite of the foreign technicians our water supply system had broken down. The town had grown too fast, and too many people were still coming in; in the shanty towns the emergency stand-pipes used to run all day long; and water was now rationed everywhere. Some of the swimming pools – and we didn't have so many – had been drained. In some the filtering machinery had simply been turned off – economy or inexperience – and those pools had become choked with brilliant green algae and wilder growths, and looked like poisonous forest ponds. But the swimming pools existed, whatever their condition, and people could talk about them as they did because here we liked the idea of the swimming pool better than the thing itself. Even when the pools worked they hadn't been used much – it was as if we hadn't yet learned to fit this bothersome luxury into our day-to-day life.

I reported the Hellenic Club chatter back to Mahesh, expecting

him to share my attitude or at least to see the joke, bad as the joke
was for us.

But Mahesh didn't see the joke. He too made the point about
the superior quality of our life in the town.

He said, 'I'm glad Noimon has gone. Let him get a taste of the
good life out there. I hope he relishes it. Shoba has some Ismaili
friends in London. They're having a *very* nice taste of the life over
there. It isn't all Harrods. They've written to Shoba. Ask her.
She will tell you about her London friends. What they call a big
house over there would be like a joke to us here. You've seen the
salesmen at the van der Weyden. That's expenses. Ask them how
they live back home. None of them live as well as I live here.'

I thought later that it was the 'I' in Mahesh's last sentence that
offended me. Mahesh could have put it better. That 'I' gave me a
glimpse of what had enraged Indar about his lunch with Mahesh
and Shoba. Indar had said: 'They don't know who I am or what
I've done. They don't even know where I've been.' He had seen
what I hadn't seen: it was news to me that Mahesh thought he
was living 'well', in the way he meant.

I hadn't noticed any great change in his style. He and Shoba
still lived in their concrete flat with the sitting room full of shiny
things. But Mahesh wasn't joking. Standing in his nice clothes by
his imported coffee machine in his franchise-given shop, he really
thought he was something, successful and complete, really thought
he had made it and had nowhere higher to go. Bigburger and the
boom – and Shoba, always there – had destroyed his sense of
humour. And I used to think of him as a fellow survivor!

But it wasn't for me to condemn him or the others. I was like
them. I too wanted to stay with what I had; I too hated the idea
that I might have been caught. I couldn't say, as they did, that
all was still for the best. But that, in effect, was my attitude. The
very fact that the boom had passed its peak, that confidence had
been shaken, became for me a good enough reason for doing
nothing. That was how I explained the position to Nazruddin
when he wrote from Uganda.

Nazruddin hardly wrote. But he was still gathering experience, his mind was still ticking over; and though his letters made me nervous before I opened them, I always read them with pleasure, because over and above his personal news there was always some new general point that Nazruddin wanted to make. We were still so close to our shock about Noimon that I thought, when Metty brought the letter from the post office, that the letter was going to be about Noimon or about the prospects for copper. But it was about Uganda. They were having their problems there too.

Things were bad in Uganda, Nazruddin wrote. The army people who had taken over had appeared to be all right at first, but now there were clear signs of tribal and racial troubles. And these troubles weren't just going to blow over. Uganda was beautiful, fertile, easy, without poverty, and with high African traditions. It ought to have had a future, but the problem with Uganda was that it wasn't big enough. The country was now too small for its tribal hatreds. The motor-car and modern roads had made the country too small; there would always be trouble. Every tribe felt more threatened in its territory now than in the days when everybody, including traders from the coast like our grandfathers, went about on foot, and a single trading venture could take up to a year. Africa, going back to its old ways with modern tools, was going to be a difficult place for some time. It was better to read the signs right rather than to hope that things would work out.

So for the third time in his life Nazruddin was thinking of moving and making a fresh start, this time out of Africa, in Canada. 'But my luck is running out. I can see it in my hand.'

The letter, in spite of its disturbing news, was in Nazruddin's old, calm style. It offered no direct advice and made no direct requests. But it was a reminder – as it was intended to be, especially at this time of upheaval for him – of my bargain with Nazruddin, my duty to his family and mine. It deepened my panic. At the same time it strengthened my resolve to stay and do nothing.

I replied in the way I have said, outlining our new difficulties in the town. I took some time to reply, and when I did I found myself writing passionately, offering Nazruddin the picture of myself as someone incompetent and helpless, one of his 'mathematicians'.

And nothing that I wrote wasn't true. I was as helpless as I presented myself. I didn't know where I could go on to. I didn't think – after what I had seen of Indar and other people in the Domain – that I had the talent or the skills to survive in another country.

And it was as if I had been caught out by my own letter. My panic grew, and my guilt, and my feeling that I was provoking my own destruction. And out of this, out of a life which I felt to be shrinking and which became more obsessed as it shrank, I began to question myself. Was I possessed by Yvette? Or was I – like Mahesh with his new idea of what he was – possessed by myself, the man I thought I was with Yvette? To serve her in the way I did it was necessary to look outward from myself. Yet it was in this selflessness that my own fulfilment lay; I doubted, after my brothel life, whether I could be a man in that way with any other woman. She gave me the idea of my manliness I had grown to need. Wasn't my attachment to her an attachment to that idea?

And, oddly involved with this idea of myself, and myself and Yvette, was the town itself – the flat, the house in the Domain, the way both our lives were arranged, the absence of a community, the isolation in which we both lived. In no other place would it be just like this; and perhaps in no other place would our relationship be possible. The question of continuing it in another place never arose. That whole question of another place was something I preferred not to think about.

The first time she had come back to the flat after dinner at the house I felt I had been given some idea of her own needs, the needs of an ambitious woman who had married young and come out to the wrong country, cutting herself off. I had never felt I could meet those needs. I had grown to accept, and be excited by, the idea that I was an encumbrance that had become a habit. Perhaps she was for me too. But I had no means of finding out and didn't particularly want to. The isolation that kept me obsessed had become something I saw as necessary.

In time it would all go; we would both return to our interrupted lives. That was no tragedy. That certainty of the end – even while the boom slackened and my fifteen dropped to fourteen, and Nazruddin and his uprooted family tried to establish themselves in Canada – was my security.

Quite suddenly, Shoba left us to go and visit her family in the east. Her father had died. She had gone for the cremation.

I was surprised when Mahesh told me. Not by the death, but by the fact that Shoba could go back to her family. That wasn't at all what I had been led to believe. Shoba had presented herself as a runaway, someone who had gone against the rules of her community by marrying Mahesh, and was living in this remote place to hide from her family's vengeance.

When she had first told me her story – it had been at lunch on a still, silent day during the rebellion – she had said that she had to be cautious with strangers. It had occurred to her that her family might hire someone, of any race, to do what they had threatened: to disfigure her or to kill Mahesh. Acid on the face of the woman, the killing of the man – they were the standard family threats on these occasions, and Shoba, conventional in so many ways, wasn't too displeased to let me know that the threats had been made in her case. Usually these threats were meaningless, and made only to satisfy convention; but sometimes they could be carried out to the letter. However, as time passed, and Shoba appeared to be forgetting some of the details of her first story, I stopped believing in that drama of the hired stranger. But I took it as settled that Shoba had been disowned by her family.

In my own predicament I had always been conscious of Shoba's example, and it was a let-down to discover that she had kept her lines of communication open. As for Mahesh, he began to behave like the mourning son-in-law. It might have been his way of making a public drama out of the business, taking expensive orders for coffee and beer and Bigburgers (the prices these days!) with an air of tenderness and sorrow. It might have been his way of showing sympathy for Shoba and respect for the dead. But it was also a little bit like the behaviour of a man who felt he had at last earned his place. Well!

But then the joke turned sour. Shoba was to have been away for two months. She returned after three weeks, and then she

seemed to go into hiding. There were no invitations to me to lunch;
that arrangement – almost that tradition now – at last came to an
end. She had hated the political situation in the east, Mahesh said.
She had never liked Africans and had come back raging about
thieving and boastful politicians, the incessant lies and hate on the
radio and in the newspapers, the bag-snatchings in daylight, the
nightly violence. She was appalled by the position of her family,
whom she had grown up thinking of as solid and secure. All this,
combined with her grief for her father, had made her strange. It
was better for the time being, Mahesh said, for me to stay away.

But that hardly seemed explanation enough. Was there something more than political and racial rage, and grief for the father
whom at one time she had shamed? Was there perhaps a new
vision of the man she had chosen and the life she had been living?
Some regret for the family life she now saw she had missed, some
greater grief for the things she had betrayed?

The air of mourning that Mahesh, in Shoba's absence, had
been so glad to put on became a deep and real gloom after Shoba's
return; and then this gloom became shot through with irritations.
He began to show his age. The confidence, which had irritated
me, left him. I grieved for it, grieved that he should have enjoyed
it for so short a time. And he, who had spoken so sharply about
Noimon, and spoken with such pride about the way he lived here,
now said, 'It's junk, Salim. It's all turning to junk again.'

No longer able to lunch with them or visit their flat, I took to
dropping in at Bigburger on some evenings to exchange a few
words with Mahesh. One evening I saw Shoba there.

She was sitting at the counter, against the wall, and Mahesh
was sitting on the stool next to hers. They were like customers in
their own place.

I greeted Shoba, but there was no warmth in her acknowledge-
ment. I might have been a stranger or someone she barely knew.
And even when I sat down next to Mahesh she continued to be
distant. She seemed not to be seeing me. And Mahesh appeared
not to notice. Was she rebuking me for those things she had
grown to condemn in herself?

I had known them both for so long. They were part of my life, however much my feelings about them shifted about. I could see the tightness and pain and something like illness in Shoba's eyes. I could also see she was acting a little. Still, I was hurt. And when I left them – no cry of 'Stay!' from either of them – I felt cast out and slightly dazed. And every familiar detail of street life at night – the cooking fires gilding the thin, exhausted-looking faces of the people who sat around them, the groups in the shadows below the shop awnings, the sleepers and their boundary markers, the ragged lost lunatics, the lights of a bar fanning out over a wooden walkway – everything had a different quality.

A radio was on in the flat. It was unusually loud, and as I went up the external staircase I had the impression that Metty was listening to a football match commentary from the capital. An echoing voice was varying its pace and pitch, and there was the roar of a crowd. Metty's door was open and he was sitting in pants and singlet on the edge of his cot. The light from the central hanging bulb in his room was yellow and dim; the radio was deafening.

Looking up at me, then looking down again, concentrating, Metty said, 'The President.'

That was clear, now that I had begun to follow the words. It explained why Metty felt he didn't have to turn the radio down. The speech had been announced – I had forgotten.

The President was talking in the African language that most people who lived along the river understood. At one time the President's speeches were in French. But in this speech the only French words were *citoyens* and *citoyennes*, and they were used again and again, for musical effect, now run together into a rippling phrase, now called out separately, every syllable spaced, to create the effect of a solemn drum beat.

The African language the President had chosen for his speeches was a mixed and simple language, and he simplified it further, making it the language of the drinking booth and the street brawl, converting himself, while he spoke, this man who kept everybody dangling and imitated the etiquette of royalty and the graces of de Gaulle, into the lowest of the low. And that was the attraction of the African language in the President's mouth. That regal and musical use of the lowest language and the coarsest expressions was what was holding Metty.

Metty was absorbed. His eyes, below the yellow highlights on his forehead, were steady, small, intent. His lips were compressed and in his concentration he kept working them. When the coarse expressions or the obscenities occurred, and the crowd roared, Metty laughed without opening his mouth.

The speech, so far, was like many others the President had made. The themes were not new: sacrifice and the bright future; the dignity of the woman of Africa; the need to strengthen the revolution, unpopular though it was with those black men in the towns who dreamed of waking up one day as white men; the need for Africans to be African, to go back without shame to their democratic and socialist ways, to rediscover the virtues of the diet and medicines of their grandfathers and not to go running like children after things in imported tins and bottles; the need for vigilance, work and, above all, discipline.

This was how, while appearing just to restate old principles, the President also acknowledged and ridiculed new criticism, whether it was of the madonna cult or of the shortage of food and medicines. He always acknowledged criticism, and he often anticipated it. He made everything fit; he could suggest he knew everything. He could make it appear that everything that was happening in the country, good or bad or ordinary, was part of a bigger plan.

People liked to listen to the President's speeches because so much was familiar; like Metty now, they waited for the old jokes. But every speech was also a new performance, with its own dramatic devices; and every speech had a purpose. This speech was of particular concern to our town and region. That was what the President said, and it became one of the dramatic devices of the later part of the speech: he broke off again and again to say that he had something to say to the people of our town and region, but we had to wait for it. The crowd in the capital, recognizing the device as a device, a new piece of style, began to roar when they saw it coming.

We in the region liked our beer, the President said. He liked it better; he could out-drink anyone of us any day. But we mustn't get pissed too soon; he had something to say to us. And it was known that the statement the President was going to make was about our Youth Guard. For a fortnight or more we had been waiting for this statement; for a fortnight he had kept the whole town dangling.

The Youth Guard had never recovered their prestige after the failure of the book march. Their children's marches on Saturday afternoons had grown raggeder and thinner, and the officers had found that they had no means of compelling children to take part. They had kept on with the Morals Patrol. But the night-time crowds were now more hostile; and one evening an officer of the Guard had been killed.

It had begun as a squabble with some pavement sleepers who had barred off a stretch of pavement in a semi-permanent way with concrete blocks looted from a building site. And it could easily have ended as a shouting match, no more. But the officer had stumbled and fallen. By that fall, that momentary appearance of helplessness, he had invited the first blow with one of the concrete blocks; and the sight of blood then had encouraged a sudden, frenzied act of murder by dozens of small hands.

No one had been arrested. The police were nervous; the Youth Guard were nervous; the people of the streets were nervous. There was talk a few days later that the army was going to be sent in to beat up some of the shanty towns. That had caused a little scuttle back to the villages; the dugouts had been busy. But nothing had happened. Everyone had been waiting to see what the President would do. But for more than a fortnight the President had said and done nothing.

And what the President said now was staggering. The Youth Guard in our region was to be disbanded. They had forgotten their duty to the people; they had broken faith with him, the President; they had talked too much. The officers would lose their stipend; there would be no government jobs for any of them; they would be banished from the town and sent back to the bush, to do constructive work there. In the bush they would learn the wisdom of the monkey.

'*Citoyens-citoyennes*, monkey smart. Monkey smart like shit. Monkey can talk. You didn't know that? Well, I tell you now. Monkey can talk, but he keep it quiet. Monkey know that if he talk in front of man, man going to catch him and beat him and make him work. Make him carry load in hot sun. Make him paddle boat. *Citoyens! Citoyennes!* We will teach these people to be like monkey. We will send them to the bush and let them work their arse off.'

14

It was the Big Man's way. He chose his time, and what looked like a challenge to his authority served in the end to underline his authority. He showed himself again as the friend of the people, the *petit peuple,* as he liked to call them, and he punished their oppressors.

But the Big Man hadn't visited our town. Perhaps, as Raymond said, the reports he had been receiving were inaccurate or incomplete. And this time something went wrong. We had all thought of the Youth Guard as a menace, and everybody was happy to see them go. But it was after the disbanding of the Youth Guard that things began to get bad in our town.

The police and other officials became difficult. They took to tormenting Metty whenever he took the car out, even on the short run to the customs. He was stopped again and again, sometimes by people he knew, sometimes by people who had stopped him before, and the car's documents were checked, and his own papers. Sometimes he had to leave the car where it was and walk back to the shop to get some certificate or paper he didn't have. And it didn't help if he had all the papers.

Once, for no reason at all, he was taken to police headquarters, fingerprinted, and – in the company of other dispirited people who had been picked up – made to spend a whole afternoon with blackened hands in a room with backless wooden benches, a broken concrete floor, and blue distempered walls grimy and shining from the heads and shoulders that had rubbed against them.

The room, from which I rescued him late in the afternoon, having spent a lot of time tracking him down, was in a rough concrete and corrugated-iron shed at the back of the main colonial building. The floor was just a few inches above the ground; the door was open, and chickens were scratching about in the bare yard. But rough and homely and full of afternoon light as it was, the room hinted at the jail. The one table and chair belonged to the officer in charge, and these scrappy pieces of furniture emphasized the deprivation of everybody else.

The officer was sweating under the arms in his over-starched uniform, and he was writing very slowly in a ledger, shaping one letter at a time, apparently entering details from the blotched finger-print sheets. He had a revolver. There was a photograph of the President showing his chief's stick; and above it on the blue wall, high up, where the uneven surface was dusty rather than grimy, was painted *DISCIPLINE AVANT TOUT*, Discipline Above All.

I didn't like that room, and I thought it would be better after that for Metty not to use the car and for me to be my own customs clerk and broker. But then the officials turned their attention to me.

They dug up old customs declarations forms, things that had been sealed and settled in the standard way long ago, and brought them to the shop and waved them in my face like unredeemed IOUs. They said they were under pressure from their superiors and wanted to go through certain details with me again. At first they were shy, like wicked schoolboys; then they were conspiratorial, like friends wanting to do me a secret good turn; then they were aggressive, like wicked officials. Others wanted to check my stock against my customs declarations and my sales receipts; others said they wanted to investigate my prices.

It was harassment, and the purpose was money, and money fast, before everything changed. These men had sniffed some change coming; in the disbanding of the Youth Guard they had seen signs of the President's weakness rather than strength. And in this situation there was no one I could appeal to. Every official was willing, for a consideration, to give assurances about his own

226

conduct. But no official was high enough or secure enough to guarantee the conduct of any other official.

Everything in the town was as it had been – the army was in its barracks, the photographs of the President were everywhere, the steamer came up regularly from the capital. But men had lost or rejected the idea of an overseeing authority, and everything was again as fluid as it had been at the beginning. Only this time, after all the years of peace and goods in all the shops, everyone was greedier.

What was happening to me was happening to every other foreign businessman. Even Noimon, if he had still been around, would have suffered. Mahesh was gloomier than ever. He said, 'I always say: you can hire them, but you can't buy them.' It was one of his sayings; it meant that stable relationships were not possible here, that there could only be day-to-day contracts between men, that in a crisis peace was something you had to buy afresh every day. His advice was to stick it out. And there was nothing else we could do.

My own feeling – my secret comfort during this time – was that the officials had misread the situation and that their frenzy was self-induced. Like Raymond, I had grown to believe in the power-wisdom of the President, and was confident he would do something to reassert his authority. So I prevaricated and didn't pay, seeing no end to paying if I should start.

But the patience of the officials was greater than mine. It is no exaggeration to say that not a day passed now without some official calling. I began to wait for their calls. It was bad for my nerves. In the middle of the afternoon, if no one had yet called, I could find myself sweating. I grew to hate, and fear, those smiling *malin* faces pushed up close to mine in mock familiarity and helpfulness.

And then the pressure eased. Not because the President acted, as I had been hoping. But because violence had come to our town. Not the evening drama of street brawls and murders, but a steady, nightly assault in different areas on policemen and police stations and officials and official buildings.

It was this, no doubt, that the officials had seen coming – and

I hadn't. This was what had made them greedy to grab as much as they could while they could. One night the statue of the African madonna and child in the Domain was knocked off its pedestal and smashed, as the colonial statues had once been smashed, and the monument outside the dock gates. After this the officials began to make themselves scarce. They stayed away from the shop; they had too many other things to do. And though I couldn't say things were better, yet the violence came as a relief and for a while, to me as well as to the people I saw in the streets and squares, was even exhilarating, the way a big fire or a storm can be exhilarating.

In our overgrown, overpopulated, unregulated town we had any number of violent outbursts. There had been riots about water, and on many occasions in the shanty towns there had been riots when someone had been killed by a car. In what was happening now there was still that element of popular frenzy; but it was also clear that it was more organized, or that at least it had some deeper principle. Some prophecy, perhaps, had been making the rounds of the *cités* and shanty towns and had found confirmation in the dreams of various people. It was the kind of thing the officials would have got wind of.

One morning, when he brought me coffee, Metty, looking serious, gave me a piece of newsprint, folded small and carefully, and dirty along the outer creases. It was a printed leaflet and had obviously been folded and unfolded many times. It was headlined 'The Ancestors Shriek', and was issued by something called The Liberation Army.

The ANCESTORS shriek. Many false gods have come to this land, but none have been as false as the gods of today. The cult of the woman of Africa kills all our mothers, and since war is an extension of politics we have decided to face the ENEMY with armed confrontation. Otherwise we all die forever. The ancestors are shrieking. If we are not deaf we can hear them. By ENEMY we mean the powers of imperialism, the multi-nationals and the puppet powers that be, the false gods, the capitalists, the priests and teachers who give false interpretations. The law encourages crime. The schools teach ignorance and people practise ignorance in preference to their true culture. Our soldiers and guardians have been given false desires and false greeds and the foreigners now qualify us everywhere as thieves. We are ignorant of ourselves and mislead ourselves. We are marching to death. We have forgotten the TRUTHFUL LAWS. We of the LIBERA-TION ARMY have received no education. We do not print books and make speeches. We only know the TRUTH, and we acknowledge this land as the land of the people whose ancestors now shriek over it. OUR PEOPLE must understand the struggle. They must learn to die with us.

Metty said he didn't know where the leaflet came from. Some-body had just given it to him the night before. I thought he knew more than he said, but I didn't press him.

We didn't have many printeries in the town, and it was clear to me that the leaflet – very badly printed, the type broken and mixed – came from the printing shop that used to do the weekly newspaper of the Youth Guard. That, while it lasted, had been our only local paper, and it was a nonsense sheet – like the wall newspaper of a school, with meaningless advertisements from traders and businessmen and even stall-holders in the market, and a few items of so-called news (more like open blackmail) about people breaking traffic rules or using government vehicles as night taxis or building shacks where they shouldn't.

Still, it was very strange. The officers of the Youth Guard, while they had been serving the President, had been hateful to the people they tried to police. Now, humiliated by the President in that 'monkey' speech, stripped of power and jobs, they offered themselves to the people as humiliated and anguished men of the region, as defenders of the people of the region. And the people were responding.

It was like the time before the rebellion. But there had been no leaflets then, no leaders as young and educated as these. And there was something else. At the time of the rebellion the town was just beginning to be re-established, and the first disturbances took place far away, in the villages. Now everything was happening in the town itself. There was a lot more blood as a result; and the violence, which at first seemed directed against the authorities alone, became more general. African stalls and shops in the outer areas were attacked and looted. People began to be killed in horrible ways, by rioters and police and shanty-town criminals.

Africans and the outer areas first, foreigners and the centre later – that was the way I saw things happening here. So that, having just been freed from a kind of official blackmail against which there was no appeal, I once again had to think of myself as exposed, with nothing to hold on to. I took this fear with me into the familiar streets, this feeling that I was now physically vulnerable. The streets had always been dangerous. But not for me. As an outsider I had so far been allowed to be separate from the violence I observed.

The strain was great. It corrupted everything, and for the first time I considered the idea of flight. If there had been a safe house waiting for me in some far city which would have allowed me in, I believe I might have left during this time. Once there was such a house; once there were several such houses. But there was no such house now. The news from Nazruddin was disheartening. His year in Canada had been bad, and he was uprooting his family yet again, and going to England. The outside world no longer offered refuge; it had remained for me the great unknown and was, increasingly, perilous. What I had once falsely written to Nazruddin had come true. I was in no position to act. I had to stay where I was.

And, forgetting goals, I kept on, living my life – I had learned that years ago from Mahesh. And more and more it happened, in my dealings with people I knew well, that I forgot to study their faces, forgot my fear. In this way fear, the feeling that everything could at any moment go, became background, a condition of life, something you had to accept. And I was made almost calm by something a German from the capital, a man in his late fifties, said to me at the Hellenic Club one afternoon.

He said, 'In a situation like this you can't spend all your time being frightened. Something may happen, but you must make yourself think of it as a bad road accident. Something outside your control, that can happen anywhere.'

Time passed. No explosion came, no cataclysm such as I had been expecting at the beginning. Fires didn't burn in the centre; the rebels' means were limited. The assaults and killings continued; the police made their retaliatory raids; and something like a balance was achieved. Two or three people were killed every night. But, strangely, it all began to seem far away. The very size and unregulated sprawl of the town muffled all but the most extraordinary events; people in the streets and squares no longer waited for news. News, in fact, was scarce. The President made no statement, and nothing was reported on the radio or in the newspapers from the capital.

In the centre of the town life went on as before. The businessman who came in from the capital by air or by the steamer and put up at the van der Weyden, and went to the better-known restaurants and night clubs and asked no questions, would not have guessed that the town was in a state of insurrection, that the insurrection had its leaders and – though their names were known only in their own districts – its martyrs.

For some time Raymond had been like a stunned man. At some moment he seemed to have decided that he wasn't going to be called back to the President's favour, and he had stopped waiting, stopped reading the signs. At dinner in the house he no longer analysed or explained events; he no longer tried to make the pieces fit together.

He didn't talk about history or about Theodor Mommsen. I didn't know what he was doing in his study, and Yvette couldn't tell me; she wasn't too interested. At one time I got the impression that he was reading old things he had written. He mentioned a diary he had kept when he had first come out to the country. He had forgotten so many things, he said; so many things were doomed to be forgotten. That used to be one of his dinner-table themes; he seemed to recognize that, and broke off. Later he said,

'Strange, reading those diaries. In those days you used to scratch yourself to see whether you bled.'

The insurrection added to his confusion; and after the madonna statue in the Domain had been smashed he became very nervous. It wasn't the President's habit to appear to support those of his men who had been attacked; he tended to dismiss them. And Raymond now lived in fear of dismissal. This was what it had come down to for him – a job, a house, his livelihood, simple security. He was a defeated man, and the house in the Domain was like a house of death.

The loss was mine as well. That house was important to me; and much, as I now saw, depended on the health and optimism of both the people who lived in it. A defeated Raymond made nonsense of my evenings there. Those evenings in the house were part of my relationship with Yvette; they couldn't simply be transferred to another site. That would have meant a new geography, another kind of town, another kind of relationship, not the one I had.

My life with Yvette depended on the health and optimism of all three of us. I was astonished by this discovery. I had discovered it first about myself, when I was under pressure from the officials. I wanted to hide from her then. I felt I could go to her, and be with her in the way I wanted, only in strength, as I had always gone to her. I couldn't present myself to her as a man tormented and weakened by other men. She had her own cause for restlessness; I knew that, and I couldn't bear the idea of the lost coming together for comfort.

It was at this time – as though we understood one another – that we began to space out our meetings. The first days without Yvette, the first days of solitude, subsiding excitement and clear vision, were always a relief. I could even pretend that I was a free man and that it was possible to do without her.

Then she would telephone. The knowlege that I was still needed would be like satisfaction enough, and would be converted, while I waited for her in the flat, into irritation and self-disgust, which would continue right up to the moment when, after pattering up the external staircase, she came into the sitting room, all the strain of Raymond and the intervening days showing on her face. Then very soon, in my own mind, the intervening days would drop away; time would telescope. Physically now I knew her so well; one occasion would very soon seem linked to the last.

But that idea of continuity, however overpowering at those intimate, narrow moments, was an illusion, as I knew. There were the hours and days in her house, with Raymond; there was her own privacy, and her own search. She had less and less news. There were events now we didn't share, and there were fewer things that could be told me without some gloss or explanation.

She telephoned me now every ten days. Ten days seemed to be the limit beyond which she couldn't go. It occurred to me on one of these days – when, the big foam bed already straightened, she was making up her face and considering parts of herself in the dressing-table mirror, before going back to the Domain – it occurred to me then that there was something bloodless about our relationship just at that moment. I might have been a complaisant father or husband, or even a woman friend, watching her prepare herself for a lover.

An idea like that is like a vivid dream, fixing a fear we don't want to acknowledge, and having the effect of a revelation. I suppose that, thinking of my own harassment and Raymond's defeat, I had begun to consider Yvette a defeated person as well, trapped in the town, as sick of herself and the wasting asset of her body as I was sick of myself and my anxieties. Now, looking at Yvette in front of the dressing-table mirror, seeing her bright with more than I had just given her, I saw how wrong I had been. Those blank days when she was away from me, those days about which I didn't inquire, would have been full of possibilities for her. I began to wait for confirmation. And then, two meetings later, I thought I found it.

I knew her so well. With her, even now, I had never ceased to look outward from myself. No other way would have had meaning, no other way would have been possible. What she drew out of me remained extraordinary to me. Her responses were part of the gift, and I had grown used to them as they had developed; I had learned to gauge them finely. On each occasion I was aware of her sensual memory of me beginning to work, linking the present to the past. But now, on the occasion I speak of, her responses were confused. Something had intervened; some new habit had begun to form, breaking up the delicate membrane of older memory. It was what I had been expecting. It had to be, one day. But the moment was like poison.

Afterwards came that bloodless interlude. The big foam bed had been made up – that housewifely service still, after what used to be passion. I was standing. She was standing too, considering her lips in the mirror.

She said, 'You make me look so good. What will I do without you?' That was a standard courtesy. But then she said, 'Raymond will want to make love to me when he sees me looking like this.' And that was unusual, not like her at all.

I said, 'Does it excite you?'

'Older men are not as repulsive as you seem to think. And I am a woman, after all. If a man does certain things to me I react.'

She didn't mean to wound me, but she did. And then I thought: 'But she's probably right. Raymond's like a whipped boy. It's all he can turn to now.'

I said, 'I suppose we've made him suffer.'

'Raymond? I don't know. I don't think so. He's never given any sign. Of course, he may tell himself something different now.'

I walked with her to the landing – the shadow of the house over the yard, the trees above the houses and the wooden out-buildings, the golden afternoon light, the dust in the air, the flamboyant blooms, the cooking smoke. She hurried down the wooden steps to where the sunlight, slanting between the houses, struck full on her. Then, above the noises of the surrounding yards, I heard her drive off.

And it was only some days later that I thought how strange it was for us to have talked of Raymond at that moment. I had talked of Raymond's pain when I was thinking of my own, and Yvette had talked of Raymond's needs when she was thinking of her own. We had begun to talk, if not in opposites, at least indirectly, lying and not lying, making those signals at the truth which people in certain situations find it necessary to make.

I was in bed one evening, about a week later, reading in one of my encyclopaedia magazines about the 'big-bang' origin of the universe. It was a familiar topic; I liked reading in my encyclopaedias about things I had read in other encyclopaedias. This kind of reading wasn't for knowledge; I read to remind myself in an easy and enjoyable way of all the things I didn't know. It was a form of drug; it set me dreaming of some impossible future time when, in the middle of every kind of peace, I would start at the beginning of all subjects and devote my days and nights to study.

I heard a car door slam. And I knew, before I heard the footsteps on the staircase, that it was Yvette, wonderfully arrived at this late hour, without warning. She hurried up the steps; her shoes and clothes made an extraordinary amount of noise in the passage; and she pushed the bedroom door open.

She was carefully dressed, and her face was flushed. There must have been some function she had been at. Dressed as she was, she threw herself on the bed and embraced me.

She said, 'I took a chance. All through dinner I was thinking about you, and as soon as I could I slipped away. I had to. I wasn't sure you would be here, but I took the chance.'

I could smell the dinner and the drink on her breath. It had all been so quick – from the sound of the car door to this: Yvette on the bed, the empty room transformed, Yvette in that exclamatory, delighted mood which was like the mood that had overtaken her the first time we had come back to the flat after dinner at the Domain. I found myself in tears.

She said, 'I can't stay. I'll just give the god a kiss and go.'

Afterwards she remembered the clothes of which so far she had been quite careless. Standing before the mirror, she raised her skirt to pull down her blouse. I, at her insistence, stayed in the bed.

Holding her head to one side, looking at the mirror, she said, 'I thought you might have been in your old haunts.'

She seemed to be talking more mechanically now. The mood she had brought to the room had left her. At last she was ready. When she looked from the mirror to me she seemed once again, though, to be genuinely pleased with herself and with me, pleased at her little adventure.

She said, 'I'm sorry. But I have to go.' When she was almost at the door she turned and smiled and said, 'You don't have a woman hidden in the cupboard, do you?'

It was so out of character. It was so much the kind of thing I had heard from whores who thought they should pretend to be jealous in order to please. It blasted the moment. Opposites: again this communication by opposites. That woman in the cupboard: that other person outside. That journey out from the Domain: that other journey back. Affection, just before betrayal. And I had been in tears.

It exploded then, all that had been building up in me since she had begun to straighten her clothes. And I was out of the bed, and between her and the door.

'Do you think I'm Raymond?'

She was startled.

'Do you think I'm Raymond?'

This time she was given no chance to reply. She was hit so hard and so often about the face, even through raised, protecting arms, that she staggered back and allowed herself to fall on the floor. I used my foot on her then, doing that for the sake of the beauty of her shoes, her ankles, the skirt I had watched her raise, the hump of her hip. She turned her face to the floor and remained still for a while; then with a deep breath such as a child draws before it screams, she began to cry, and that wail after a time broke into real, shocking sobs. And it was like that in the room for many minutes.

I was sitting, among the clothes I had taken off before going to bed, in the round-backed Windsor chair against the wall. The palm of my hand was stiff, swollen. The back of my hand, from little finger to wrist, was aching; bone had struck bone. Yvette raised herself up. Her eyes were slits between eyelids red and swollen with real tears. She sat on the edge of the foam mattress, at the corner of the bed, and looked at the floor, her hands resting palm outwards on her knees. I was wretched.

She said after a time, 'I came to see you. It seemed such a good thing to do. I was wrong.'

Then we said nothing.

I said, 'Your dinner?'

She shook her head slowly. Her evening was ruined; she had given it up – but how easily! And that head-shaking gesture made me enter into her earlier joy, now gone. My error: I was too ready to see her as someone lost.

She prised her shoes off, using one foot against the other. She stood up, undid her skirt and took it off. Then, just as she was, with her hair done up, her blouse on, she got into the bed, pulled the top cotton sheet over herself and moved to the far side of the bed, always hers. She settled her fluffed-out head on the pillow, turned her back to me; and the encyclopaedia magazine that had remained on that side of the bed fell to the floor with its own little noise. And that was how, at this time of farewell, in this parody of domestic life, we stayed for a while, oddly reposed.

She said after some time, 'Aren't you coming?'

I was too nervous to move or talk.

A while later, turning to me, she said, 'You can't keep sitting on that chair.'

I went and sat on the bed beside her. Her body had a softness, a pliability, and a great warmth. Only once or twice before I had known her like that. At this moment! I held her legs apart. She raised them slightly – smooth concavities of flesh on either side of the inner ridge – and then I spat on her between the legs until I had no more spit. All her softness vanished in outrage. She shouted, 'You can't do that!' Bone struck against bone again; my hand ached at every blow; until she rolled across the bed to the other side and, sitting up, began to dial on the telephone. Who was she telephoning at this hour? Who could she turn to, who was she so sure of?

She said, 'Raymond. Oh, Raymond. No, no. I'm all right. I'm sorry. I'm coming right away.'

She put on her skirt and shoes, and through the door that she left open she swung out into the passage. No pause, no hesitation: I heard her pattering down the staircase – what a sound now! The bed, where nothing had occurred, was in a mess – for the first time, after she had been: I had had the last of that housewifely service. There were the marks of her head on the pillow, the gathers in the sheet from her movements: things now rare, indescribably precious to me, those relics in cloth that would go so soon. I lay down where she had lain, to get her smell.

Outside the door Metty said, 'Salim?' He called again, 'Salim.' And he came in, in pants and vest.

I said, 'Oh, Ali, Ali. Terrible things happened tonight. I spat on her. She made me spit on her.'

'People quarrel. After three years a thing doesn't just end like this.'

'Ali, it isn't that. I couldn't do anything with her. I didn't want her, I didn't want her. That is what I can't bear. It's all gone.'

'You mustn't stay inside. Come outside. I will put on my pants and shirt and I will walk with you. We will walk together. We will walk to the river. Come, I will walk with you.'

The river, the river at night. No, no.

'I know more things about your family than you, Salim. It is better for you to walk it off. It is the best way.'

'I'll stay here.'

He stood about for a little, then he went to his room. But I knew that he was waiting and watching. All the back of my swollen hand was aching; my little finger felt dead. The skin was blue-black in parts – that too now a relic.

I was ready when the telephone rang.

'Salim, I didn't want to leave. How are you?'

'Dreadful. And you?'

'When I left I drove slowly. Then after the bridge I drove very fast, to get back here to telephone you.'

'I knew that you would. I was waiting for it.'

'Do you want me to come back? The road is quite empty. I can be back in twenty minutes. Oh, Salim. I look dreadful. My face is in an awful state. I will have to hide for days.'

'You will always look wonderful to me. You know that.'

'I should have given you some Valium when I saw how you were. But I thought about that only when I was in the car. You must try to sleep. Make some hot milk and try to sleep. It helps to have a hot drink. Let Metty make some hot milk for you.'

Never closer, never more like a wife, than at this moment. It was easier to talk on the telephone. And when that was over, I began to watch through the night, waiting for daylight and another telephone call. Metty was sleeping. He had left the door of his room open, and I heard his breathing.

There came a moment, with the coming of the light, when suddenly the night became part of the past. The brush-strokes on the white-painted window panes began to show, and at that time, out of my great pain, I had an illumination. It didn't come in words; the words I attempted to fit to it were confused and caused the illumination itself to vanish. It seemed to me that men were born only to grow old, to live out their span, to acquire experience. Men lived to acquire experience; the quality of the experience was immaterial; pleasure and pain – and, above all, pain – had no meaning; to possess pain was as meaningless as to chase pleasure. And even when the illumination vanished, became as thin and half nonsensical as a dream, I remembered that I had had it, that knowledge about the illusion of pain.

The light brightened through the white-painted windows. The disturbed room changed its character. It seemed to have become stale. The only true relic was now my aching hand, though if I had looked I would have found a hair or two from her head. I dressed, went downstairs and, giving up the idea of a morning walk, began to drive about the awakening town. I felt refreshed by the colours; I thought this early morning drive was something I should have done more often.

Just before seven I went to the centre, to Bigburger. Sacks and boxes of uncollected rubbish were on the pavement. Ildephonse was there, the jacket of his uniform now as worn as the décor. Even at this early hour Ildephonse had been drinking; as with most Africans, he needed just a little of the weak local beer to top up and get high. He had known me for years; I was the first customer of the day; yet he hardly acknowledged me. His beer-glazed eyes stared past me at the street. In one of the lines or furrows of his lower lip he had fitted a toothpick, very precisely, very snugly, so he could talk or let his lower lip fall without the toothpick being disturbed; it was like a trick.

I called him back from wherever he was, and he gave me a cup of coffee and a slice of processed cheese in a roll. That was two hundred francs, nearly six dollars; prices were ridiculous these days.

A few minutes before eight Mahesh came. He had been letting himself go. He had always been proud of his smallness and spareness. But he wasn't as spare as he had been; I could just begin to see him as a simpler kind of small fat man.

The effect of his arrival on Ildephonse was electric. The glazed look left Ildephonse's eyes, the toothpick disappeared, and he began to jump about, smiling and welcoming the early morning customers, mainly guests from the van der Weyden.

I was hoping that Mahesh would notice my condition. But he made no reference to it; he didn't even seem surprised to see me.

He said, 'Shoba wants to see you, Salim.'

'How is she?'

'She is better. I think she is better. She wants to see you. You must come to the flat. Come for a meal. Come for lunch. Come for lunch tomorrow.'

Zabeth helped me to get through the morning. It was her shopping day. Her business had gone down since the insurrection, and her news these days was of trouble in the villages. Young men were being kidnapped here and there by the police and the army: it was the new government tactic. Though nothing appeared in the newspapers, the bush was now again at war. Zabeth seemed to be on the side of the rebels, but I couldn't be sure; and I tried to be as neutral as I could.

I asked about Ferdinand. His time in the capital as an administrative cadet was over. He was due for some big post soon, and the last I had heard from Zabeth was that he was being considered as a successor to our local Commissioner, who had been sacked shortly after the insurrection had broken out. Ferdinand's mixed tribal ancestry made him a good choice for the difficult post.

Zabeth, speaking the big title quite calmly (I thought of the old subscription book for the lycée gymnasium, and of the days when the governor of the province signed by himself on a whole page, like royalty), Zabeth said, 'I suppose Fer'nand will be Commissioner, Salim. If they let him live.'

'If he lives, Beth?'

'If they don't kill him. I don't know whether I would like him to take that job, Salim. Both sides would want to kill him. And the President will want to kill him first, as a sacrifice. He is a jealous man, Salim. He will allow nobody to get big in this place. It is only his photo everywhere. And look at the papers. His photo is bigger than everybody else's every day. Look.'

The previous day's paper from the capital was on my desk, and the photograph Zabeth pointed to was of the President addressing government officials in the southern province.

'Look, Salim. He is very big. The others are so small you can scarcely see them. You can't tell who is who.'

The officials were in the regulation dress devised by the President – short-sleeved jackets, cravats in place in of shirts and ties. They sat in neat packed rows and in the photograph they did look alike. But Zabeth was pointing out something else to me. She didn't see the photograph as a photograph; she didn't interpret distance and perspective. She was concerned with the actual space occupied in the printed picture by different figures. She was, in fact, pointing out something I had never noticed: in pictures in the newspapers only visiting foreigners were given equal space with the President. With local people the President was always presented as a towering figure. Even if pictures were of the same size, the President's picture would be of his face alone, while the other man would be shown full length. So now, in the photograph of the President addressing the southern officials, a photograph taken from over the President's shoulder, the President's shoulders, head and cap occupied most of the space, and the officials were dots close together, similarly dressed.

'He is killing those men, Salim. They are screaming inside, and he knows they're screaming. And you know, Salim, that isn't a fetish he's got there. It's nothing.'

She was looking at the big photograph in the shop, which showed the President holding up his chief's stick, carved with various emblems. In the distended belly of the squat human figure half-way down the stick the special fetish was thought to be lodged.

She said, 'That's *nothing*. I'll tell you about the President. He's got a man, and this man goes ahead of him wherever he goes. This man jumps out of the car before the car stops, and everything that is bad for the President follows this man and leaves the President free. I saw it, Salim. And I will tell you something. The man who jumps out and gets lost in the crowd is white.'

'But the President hasn't been here, Beth.'

'I saw it, Salim. I saw the man. And you mustn't tell me that you don't know.'

Metty was good all that day. Without referring to what had happened, he handled me with awe (awe for me as a violent, wounded man) and tenderness – I recalled moments like this from our own compound life on the coast, after some bad family quarrel. I suppose he recalled such moments too, and fell into old ways. I began in the end to act for him, and that was a help.

I allowed him to send me home to the flat in the middle of the afternoon; he said he would close up. He didn't go to his family afterwards, as was his custom. He came to the flat and discreetly let me know that he was there, and staying. I heard him tiptoeing about. There was no need for that, but the attention comforted me; and on that bed, where from time to time I caught some faint scent from the day before (no, that day itself), I began to sleep.

Time moved in jerks. Whenever I awakened I was confused. Neither the afternoon light nor the noisy darkness seemed right. So the second night passed. And the telephone didn't ring and I didn't telephone. In the morning Metty brought me coffee.

I went to Mahesh and Shoba's for lunch – it seemed to me that I had been to Bigburger and received that invitation a long time ago.

The flat, with its curtains drawn to keep out the glare, with its nice Persian carpets and brass, and all its other fussy little pieces, was as I remembered it. It was a silent lunch, not especially a lunch of reunion or reconciliation. We didn't talk about recent events. The topic of property values – at one time Mahesh's favourite topic, but now depressing to everybody – didn't come up. When we did talk, it was about what we were eating.

Towards the end Shoba asked about Yvette. It was the first time she had done so. I gave her some idea of how things were. She said, 'I'm sorry. Something like that may not happen to you again for twenty years.' And after all that I had thought about Shoba, her conventional ways and her malice, I was amazed by her sympathy and wisdom.

Mahesh cleared the table and prepared the Nescafé – so far I had seen no servant. Shoba pulled one set of curtains apart a little, to let in more light. She sat, in the extra light, on the modern settee – shiny tubular metal frame, chunky padded arm-rests – and asked me to sit beside her. 'Here, Salim.'

She looked carefully at me while I sat down. Then, lifting her head a little, she showed me her profile and said, 'Do you see anything on my face?'

I didn't understand the question.

She said, 'Salim!' and turned her face full to me, keeping it lifted, fixing her eyes on mine. 'Am I still badly disfigured? Look around my eyes and my left cheek. Especially the left cheek. What do you see?'

Mahesh had set down the cups of coffee on the low table and was standing beside me, looking with me. He said, 'Salim can't see anything.'

Shoba said, 'Let him speak for himself. Look at my left eye. Look at the skin below the eye, and on the cheekbone.' And she held her face up, as though posing for a head on a coin.

Looking hard, looking for what she wanted me to find, I saw that what I had thought of as the colour of fatigue or illness below her eye was also in parts a very slight staining of the skin, a faint lividness on her pale skin, just noticeable on the left cheekbone. And having seen it, after having not seen it, I couldn't help seeing it; and I saw it as the disfigurement she took it to be. She saw that I saw. She went sad, resigned.

Mahesh said, 'It isn't so bad now. You *made* him see it.'

Shoba said, 'When I told my family that I was going to live with Mahesh, my brothers threatened to throw acid on my face. You could say that has come to pass. When my father died they sent me a cable. I took that as a sign that they wanted me to go back home for the ceremonies. It was a terrible way to go back – my father dead, the country in such a state, the Africans being so awful. I saw everybody on the edge of a precipice. But I couldn't tell them that. When you asked them what they were going to do, they would pretend that it was all all right, there was nothing to worry about. And you would have to pretend with them. Why are we like that?

'One morning I don't know what possessed me. There was this Sindhi girl who had studied in England – as she said – and had set up a hairdresser's shop. The sun is very bright in the highlands there, and I had done a lot of driving about, visiting old friends and just driving about, getting out of the house. Every place I used to like, and went to see, I began to hate, and I had to stop. I suppose it was that driving about that had darkened and blotched my skin. I asked the Sindhi girl whether there wasn't some cream or something I could use. She said she had something. She used this something. I cried out to her to stop. She had used peroxide. I ran home with my face scorched. And that house of death became for me truly a house of grief.

'I couldn't stay after that. I had to hide my face from everybody. And then I ran back here, to hide as before. Now I can go nowhere. I only go out at night sometimes. It has got better. But I still have to be careful. Don't tell me anything, Salim. I saw the truth in your eyes. I can't go abroad now. I so much wanted to go, to get away. And we had the money. New York, London, Paris. Do you know Paris? There is a skin specialist there. They say he peels your skin better than anybody else. That would be nice, if I could get there. And then I could go anywhere. Suisse, now – how do you say it in English?'

'Switzerland.'

'You see. Living in this flat, I'm even forgetting my English. That would be a nice place, I always think, if you could get a permit.'

All the while Mahesh looked at her face, half encouraging her, half irritated with her. His elegant red cotton shirt with the stiff, nicely shaped collar was open at the neck – it was part of the stylishness he had learned from her.

I was glad to get away from them, from the obsession they had forced on me in their sitting room. Peeling, skin – the words made me uneasy long after I had left them.

Their obsession was with more than a skin blemish. They had cut themselves off. Once they were supported by their idea of their high traditions (kept going somewhere else, by other people); now they were empty in Africa, and unprotected, with nothing to fall back on. They had begun to rot. I was like them. Unless I acted now, my fate would be like theirs. That constant questioning of mirrors and eyes; compelling others to look for the blemish that kept you in hiding; lunacy in a small room.

I decided to rejoin the world, to break out of the narrow geography of the town, to do my duty by those who depended on me. I wrote to Nazruddin that I was coming to London for a visit, leaving him to interpret that simple message. What a decision, though! When no other choice was left to me, when family and community hardly existed, when duty hardly had a meaning, and there were no safe houses.

I left eventually on a plane which travelled on to the east of the continent before it turned north. This plane stopped at our airport. I didn't have to go to the capital to take it. So even now the capital remained unknown to me.

I fell asleep on the night flight to Europe. A woman in the window seat, going out to the aisle, rubbed against my legs and awakened me. I thought, 'But that's Yvette. She's with me, then. I'll wait for her to come back.' And wide awake, for ten or fifteen seconds I waited. Then I understood that it had been a waking dream. That was pain, to understand that I was alone, and flying to quite a different destiny.

15

I HAD never travelled on an aeroplane before. I half remembered what Indar had said about aeroplane travel; he had said, more or less, that the aeroplane had helped him to adjust to his homelessness. I began to understand what he meant.

I was in Africa one day; I was in Europe the next morning. It was more than travelling fast. It was like being in two places at once. I woke up in London with little bits of Africa on me – like the airport tax ticket, given me by an official I knew, in the middle of another kind of crowd, in another kind of building, in another climate. Both places were real; both places were unreal. You could play off one against the other; and you had no feeling of having made a final decision, a great last journey. Which, in a way, was what this was for me, though I only had an excursion ticket, a visitor's visa, and I had to go back within six weeks.

The Europe the aeroplane brought me to was not the Europe I had known all my life. When I was a child Europe ruled my world. It had defeated the Arabs in Africa and controlled the interior of the continent. It ruled the coast and all the countries of the Indian Ocean with which we traded; it supplied our goods. We knew who we were and where we had come from. But it was Europe that gave us the descriptive postage stamps that gave us our ideas of what was picturesque about ourselves. It also gave us a new language.

Europe no longer ruled. But it still fed us in a hundred ways with its language and sent us its increasingly wonderful goods, things which, in the bush of Africa, added year by year to our idea of who we were, gave us that idea of our modernity and development, and made us aware of another Europe – the Europe of great cities, great stores, great buildings, great universities. To that Europe only the privileged or the gifted among us journeyed. That was the Europe Indar had gone to when he had left for his famous university. That was the Europe that someone like Shoba had in mind when she spoke of travelling.

But the Europe I had come to – and knew from the outset I was coming to – was neither the old Europe nor the new. It was something shrunken and mean and forbidding. It was the Europe where Indar, after his time at the famous university, had suffered and tried to come to some resolution about his place in the world; where Nazruddin and his family had taken refuge; where hundreds of thousands of people like myself, from parts of the world like mine, had forced themselves in, to work and live.

Of this Europe I could form no mental picture. But it was there in London; it couldn't be missed; and there was no mystery. The effect of those little stalls, booths, kiosks and choked grocery shops – run by people like myself – was indeed of people who had squashed themselves in. They traded in the middle of London as they had traded in the middle of Africa. The goods travelled a shorter distance, but the relationship of the trader to his goods remained the same. In the streets of London I saw these people, who were like myself, as from a distance. I saw the young girls selling packets of cigarettes at midnight, seemingly imprisoned in their kiosks, like puppets in a puppet theatre. They were cut off from the life of the great city where they had come to live, and I wondered about the pointlessness of their own hard life, the pointlessness of their difficult journey.

What illusions Africa gave to people who came from outside! In Africa I had thought of our instinct and capacity for work, even in extreme conditions, as heroic and creative. I had contrasted it with the indifference and withdrawal of village Africa. But now in London, against a background of busyness, I saw this instinct purely as instinct, pointless, serving only itself. And a feeling of rebellion possessed me, stronger than any I had known in my childhood. To this was added a new sympathy for the rebellion

Indar had spoken of to me, the rebellion he had discovered when he had walked beside the river of London and had decided to reject the ideas of home and ancestral piety, the unthinking worship of his great men, the self-suppression that went with that worship and those ideas, and to throw himself consciously into the bigger, harder world. It was the only way I could live here, if I had to live here.

Yet I had had my life of rebellion, in Africa. I had taken it as far as I could take it. And I had come to London for relief and rescue, clinging to what remained of our organized life.

Nazruddin wasn't surprised by my engagement to his daughter Kareisha. He had always, as I realized with dismay, held fast to that idea of my faithfulness which years before he had seen in my hand. Kareisha herself wasn't surprised. In fact, the only person who seemed to examine the event with some astonishment was myself, who marvelled that such a turn in my life could occur so easily.

The engagement came almost at the end of my time in London. But it had been taken as settled from the start. And, really, it was comforting, in the strange big city, after that fast journey, to be taken over by Kareisha, to have her call me by my name all the time, to have her lead me about London, she the knowing one (Uganda and Canada behind her), I the primitive (acting up a little).

She was a pharmacist. That was partly Nazruddin's doing. With his experience of change and sudden upheaval, he had long ago lost faith in the power of property and business to protect people; and he had pushed his children into acquiring skills that could be turned to account anywhere. It might have been her job that gave Kareisha her serenity, extraordinary for an unmarried woman of thirty from our community; or it might have been her full family life, and the example of Nazruddin, still relishing his experiences and looking for new sights. But I felt more and more that at some stage in Kareisha's wanderings there must have been a romance. At one time the idea would have outraged me. I didn't mind now. And the man must have been nice. Because he had left Kareisha with an affection for men. This was new to me – my experience of women was so limited. I luxuriated in this affection of Kareisha's, and acted out my man's role a little. It was wonderfully soothing.

Acted – there was a lot of that about me at this time. Because always I had to go back to my hotel (not far from their flat) and there I had to face my solitude, the other man that I also was. I hated that hotel room. It made me feel I was nowhere. It forced old anxieties on me and added new ones, about London, about this bigger world where I would have to make my way. Where would I start? When I turned the television on, it wasn't to marvel. It was to become aware of the great strangeness outside, and to wonder how those men on the screen had had themselves picked out from the crowd. And always in my mind then was the comfort of 'going back', of taking another aeroplane, of perhaps not having, after all, to be here. The decisions and the pleasures of the day and early evening were regularly cancelled out by me at night.

Indar had said about people like me that when we came to a great city we closed our eyes; we were concerned only to show that we were not amazed. I was a little like that, even with Kareisha to guide me around. I could say that I was in London, but I didn't really know where I was. I had no means of grasping the city. I knew only that I was in the Gloucester Road. My hotel was there; Nazruddin's flat was there. I travelled everywhere by underground train, popping down into the earth at one place, popping up at another, not able to relate one place to the other, and sometimes making complicated interchanges to travel short distances.

The only street I knew well was the Gloucester Road. If I walked in one direction I came to more buildings and avenues and got lost. If I walked in the other direction I went past a lot of tourist eating places, a couple of Arab restaurants, and came to the park. There was a wide, sloping avenue in the park with boys skateboarding. At the top of the slope there was a big pond with a paved rim. It looked artificial, but it was full of real birds, swans and different kinds of ducks; and that always struck me as strange, that the birds didn't mind being there. Artificial birds, like the lovely celluloid things of my childhood, wouldn't have been out of place. Far away, all around, beyond the trees, were the buildings.

There you really did have an idea of the city as something made by man, and not as something that had just grown by itself and was simply there. Indar had spoken of that, too; and he was right. It was so easy for people like us to think of great cities as natural growths. It reconciled us to our own shanty cities. We slipped into thinking that one place was one thing, and another place another thing.

In the park on fine afternoons people flew kites, and sometimes Arabs from the embassies played football below the trees. There were always a lot of Arabs about, fair-skinned people, real Arabs, not the half-African Arabs of our coast; one of the news-stands outside the Gloucester Road station was full of Arabic papers and magazines. Not all of the Arabs were rich or clean. Sometimes I saw little groups of poor Arabs in dingy clothes squatting on the grass in the park or on the pavements of the streets near by. I thought they were servants, and that seemed to me shameful enough. But then one day I saw an Arab lady with her slave.

I spotted the fellow at once. He had his little white cap on and his plain white gown, proclaiming his status to everybody, and he was carrying two carrier bags of groceries from the Waitrose supermarket on the Gloucester Road. He was walking the regulation ten paces ahead of his mistress, who was fat in the way Arab women like to be, with blue markings on her pale face below her gauzy black veil. She was pleased with herself; you could see that being in London and doing this modern shopping with other housewives at the Waitrose supermarket had excited her. For a moment she thought I was an Arab and she gave me a look, through her gauzy veil, which was meant to get back a look of approval and admiration from me.

As for the fellow carrying the groceries, he was a thin, fair-skinned young man, and I would have said that he had been born in the house. He had the vacant, dog-like expression that house-born slaves, as I remembered, liked to put on when they were in public with their masters and performing some simple task. This fellow was pretending that the Waitrose groceries were a great burden, but this was just an act, to draw attention to himself and the lady he served. He too had mistaken me for an Arab, and when we crossed he had dropped the burdened-down expression and given me a look of wistful inquisitiveness, like a puppy that wanted to play but had just been made to understand that it wasn't play-time.

I was going to the Waitrose place to get a gift of wine for Nazruddin. He hadn't lost his taste for wine and good food. He was happy to be my guide in these matters; and indeed, after years of that Portuguese stuff in Africa, white and meaningless or red and acrid, the range of wines in London was a small daily excitement for me. At dinner in the flat (and before television: he watched for a couple of hours every night) I told Nazruddin about the slave in white. He said he wasn't surprised; it was a new feature of life in the Gloucester Road; for a couple of weeks he had been noticing a grubby fellow in brown.

Nazruddin said: 'In the old days they made a lot of fuss if they caught you sending a couple of fellows to Arabia in a dhow. Today they have their passports and visas like everybody else, and walk past immigration like everybody else, and nobody gives a damn.

'I'm superstitious about the Arabs. They gave us and half the world our religion, but I can't help feeling that when they leave Arabia terrible things are about to happen in the world. You just have to think of where we come from. Persia, India, Africa. Think of what happened there. Now Europe. They're pumping the oil in and sucking the money out. Pumping the oil in to keep the system going, sucking the money out to send it crashing down. They need Europe. They want the goods and the properties and at the same time they need a safe place for their money. Their own countries are so dreadful. But they're destroying money. They're killing the goose that lays the golden egg.

'And they aren't the only ones. All over the world money is in flight. People have scraped the world clean, as clean as an African scrapes his yard, and now they want to run from the dreadful places where they've made their money and find some nice safe country. I was one of the crowd. Koreans, Filipinos, people from Hong Kong and Taiwan, South Africans, Italians, Greeks, South Americans, Argentines, Colombians, Venezuelans, Bolivians, a lot of black people who've cleaned out places you've never heard of,

Chinese from everywhere. All of them are on the run. They are frightened of the fire. You mustn't think it's only Africa people are running from.

'Mostly nowadays, since Switzerland closed down, they are going to the United States and Canada. And they are waiting for them there, to take them to the cleaners. There they meet the experts. The South Americans are waiting for the South Americans, the Asians for the Asians, the Greeks for the Greeks. And they take them to the cleaners. In Toronto, Vancouver, California. As for Miami, that is one big cleaning establishment.

'I knew about this before I went to Canada. I didn't let anybody sell me a million-dollar villa in California or an orange grove in Central America or a piece of swamp in Florida. You know what I bought instead? You wouldn't believe it. I bought an oil well, part of one. The man was a geologist. Advani introduced him to me. They said they wanted ten of us to form a little private oil company. They wanted to raise a hundred thousand dollars, everybody putting up ten. The authorized capital, though, was to be more than that, and the arrangement was that if we struck oil the geologist was to buy the rest of the shares at nominal rates. That was fair. It was his stake, his work.

'The stake was in order, the land was there. In Canada you can just go and do your own drilling. You can hire the equipment, and it doesn't cost all that much. Thirty thousand for a trial well, depending on where you want to drill. And they don't have the fruits-of-the-earth legislation you have where you are. I checked it all out. It was a risk, but I thought it was only a geological risk. I put up my ten. And guess what. We struck oil. Overnight, then, my ten was worth two hundred – well, say a hundred. But since we were a private company the profit was only a paper profit. We could only sell to one another, and none of us had that kind of money.

'The geologist exercised his options and bought up the remaining shares of the company for virtually nothing. So he acquired control of our company – but all that was in the agreement. Then he bought a semi-bankrupt mining company. We wondered about this, but we didn't question the wisdom of our man now. Then he disappeared to one of the black islands. He had linked the two companies in some way, borrowed a million dollars for our company on the strength of our oil, and transferred the money on some pretext to his own company. He left us with the debt. The oldest trick in the book, and the nine of us stood and watched while it was happening as though we were watching a man dig a hole in the road. To add insult to injury, we found out that he hadn't put up his ten. He had done it all with our money. Now I suppose he is moving heaven and earth to transfer his million to some safe place. Anyway, that was how I achieved the impossible, converting ten into a debt of a hundred.

'In time the debt will settle itself. The oil is there. I might even get my ten back. The trouble with people like us, running about the world with money to hide, is that we are good about business only in our own places. Still. The oil was only a sideline. What I was trying to do was to run a movie theatre, an ethnic theatre. You know the word? It means all the foreign groups in a place. It was very ethnic where I was, but I suppose I got the idea only because there was a theatre for sale, and it seemed a nice downtown property to get.

'Everything was working when I looked at the place, but when I took over I found we couldn't get a clear picture on the screen. At first I thought it just had to do with the lenses. Then I realized that the man who had sold me the place had changed the equipment. I went to him and said, "You can't do this." He said, "Who are you? I don't know you." So. Well, we straightened out the projectors in the end, we improved the seating and so on. Business wasn't too good. An ethnic theatre downtown wasn't such a good idea. The thing about some of those ethnic groups over there is that they don't like moving around too much. They just want to go home as fast as they can and stay there. The pictures that did well were the Indian pictures. We got a lot of Greeks then. The Greeks love Indian pictures. Did you know that? Anyway. We struggled through the summer. The cold weather came. I threw some switches for the heating. Nothing came on. There was no heating system. Or what was there had been taken away.

'I went to the man again. I said, "You sold me the theatre as a going concern." He said, "Who are you?" I said, "My family have been traders and merchants in the Indian Ocean for centuries, under every kind of government. There is a reason why we have lasted so long. We bargain hard, but we stick to our bargain. All our contracts are oral, but we deliver what we promise. It isn't because we are saints. It is because the whole thing breaks down otherwise." He said, "You should go back to the Indian Ocean."

'When I left him I walked very fast. I stumbled on an unevenness in the pavement and turned my ankle. I took that as a sign. My luck had run out; I knew that it had to. I didn't feel I could stay in that country. I felt the place was a hoax. They thought they were part of the West, but really they had become like the rest of us who had run to them for safety. They were like people far away, living on other people's land and off other people's brains, and that was all they thought they should do. That was why they were so bored and dull. I thought I would die if I stayed among them.

'When I came to England all my instincts were to go into light engineering. A small country, good roads and railways, power, every kind of industrial facility. I thought that if you identified some area, got in good equipment, and employed Asians, you couldn't lose. Europeans are bored with machines and factories. Asian people love them; they secretly prefer factories to their family life. But after Canada I had lost my nerve. I thought I would play safe. I thought I would go into property. That was how I came to the Gloucester Road.

'It is one of the centres of the tourist trade in London, as you see. London is destroying itself for its tourist trade – you can see that here. Hundreds of houses, thousands of flats, have been emptied to provide hotels, hostels and restaurants for the tourists. Private accommodation is getting scarcer. I thought I couldn't lose. I bought six flats in a block. I bought at the height of the boom. Prices have now dropped twenty-five per cent, and interest rates have risen from twelve per cent to twenty and even twenty-four per cent. Do you remember the scandal on the coast when it came out that Indar's people were lending money at ten and twelve per cent? I feel I no longer understand money. And the Arabs are in the streets outside.

'I have to charge ridiculous rents to break even. And when you charge ridiculous rents you attract strange people. This is one of my souvenirs. It is a betting slip from one of the betting shops in the Gloucester Road. I keep it to remind myself of a simple girl who came down from the north. She got her Arabs mixed up. The Arab she became involved with was one of the poor ones, from Algeria. She used to dump her rubbish outside her flat door. The Algerian used to gamble on the horses. That was how they were going to make the big time.

'They won, and then they lost. They couldn't pay the rent. I reduced it. They still couldn't pay. There were complaints about the rubbish and the quarrels, and the Algerian was in the habit of pissing in the lift when he was locked out. I asked them to leave. They refused, and the law was on their side. I had a new lock put in one day when they were out. When they came back they simply called the police, and the police opened up for them. To prevent me getting in again, they put in another lock. By this time, on that door, key-holes and their metal surrounds were like buttons down a shirt front. I gave up.

'Every kind of bill was unpaid. I went up one morning and knocked. The flat was full of whispers, but no one opened. The lift was close to the flat door. I opened the door of the lift and closed it. They thought I had gone down, and sure enough they opened up to check. I put my foot in the door and went in. The little flat was full of poor Arabs in singlets and horribly coloured pants. There was bedding all over the floor. The girl wasn't with them. They had sent her away, or she had left. So for two months, while I had been paying twenty per cent interest and other charges, I had been giving free shelter to a whole tentful of poor Arabs. They are a strange people racially. One of them had bright red hair. What were they doing in London? What were they expecting to do? How are they going to survive? What place is there in the world for people like that? There are so many of them.

'Here is another girl who ran out on me. Seven hundred pounds went with her. She came from Eastern Europe. Refugee? But she was a woman. She must have spent quite a bit of money to get these photographic cards printed. Here she is, up to her neck in water – I don't know why she thought she should put that on her card. And here she is, pretending to thumb a lift, in a kind of button-up dungaree open at the top, and showing a little breast. Here she is wearing a big black bowler hat and black leather trousers and sticking out her little bottom. "Erika. Model-Actress-Singer-Dancer. Hair: Red. Eyes: Grey-Green. Specialities: Fashion-Cosmetic-Footwear-Hands-Legs-Teeth-Hair. 5′ 9″. 32–25–33." All that, and nobody wants to buy. All that happened to her was that she became pregnant, ran up a telephone bill of £1200 – twelve hundred pounds! – and ran away one night, leaving these picture cards of herself. A big pile. I couldn't bear to throw them all away. I felt I should keep one, for her sake.

'What happens to these people? Where do they go? How do they live? Do they go back home? Do they have homes to go back to? You've talked a lot, Salim, about those girls from East Africa in the tobacco kiosks, selling cigarettes at all hours of the night. They've depressed you. You say they don't have a future and that they don't even know where they are. I wonder whether that isn't their luck. They expect to be bored, to do what they do. The people I've been talking about have expectations and they know they're lost in London. I suppose it must be dreadful for them when they have to go back. This area is full of them, coming to the centre because it is all they know about and because they think it's smart, and trying to make something out of nothing. You can't blame them. They're doing what they see the big people doing.

'This place is so big and busy you take some time to see that very little is happening. It's just keeping itself going. A lot of people have been quietly wiped out. There's no new money, no real money, and this makes everybody more desperate. We've come here at the wrong time. But never mind. It's the wrong time everywhere else too. When we were in Africa in the old days, consulting our catalogues and ordering our goods and watching the ships unload in the harbour, I don't suppose we thought it would be like this in Europe, or that the British passports we took out as protection against the Africans would actually bring us here, and that the Arabs would be in the streets outside.'

That was Nazruddin. Kareisha said, 'I hope you know you've been listening to the story of a happy man.' She didn't have to tell me.

Nazruddin was all right. He had made himself at home in the Gloucester Road. The London setting was strange, but Nazruddin appeared to be as he had always been. He had moved on from fifty to sixty, but he didn't look particularly older. He still wore his old-style suits; and the broad lapels (with the curling tips) which I associated with him were back in fashion. I didn't think he doubted that his property venture would eventually right itself. What oppressed him (and made him talk about his luck running out) was his inactivity. But he had found in the half a mile or so of the Gloucester Road, between the underground railway station and the park, the perfect retirement resort.

He bought his newspaper in one shop, read it with morning coffee in a tiny café that also offered old water-colour paintings for sale; took a turn in the park; shopped for delicacies in the various food shops. Sometimes he gave himself the luxury of tea or a drink in the big, old-fashioned lounge of the red-brick hotel near the station. Sometimes he went to the Arab or Persian 'Dancing Room'. And there was the nightly excitement of television in the flat. The population of the Gloucester Road was cosmopolitan, always shifting, with people of all ages. It was a friendly, holiday place, and Nazruddin's days were full of encounters and new observations. He said it was the best street in the world; he intended to stay there as long as he was allowed to.

He had chosen well once again. That had always been his gift, to suggest that he had chosen well. At one time it had made me anxious to find the world he had found. Nazruddin's example, or the way in which I had secretly interpreted his experience, had after all helped to determine my life. Now in London, glad though I was to find him in good spirits, that gift of his depressed me. It made me feel that after all these years I had never caught up with him, and never would; that my life would always be unsatisfactory. It could send me back to my hotel room in an agony of solitude and dread.

Sometimes as I was falling asleep I was kicked awake by some picture that came to me of my African town – absolutely real (and the aeroplane could take me there tomorrow), but its associations made it dreamlike. Then I remembered my illumination, about the need of men only to live, about the illusion of pain. I played off London against Africa until both became unreal, and I could fall asleep. After a time I didn't have to call up the illumination, the mood of that African morning. It was there, beside me, that remote vision of the planet, of men lost in space and time, but dreadfully, pointlessly busy.

It was in this state of indifference and irresponsibility – like the lost Gloucester Road people Nazruddin had spoken about – that I became engaged to Kareisha.

One day, near the end of my time in London, Kareisha said, 'Have you been to see Indar? Are you going to see him?'

Indar! His name had come up often in our talk, but I didn't know that he was in London.

Kareisha said, 'That's just as well. I wouldn't recommend a visit or trying to get in touch or anything like that. He can be difficult and aggressive when he's in the mood, and it isn't funny. He's been like that ever since his outfit folded.'

'His outfit folded?'

'About two years ago.'

'But he knew it was going to fold. He talked as though he expected it to fold. Lecturers, universities, African interchange – he knew the excitement couldn't last, that no local government really cared one way or the other. But I thought he had his plans. He said he could exploit himself in lots of other ways.'

Kareisha said: 'It was different when the time came. He cared more about his outfit than he pretended. Of course there are many things he can do. But he's determined not to do them. He can get a job in a university, certainly in America. He has the contacts. He can write for the papers. We don't talk about it now when we see him. Naz' says Indar's become help-resistant. The trouble is he invested too much in that outfit of his. And after it folded he had that bad experience in America. A bad experience for him any- way.

'You know Indar. You know that when he was young the most important thing to him was that his family was rich. You remember the house they lived in. When you live in a house like that I suppose you think ten or twelve or twenty times a day that you are very rich or that you are richer than nearly everybody else. And you remember how he used to get on. Not talking about money, but it was always there. You would say that he felt that money had made him holy. All rich people are like that, I suppose. And that was one idea about himself that Indar never lost. His outfit didn't give him back his money but it made him holy again. It raised him up again above everybody else and made him equal with the big boys of Africa, being a guest of the government in this place and that place, meeting foreign ministers and presidents. So it was a blow when the outfit folded, when the Americans decided there was nothing in it for them.

'Indar went to America, to New York. Being Indar, he stayed in an expensive hotel. He saw his American people. They were all very nice. But he didn't like the direction in which they were pushing him. He felt they were pushing him towards smaller things and he pretended not to notice. I don't know what Indar was expecting from these people. No, I know. He was hoping to be made one of them, to keep on at the old level. He thought that was his due. He was spending a lot of money, and the money was running out. One day, much against his will, he even looked at cheaper hotels. He didn't want to do that because he thought that even to start looking for cheaper hotels was to admit that it soon might be over for him. He was appalled by the cheaper hotels. In New York you drop fast, he said.

'There was one man in particular he used to deal with. He had met this man in London right at the beginning, and they had become friends. It wasn't always like that. In the beginning he had thought the man foolish and had been aggressive with him. That used to embarrass Indar, because it was this man who had brought him out of the mess he was in the first time in London. This man had given Indar back his confidence then, had made him think positively about Africa and himself. It was this man who had drawn the good ideas out of Indar. Indar had grown to depend on this man. He thought of him as his equal, and you will know what I mean by that.

'They used to meet in New York. Lunch, drinks, meetings in the office. But nothing seemed to be happening. It was always just back to the hotel, and waiting. Indar was getting lower. The man invited Indar to dinner one evening at his apartment. It was an expensive-looking building. Indar gave his name downstairs and took the elevator up. The elevator-man waited and watched until the apartment door was opened and Indar was let in. When Indar went inside he was stunned.

'He had thought of the man as his equal, his friend. He had opened himself to the man. He found now that the man was immensely rich. He had never been in a richer room. You or I would have found it interesting, the money. Indar was shattered. It was only there, in the rich apartment with the costly objects and pictures, that Indar understood that while he had opened himself to the man, and talked of all the little things that made him anxious, he had received very little of that in return. This man was much, much holier. It was more than Indar could bear. He felt he had been cheated and fooled. He had grown to depend on this man. He tested his ideas on him; he looked to him for moral support. He thought of this man as someone like himself. He felt he had been led on all these years, and exploited in the worst way. All that optimism dragged out of him, after he had lost so much. All those constructive ideas! Africa! There was nothing of Africa in that apartment, or in the dinner party. No danger, no loss. The private life, the life with friends, was quite different from the life outside. I don't know what Indar expected.

'During the dinner he focused all his resentment on a young woman. She was the wife of a very old journalist who had written books that had made a lot of money at one time. Indar hated her. Why had she married the old man? What was the joke? Because apparently the dinner had been arranged around her and the man she was having an affair with. They didn't keep it too secret, and the old man pretended not to notice. He just kept babbling on about French politics in the 1930s, still keeping himself in the centre of things, though, telling about the important people he had met and what they had told him personally. No one paid him the slightest attention, but he didn't mind.

'Still, he had been a famous man. Indar thought a lot about that. He was trying to put himself on the old man's side, to hate the others better. Then the old man noticed who Indar was and he began to talk about India in the old days and his meeting with Gandhi in some famous mud hut. As you know, Gandhi and Nehru aren't Indar's favourite subjects. He decided he wasn't doing any social work that night, and he was very rough with the old man, much rougher than anybody else had been.

'So at the end of the dinner Indar was in a state. He thought about the cheap hotels he had looked at, and as he was going down in the elevator he had a wild panic. He thought he was going to pass out. But he got outside all right, and there he calmed down. He had got a simple idea. The idea was that it was time for him to go home, to get away.

'And that's how it has been with him. From time to time that is all he knows, that it is time for him to go home. There is some dream village in his head. In between he does the lowest kind of job. He knows he is equipped for better things, but he doesn't want to do them. I believe he enjoys being told he can do better. We've given up now. He doesn't want to risk anything again. The idea of sacrifice is safer, and he likes the act. But you will see for yourself, when you come back.'

Kareisha, talking about Indar, touched me more than she knew. That idea of going home, of leaving, the idea of the other place – I had lived with it in various forms for many years. In Africa it had always been with me. In London, in my hotel room, I had allowed it on some nights to take me over. It was a deception. I saw now that it comforted only to weaken and destroy.

That illumination I held on to, about the unity of experience and the illusion of pain, was part of the same way of feeling. We fell into it – people like Indar and myself – because it was the basis of our old way of life. But I had rejected that way of life – and just in time. In spite of the girls in the cigarette kiosks, that way of life no longer existed, in London or Africa. There could be no going back; there was nothing to go back to. We had become what the world outside had made us; we had to live in the world as it existed. The younger Indar was wiser. Use the aeroplane; trample on the past, as Indar had said he had trampled on the past. Get rid of that idea of the past; make the dreamlike scenes of loss ordinary.

That was the mood in which I left London and Kareisha, to go back to Africa, to wind up there, realize as much as I could of what I had. And make a fresh start somewhere else.

I got to Brussels in the late afternoon. The plane for Africa was leaving from there at midnight. I felt afresh the drama of aeroplane travel – London vanished, Africa to come, Brussels now. I gave myself dinner and went to a bar afterwards, a place with women. All the excitement lay in the idea of the place rather than the place itself. What followed, some time later, was brief and meaningless and reassuring. It didn't lessen the value of what I had had in Africa – that was no delusion; that remained true. And it removed the special doubt I felt about my engagement to Kareisha, whom I had not yet even kissed.

The woman, naked, unruffled, stood in front of a long mirror and looked at herself. Fat legs, roundish belly, chunky breasts. She said, 'I've begun to do yoga with a group of friends. We have a teacher. Do you do yoga?'

'I play a lot of squash.'

She paid no attention. 'Out teacher says that a man's psychic fluids can overpower a woman. Our teacher says that after a dangerous encounter a woman can become herself again by clapping her hands hard or by taking a deep breath. Which method do you recommend?'

'Clap your hands.'

She faced me as she might have faced her yoga teacher, drew herself up, half closed her eyes, pulled her outstretched arms back, and brought her hands violently together. At the sound, startling in the over-furnished little room, she opened her eyes, looked surprised, smiled as though she had been joking all along, and said, '*Go!*' When I was out in the street I took a deep breath, and went straight to the airport to catch the midnight plane.

IV

Battle

16

THE dawn came suddenly, in the west pale blue, in the east red with thick horizontal bars of black cloud. And for many minutes it was like that. The scale, the splendour – six miles above the earth! We came down slowly, leaving the upper light. Below the heavy cloud Africa showed as a dark-green, wet-looking land. You could see that it was barely dawn down there; in the forests and creeks it would still be quite dark. The forested land went on and on. The sun struck the bottom of the clouds; it was light when we touched down.

So at last I had come to the capital. It was a strange way to come to it, after such a roundabout journey. If I had come to it fresh from my up-river town it would have seemed immense, rich, a capital. But after Europe, and with London still close to me, it seemed flimsy in spite of its size, an echo of Europe, and like make-believe, at the end of all that forest.

The more experienced among the European passengers, paying no attention to the big photograph of the President with his chief's stick, made a rush at the immigration and customs officials and appeared to force their way through. I wondered at their confidence, but they were mainly people with protection – embassy people, people working on government projects, people working for big companies. My own passage was slower. When I was through, the terminal building was almost empty. The airline posters and the photograph of the President had no one to look at them. Most of the officials had disappeared. And it was fully morning.

It was a long drive into the town. It was like the drive, in my own town, from the Domain to the town centre. But the land was hillier here and everything was on a larger scale. The shanty towns and *cités* (with the maize plantings between houses) were bigger; there were buses, even a railway train with old-fashioned open coaches; there were factories. All along the road were big boards about ten feet high, uniformly painted, each with a separate saying or maxim of the President. Some of the painted portraits of the President were literally as big as a house. We had had nothing like that in our town. Everything in our town, as I realized, was on a smaller scale.

Portraits, maxims, occasional statues of the African madonna – they continued all the way to the hotel. If I had come to the capital fresh from our town I would have felt choked. But after Europe, and after what I had seen of the country from the air, and still with my sense of the flimsiness of the capital, my attitude was different, and I was surprised by it. There was to me an element of pathos in those maxims, portraits and statues, in this wish of a man of the bush to make himself big, and setting about it in such a crude way. I even felt a little sympathy for the man who was making such a display of himself.

I understood now why so many of our later visitors at the Domain found our country, and our awe of the President, comic. What I saw on the road from the airport didn't seem comic, though. I felt it more as a shriek. I had just come from Europe; I had seen the real competition.

Overnight I had changed one continent for another, and this odd sympathy for the President, this vision of the impossibility of what I thought he was trying to do, came just at the moment of arrival. The sympathy wore off as the town became more familiar and I began to see it as a larger version of my own town. The sympathy, in fact, began to wear off when I got to the new big hotel (air-conditioned, shops in the lobby, a swimming pool no one was using) and found it full of secret police. I can't imagine that they had much to do there. They were there to show themselves to visitors. And also because they liked being in the smart new hotel; they wanted to show themselves to visitors in that modern setting.

It was pathetic; or you could make a joke of it. But those men weren't always funny. Already, then, the tensions of Africa were returning to me.

This was the President's city. This was where he had grown up and where his mother had worked as a hotel maid. This was where, in colonial days, he had got his idea of Europe. The colonial city, more extensive than ours, with many residential areas rich with decorative, sheltering trees now fully grown, was still to be seen. It was with this Europe that, in his own buildings, the President wished to compete. The city, while decaying in the centre, with dirt roads and rubbish mounds just at the back of the great colonial boulevards, was yet full of new public works. Large areas near the river had been turned into Presidential reserves – palaces with great walls, gardens, state houses of various sorts.

In the Presidential gardens near the rapids (the rapids here matching ours, a thousand miles up river) the statue of the European explorer who had charted the river and used the first steamer had been replaced by a gigantic statue of an African tribesman with spear and shield, done in the modern African style – Father Huismans would have had no time for it. Beside this statue was a smaller one of an African madonna with a bowed, veiled head. Near by were the graves of the earliest Europeans: a little dead settlement, out of which it had all grown, out of which our own town had been seeded. Simple people, with simple trades and simple goods, but agents of Europe. Like the people who came now, like the people on the aeroplane.

The rapids made a constant, unchanging noise. The water hyacinths, the 'new thing in the river', beginning so far away, in the centre of the continent, bucked past in clumps and tangles and single vines, here almost at the end of their journey.

The next morning I went back to the airport, to take the up-country plane. By now I was more in tune with the place, and the spread of the capital made a greater impression on me. Always, beside the airport road, there was some new settlement. How did all these people live? The hilly land had been scraped clean, cut up, eroded, exposed. Had there been forest here? The posts that supported the President's maxim-boards were often set in bare clay. And the boards themselves, spattered with mud from the road and dust-blown at the bottom, not as fresh as they had seemed to me the previous morning, were like part of the desolation.

At the airport, in the section for internal flights, the departures board announced my flight and one other. The board was electrically operated and, according to a sign it carried, made in Italy. It was a modern piece of equipment; it was like the boards I had seen in the airports of London and Brussels. But below it, around the checking-in desks and weighing machines, was the usual scramble; and what was being checked in, with a lot of shouting, was like the cargo of a market jitney: metal trunks, cardboard boxes, cloth bundles, sacks of this and that, big enamel basins tied up in cloth.

I had my ticket and it was in order, but my name wasn't on the passenger list. Some francs had to pass first. And then, just as I was going out to the plane, a security man in plain clothes who was eating something asked for my papers and decided that they had to be examined more closely. He looked very offended and sent me to wait in an empty little inner room. This was standard procedure. The offended, sideways look, the little private room – this was how middle-rank officials let you know they were going to take some money off you.

But this fellow didn't get anything, because he played the fool and kept me waiting in that little room so long, without coming to collect, that he delayed the flight and was bawled out by an airline man, who, clearly knowing where I was to be found, burst into the little room, shouted to me to get out at once, and sent me running across the asphalt to the plane, last man in, but lucky.

In the front row was one of the airline's European pilots, a small, middle-aged, family man; beside him was a little African boy, but it was hard to tell whether there was any connection. Some rows behind there was a group of six or eight Africans, men in their thirties, with old jackets and shirts buttoned right up, who were talking loudly. They were drinking whisky, straight from the bottle – and it was nine in the morning. Whisky was expensive here, and these men wanted everybody to know that they were drinking whisky. The bottle was passed to strangers; it was even passed to me. These men were not like the men of my region. They were bigger, with different complexions and features. I couldn't understand their faces; I saw only their arrogance and drunkenness. Their talk was boastful; they wanted the rest of us to know that they were men who owned plantations. They were like people who had just come into money, and the whole thing struck me as odd.

It was a simple flight, two hours, with a half-way stop. And it seemed to me, with my experience of intercontinental travel, that we had just begun to cruise above the white clouds when we began coming down for that stop. We saw then that we had been following the river – brown, rippled and wrinkled and streaked from this height, with many channels between long thin islands of green. The aeroplane shadow moved over the forest top. That top became less even and tight as the aeroplane shadow grew bigger; the forest we came down to was quite ragged.

After we landed we were told to leave the aeroplane. We went to the small building at the edge of the airfield, and while we were there we saw the aeroplane turn, taxi, and fly away. It was needed for some Presidential service; it would come back when it had done that service. We had to wait. It was only about ten. Until about noon, while the heat built up, we were restless. Then we settled down – all of us, even the whisky-drinkers – to wait.

We were in the middle of bush. Bush surrounded the cleared area of the airfield. Far away a special density about the trees marked the course of the river. The aeroplane had shown how complex it was, how easy it would be to get lost, to waste hours paddling up channels that took you away from the main river. Not many miles from the river people would be living in villages more or less as they had lived for centuries. Less than forty-eight hours before, I had been in the over-trampled Gloucester Road, where the world met. Now, for hours, I had been staring at bush. How many miles separated me from the capital, from my own town? How long would it take to do the distance by land or by water? How many weeks, how many months, and against what dangers?

It clouded over. The clouds grew dark and the bush grew dark.

The sky began to jump with lightning and thunder; and then the rain and the wind came, driving us in from the verandah of the little building. It rained and stormed. The bush vanished in the rain. It was rain like this that fed these forests, that caused the grass and bright green weeds around the airfield building to grow so high. The rain slackened, the clouds lifted a little. The bush revealed itself again, one line of trees behind another, the nearer trees darker, the further trees fading line by line into the grey colour of the sky.

Empty beer bottles covered the metal tables. Not many people were moving about; nearly everyone had found the place where he was going to stay. No one was talking much. The middle-aged Belgian woman whom we had found in the building waiting to join our flight was still absorbed in the French paperback of *Peyton Place*. You could see that she had shut the bush and weather out and was living somewhere else.

The sun came out and glittered on the tall wet grass. The asphalt steamed, and for a while I watched that. Later in the afternoon one half of the sky went black, while the other half stayed light. The storm that began with vivid lightning in the black half then spread to us and it became dark and chill and very damp. The forest had become a place of gloom. There was no excitement in this second storm.

One of the African passengers, an elderly man, appeared with a grey felt hat and a blue bath robe of towelling material over his suit. No one paid him too much attention. I just noted his oddity, and thought, 'He's using a foreign thing in his own way.' And something like that went through my head when a bare-footed man turned up wearing a fireman's helmet with the transparent plastic visor pulled down. He was an old man with a shrunken face; his brown shorts and grey check shirt were ragged and soaked through. I thought: 'He's found a ready-made dancing mask.' He went from table to table, checking the beer bottles. When he decided that a bottle was worth emptying he raised the visor of his mask and drank.

It stopped raining, but it remained dark, the darkness of late afternoon. The aeroplane, at first only a brown smoke trail in the

sky, appeared. When we went out to the wet field to board it I saw
the man with the fireman's helmet – and a companion, also
helmeted – standing unsteadily beside the gangway. He was, after
all, a fireman.

As we rose we saw the river, catching the last of the light. It was
gold-red, then red. We followed it for many miles and minutes,
until it became a mere sheen, a smoothness, something extra black
between the black forests. Then it was all black. Through this
blackness we flew to our destination. The journey, which had
seemed so simple in the morning, had acquired another quality.
Distance and time had been restored to it. I felt I had been travelling for days, and when we began to go down again, I knew that I
had travelled far, and I wondered how I had had the courage to
live for so long in a place so far away.

And then, suddenly, it was easy. A familiar building; officials I
knew and could palaver with; people whose faces I understood;
one of our old disinfected taxis; the well-known lumpy road to the
town, at first through bush which had distinguishing features,
then past the squatters' settlements. After the strangeness of the
day, it was like organized life again.

We passed a burnt-out building, a new ruin. It had been a
primary school, never much of a place, more like a low shed, and
I might have missed it in the dark if the driver hadn't pointed it out
to me; it excited him. The insurrection, the Liberation Army –
that was still going on. It didn't lessen my relief at being in the
town, seeing the night-time pavement groups, and finding myself,
so quickly after arrival, something of the forest gloom still on
me, in my own street – all there, and as real and as ordinary as
ever.

It was a shock, a puncturing, to find Metty cold. I had made
such a journey. I wanted him to know; from him I had been expecting the warmest welcome. He must have heard the slam of the
taxi door and my palaver with the driver. But Metty didn't come
down. And all that he said when I went up the external staircase,
and found him standing in the doorway of his room, was: 'I didn't
expect to see you back, *patron*.' The whole journey seemed to turn
sour then.

Everything was in order in the flat. But about the sitting room and especially the bedroom there was something – perhaps an extra order, an absence of staleness – that made me feel that Metty had been spreading himself in the flat in my absence. The telegram that I had sent him from London must have caused him to retreat. Did he resent that? Metty? But he had grown up in our family; he knew no other life. He had always been with the family or with me. He had never been on his own, except on his journey up from the coast, and now.

He brought me coffee in the morning.

He said, 'I suppose you know why you come back, *patron.*'

'You said this last night.'

'Because you have nothing to come back to. You don't know? Nobody told you in London? You don't read the papers? You don't have anything. They take away your shop. They give it to Citizen Théotime. The President made a speech a fortnight back. He said he was radicalizing and taking away everything from everybody. All foreigners. The next day they put a padlock on the door. And a few other doors as well. You didn't read that in London? You don't have anything, I don't have anything. I don't know why you come back. I don't think it was for my sake.'

Metty was in a bad way. He had been alone. He must have been beside himself waiting for me to come back. He was trying to provoke some angry response from me. He was trying to get me to make some protective gesture. But I was as lost as he was.

Radicalization: two days before, in the capital, I had seen the word in a newspaper headline, but I hadn't paid attention. I had thought of it as just another word; we had so many. Now I understood that radicalization was the big new event.

And it was as Metty had said. The President had sprung another of his surprises, and this surprise concerned us. I – and others like me – had been nationalized. Our businesses had ceased to be ours, by decree, and were being given out by the President to new owners. These new owners were called 'state trustees'. Citizen Théotime had been made the state trustee of my business; and Metty said that for the last week the man had actually been spending his days in the shop.

'What does he do?'

'Do? He's waiting for you. He'll make you the manager. That is what you have come back for, *patron*. But you will see. Don't hurry yourself. Théo doesn't come to work too early.'

When I went to the shop I saw that the stock, which had gone down in six weeks, was displayed in the old way. Théo hadn't touched that. But my desk had been moved from its place next to the pillar in the front of the shop to the store-room at the back. Metty said that had happened on the first day. Citizen Théo had decided that the store-room was to be his office; he liked the privacy.

In the top drawer of the desk (where I used to keep Yvette's photographs, which had once transformed the view of the market square for me) there were many tattered French-African photo-novels and comic books: Africans shown living very modern lives, and in the comic books they were drawn almost like Europeans – in the last two or three years there had been a lot of this French-produced rubbish around. My own things – magazines, and shop documents I had thought Metty would need – were in the two bottom drawers. They had been handled with care; Théo had had that grace. Nationalization: it had been a word. It was shocking to face it in this concrete way.

I waited for Théo.

And when the man came I could see that he was embarrassed and his first impulse, when he saw me through the glass, was to walk past the door. I had known him years before as a mechanic; he used to look after the vehicles in the health department. Then, because he had certain tribal connections, he had risen politically, but not very high. He would have had trouble signing his name. He was about forty, undistinguished in appearance, with a broad, dark-brown face beaten up and spongy with drink. He was drunk now. But only on beer; he hadn't yet moved on to whisky. Nor had he moved on to the regulation official dress of short-sleeved jacket and cravat. He stuck to trousers and shirt. He was, really, a modest man.

I was standing where my desk used to be. And it occurred to me, noticing how sweated and grimy Théo's white shirt was, that it was like the time when the schoolboys, treating me like prey, used to come to the shop to try to get money out of me in simple ways. Théo was sweating through the pores on his nose. I don't believe he had washed his face that morning. He looked like a man who had added fresh drink, and nothing else, to a bad hangover.

He said, 'Mis' Salim. Salim. Citizen. You mustn't take this personally. It has not come about through any wish of mine. You know that I have the highest regard for you. But you know what the situation was like. The revolution had become' – he fumbled for the word – '*un pé pourrie*. A little rotten. Our young people were becoming impatient. It was necessary' – trying to find the right word, he looked confused, clenched his fist and made a clumsy cuffing gesture – 'it was necessary to radicalize. We had absolutely to radicalize. We were expecting too much of the President. No one was willing to take responsibility. Now responsibility has been forced on the people. But you will suffer in no way. Adequate compensation will be paid. You will prepare your own inventory. And you will continue as manager. The business will run as before. The President insists on that. No one is to suffer. Your salary will be fair. As soon as the Commissioner arrives, the papers will come through.'

After his hesitant start, he had spoken formally, as though he had prepared his words. At the end he became embarrassed again. He was waiting for me to say something. But then he changed his mind and went to the store-room, his office. And I left, to go and look for Mahesh at Bigburger.

There it was business as usual. Mahesh, a little plumper, was pulling coffees, and Ildephonse was jumping about and serving late breakfasts. I was surprised.

Mahesh said, 'But this has been an African company for years. It can't be radicalized any more. I just manage Bigburger for 'Phonse and a few others. They formed this African company and they gave me a little part in it, as manager, and then they bought a lease from me. That was during the boom. They owe the bank a lot. You wouldn't believe it when you look at 'Phonse. But it's true. That happened in a lot of places after Noimon sold out to the government. That gave us an idea which way the wind was blow-ing, and some of us decided to compensate ourselves in advance. It was easy enough then. The banks were flush with money.'

'Nobody told me.'

'It wasn't the kind of thing people would talk a lot about. And your thoughts were elsewhere.'

That was true. There had been a coolness between us at that time; we had both been scratchy after Noimon's departure.

I said, 'What about the Tivoli? All that new kitchen equipment. They invested so much.'

'That's crippled with debt. No African in his right mind would want to be the trustee of that. They queued up for yours, though. That was when I knew you hadn't done anything. Théotime and another man actually came to blows, right here in Bigburger. There were a lot of fights like that. It was like a carnival after the President announced the measures. So many people just going into places, not saying anything to the people inside, just making marks on doors or dropping pieces of cloth on the floor, as though they were claiming a piece of meat in the market. It was very bad for a few days. One Greek burnt down his coffee plantation. They've calmed down now. The President issued a statement, just to let everybody know that what the Big Man gives the Big Man can take away. That's how the Big Man gets them. He gives and he takes back.'

I spent the rest of the morning at Bigburger. It was strange for me, wasting the working day in chat, giving news, asking for news, watching the coming and going in Bigburger and the van der Weyden across the road, and all the time feeling myself separated from the life of the town.

Mahesh had little to tell me about Shoba. There was no change there. She still hid with her disfigurement in the flat. But Mahesh no longer fought against that situation or seemed irritated by it. It didn't make him unhappy – as I had feared it might – to hear about London and my travels. Other people travelled; other people got away; he didn't. For Mahesh it had become as simple as that.

I became Théotime's manager. He seemed relieved and happy, and agreed to the salary I suggested for myself. I bought a table and chair and set them next to the pillar, so that it was almost like old times. I spent many days assembling old invoices, checking stock, and preparing the inventory. It was a complicated document, and of course it was padded. But Théotime approved it so readily (sending me out of the store-room while he struggled to sign *Cit: Theot:*) that I felt that Mahesh was right, that no compensation was going to be paid, that the most I could expect, if anybody remembered, were government bonds.

The inventory only reminded me of what I had lost. What remained? In a bank in Europe I had about eight thousand dollars, proceeds from my gold dealings in the old days; that money had just stayed and rotted, losing value. There was the flat in the town, for which there would be no buyer; but the car would fetch a few thousand dollars. And I had about half a million local francs in various banks – about fourteen thousand dollars at the official rate of exchange, and half that on the free market. That was all; it wasn't a great deal. I had to make more, as fast as I could; and the little I had, I had to get out of the country.

As manager in the shop I had opportunities; but they were not extraordinary. And so I began to live dangerously. I began to deal in gold and ivory. I bought, stored, and sold; or acting for bigger operators (who paid directly to my bank in Europe), I stored and shipped on, for a percentage. It was dangerous. My suppliers, and sometimes the poachers, were officials or army people, and these people were always dangerous to deal with. The rewards were not great. Gold only sounds expensive; you have to handle kilos before your percentage amounts to anything. Ivory was better, but ivory was more difficult to store (I continued to use the hole at the bottom of the staircase in my yard) and trickier to ship. For shipping I used one of the ordinary market vans or jitneys, sending the stuff (larger tusks in mattress consignments, smaller pieces in sacks of cassava) with other goods, always doing so now in the name of Citizen Théotime, and sometimes getting Théotime himself to pull a little political rank and give the driver a good talking-to in public.

Money could be made. But to get it out of the country was another matter. Money can be got out of countries like these only if you deal in very large sums and can get high officials or ministers to take an interest; or if there is a certain amount of business activity. There was little activity now, and I had to depend on visitors who for various reasons needed local currency. There was no other way. And I had to trust these people to pay up when they got back to Europe or the United States.

It was a slow, tout-like, humiliating business. I wish I could say that I discovered certain rules about human behaviour. I wish I could say that people of a certain class or country were to be trusted and people of another class and country not trusted. That would have made it much simpler. It was a gamble each time. I lost two-thirds of my money in this way; I gave it away to strangers.

I was in and out of the Domain on this money business; it was there that I made many of my contacts. At first it made me uneasy to be there. But then I proved Indar's point about trampling on the past: the Domain quickly ceased to be what it had been for me. It became a place where honourable people – many of them first-time law-breakers, who were later to use their respect for the law to cheat me with a clear mind – tried to get better rates than the ones we had agreed. What was common to these people was their nervousness and contempt, contempt for me, contempt for the country. I was half on their side; I envied them the contempt that it was so easy for them to feel.

One afternoon I saw that Raymond and Yvette's house had a new tenant, an African. The house had been closed since I had come back. Raymond and Yvette had gone away; no one, not even Mahesh, could tell me where or in what circumstances. The doors and windows of the house were wide open now, and that emphasized the shoddiness of the construction.

The new man, barebacked, was forking up the ground just in front of the house, and I stopped to have a chat. He was from somewhere down river, and friendly. He told me he was going to grow maize and cassava. Africans didn't understand large-scale agriculture; but they were passionate planters in this smaller way, growing food for the house and liking to grow it very close to the house. He noted my car; he remembered his bare back. He told me he worked for the government corporation that ran the steamer service. And, to give me some idea of his standing, he said that whenever he travelled on the steamer he travelled first class and free. That big government job, this big government house in the famous Domain – he was a happy man, pleased with what he had been granted, and asking for nothing else.

There were more households like his in the Domain now. The polytechnic was still there, but the Domain had lost its modern 'show-place' character. It was scruffier; every week it was becoming more of an African housing settlement. Maize, which in that climate and soil sprouted in three days, grew in many places; and the purple-green leaves of the cassava, which grew from a simple cutting even if you planted it upside down, created the effect of garden shrubs. This piece of earth – how many changes had come to it! Forest at a bend in the river, a meeting place, an Arab settlement, a European outpost, a European suburb, a ruin like the ruin of a dead civilization, the glittering Domain of new Africa, and now this.

While we were speaking, children began to appear from the back of the house – country children still, bending a knee at the sight of the adult, before coming up shyly to listen and watch. And then a large Doberman came bounding out at me.

The man with the fork said, 'Don't worry. He'll miss you. He can't see very well. A foreigner's dog. He gave it to me when he went away.'

It was as he said. The Doberman missed me by about a foot, ran on a little way, stopped, raced back, and then was all over me, wagging his docked tail, beside himself with joy at my foreigner's smell, momentarily mistaking me for somebody else.

I was glad for Raymond's sake that he had gone away. He wouldn't have been safe in the Domain or the town now. The curious reputation that had come to him in the end – of being the white man who went ahead of the President, and drew on himself the bad things that should have fallen on the President – that reputation might have encouraged the Liberation Army to kill him, especially now, when the President was said to be planning to visit the town, and the town was being made ready for that visit.

The rubbish hills in the centre were being carted away. The

corrugated streets were being levelled and graded. And paint! It was everywhere in the centre, slapped on to concrete and plaster and timber, dripping on the pavements. Someone had unloaded his stock – pink and lime and red and mauve and blue. The bush was at war; the town was in a state of insurrection, with nightly incidents. But suddenly in the centre it seemed like carnival time.

17

CITIZEN THÉOTIME would come in in the mornings, red-eyed and tormented-looking, high on his breakfast beer, with a couple of comic books or photo-novels to see him through office hours. There was an informal system of magazine exchange in the town; Théo always had something new to look at. And, oddly, his comic books or photo-novels, tightly rolled up, gave him a busy, business-like air when he came into the shop. He went straight to the store-room, and could stay there without coming out for the whole morning. At first I thought it was because he wanted to be out of the way and not to be any trouble. But then I understood that it was no hardship for him. He liked being in the dark store-room with nothing in particular to do, just looking at his magazines when the mood took him, and drinking his beer.

Later, when he became easier and less shy with me, his store-room life became fuller. He began to be visited by women. He liked them to see him as a real *directeur*, with a staff and an office; and it pleased the women too. A visit could take up a whole after-noon, with Théotime and the woman chatting in the way people chat when they are sheltering from the rain – with long pauses and long hypnotized stares in different directions.

It was an easy enough life for Théotime, easier than anything he could have imagined when he was a mechanic in the health department. But as he gained confidence, and lost his fear that the shop might be taken away from him by the President, he became difficult.

It began to worry him that as a *directeur* he didn't have a car.

Some woman had perhaps given him the idea, or it might have been the example of other state trustees, or it might have been something he had got from his comic books. I had a car: he began to ask for lifts, and then he required me to drive him to and from his house. I could have said no. But I told myself it was a small thing to do to keep him quiet. The first few times he sat in the front; then he sat in the back. This was a four-times- a-day duty.

He didn't stay quiet for long. It might have been my easiness, my wish to appear unhumiliated: Théotime was soon looking for new ways of asserting himself. The trouble now was that he didn't know what to do. He would have liked to live out his role in fact – to take over the running of the shop, or to feel (while enjoying his store-room life) that he was running the shop. He knew, though, that he knew nothing; he knew that I knew he knew nothing; and he was like a man enraged by his own helplessness. He made constant scenes. He was drunken, aggrieved and threatening, and as deliberately irrational as an official who had decided to be *malin*.

It was strange. He wanted me to acknowledge him as the boss. At the same time he wanted me to make allowances for him as an uneducated man and an African. He wanted both my respect and my tolerance, even my compassion. He wanted me, almost, to act out my subordinate role as a favour to him. Yet if, responding to his plea, I did so, if I took some simple shop document to him, the authority he put on then was very real. He added it to his idea of his role; and he would use that authority later to extort some new concession. As he had done with the car.

It was worse than dealing with a *malin* official. The official who pretended to be offended – and bawled you out, for instance, for resting your hand on his desk – was only asking for money. Théotime, moving quickly from a simple confidence in his role to an understanding of his helplessness, wanted you to pretend that he was another kind of man. It wasn't funny. I had resolved to be calm about my dispossession, to keep my mind on the goal I had given myself. But it wasn't easy to be calm. The shop became a hateful place to me.

It was worse for Metty. The little services that he had done for

Théotime in the beginning became things that he was required to do, and they multiplied. Théotime began sending Metty out on quite pointless errands.

Late one evening, when he came back to the flat after being with his family, Metty came into my room and said, 'I can't take it, *patron*. I will do something terrible one of these days. If Théo doesn't stop it, I'll kill him. I'd rather hoe in the fields than be his servant.'

I said, 'It won't last long.'

Metty's face twisted with exasperation, and he did a silent stamp with one foot. He was close to tears. He said, 'What do you mean? What do you mean?' and went out of the room.

In the morning I went to collect Théotime to drive him to the shop. As a well-to-do and influential local man, Théotime had three or four families in different parts of the town. But since becoming a state trustee he had (like other trustees) picked up a number of new women, and he lived with one of them in one of the little back houses in a *cité* yard – bare red ground intersected with shallow black drains all down one side, scraped-up earth and rubbish pushed to the edge, mango and other trees scattered about, cassava and maize and clumps of banana between the houses.

When I blew the horn, children and women from the various houses came out and watched while Théotime walked to the car, with his comic book rolled up. He pretended to ignore the watchers and spat casually on the ground once or twice. His eyes were reddened with beer and he tried to look offended.

We drove out of the bumpy *cité* lane to the levelled red main road, where the buildings were freshly painted for the President's visit – each building done in one colour (walls, window frames, doors), and each building a different colour from its neighbour.

I said, 'I want to talk to you about Citizen Metty's duties in our establishment, citizen. Citizen Metty is the manager's assistant. He is not a general servant.'

Théotime had been waiting for this. He had a speech prepared. He said, 'You astonish me, citizen. I am the state trustee, appointed by the President. Citizen Metty is an employee of a state establishment. It is for me to decide how the half-caste is to be used.' He used the word *métis*, using it to play on the adopted name of which Metty had once been so proud.

The vivid colours of the buildings became even more unreal to me. They became the colours of my rage and anguish.

I had been growing smaller and smaller in Metty's eyes, and now I failed him altogether. I could no longer offer him the simple protection he had asked for – Théotime made that plain during the course of the day. So the old contract between Metty and myself, which was the contract between his family and mine, came to an end. Even if I had been able to place him in another establishment in the town – which I might have been able to do in the old days – it would have meant that our special contract was over. He seemed to understand this, and it made him unbalanced.

He began to say, 'I am going to do something terrible, Salim. You must give me money. Give me money and let me go away. I feel I'm going to do something terrible.'

I felt his pain as an extra pressure on myself. I mentally added his pain to mine, made it part of my own. I should have thought more of him. I should have made him stay away from the shop, and given him an allowance from my own salary, while that lasted. It was, really, what he wanted. But he didn't put it like that. He involved it in that wild idea of going away, which only frightened me and made me think: 'Where is he going to go?'

So he continued to go to the shop and Théotime, and became more and more tormented. When he said to me one evening, 'Give me some money and I will go away,' I said, thinking of the situation in the shop, and trying to find comforting words, 'It isn't going to last forever, Metty.' This made him scream, '*Salim!*' And the next morning, for the first time, he didn't bring me coffee.

That happened at the beginning of the week. On Friday afternoon, after closing up the shop and driving Théotime to his yard, I came back to the flat. It was a place of desolation for me now. I no longer thought of it as my own. Since that morning in the car with Théotime I had felt a nausea for the bright new colours of the town. They were the colours of a place that had become strange and felt far away from everywhere else. That feeling of strangeness extended to everything in the flat. I was thinking of going to the

Hellenic Club – or what remained of it – when I heard car doors slam.

I went out to the landing and saw police in the yard. There was an officer – his name was Prosper: I knew him. One of the men with him had a fork, another a shovel. They knew what they had come for, and they knew exactly where they had to dig – below the external staircase. I had four tusks there.

My mind raced, made links. Metty! I thought, 'Oh, Ali! What have you done to me?' I knew it was important to let someone know. Mahesh – there was no one else. He would be at his flat now. I went to the bedroom and telephoned. Mahesh answered, and I only had time to say, 'Things are bad here,' before I heard footsteps coming up. I put the phone down, went to the bathroom, pulled the lavatory chain, and went out to see the round-faced Prosper coming up alone, smiling.

The face came up, smiling, and I retreated before it, and this was how, not saying anything, we moved down the passage before I turned and led Prosper into the white sitting room. He couldn't hide his pleasure. His eyes glittered. He hadn't yet decided how to behave. He hadn't yet decided how much to ask for.

He said, 'The President is coming next week. Did you know that? The President is interested in conservation. This is why this is very serious for you. Anything might happen to you if I send in my report. This is certainly going to cost you a couple of thousand.'

This seemed to me very modest.

He noticed my relief. He said, 'I don't mean francs. I mean dollars. Yes, this is going to cost you three or four thousand dollars.'

This was outrageous. Prosper knew it was outrageous. In the old days five dollars was considered pretty good; and even during the boom you could get many things done for twenty-five dollars. Things had changed since the insurrection, of course, and had become very bad with the radicalization. Everyone had become more greedy and desperate. There was this feeling of everything running down very fast, of a great chaos coming; and some people could behave as though money had already lost its value. But even so, officials like Prosper had only recently begun to talk in hundreds.

I said, 'I don't have that kind of money.'

'I thought you would say that. The President is coming next week. We are taking a number of people into preventive detention. That is how you will go in. We will forget the tusks for the time being. You will stay in until the President leaves. You might decide then that you have the money.'

I packed a few things into a canvas hold-all and Prosper drove me in the back of his Land-Rover through the brightly coloured town to police headquarters. There I learned to wait. There I decided that I had to shut out thoughts of the town and stop thinking about time, that I had as far as possible to empty my mind.

There were many stages in my progress through the building, and I began to look upon Prosper as my guide to this particular hell. He left me for long periods sitting or standing in rooms and corridors, which gleamed with new oil paint. It was almost a relief to see him coming back to me with his chunky cheeks and his stylish briefcase.

It was near sunset when he led me to the annexe in the yard at the back, where I had once gone to rescue Metty, and where I now had to be fingerprinted myself, before being taken to the town jail. The walls had been a dusty blue, I remembered. Now they were a brilliant yellow, and *DISCIPLINE AVANT TOUT*, Discipline Above All, had been freshly painted in big black letters. I lost myself contemplating the bad, uneven lettering, the graining of the photograph of the President, the uneven surface of the yellow wall, the dried yellow spattering on the broken floor.

The room was full of young men who had been picked up. It was a long time before I was fingerprinted. The man at the table behaved like an overworked man. He didn't seem to look at the faces of the people he fingerprinted.

I asked whether I couldn't get the ink off my hands. It wasn't a wish to be clean, I decided after I had asked. It was more a wish to appear calm, unhumiliated, to feel that the events were normal. The man at the table said yes, and from a drawer brought out a pink plastic soap-dish with a slender-waisted wafer of soap

streaked with black lines. The soap was quite dry. He told me I
could go outside and use the stand-pipe.

I went out into the yard. It was now dark. Around me were trees,
lights, cooking smoke, evening sounds. The stand-pipe was near the
open garage shed. The ink, surprisingly, washed out easily. A rage
began to possess me when I went back and gave the man his soap
and saw the others who were waiting with me in that yellow room.

If there was a plan, these events had meaning. If there was law,
these events had meaning. But there was no plan; there was no law;
this was only make-believe, play, a waste of men's time in the
world. And how often here, even in the days of bush, it must have
happened before, this game of warders and prisoners in which
men could be destroyed for nothing. I remembered what Raymond
used to say – about events being forgotten, lost, swallowed up.

The jail was on the road to the Domain. It was set a good way
back, and in the space in front there had grown up a market and a
settlement. This was what registered – the market and the settlement – when you drove by. The concrete jail wall, no more than
seven or eight feet high, was a white background. It had never
seemed like a real jail. There was something artificial and even
quaint about it: this new jail in this new settlement, all so rough
and temporary-looking, in a clearing in the bush. You felt that the
people who had built it – village people, establishing themselves in
a town for the first time – were playing at having a community and
rules. They had put up a wall just taller than a man and put some
people behind it; and, because they were village people, that was
jail enough for them. In another place a jail would have been a
more elaborate thing. This was so simple: you felt that what went
on behind the low wall matched the petty market life in front.

Now, at the end of the lane, after the lights and radios of the
little huts and shacks and stalls and drinking booths, that jail
opened to let me in. A wall taller than a man is a high wall. Below
electric lights the outside wall gleamed with new white paint; and
again, but in large black letters about two feet high, was *DIS-
CIPLINE AVANT TOUT*. I felt damned and mocked by the
words. But that was how I was expected to feel. What a complicated lie those words had become! How long would it take to work

back from that, through all the accumulated lies, to what was simple and true?

Inside, behind the jail gates, there was silence and space: a large, bare, dusty yard with rough low buildings of concrete and corrugated iron arranged in squares.

The barred window of my cell looked out on a bare courtyard, lit by electric lamps high up on poles. There was no ceiling to my cell; there was only the corrugated-iron roof. Everything was rough, but everything held. It was Friday night. And of course Friday was the day to pick people up: nothing would happen over the weekend. I had to learn to wait, in a jail that was suddenly real, and frightening now because of its very simpleness.

In a cell like mine you very quickly become aware of your body. You can grow to hate your body. And your body is all you have: this was the curious thought that kept floating up through my rage.

The jail was full. I found that out in the morning. Quite a time before, I had heard from Zabeth and others about the kidnapping operations in the villages. But I had never suspected that so many young men and boys had been picked up. Worse, it had never occurred to me that they were being kept in the jail past which I drove so often. In the newspapers there was nothing about the insurrection and the Liberation Army. But this was all that the jail – or the part of it I was in – was about. And it was awful.

It had sounded, bright and early in the morning, like a class of some sort: people being taught poems by many instructors. The instructors were warders with big boots and sticks; the poems were hymns of praise to the President and the African madonna; the people being compelled to repeat the lines were those young men and boys from the villages, many of whom had been trussed up and dumped in the courtyard and were being maltreated in ways I don't want to describe.

These were the dreadful sounds of the early morning. Those poor people had also been trapped and damned by the words on the white jail wall. But you could tell, from their faces, that in their minds and hearts and souls they had retreated far. The frenzied warders, Africans themselves, seemed to understand this, seemed to know that their victims were unreachable.

Those faces of Africa! Those masks of childlike calm that had brought down the blows of the world, and of Africans as well, as now in the jail: I felt I had never seen them so clearly before. Indifferent to notice, indifferent to compassion or contempt, those faces were yet not vacant or passive or resigned. There was, with the prisoners as well as with their active tormentors, a frenzy. But the frenzy of the prisoners was internal; it had taken them far beyond their cause or even knowledge of their cause, far beyond thought. They had prepared themselves for death not because they were martyrs; but because what they were and what they knew they were was all they had. They were people crazed with the idea of who they were. I never felt closer to them, or more far away.

All day, through the mounting and then lessening heat of the sun, those sounds continued. Beyond the white wall was the market, the outside world. Every image that I had of that world outside was poisoned for me by what was going on around me. And the jail had seemed quaint. I had thought that the life of the jail would match the market life outside. Yvette and I had stopped at a stall one afternoon to buy sweet potatoes. At the next stall a man was selling hairy orange-coloured caterpillars – he had a big white basinful. Yvette had made a face of horror. He, the vendor, laughing, had lifted his basin and pushed it into the window of the car, offering it all as a gift; later, he had held a squirming caterpillar over his mouth and pretended to chew.

All that life was going on outside. While here the young men and boys were learning discipline and hymns to the President. There was a reason for the frenzy of the warders, the instructors. I heard that an important execution was to take place; that the President himself was going to attend it when he came to the town; and that he would listen then to the hymns sung by his enemies. For that visit the town had burst into bright colour.

I felt that almost nothing separated me from those men in the courtyard, that there was no reason why I shouldn't be treated like them. I resolved to maintain and assert my position as a man apart, a man waiting to be ransomed. The idea came to me that it was important for me not to be touched physically by a warder. To be touched in one way might lead to more terrible things. I determined to do nothing to provoke any physical contact, however slight. I became cooperative. I obeyed orders almost before they were given. So at the end of my weekend, with my rage and obedience, my exposure to the sights and sounds of the courtyard, I was a hardened jailbird.

Prosper came for me on Monday morning. I was expecting someone to come. But I wasn't expecting Prosper, and he didn't look too happy. The loot-glitter had gone from his eyes. I sat beside him in his Land-Rover and he said, almost companionably, as we drove through the jail gates, 'This business could have been settled on Friday. But you've made it much worse for yourself. The Commissioner has decided to take a particular interest in your case. All I can say is that I hope it goes well for you.'

I didn't know whether this was good news or bad news. The Commissioner might have been Ferdinand. His appointment had been announced some time before, but so far he had not appeared in the town; and it was possible that the appointment had been rescinded. If it was Ferdinand, however, this wasn't the best way for me to meet him.

Ferdinand, progressing through the world, had, as I remembered, accepted all his roles, and lived them out: lycée boy, polytechnic student, new man of Africa, first-class passenger on the steamer. After four years, after his time as an administrative cadet in that capital so dominated by the President, where would he be? What would he have learned? What idea would he have about himself as one of the President's officials? In his own eyes he would have risen; I would have got smaller. It had always unsettled me a little – the knowledge that the gap between us would get bigger as he grew older. I had often thought how ready-made and easy the world was for him, the village boy, starting from nothing.

Prosper delivered me to the people in the front office of the secretariat. There was a wide verandah all around the inner courtyard, and on three sides the verandah was screened from the sun by big reed blinds. It gave an odd feeling, walking through the thin stripes of light and shadow, watching them appear to move over you as you moved. The orderly let me into a room where, after the shifting verandah dazzle, spots of light momentarily danced before my eyes; and then I was let into the inner office.

It was Ferdinand, strange in his polka-dotted cravat and short-sleeved jacket, and unexpectedly ordinary. I would have expected style, a certain heartiness, a little arrogance, a little showing off. But Ferdinand looked withdrawn and ill, like a man recovering from fever. He wasn't interested in impressing me.

On the newly painted white wall was a larger-than-life photograph of the President, just the face – that was a face full of life. Below that face, Ferdinand seemed shrunken, and characterless in the regulation uniform that made him look like all those officials who appeared in group photographs in the newspapers. He was, after all, like other high officials. I wondered why I thought he would be different. These men, who depended on the President's favour for everything, were bundles of nerves. The great power they exercised went with a constant fear of being destroyed. And they were unstable, half dead.

Ferdinand said, 'My mother told me you had gone away. I was surprised to hear that you were still here.'

'I went to London for six weeks. I haven't seen your mother since I've come back.'

'She's given up the business. And you must do that too. You must go. You must go right away. There's nothing here for you. They've taken you into jail now. They haven't done that before. Do you know what it means? It means they'll take you in again. And I won't always be here to get you out. I don't know how much Prosper and the others wanted from you. But next time it will be more. That's all that it is about now. You know that. They haven't done anything to you in jail. That's only because it hasn't occurred to them. They still think you are not that kind of man. You are a foreigner; they are not interested in you in that way; they just beat up bush people. But one day they will rough you up and then they will discover that you are like everybody else, and then very bad things will happen to you. You must go. Forget everything and go. There are no aeroplanes. All the seats have been reserved for officials coming up for the President's visit. That's standard security for these visits. But there's a steamer on Tuesday. That's tomorrow. Take it. It may be the last. The place will be full of officials. Don't draw attention to yourself. Don't take too much luggage. Don't tell anyone. I will keep Prosper busy at the airport.'

'I will do what you say. And how are you, Ferdinand?'

'You don't have to ask. You mustn't think it's bad just for you. It's bad for everybody. That's the terrible thing. It's bad for Prosper, bad for the man they gave your shop to, bad for everybody. Nobody's going anywhere. We're all going to hell, and every man knows this in his bones. We're being killed. Nothing has any meaning. That is why everyone is so frantic. Everyone wants to make his money and run away. But where? That is what is driving people mad. They feel they're losing the place they can run back to. I began to feel the same thing when I was a cadet in the capital. I felt I had been used. I felt I had given myself an education for nothing. I felt I had been fooled. Everything that was given to me was given to me to destroy me. I began to think I wanted to be a child again, to forget books and everything connected with books. The bush runs itself. But there is no place to go to. I've been on tour in the villages. It's a nightmare. All these airfields the man has built, the foreign companies have built – nowhere is safe now.'

His face had been like a mask at the beginning. Now he was showing his frenzy.

I said, 'What are you going to do?'

'I don't know. I will do what I have to do.'

That had always been his way.

On his desk there was a glass paperweight – small flowers set in a half sphere of crystal. He put the paperweight on the flat palm of his left hand and looked at it.

He said, 'And you must go and get your steamer ticket. That was where we last met. I've often thought about that day. There were four of us on the steamer. It was midday. We drank beer in the bar. There was the director's wife – you left with her. There was the lecturer who was your friend. He travelled down with me. That was the best time. The last day, the day of leaving. It was a good journey. It became different at the other end. I've had a dream, Salim. I've had a terrible dream.'

He took the paperweight off his palm and rested it on the desk again.

He said, 'An execution is to take place at seven in the morning. That is what we are meeting for. We are going to witness the execution. It is one of us who is going to be executed, but the man doesn't know. He thinks he is going to watch. We are meeting in a place I can't describe. It may be a family place – I feel the presence of my mother. I am in a panic. I have soiled something in a shameful way and I am trying hard to clean it or to hide it, because I have to be at the execution at seven. We wait for the man. We greet him in the usual way. Now here is the problem in the dream. Are we going to leave the man alone, to be driven alone to the place of his execution? Will we have the courage to be with him, to talk in a friendly way to the last? Should we take one car, or should we go in two cars?'

'You must go in one car. If you go in two, it means you are half-way to changing your mind.'

'Go and get your steamer ticket.'

The steamer office was famous for its erratic hours. I sat on the wooden bench outside the door until the man came and opened up. The *cabine de luxe* was free; I booked it. This took most of the morning. The market outside the dock gates had built up: the steamer was due that afternoon. I thought of going to see Mahesh at Bigburger, but decided against it. The place was too open and central, and there were too many officials there at lunch time. It was strange, having to think of the city in this way.

I had a snack at the Tivoli. It looked a little demoralized these days, as though awaiting radicalization. But it had kept its European atmosphere, and there were European artisans and their families at the tables and men drinking beer at the bar. I thought: 'What is going to happen to these people?' But they were protected. I bought some bread and cheese and a few expensive tins – my last shopping in the town – and decided to spend the rest of the time at the flat. I wanted to do nothing else. I had no wish to go anywhere or look at anything or talk to anyone. Even the thought of having to telephone Mahesh was like a burden.

Late in the afternoon there were footsteps on the external staircase. Metty. I was surprised. Normally at this time he was with his family.

He came into the sitting room and said, 'I heard they let you out, Salim.'

He looked wretched and confused. He must have spent some bad days after reporting me to Prosper. That was what he wanted me to talk about. But I didn't want to talk about it. The shock of that moment of three days before had vanished. My head was full of other things.

We didn't talk. And soon it was as though we had nothing to talk about. There had never been a silence like this between us before. He stood around for a little, went to his room, then came back.

He said, 'You must take me with you, Salim.'

'I'm not going anywhere.'

'You can't leave me here.'

'What about your family? And how can I take you with me, Metty? The world isn't like that nowadays. There are visas and passports. I can hardly arrange these things for myself. I don't know where I'm going or what I'll do. I hardly have any money. I'm scarcely able to look after myself.'

'It's going to be bad here, Salim. You don't know what they're talking about outside. It's going to be very bad when the President comes. At first they were only going to kill government people. Now the Liberation Army say that isn't enough. They say they have to do what they did the last time, but they have to do it better this time. At first they were going to have people's courts and shoot people in the squares. Now they say they have to do a lot more killing, and everybody will have to dip their hands in the blood. They're going to kill everybody who can read and write, everybody who ever put on a jacket and tie, everybody who put on a *jacket de boy*. They're going to kill all the masters and all the servants. When they're finished nobody will know there was a place like this here. They're going to kill and kill. They say it is the only way, to go back to the beginning before it's too late. The killing will last for days. They say it is better to kill for days than to die forever. It is going to be terrible when the President comes.'

I tried to calm him down. 'They always talk like this. Ever since the insurrection they've been talking of the morning when the whole thing is going to go up in flames. They talk like that because that is what they would like to happen. But nobody knows what is going to happen. And the President is smart. You know that. He must know they're preparing something for him here. So he'll get them excited, and then he may not come. You know the President. You know how he plays on the people.'

'The Liberation Army isn't just those boys in the bush, Salim. Everybody's in it. Everybody you see. How am I going to make out alone?'

'You have to take your chance. That's what we've always done. Everybody has done that here. And I don't think they'll trouble you – you don't frighten them. Hide the car, though. Don't tempt them with it. Whatever they say about going back to the beginning, they'll be interested in the car. If they remember and ask you about it, tell them to ask Prosper. And always remember that the place is going to start up again.'

'How am I going to live then? When there is no shop, and I have no money? You gave me no money. You gave it away to other people, even when I was asking you.'

I said, 'Ali! I gave it away. You're right. I don't know why I did that. I could have given some of it to you. I don't know why I didn't. I never thought of it. I never thought of you in that way. You've just made me think of it. It must have driven you crazy. Why didn't you tell me?'

'I thought you knew what you were doing, Salim.'

'I didn't. I don't know now. But after this is over you'll have the car and you'll have the flat. The car will be worth quite a lot, if you keep it. And I'll send you money through Mahesh. That will be very easy to arrange.'

He wasn't comforted. But it was all I could do now. He recognized that and didn't press me any further. Then he left to go to his family.

In the end I didn't telephone Mahesh; I thought I would write him later. Security at the docks the next morning wasn't extraordinary.

But the officials were tense. They were like people with a job to do; and that was to my advantage. They were less interested in a foreigner who was leaving than in the African strangers in the market encampment around the monument and the dock gates. Still, I was constantly stopped.

A woman official said, when she gave me back my papers, 'Why are you leaving today? The President is coming this afternoon. Wouldn't you like to see him?' She was a local woman. Was there irony in her voice? I was careful to take all irony out of mine. I said, 'I would like to, citizen. But I have to go.' She smiled and waved me on.

At last I went aboard the steamer. It was hot in my *cabine de luxe*. The door faced the river, which dazzled; and the sun fell on the deck. I went around to the shaded side, that overlooked the quay. That wasn't a good idea.

A soldier on the quay began to gesture at me. Our eyes met, and he began to scramble up the gangway. I thought: 'I mustn't be alone with him. I must have witnesses.'

I went down to the bar. The barman was standing in front of his empty shelves. A fat man with big, smooth arms, a steamer official of some sort, was drinking at a table.

I sat at a table in the centre, and the soldier soon appeared in the doorway. He remained there for a while, nervous of the fat man. But then, overcoming his nervousness, he came to my table, leaned over and whispered, '*C'est moi qui a réglé votre affaire.* I fixed it for you.'

It was a smiling request for money, from a man who might soon have to fight a battle. I did nothing; the fat man stared. The soldier felt the fat man's stare and began to back away, smiling, saying with his gestures that I was to forget his request. But I took care after that not to show myself.

We left at about midday. The passenger barge was not towed behind these days – that was now considered a colonial practice. Instead, the barge was lashed to the forward part of the steamer. The town was soon past. But for some miles that bank, though overgrown, still showed where in colonial days people had laid out estates and built great houses.

After the morning heat it had turned stormy, and in the silver storm-light the overgrown, bushy bank was brilliant green against the black sky. Below this brilliant green the earth was bright red. The wind blew, and ruffled away reflections from the river surface near the bank. But the rain that followed didn't last long; we sailed out of it. Soon we were moving through real forest. Every now and then we passed a village and market dugouts poled out to meet us. It was like that all through the heavy afternoon.

The sky hazed over, and the sinking sun showed orange and was reflected in a broken golden line in the muddy water. Then we sailed into a golden glow. There was a village ahead – you could tell from the dugouts in the distance. In this light the silhouettes of the dugouts and the people in them were blurred, not sharp. But these dugouts, when we came to them, had no produce to sell. They were desperate only to be tied up to the steamer. They were in flight from the river banks. They jammed and jostled against the sides of the steamer and the barge, and many were swamped. Water hyacinths pushed up in the narrow space between the steamer and the barge. We went on. Darkness fell.

It was in this darkness that abruptly, with many loud noises, we stopped. There were shouts from the barge, the dugouts with us, and from many parts of the steamer. Young men with guns had boarded the steamer and tried to take her over. But they had failed; one young man was bleeding on the bridge above us. The fat man, the captain, remained in charge of his vessel. We learned that later.

At the time what we saw was the steamer searchlight, playing on the river bank, playing on the passenger barge that had snapped loose and was drifting at an angle through the water hyacinths at the edge of the river. The searchlight lit up the barge passengers who, behind bars and wire-guards, as yet scarcely seemed to understand that they were adrift. Then there were gunshots. The searchlight was turned off; the barge was no longer to be seen. The steamer started up again and moved without lights down the river, away from the area of battle. The air would have been full of moths and flying insects. The searchlight, while it was on, had shown thousands, white in the white light.